M000166231

# MERCENARY

GANGSTERS OF NEW YORK, BOOK 3

## BELLA DI CORTE

Bella Di Corte

Copyright © 2020 by Bella Di Corte

All rights reserved.

No part of this book may be reproduced in any form or by any electronic or mechanical means, including information storage and retrieval systems, without written permission from the author, except for the use of brief quotations in a book review.

**This book is a work of fiction.**

Names of characters, places, and events are the construction of the author, except those locations that are well-known and of general knowledge, and all are used fictitiously. Any resemblance to persons living or dead is coincidental, and great care was taken to design places, locations, or businesses that fit into the regional landscape without actual identification; as such, resemblance to actual places, locations, or businesses is coincidental. Any mention of a branded item, artistic work, or well-known business establishment, is used for authenticity in the work of fiction and was chosen by the author because of personal preference, its high quality, or the authenticity it lends to the work of fiction; the author has received no remuneration, either monetary or in-kind, for use of said product names, artistic work, or business establishments, and mention is not intended as advertising, nor does it constitute an endorsement. The author is solely responsible for content.

**Disclaimer:**

Material in this work of fiction is of graphic sexual and violent natures and is not intended for audiences under 18 years of age.

Copyright © 2020 by Bella Di Corte

Editing by: Alisa Carter

Cover Designed by: Najla Qamber Designs

Model: Richard Deiss

Photographer: Michelle Lancaster

*To the Alcinas of the world.*
*That little light of yours...let it shine.*

"Why waltz with a guy for ten rounds if you can knock him out in one?"— Rocky Marciano

# FOREWARD

Dear Reader,

If you're familiar with my writing, you probably know that I usually add touches of the Italian/Sicilian language to my books where it's necessary. I love the language, the people, and the culture, and not only because I grew up a part of it.

I believe adding touches of the language (and not only hand gestures) is as impactful as describing the baroque architecture of an old church, the scents of lemon and orange in a warm Sicilian fruit grove, the noises you hear when you're taking a stroll in a particularly lively piazza. However, I do not speak Italian or Sicilian. Luckily, I have a wonderful friend in Sicily who does. She's one of my beta readers, and she's always willing to check over my translations so that you get a taste of a true Italian experience.

I appreciate her so much that I decided she needed to be recognized in one of my books—I hope as you read on, you'll feel Anna is as amazing as I think she is.

No matter how hard we try, though, sometimes languages do get lost in translation. There are many different dialects in Italy —some even specific to different villages. So any mistakes found in this book are my sole responsibility. (Also, Google translate might not work on a few of them, but my hope is that the sentence will give meaning to the word, or that the actual translation I've added will.)

*Grazie*, Anna, for being so gracious with your time. Thank you for being such a *meravigliosa amici*.

XoXo,
 Bella

# THE
# FAUSTI
## FAMILY

Faustis who are either mentioned or make an appearance in Mercenary:

Marzio Fausti (deceased) was the head of the infamous Fausti *famiglia* in Italy. He has five sons: **Luca, Ettore, Lothario, Osvaldo,** and **Niccolo.**

Luca Fausti (incarcerated) is the eldest son of Marzio Fausti and he has four sons: **Brando, Rocco, Dario,** and **Romeo.**

Brando Fausti is married to **Scarlett Rose Fausti.** (The Fausti Family)

Rocco Fausti is married to **Rosaria Caffi.**

Romeo Fausti is **Brando** and **Rocco's** youngest brother.

Guido Fausti: A **solider** in the Fausti Family.

Tito Sala, MD is connected to the Faustis by marriage. He is married to **Lola Fausti.**

# MACHIAVELLIAN & MARAUDER

## APPEARANCES OR MENTIONS FROM THE GANGSTERS OF NEW YORK

**Appearances (or mentions) from the Machiavellian cast:**

**Arturo Lupo Scarpone:**

He is the head of the Scarpone family; one of the five families of New York.

He has two sons: **Vittorio Lupo Scarpone** (mother, **Noemi**) and **Achille Scarpone** (mother, **Bambi**).

---

**Vittorio Lupo Scarpone:**

He is married to **Mariposa Flores Macchiavello**.

He is the son of **Arturo** and **Noemi**.

His maternal grandfather, **Pasquale Ranieri**, was a world renown poet and novelist from Sicily. He had five daughters (who all, but Noemi, live in Italy): **Noemi Ranieri Scarpone, Stella, Eloisa, Candelora,** and **Veronica**.

He has one brother: **Achille Scarpone**

**Vittorio/Mac goes by a list of names: Capo** (Mari),

Amadeo (In Italy, mostly by his family), **Mac Macchiavello** (In New York and the rest of the world), or simply, **Ghost**.

---

**Achille Scarpone:**

He is the son of **Arturo** and **Bambi**.

He has four sons: **Armino, Justo, Gino, and Vito** (Only **Armino** and **Vito** are mentioned by name in Mac.)

He has one brother: **Vittorio Lupo Scarpone**

---

Tito Sala (married to **Lola Fausti**) is **Pasquale Ranieri's** first cousin.

---

**Appearances from the Marauder cast:**

Cashel 'Cash' Kelly and his wife **Keely Ryan Kelly.**

Cash & Keely's two children: **Connolly and Ryan Kelly.**

Harrison 'Harry Boy' Ryan: He is **Keely's** brother.

# MERCENARY'S CAST

## Emilio Capitani:

He is the head of the Capitani family; one of the five families of New York.

His wife is **Teresa Capitani.**

**Emilio** and **Teresa** have three daughters: **Concetta** (Bianca's mother), **Emilia,** and **Luna.**

---

## Silvio and Silvio "Junior" Napoli:

**Silvio Sr** is one of **Emilio Capitani's underbosses.**

**Junior** is a made man in the family. He is a **solider.**

---

## Men who make appearances in the book:

**Adriano Lima:** **Corrado Capitani's** cousin. He is a **Capo** in the family.

**Nunzio Bruno:** **Corrado Capitani** knows him from childhood. He was born in Sicily and belongs to a family there.

**Nicodemo Leonardi:** **Corrado Capitani** knows him from childhood. He is from Sicily, but does not belong to a family.

**Calcedonio Badalamenti:** **Corrado Capitani's** underboss.

**Francesco Di Pisa:** **Corrado Capitani's** *consigliere*.

**Carmine Messina:** **Emilio Capitani's** *consigliere*.

**Vito:** Close friend of **Silvio's**. **Junior's** godfather. He is a **Capo** in the family.

**Baggio:** He was a part of **Adriano's** crew. Then he was promoted to **Capo** in **Adriano's** absence.

---

### The Parisi *Famiglia*:

**Giuseppe** and **Angela Parisi** have two daughters: **Alcina** (Alchena) and **Anna**. **Giuseppe** and **Angela** live in Forza d'Agrò (Sicily).

**Anna** is married to **Fabrizio Pappalardo**. They live in Bronte (Sicily).

# HIERARCHY
A DEEPER LOOK INTO THIS WORLD OF OURS:

**Boss (Godfather or Don):** Head of the family.

*Consigliere*: Chief advisor to the Boss.

**Underboss:** Second in command under the Boss.

**Capo (or** *caporegime*)**:** The captain or lieutenant of a division within the family. **Capos** head a crew of **soldiers** and report directly to a **boss** or **underboss**, who hands down the orders.

**Soldiers:** The lowest-ranking members of the hierarchy. They do most of the dirty work and hope to make a name for themselves as they rise in ranks in the family. Loyalty is very important.

**Associates:** Not actual members of a family. They mostly do business with them. They are not protected like a made man. Anyone can be an associate, but only Italians and Sicilians can become made men.

# MERCENARY

*noun*

1. a professional soldier hired to serve in a foreign army.

# INTRODUCTION

Allow me to introduce myself.

My name is Corrado Alessandro Capitani, but you can call me Scorpio, or even Don Corrado.

Because that other name, *Palermo*, I refuse to claim.

Why?

Because it never fucking claimed me.

# 1

## CORRADO

The moment the bum ran from me under the light of the moon, I knew my life was never going to be the same.

I was in Vegas with my cousin Bugsy. He ran one of the most well-known casinos along the strip, *Paradiso*. His grandfather was my grandfather's little brother, and even though they lived in different states—mine in New York; his in Vegas—they both ran their territories with an iron fist.

No move was made without permission. They knew all, approved or not, and there was hell to pay if you disobeyed or failed to get the okay. Especially when the mark was connected and could start a war. But there was a reason why Giordano Capitani was called Bugsy: he was fucking buggy, and his temper came before his thoughts. Usually when he lost control, though, it was for a good reason.

The sack of shit he was beating to death along this desert road deserved every whack with the bat. Bugsy had caught him selling women, using his casino as an auctioning block. And Bugsy had once considered the fucking bum a friend.

Our grandfathers were old-school, which meant, rule number one: no flesh for sale unless the woman was doing the selling. But before Bugsy sought permission from Old Gio to whack this guy, he lost his mind and chased the fucking bum down. The bum was lucky he made it out of the casino, but he knew Bugsy wouldn't run after him in his place of business. He trailed him all the way here, until he was finally able to run him off the road.

The bum took off running, kicking up sand as he did. Where he planned on running to? Who the fuck knew. Maybe to the car Bugsy ran off the road, but his steps were not headed that way. In a straight shot, there seemed to be nothing around here for miles. Nothing but cactuses and things that came out at night, because they were too smart to burn in the searing sun all day.

Unlike the fuck who ran from me.

He was not smart.

Apparently, the bum who'd been selling flesh for a pound didn't come alone. After his associate unloaded on a few cacti, —either a shit shot or he couldn't control his trigger finger with the way his hand trembled—he took one look at the empty pistol, one look at me, flung the gun at my face and then took off.

No one ran from me and got away. I was too quick, and if they happened to get the jump, I always found them. Then I'd drag them back to the hell they had escaped from.

"Why waltz with a guy for ten rounds if you can knock him out in one?" was a quote I lived by.

I was about to knock this motherfucker out for the count. Maybe I would've gone easy on him, but because he was a coward, this night wasn't ending well for him. My designer shoes were filled with sand from running in this fucking endless sandbox, and it irritated me. I could've ended this easily—the gun in my pocket was hot—but there was no honor in shooting a man in his back. He'd face me.

If he got the best of me, we'd either meet again or he'd send me packing in a body bag. I was still standing, which meant no one had gotten me yet.

Having enough of the game, I stretched my arm out, grabbing him by his collar. He was short, but he was built like a bull. He kept trying to use his weight to tear out of my hold, probably wishing he had bought a shirt from the superstore instead of the designer one covering his shoulders. One he could probably afford by selling a few women.

He was breathing heavily. I could smell garlic on his breath. He was opening and closing his mouth, trying to get a few words out, but due to his lack of physical activity and the shirt pressing into his throat, he couldn't get anything out but wheezes.

"No use in running," I said, my voice clear and sharp. "You have nowhere to run to."

He lifted his hands, in surrender, and I released my hold, giving him the opportunity to face me. Man to man.

He did, turning slowly, his hands still raised. When he faced me, he held the phone out, which he'd been running with. The picture on the screen was of Bugsy and me. Bugsy was in motion, swinging the bat that took out the made man's kneecaps. I was next to him, watching. This fucking guy had sent it to a few people.

I smiled at him in the glow of the moon. Once his eyes focused, he noticed the tattoo on my hand and on my neck.

"God h-h-help m-m-me," he said, making the sign of the cross.

It was game over for this guy, but it was only the beginning for me. The full moon over my head was the start of something much wilder than I could've ever imagined—I felt the madness moving in my blood, urging my finger to move, to put pressure on the trigger.

*Bing.*

*Bam.*

*Boom.*

Game over.

The scorpion wins.

## 2

## CORRADO

Music floated from outside of my grandparent's house as I pulled up. One of my old uncles sang a classic Italian ballad from the backyard. I had the windows rolled down in my '58 Cadillac Coupe Deville, trying to rid it of the smell of my cousin Adriano's cheap cologne.

Another one of my cousins had gotten married, and for a man dressed in a pricy custom-made suit to attend the event, Adriano had no taste when it came to cologne. It was fucking offensive.

The thing about Italian families—they are usually large. It doesn't matter how far down the line the cousin or whoever is. Fourth? Great-great? Still as close as first. Numbers don't matter when it comes to family. A title is a title. Just like a leaf on a tree is still part of that tree, no matter how far from the root.

Bugsy once told me, "We don't have friends. We have cousins."

It seemed like the entire *famiglia* had come out to celebrate my cousin Bianca's wedding. There were too many people to keep count. They were vetted at the entry gate, and then led to an archway that led to the backyard. Guests were backed up, all trying to get to the source of the music at once.

Basically, Sunday dinner on a more lavish scale.

My grandparents had spared no cost when it came to this wedding. They had three daughters. Two were no longer living, and the third was dead to my grandfather in a sense.

Bianca's mother had suffered a stroke and died not long after. My grandparents felt it was their duty to step in and take care of what my aunt couldn't.

My mother hadn't stepped foot in this house since a couple of days after I was born. My grandmother went to see her occasionally, but the relationship between my mother and grandfather was nonexistent. They didn't speak. Hadn't since she left his house and never looked back.

Neither one of them would tell me the reason. I got the feeling it had to do with me, but neither would speak on it.

One of my cousins had told me it had to do with my mother getting pregnant out of wedlock, but her husband had married her, so I couldn't see my grandfather refusing to speak to her because of it. Not after all of this time.

I called my father "her husband" because he was never a father to me. He treated me like the bastard son of an enemy, so I never felt he deserved the title. It was earned, just like everything else in this life.

He was straight with the title, too. So that was how we addressed each other. Her husband. Her son.

My grandfather was more of a father to me, and after he heard the way her husband had been treating me when I was a kid from an older cousin, her husband stuck to himself, and we rarely spoke a word to each other.

My mother got the message. If there was something she needed help with, in regards to me, my grandfather handled it. He even changed my last name to his.

"*Oh, mamma!*" the cheer went up from the backyard. *La la la la la* followed right after.

I watched the flow of the crowd, already starting to clap even before they made it to the center of the celebration. I was watching for Bugsy.

After we returned from the desert, the night the moon was full and blood was spilled underneath it, there was already a message waiting for me at *Paradiso*. My grandfather had sent an order, one word—home.

I was ordered to go straight to the Primo Club, a place where he frequently did business. After I'd met my grandfather there, we went straight from the club to his home, where he had me sit across from his desk. He eyed the tattoo on my neck and on my hand. He was a traditional man, stuck in traditional ways, and he always dressed the part. He didn't like the tattoos on my body.

"You will go to Sicily," he had said, his eyes hard on mine. "Until the situation can be taken care of."

The situation. The bum that Bugsy had killed was connected, and he was making some men some serious cash. There were rules to consider, as well. A made man never touched another made man unless it was approved. The guy I'd killed, Garlic Breath, was an associate, but also an informant. The picture he'd taken was sent to all parties involved. I had a feeling my grandfather was going to argue that I didn't actually kill the made man, Bugsy did. I killed the associate, who was not protected like a made man. Besides, he was a rat. I did them all a favor. Unless it brought some heat down on the family.

"With all due respect," I'd said, sitting forward, fixing my suit and tie, "a man who runs is a coward. I refuse to run."

We watched each other until he nodded once. "We will see how this goes." Then he looked at his other underboss, Silvio, and nodded.

There would be men around me twenty-four/seven because

of who the bum was and what he had meant to them. There was no use in arguing. My grandfather and I had conversations, but only if the lines of communication were open. He'd closed it with that nod.

Besides, arguing wasn't allowed. Punishment was to be taken like a man. And to have men surround me constantly was the equivalent of serving time for a man like me.

It had been a week since that conversation, and my grandfather hadn't said anything about it since. That could mean he was taking care of the situation, or it could mean something else—he was dealing with another situation that took his attention.

All five families were getting hit lately. One family blamed another, because there were things that tipped us off on each. The Scarpones were at the center of the distrust, even though they claimed to have nothing to do with what was going on. They were getting hit hard, too.

Silvio thought they were staging the hits on their own shit, just to make it look a certain way, but my grandfather didn't believe they were that smart. He said only one man was smart enough to pull this off: Vittorio Scarpone.

Vittorio was the son of Arturo, the head of the Scarpones. Vittorio had had his throat slit years ago. His own father had ordered the hit. Vittorio didn't kill a man named Corrado Palermo and his family when Arturo gave the order, after Palermo tried to slit Arturo's throat.

There was just one issue with the theory that Vittorio Scarpone had arranged the mayhem that ensued: He was supposed to be dead.

I sat back in my seat, checking my rearview mirror. Silvio was coming toward my car, a cigar hanging out of the side of his mouth. Silvio had been around since before I was born and had about thirty years on me. He had started out like everyone else and worked his way up. He wasn't blood, but he might as well have been. My grandfather considered him family.

Silvio stopped at the window, leaning in some, smoke blowing in the car. The sweet smell paired perfectly with the scent of the old leather seats. "Afraid you gonna catch the garter?" He grinned at me.

"I'm quick," I said, returning the grin. "If I can dodge a bullet, I can dodge that fucking luck."

"Don Emilio has taught you everything but the most important thing." He laughed. "That a woman is quicker than a bullet."

"None have hit me yet. A woman or a bullet."

"What the fuck is wrong with you?" He used the car to lift himself straight, blowing out another ring of smoke. "You just jinxed yourself."

"Bullshit," I said, shutting the car off. I stepped out and shut the door, pocketing my keys. "I'm stating facts. Even fate can't argue with those."

"You willin' to bet your balls on it?"

We both turned to look at his son, a mini version of him, Silvio Junior, or as everyone called him, Junior. His nickname was "The Bull," though behind his back, most of the guys called him "No Nuts."

No Nuts had been sent to Sicily after he'd killed the wrong guy and caused some issue between our family and another. It was a straight hit—bing, bam, boom, done—but somehow he got the cars mixed up. He didn't bother to check the car's license plate. So instead of killing an associate, he killed someone important to another family.

Silvio had gone to my grandfather and asked a favor of him after: to hide No Nuts until things could get straightened out. While No Nuts was there, he fell for a Sicilian girl, who didn't seem to feel the same about him. She castrated him and then ran and hid.

No Nuts lost his mind when he lost his balls, like they were directly connected, and no one could locate her or them since —the woman or his nuts.

We both shivered, cupping ours, protecting them from evil. That poor motherfucker was the poster boy for ball loss. I couldn't be sure, but after he came home, it seemed like his eyes had crossed some as a side effect.

"Poor bastard." Silvio shook his head. "That bitch is going to pay. You can't run and hide forever. Your bad deeds always catch up to you." He stared at No Nuts for a second before he shook his head. "Don Emilio sent me out to get you. He wants pictures done of the family."

We watched No Nuts dancing around a bunch of cars, mouthing the words to "Mambo Italiano," before we went to find my grandfather in the mix of the crowd.

THERE WERE MORE people than I thought. Most of them were crowded around my grandparents, watching as they danced to a slow song. Once the dance was over, and so were the pictures, my grandfather and I headed toward his office.

One foot inside of the house, and it was like taking a step back in time. Most of the furniture had been imported from Sicily. Some had been passed down through the generations. The only difference was that the entire house had been decorated with flowers for the wedding.

I followed my grandfather up the steps, eyeing the hand-carved cross and then a picture of my aunts and mother. It was an oil painting done years ago, when they were just kids. They were all pretty close in age.

My mother, Emilia, and the little girl sitting close to her in the painting, Luna, were the closest in age and in life. My grandmother told me that wherever Luna went, so did Emilia.

Emilia treated her little sister like a baby doll. Luna died not long after I was born. From what Silvio had told me, my mother and grandfather were never the same after. Luna was the baby.

When I realized my grandfather had reached the top of the stairs, I started moving again, meeting him in his office. I wasn't surprised that my uncle Carmine was already in the sitting area, Tito Sala next to him.

Uncle Carmine was my grandmother's sister's husband, and my grandfather's *consigliere*. He counseled my grandfather on issues. Tito Sala had done the same for the Fausti family at one time.

The Faustis were the bosses of the bosses. Most people assumed men of such high ranking didn't exist any longer, but the Fausti *famiglia* existed, and in the old country. Italy. When the worst of the worst couldn't be controlled, or issues like the ones going on between the five families cropped up, their leaders stepped in.

Most of the time, though, it was their lower-ranking men who dealt with the petty shit. If their *capo dei capi—bosses of all bosses*—stepped in, it meant that the entire organization was close to the end. That's why the family always stepped in before it could even get that close.

Marzio Fausti had been the *capo dei capi* for as long as I could remember. But he'd been killed, and his son, Lothario, was acting in his place until a new leader was announced officially. They were sniffing around more than usual lately because of the issues between the five families.

Tito Sala could be here for the wedding, or he could be here to judge the mood and report back to Rocco, who was in our area as of late. Then Rocco would pass that information on to whoever in his family.

I greeted Uncle Carmine and then Tito Sala. They both took a seat after we all shook hands. My grandfather took his seat at the head of the desk. I took the seat across from him, glancing down at my phone for a brief second.

My mother had tried to call me during the church service. The missed call was stuck on my screen, and it showed a voicemail. I turned my eyes up before my grandfather demanded my attention.

He looked me straight in the eye. "You and I, along with the men in this room, know I have prepared you all of these years to take over."

It wasn't the norm to have two men prepared to take one spot, but my grandfather had taught Silvio the same as he had taught me over the years. He had groomed us both for the position he held in the family.

Our family was separated into two factions. Silvio ran one. I ran the other. One governing body separated into two territories.

My grandfather's intro into this conversation had me thinking. Had he been thinking about retirement? He was ninety years old, and he was growing older by the day.

I nodded. "Yes."

He stroked his chin thoughtfully. The weight of his stare felt even heavier with whatever he was thinking. "I did not want you to be a part of this life. I wanted you to go to college. To get a degree. To take a different road. I had hoped Silvio would one day take my place. That he would one day sit in this seat." He knocked on the desk once with his pointer finger. "But as you grew older, there was no denying the blood that ran through your veins. Mine. You are a born leader, Corrado. But there is one thing a leader should learn before he takes this seat. He cannot rule alone."

He paused and the air in the room stilled. "There is one thing you must do before you take this seat. Before you will be called Don Capitani. Before you secure your vote: take a bride."

I took out my gun and slid it toward him. "Shoot me."

None of the men even grinned.

"Put that away!" My grandfather waved his hand. "This is not a joking matter. You must prove to the men that you will settle down. Be responsible enough to rule this family the way I did, but even better."

Our eyes met and clashed in a silent battle, even though I knew I was going to lose. His mind was made up. He wouldn't give me his vote, his blessing, unless I did what I said I would never do. Get married.

Uncle Carmine cleared his throat, but my stare still didn't leave my grandfather's. "The men call you Scorpio, the man who never allows an enemy to defeat him. You have to learn that you are not immune to rules or being ruled on occasion."

So the three of them—my grandfather, uncle Carmine, and Tito—had come up with this, after what had happened in Vegas.

I thought of Bugsy, who hadn't showed his face at this wedding. I grinned. My grandfather and his were usually of the same mind when it came to punishment. His was just more fucking showy about it. He was probably rolling the dice on Bugsy's future right now, or already had.

My grandfather gave me a slight grin. He knew my thoughts and was confirming them.

"With all due respect," I said, "I can't say I feel the punishment fits the crime." Even though I couldn't be disrespectful, even raise my voice, I had to try once more.

"Punishment," Tito said, tasting the word with the thought of vows fresh on his tongue. He had a good marriage and a romantic nature, so it made sense that he wouldn't understand my hesitation toward being forced into it.

I could've said no, but I had two choices: take a bride or lose my grandfather's vote to Silvio. Even though the men would vote, my grandfather was a great boss, and the men respected him. They wanted to keep the family as is, or make it even greater. His opinion mattered and could sway the election either way.

The men liked my numbers. I brought in more than any man outside of Capone, and at a much younger age. Money and men came to me, which I knew bothered Silvio. He was older and couldn't bring in half of what I did.

However, this life had many tests, and I'd passed all of them. I always would.

"You will choose for me," I said to my grandfather.

"I will arrange it."

Arranged marriages were not uncommon in our culture, and since this was supposed to be about teaching me boundaries, and nothing else, let him decide on my behalf. I'd claim my seat, become the man I was born to be, and the rest would fall into place.

One hard knock came at the door. My grandfather took a minute before he nodded at uncle Carmine to answer it. The whispers were lost among the noises in the house and the music coming from outside. Tarantella played.

A minute later, uncle Carmine came back in. He seemed to be a completely different man. The minute it took him to answer the door and come back had aged him somehow. It was a look I'd never forget. Like he'd been drained of blood.

My grandfather noticed and his posture went rigid.

"Emilio," Uncle Carmine said, putting a hand on my grandfather's shoulder, squeezing. He looked between the two of us. "Emilia." He hesitated on my mother's name. Then he cleared his throat. "She has been murdered."

The mandolin sneaking in through the open door seemed to cry.

# 3

# CORRADO

Rain started to fall after they lowered my mother into the ground and sealed her in forever. She and her husband both. They killed him as soon as he'd opened the door to their house. He was on blood thinners, and it didn't take much to make him bleed out.

My mother—Emilia—they beat her until she could no longer get up. Then strangled her for not talking.

I looked down at my phone, rain splattering against the screen, and pressed a few buttons. I hit speaker so I could hear her voice.

"Corrado," she had said. "This is your mother. I haven't heard from you—" She stopped talking. I could hear her breathing and a rush of voices from the other side.

"Where is she? Who the fuck is she? Palermo's kid!"

"Fuck you!" she spat at the man.

There was more than one. They were yelling back and forth. The pottery she made and sold crashed to the floor in the background. Then everything went quiet, and my entire life seemed to go dead.

When I returned to the land of the living, I was a new man.

The autopsy report gave the reason for death, but it also said that my mother—Emilia—had never had any children. I demanded a DNA test for her husband, and it turned out, the fucker wasn't my father.

The woman I believed to be my mother was my aunt.

My grandmother finally broke down and told me the truth.

Emilia and Luna left New York when they were young against my grandparents' wishes and went to Las Vegas. Luna became pregnant with me after she got there. Luna must've either fallen in love with the bastard or was afraid of him, because she refused to give up his name. Even to my grandfather. He refused to talk to either one of them after. When I was only a few months old, Luna died in a car accident.

Emilia brought me back to New York, and my grandfather demanded to know my father's name. She refused to give it to him. That was when he told her he would take care of me, but until she told him the truth, he wouldn't speak to her.

He'd never speak to her again, because she went to the grave with the secret.

Tito Sala had told me who my biological father was because he thought I deserved to know after Emilia's murder: Corrado Palermo.

Palermo was a capo in the Scarpone family who'd tried to kill his boss—Arturo—by slitting his throat. Palermo married after I was born, and after doing some research, I discovered he'd had a daughter with his Sicilian wife.

Which meant I had a sister.

A sister that no one, not even me, had a clue what had happened to. Corrado and his wife had been murdered, but the little girl was never found. Marietta Bettina Palermo was her name. We were thirteen years apart in age.

Somehow the Scarpones must've gotten wind of something they either forgot or had just discovered—or they had left it alone all of these years because they didn't want my grandfather to know. If he had known, he would have gone to war over his daughter. Whatever the reason, the Scarpones went after Emilia thinking she knew something about Marietta, since they had no clue about me.

There's no speaking beyond the grave, so all I had were my own deductions to rely on. My mother and aunt—either one worked for either woman—knew the trouble (always in fucking trouble) Corrado Palermo was in before the Scarpones had hidden him in Italy. The Scarpones and Corrado Palermo had been tight before he tried to slit Arturo's throat when he returned to New York. After I was born, though, my mother and aunt refused to speak his name to anyone in fear that the same fate would come for me, if I was ever connected to him. Especially since he had denied me even before birth.

Emilia knew what I'd do if she told me my true identity— I'd go looking for the motherfucker, or anyone who had anything to do with him. She knew if I got close, it was only going to bring trouble, because the Scarpones were still looking for my little sister.

Marietta had a guillotine hanging over her head before she was even born.

I wondered if she even knew who she was. Or if she did, how she had survived for this long.

It wasn't a secret in our circle that Vittorio Scarpone had been killed because he refused to end her life, so where the fuck did he take her? Why did he let her live? He was as ruthless as the rest of the Scarpones. None of them had hearts, not even for women or children.

As far as I was concerned, all Scarpone blood would be wiped clean from this earth. Saving my sister from death wouldn't stop me from killing Vittorio Scarpone, if the rumor was true, and he was still alive.

Footsteps coming up from behind me stopped me from replaying the voicemail again. I slipped my phone into my pocket before Silvio reached me. Things had been a little tense between us after my grandfather had given his support for me getting the position instead of him, as long as I met the condition.

I would.

Rain dripped from his fedora as he blew smoke out of his mouth in a white cloud that quickly disappeared. "You're causing Don Emilio unnecessary worry." He took another puff from his cigar. "Go to Sicily for a while. Just until everything cools down. He's lost enough."

I said nothing, staring as rain collected on the yellow roses left on top of the casket.

He dug in his pocket for a second and pulled out a sheet of paper. He slipped it into my palm and said, "Find her for me, and I'll tell you all you want to know about Vittorio Scarpone. The things we know." He looked behind him, to make sure we were not being overheard.

Men were placed sporadically around the graveyard, in case we were attacked. They'd come on a day when attention wasn't focused on war, but on tragedy.

There was no other focus for me. I saw, heard, and tasted nothing else but the salty tang of battle.

I squeezed the paper in my hand, crumpling it into a ball, and stuck it in my pocket. I rolled my shoulders, the fabric giving too much. The suit I wore didn't feel snug enough. "If the men in Sicily can't find one woman, you either need to find new men or let her go on principal."

He hesitated beside me for a minute. His eyes were hard on my face. "Junior needs to divorce her so he can remarry. We can't find her to do it."

I looked at him then, refusing to respond to a lie. "Let it go."

He shook his head. "Can't. We won't kill her, but she'll pay. We're owed that. And if you go to Sicily to ease Don Emilio's mind for a while, you can find her while you're there. I'll pay you with the information you want."

"He's been keeping things from me," I said, turning to face the grave again.

"For your own safety. After he found out who your father—"

Chaos erupted from different sides of the cemetery. Some of the men placed around the perimeter were running toward us. Others were running toward my grandfather's car, which waited for me with him in it.

A bullet whizzed past my head, and at the same time, the bouquet of yellow roses on top of the casket exploded in a shower of petals as it was hit over and over again.

"This way!" One of the men used his gun to point in the direction of my grandfather's armored car. It was getting hit with bullets, but it wasn't moving. They were waiting for me.

I had my gun out as we took cover from stone to stone. Every once in a while a bullet would make contact, sending shards flying in different directions. Silvio had been hit on the last run, and he was holding a hand to his arm, shaking his head.

"Bum motherfuckers!" he shouted to no one in particular, raising his gun and shooting in a direction where most of the shots were coming from.

The line of cars was close, and there was no use in waiting any longer. The longer we sat, the better the chance of them picking us off.

"Move," I said.

"Are you fucking—"

"There are more of our men around," I said. "They'll hold 'em off long enough for us to make it to the cars."

I stood and ran toward the waiting car with one man ahead of me, one behind, and two beside me. Gunfire was heavier the closer we came to the car, and the man to the right of me took a bullet in his right arm. He fell back, leaving me somewhat exposed. I shot in the direction, seeing a man duck behind a stone as I did. The man in front of me yanked the car door open and I ducked inside, the door slamming closed behind me.

My grandfather nodded once—the driver honked his horn twice—and then, like a carefully coordinated motorcade, the line of our cars started to leave the cemetery.

My grandfather looked out of the window, the gray light falling on his face like a dark cloud. It was hard not to see him in this place instead of Emilia. She had more life to her face in the casket than he did in this car.

I turned to look out of the opposite window, heavy droplets of water rushing down the pane with the speed we were going. The interior was as cool as the funeral home. It smelled like death—like the roses on the casket.

"Tell me about Vittorio Scarpone," I said.

"Enough!" he shouted. It echoed inside of the car. It was the first time I'd ever heard him raise his voice. He could order a man's life to be taken with a nod of his head. "I forbid you to go near the Scarpones. They will be taken care of. But you." He lifted his pointer finger and then let it fall. "You will be taken to the airport. Now."

"Or?"

"Or." He cleared his throat. "Or nothing." He lifted his arm, letting the jacket fall back, and looked at his watch. "Your plane leaves in an hour."

The paper in my pocket felt like money burning a hole, and nothing would stop me from earning it. The men called me Scorpio. They would soon call me Mercenary, because the information would be mine, no matter what.

# 4

## ALCINA

The light in *chiesa della Santissima Annunziata* felt amber in spirit, even though it was dreary and cold outside. I closed my eyes to it, wondering if it was a warning or something more healing. It snuck in through the black lace *mantello* I wore, either accenting the morose piece, and why I was wearing it, or defying it.

I brought my rosary to my forehead, letting it dangle in front of my face. The gold from the beads seemed to ward off the dreariness and emptiness and fill me with the warmth from the sun. I hoped this time it would stay with me.

Stay with me during the uncertain times I faced. Cling to me like a shield that would protect me from the cold wind howling outside.

My *mamma* sat next to me on the pew and chanted a whispered prayer, "*Dio...*"

My lips moved with hers, but no sound came out.

What did I want? What did I need? What was I really asking for?

An old romantic poet once told me that we don't always get what we want, but what we need.

I needed to stop running. To stop hiding. To stop living in fear of hell and to look forward to something much more heavenly. I needed to be safe. To live a life worth living.

I tried to imagine it. This new life my father, my *papà*, had arranged for me. What would this new man be like? Would he treat me the same way the bull did? Like nothing but a cow in a pasture?

A tear slipped down my *mamma*'s cheek. I wiped it before it could turn cold on her warm skin.

I had until October—when our marriage would be finalized —to come to terms with this new arrangement and accept it. I would stand in this church that my family had attended for generations, face the man who accepted the terms *papà* had set, and commit my life to a stranger. A man who could be another bull that deserved to be castrated.

*Papà* told me that I was hardheaded. That it was better to marry and live rather than to hide and be found and then killed, or worse: to be taken back to New York, never to be heard from again.

*Papà* was old school, not unfamiliar with arranged marriages, but I had never wanted that for myself. I wanted the freedom to choose. Under different circumstances, *papà* would have wanted that for me, too.

I glanced to the left, at my sister Anna, when she reached out and wove her fingers together with mine. She didn't open her eyes, but she squeezed, letting me know that she agreed. Sometimes we could read each other's thoughts, like *mamma* shed the tears that I could not.

My sister's marriage was not arranged. It was love at first sight. What most parents want for their children—the power to decide.

A woman dragging a little boy with her sat across from us. She took her seat first, him right behind, and then she told him something in a hushed whisper. He bent his head right after.

*Accussi normale. So normal.*

I found myself watching other people from time to time. Imagining that her life—or his—was much easier than mine. My grip on the rosary grew tighter. Sadness, the cold ache for something better, overwhelmed me and drug my heart deeper into darkness.

I closed my eyes to the overwhelming feeling, letting my mind get lost in the warmth of the amber, before I heard my name.

"Alcina," *mamma* whispered.

I opened my eyes to find her waiting for me. My sister stood next to her.

"Time to go," she said in Sicilian.

I sighed, standing and slipping my rosary into my pocket. I felt darkness pushing in on me as I stepped out of the doors. Night usually sheltered me and allowed me to burn brightly, as if I was a lit flame, but the cold wind struck me, and I flickered against its strength—my light as uncertain as the months to come.

# 5

# CORRADO

T he paper in my hand had become creased and worn, but I would never forget the writing that inked my memories.

*Alcina Maria Parisi*

*Around 5'5, brown hair, dark brown eyes, 25 years old*

*Parents—Giuseppe and Angela*

*Sister—Anna*

*Anna is married to...?*

*Alcina was born in Forza d'Agrò on May 8, 1995; her parents still* live there

*She was baptized at Maria S. Annunziata e Assunta*

It seemed like Silvio had scribbled down the information as Junior was telling it to him, probably trying to remember all of the things he knew about his wife and her family. There were no pictures of her, only the paper he'd ripped from a notebook in a rush.

I glanced between the paper and a sign in front of the church: *Cattedrale Maria S. Annunziata e Assunta.* It marked the location in case anyone was looking for it and needed confirmation.

From my explorations around the area, the church was also referred to as *chiesa della Santissima Annunziata*. One local told me the church had been there since the 1400s and was the second oldest church in the country. It was located in the small town of Forza d'Agrò, only about two hours from where my grandfather had sent me in Ragusa.

Forza d'Agrò looked as old as the baroque-style church. It was at the base of a mountain, and overlooking it, at the peak, was a Norman castle in ruins. The town itself had narrow streets and *casas* that looked like they belonged in another time —balconies with iron details, clothes hanging out to dry on lines, overflowing planters, wooden shutters, multicolored chipped stone, lanterns on buildings, and cobblestone alleyways. The only sign that we were in modern times was the lines running from one building to another supplying power.

In the distance towered the rough terrain of the mountains, outlined by the Ionian Sea, the part of the Mediterranean that separated southern Italy from western Greece.

I'd been coming here often ever since my arrival in Sicily— long enough that the cold of winter had turned into the warmth of summer. The day after I stepped off the plane and a few men my grandfather had been in touch with had met me, I directed them to take me here.

People don't stray from where their hearts belong, and something told me Alcina Maria Parisi was never far from hers. The problem with looking for someone who belonged to such a small community, though, was that they were wary of new people.

Whoever Silvio had looking for her had come in like a wrecking-ball, and besides a few old men willing to give me a few history lessons and stories, they gave me side-eye looks that would've pushed me off a cliff if possible.

As soon as I said her name, as expected, none of them would come near me again. They knew I didn't belong.

So I set my sights on her parents.

Her *mamma*, Angela, was a devout woman who didn't travel far from home. Her *patri, father,* owned a restaurant that had views of the sea. He watched me as closely as I watched him.

Every day I would see the man and he would see me. There was no animosity in the way he looked at me, but a smug assurance that no matter what I did, I'd never find his precious daughter. He had no fucking clue.

I'd wait here for the rest of my life for Alcina Parisi.

I narrowed my eyes against the glare of the sun breaking around the church, wondering how many times she'd stepped inside of it. How many times she'd walked the same paths I had to get to the same spot.

"This is called stalking in America, I believe," Nunzio said, blowing smoke out of his mouth. He was a trusted man who came with me wherever I went. He shook his head when I gave no answer and went to sit on a bench close to the church, in the shade.

"I need food," Adriano said, taking out a handkerchief from his pocket and wiping at his head. There was no doubt that my grandfather had sent him with me as punishment.

His cologne assaulted me in the breeze, and I turned my narrowed eyes on him. It brought back memories of Bianca's wedding. I resisted the urge to throw him in the sea—from a cliff—to rid him of the insulting smell.

Adriano stuck the handkerchief back in his pocket. "What are we doing here anyway? We've been all over this place. There's no more to see, Corrado. Let's go to the beach." He nudged me with his elbow and wiggled his thick eyebrows at me.

At the same time he nudged me, a gust of wind swept up, coming straight from the sea, and the paper in my hand was set free. My eyes collided with Angela's as the paper flew toward her. It went up the steps of the church, hitting one of the stones, and with another gust, landing at her feet.

She always wore dresses that matched the area—old in style—and leather sandals. Her hair was pulled up, dark red in the sun, gray streaks coming out on the sides.

The paper was in her hand by the time I made it up the steps and to her. She held it out for me to take without even looking at it, or maybe she had, but it didn't show on her face. The only thing that showed was a grin that I'd seen before. It made me think she had a running joke going at my expense, something only she could hear. She laughed at me every time she saw me standing around or sitting in their restaurant.

My fingers touched the paper, but when I went to take it back, she held on, not letting it go. "Tell me," she said in Sicilian. "Can you sing?"

Her mouth didn't laugh, but her eyes did—at me, at the look on my face. I could see my reflection in her dark eyes. They crinkled on the sides, a sign Tito had once told me meant that a woman kept her secrets locked up tight, and she generally had a good sense of humor, even at other people's expense.

Angela let go of the paper, without my answer, the sound of her laugher echoing behind her as she disappeared inside of the church. Everything went quiet after, except for the sound of the breeze, rustling the palm trees behind me.

---

"If I don't lose ten pounds by the time I get back to New York —" Adriano shook his head, searching for his handkerchief again "—there's no help for me. All we do is walk. I'm sweatin' buckets."

"All you do is eat," Nunzio said in accented English, shaking his head and stepping on another cigarette he had dropped on the walk. "When we are not walking."

"What's so special about this place?" Adriano looked around, wiping his neck. He stuck his handkerchief back in his pocket, the guns underneath his shirt probably ringing wet from his sweaty skin. "The beach. I need to be on the beach with some healthy fruit and a few drinks."

Nunzio lifted both of his hands, palms up, complaining behind Adriano's back as he entered into Parisi's restaurant first. The girl who usually served us waved us to our regular table. She was the only one who wasn't outright cold. I wondered how much she knew, but more so—how much would she talk if persuaded?

Giuseppe Parisi came out of the kitchen when he heard Nunzio ordering drinks. He always did. He wanted to make sure that I knew that he knew I was there.

I nodded at him, as usual, and as usual, he stared at me a moment before he started to grin—no. He wasn't grinning this time. His eyes narrowed even lower, his mouth pinched into a tight line, and his head tilted to the left, like he was studying me harder.

After a second, he threw his hand in the air, like he was disgusted, and then disappeared into the kitchen.

Nunzio had started to place our usual order with the young waitress, and I was barely listening, until Adriano nudged me with his arm. My eyes moved to the waitress, who was listening to Nunzio but staring at me.

I smiled at her and her cheeks flushed. She tucked a strand of hair behind her ear, constantly nodding at what he was saying. He was ordering seafood dishes and a bottle of Amaro Averna for after dinner. Even after he finished, she kept staring at me.

"Your name?" I asked her in Sicilian.

"Calista," she said, her voice soft, her eyes lowered. She tucked another strand of hair behind her ear.

"Ah. Beautiful." I grinned. "Ask her if she's lived here long," I said to Nunzio.

I had most of the Sicilian language, because I grew up listening to it and speaking it in certain circles, but Nunzio was born and raised in Sicily. Adriano had even less than I did.

Nunzio spoke the words to her. She nodded, answering.

"All of her life," he said to me.

"Do you know the Parisi family well?"

Nunzio looked between her and I, his eyebrows drawing down, but then asked her. As soon as the question was out, she looked toward the doors to the kitchen and then back at me. She bit her lip, going for her hair again, and nodded at me once she realized the coast was clear.

I kept my eyes connected to hers, cleared my throat, about to whisper the most important question to her, when a loud voice from the back made her jump clear off the ground.

"Calista!" Giuseppe shouted, looking between the two of us. Her name was followed by a string of Sicilian words too fast for me to follow. The girl's cheeks turned bright red and she hurried off to the kitchen. A few minutes later, she came back out and started readying a table facing the sea for what seemed like a few guests.

She refused to look at me again.

"Hah!" Giuseppe Parisi said, watching me. He crossed his arms over his chest, shaking his head.

I grinned, turning my face away from his and toward the older guy who set our food down. "Tell me what that was about," I said to Nunzio.

A piece of octopus dangled from his fork. It jiggled when he paused to answer me. "He told her to stop flirting and get back to work."

"The way he looks at you, Corrado," Adriano said, taking a bite of pasta, "you'd think he wants to poison you."

Nunzio's fork stopped close to his plate, going for another bite, and stayed that way for a minute. He looked between Giuseppe and me and then put his fork down, wiping his mouth after. He'd finally caught on to why I never ate a bite from this place. I only drank from the bottle after we opened it ourselves.

Nunzio opened his mouth but snapped it shut when Nicodemo Leonardi walked through the door of the restaurant, stopping for a second to look for me. He nodded once when he saw me, heading toward our table.

Nicodemo Leonardi had few friends but many enemies. He didn't work for one family, but for himself. Some called him "Bones."

Underneath his white dress shirt, I could see the stark black lines of ink running along his collarbone, forming the Latin words: *Veni. Vidi. Vici. "I came. I saw. I conquered."* He had the same tattoo twice, but with the words in a different place and in a different order: *I saw. I conquered. I came.*

When I was younger and I'd come to visit my grandparents' family in Italy during the summers, Tito Sala had introduced us. There were no real friends in this life, but Nicodemo and I had an understanding.

I stood, and when he was close enough, we took a hand and pulled each other closer.

His nose crinkled when I offered him the seat next to Adriano after we'd broken apart. Nicodemo moved his chair over a bit before he got comfortable. "I heard about the trouble in America," he said, declining food or drink from the waitress, who still refused to look at me. He didn't eat out many places either. "It has only gotten worse. You are a wanted man."

"You going to claim the price on my head?"

He shrugged. "If I needed the money."

Nunzio made a sound in his throat that Nicodemo didn't even bother acknowledging.

"I'm glad it's still about the dollar," I said. "I need to find someone."

"The woman," he said, sitting back a bit, getting more comfortable. "Alcina Parisi."

I nodded, refusing to say anything else. I could tell Nunzio was starting to catch on—there was a reason why I'd been coming here, searching specific areas where I could catch her scent. Adriano looked out at the water while stuffing his face, trying to listen to the man playing the *mandolino*, not a fucking clue.

I hadn't told any of the men why I was here. They reported everything back to my grandfather. If he found out about the deal between Silvio and me, they'd be ordered to take me somewhere else. Somewhere that didn't have cars small enough to fit on the street.

"Italy becomes a big place when looking for one small woman," I said.

Nicodemo grinned. The girl almost dropped the bottle of Amaro Averna in his lap when he did. She wasn't attracted to him; she was fucking scared. He didn't react, just told her in Sicilian to bring another chair to the table.

"Italy becomes a big place when one small woman doesn't want to be found," he said.

I waved a dismissive hand—neither here nor there.

"I do not understand your logic," he said, ignoring the trembling girl as she sat a chair next to Nunzio. "People talk. Word travels. I would not return to a place when *your* eyes are set on it."

I opened the bottle and poured myself a glass. I shrugged. "I'm getting to know her."

That was the fucking truth. I watched her parents do what they did every day. I imagined her walking the streets here. Going to church. Raising her voice and waving her hands when she wanted to be heard. I had a clear picture in my mind of

Alcina Parisi, though the features of her face and body were not in focus. If Junior didn't take a picture of her, I wondered how attractive she was.

"Ah," Nicodemo said, accepting a glass from me. "Your leads have turned cold, Scorpio." He nodded to the tattoo on my hand, between my thumb and pointer finger.

They had, but I needed to widen my search some, go further out. I thought she would have stayed close, but all roads led me back to Forza d'Agrò.

The four of us grew quiet as seven men entered the restaurant. I put the glass up to my mouth, watching as Giuseppe led them to the table the girl had prepared. The older man, the head, took my attention right away. He was the one calling the shots. The other ones, besides the middle-aged man who was a younger version of pops, were all muscle.

I figured Giuseppe would leave their table after he welcomed them, head back to the kitchen as usual, but instead, he took a seat. Angela served them instead of the young girl. Every once in a while, she would turn her eyes my way, catching me staring.

Her eyes were not laughing.

"Tell me," I said, nodding toward the table.

"The Balistreris," Nunzio answered, keeping his voice low. He patted the spots where his guns were hidden underneath his shirt. Then he stood. "Let us go."

I waved my hand down, ordering him to sit. "Relax and enjoy your dinner."

He glanced at their table before he took his seat again.

"A problem, *cugino*?" Nicodemo said to me. He called me that sometimes. *Cousin.*

I turned my eyes away from the table and met his stare. He didn't care either way. His eyes were asking me if I had a problem with what I was seeing. For some reason, it bothered me, Giuseppe sitting down to break bread with these men in his restaurant. He knew what kind of man I was the moment he looked at me, and I could feel that I was unwelcome from across the street.

The same feeling was strong toward these men, too, but different. Every so often he would wipe his head with a napkin when the conversation would start to heat up a bit, but mostly, it was whispers mixing in with the sound of the mandolin that would reach our table.

I wasn't listening for the meaning of words. I watched body language.

There was no doubt that they were doing business of some kind. There was also no doubt that the reason Angela served them was because she wanted to be near the conversation. She wasn't watching the old man, either, but the one I assumed to be the son.

Giuseppe stuck his pointer finger in the air and then came down with it on the table silently. He said something after, and as soon as he did, the son started to laugh—it was a fucking roar, and it messed with the sound of the mandolin.

What a fucking pity, that. It was a beautiful melody. He ruined the sound of it, like Adriano ruined the air with his cologne. It irked me.

"Incoming," Adriano said, his face red. It always was when he had a few drinks after a heavy meal.

Tito Sala took the empty seat that Nicodemo had ordered the waitress to bring. So he knew he was coming. Tito got comfortable and ordered a seafood dish with a glass of white wine. He was the messenger, sometimes, between my grandfather and me.

We said little to each other over the phone, for more than one reason. The main one was that there was some animosity on my part for him ordering me to be here. He refused to update me on the Scarpone situation, as well.

There was no way my grandfather was going to let it slide,

but I was going to take it a step further and find the ghost, Vittorio Scarpone, and finish him off if he was still alive. My grandfather respected Vittorio for some reason. I wasn't sure what it was. I didn't fucking care.

Tito glanced at the table doing business before he pushed up his glasses and turned his eyes on me. "Your grandfather has agreed to an arrangement with a bride."

"Excellent," I said. "Tell me who she is." One step closer to going home—after I had Alcina to bring with me.

"He does not know," he said. "He left it up to me."

The entire table stared at him, no one longer than me. He stared back, not caring one way or another. He got to work on his plate as soon as the young girl set it down. She relaxed some when he thanked her.

"You leave tomorrow for Bronte," he said. "You will not loaf around Italy any longer on some fool's quest." He patted his mouth with a napkin. "The pistachio harvest will begin soon. You will work."

"Fool's quest," I repeated. If Silvio had told him, I'd kill Silvio. This was between the two of us. I refused to allow my grandfather to stop me.

He nodded. "That is what I would do," he said, setting his glass down, "if I found out who my father was and wanted to kill the family who deprived me of him. But things are not always clear in life, ah? Sometimes we must have patience to find out where we're going, when we have just found out where we've been."

He took another bite. I was torn between watching him and watching the men at the table, who were rising from their seats.

"You will go to Bronte, and by October, you will be a married man," Tito continued. "This will please your grandfather. Her name matters none—or does it?"

I heard him, but my eyes locked on the son, who was

walking toward the door. We stared at each other until he left. "No," I said, absentmindedly. "It doesn't."

"*Bene*," Tito said. "We will go in the morning."

Neither Giuseppe nor Angela looked at me as they walked toward the kitchen after the men left. Her hand reaching out for her husband's shoulder was the last thing I saw before the doors closed behind them.

# 6

## CORRADO

Bronte was around an hour and a half from Forza d'Agrò, and the town was known for its pistachios. "*l'Oro della Sicilia.*" Or, *Sicily's gold*. Mount Etna towered in the distance, smoke coming from its mouth, the town lying at its feet. Lava rock was scattered from eruptions. The trees grew right out of it.

Tito told me that was why the pistachios were compared to gold, because of the volcanic soil. "It is rich," he said, as he pointed out of the window at some areas of land filled with more trees at the foothills. "It is called *sciara.*"

Nunzio drove us down an old dirt road that had worn-in tire tracks. Men and women walked the fields with straps around their necks, red buckets at the ends. Some were in the distance standing on lava rocks, balancing as they reached for the fruit along the branches. More workers walking along the road stopped and watched as we passed.

"The festival will take place in October this year," Tito said. "Fabrizio appreciates the help. His family has owned this land for generations. It is passed down."

"His last name?" I said, watching as a large villa in the

distance grew closer. It was tan stone with green shutters and a dark, wooden front door.

"Pappalardo," Tito said.

I didn't even ask if Fabrizio Pappalardo knew why I was here. Tito knew better than to tell him. There were a few people who would pay a lot of money for the information.

Tito pointed behind the main villa. "There are places for the workers to stay during the collecting months. You will take an apartment."

"We must stay close," Nunzio said, keeping his eyes on the road.

"*Sì*." Tito nodded, his wide-brimmed cap dipping with the motion. "I arranged this."

"Can we eat the pistachios?" Adriano stared at all of the buckets filled with the green gold of Sicily. "Or are they like olives straight from the tree? Tried that once and spit it clear across the field after I fucking did. Big, *huge*, mistake."

"Life is a gamble," I said.

Fabrizio Pappalardo was waiting in front of the villa as Nunzio pulled up and parked. Pappalardo was around my age, maybe a little younger, and in work clothes. He was pointing at a bag filled with pistachios that had "*Pappa*" stamped to the white fabric in red, telling one of the workers to bring it somewhere.

If he noticed what kind of men we were, he didn't outwardly show it. I was here for a reason, so I blended, leaving the suits and ties in New York. But when he saw Nicodemo, who never left the suits and ties at home, I wondered if he would take notice and start to ask questions. Then again, being connected to Tito could come with its questions, too.

Or not.

If Fabrizio had lost a few workers due to illness or accident, Tito was the kind of man who would recommend men he knew needed the work.

After Nicodemo stepped out of his car, he shook hands with Fabrizio, so they seemed to know each other. Nicodemo nodded at me before he entered the villa.

"Fucking bum," Adriano said underneath his breath as he watched the door close behind Nicodemo. "*I* stink. Imagine. I buy the best shit there is."

Adriano was pissed at Nicodemo, who had told him that he stunk and would attract flies out in the heat once he started to sweat.

Fabrizio cleared his throat to get our attention. He was all business. He directed us to a man named Fabio, who put us to work at once. We were all given buckets and gloves and told not to let the fruit drop, if we could help it. After we filled our buckets, we were to report to Fabrizio and the buckets would be poured into a bag. We were to keep picking until the day was over.

It wasn't easy work. Some of the rocks were steep, and the trees grew at an odd angle, so it took balance to keep from falling over or dropping the fruit. Sometimes branches would fall between the crevices, and I would have to stick my hand between to retrieve them. I always checked for snakes before I did.

I was quiet as I did my job, getting lost in the rhythm of it. Sometimes I would study the workings of the trees. They seemed to have deep root systems, usually with short trunks, and long, resinous branches. The leaves were like velvet and leather. The pistachios were about the size of olives and grew in pink clusters. The men called the plants *scornabecco*, and the shell after it had been separated from its husk *tignosella*.

It was easy to forget about the issues in New York while I got lost in the work. I could've been a different man— a man with regular problems.

Other times, the need to take care of the Scarpones only grew with the silence that consumed my mind. It wasn't even words that came to mind but a color. Red. It was time to bleed them fucking dry.

The urge to find Alcina was so strong that I could taste it in my mouth, like the cool water Tito gave us to drink on our lunch break.

Tito stood next to Adriano, Nunzio, and me, surveying the land under the shade of his wide-brimmed cap. We were working in a more secluded location, and I wondered if it was because Tito requested it—keeping me hidden but not.

"It is wondrous how Mother Nature works." He nodded to Mount Etna, smoke billowing out against the blue sky from its tip. "You have such a disruptive force—bigger than this entire town—yet it still gives us the best of what it is. Look at the fruit it offers."

Adriano wrinkled his nose and shook his head. "Is this all we get to eat?" He lifted the basket that Tito had brought out with cheeses, crackers, meats, and fruits. He was sprawled out on the ground, half sitting, half lying down. His cheeks were red, and nothing was coming out of his pores but sweat now.

Nunzio nodded toward the volcano, ignoring Adriano. "A volcano reminds me of an Italian woman," he said. "Fire in her veins, but even after she scalds you with her temper, she feeds you the best."

Tito smiled. "I would have to agree."

"A woman kicks me in the balls and then feeds me grapes in bed as an apology after." Adriano lifted a bunch of them, taking the bottom one in his mouth. "I'd accept it."

I grinned at the face Nunzio made. Then I took off the long-sleeved shirt I wore over my t-shirt, balling it up, using it as a pillow. I set my hands behind my head as an extra layer, closing my eyes. I fell asleep with the sun hot on my face. A few minutes later, I woke up to the sound of a long, low whistle from Adriano. I followed the sound until I met the cause of it.

A few women walked toward us with a group of children around them.

"I'd give up pasta to be with any of those women alone," Adriano said, sitting up on his elbows, watching as they walked closer.

"That's not a woman," I said, staring at one in particular. "That's a fucking weapon."

She was holding hands with a little girl she'd called Calogera. Most of the woman's long, dark brown hair was behind a scarf, but small tendrils fell from the sides, skimming her neck, where I imagined the pulse of her artery would pound against my mouth when I put it there.

The wind blew against her, rustling the dress on her body, and it sent a sweet scent in the air around me. The dress reminded me of the ones Angela usually wore, but it hugged every one of this woman's curves. The cross she wore around her neck caught the bright light and glowed gold against her tan skin.

Even in the old-style dress, she hit all the right notes.

I was Orlando Furioso when I looked at her. The sway of those hips—I licked my lips, and I could taste lemon and chocolate.

It wasn't even her face or body that was the weapon. It was those cat-shaped eyes, dark and full of secrets, that were dangerous. As unpredictable as any man I'd ever stood against.

When she was close enough and turned them on me, she stopped, even though the little girl kept pulling on her hand to keep walking. On one rough tug, she went, following the group of women who had walked ahead.

Nunzio nudged me. He nudged me again.

"She is taken," I heard Tito say in Italian. Laughter after he'd said it. Someone said the word moonstruck. And then, "*cugino sei cotto.*" *Cousin, you're cooked.*

She looked over her shoulder at me before she turned

again, moving further and further away, going deeper into the orchard.

"Her name," I said.

"Angelica," Nicodemo said, appearing beside me.

I grinned at that but said nothing.

The woman had dropped a glove she'd been carrying between the rows of pistachio trees. I picked it up, and the closer I came to her, the better I could smell her in the air. The scent of her would forever be tattooed on my memory—more permanent than the ink on my skin.

"*Signora*," I called out, my voice low but still loud enough to hear.

She stopped but didn't turn. The girl, Calogera, stuck her tongue out at me. I did the same. She laughed a little, and I grinned.

Finally, the woman turned, looking up and meeting my eyes again. I lifted the glove and told her in Sicilian that she'd dropped it. She nodded once, reached out, and I allowed her to grab it. When she went to take it back, though, I held on. She pulled a little, but after she realized I wasn't letting it go so easily, she stopped. We both held on.

"*Grazie*," she whispered. The longest fucking lashes I'd ever seen on a woman fanned when she blinked.

"*Prego*," I said.

She took the glove then, turning her back on me again, moving even faster to keep up with the other women and children.

Angelica—yeah, that didn't fit. She wasn't the princess. She was Alcina, the sorceress, luring men to her magical island.

No wonder Junior never took a picture of her. It would never do her fucking justice.

7

# ALCINA

"**W**hat are you doing?" my sister jumped into the quiet kitchen and shouted the words at me at the same time. Her boots hit the ground with a slap at the same time my heart lodged in my throat.

I jumped back from the window, my hand over my chest. I was going to pull her hair out by the roots. "What am *I* doing?" I screamed back in Sicilian. Most of our conversations were in a mixture of our native tongue and English. The longer we were in Italy, though, the less English we used.

She laughed, going to sit at the kitchen table. "You have been staring out of the same window for an hour. It is dark now. He has already gone to his place." She wiggled her eyebrows at me. "He is nice to look at, ah?"

"Nice." I rolled my eyes. "He is trouble."

The moment I saw him, I knew.

His dark amber eyes would hypnotize.

His full lips would speak the most beautiful promises.

His body? Made for pleasure. He was tall, his shoulders wide, his legs long and lean.

Everything about him was perfect. On the surface.

But if he thought that he could fool me into thinking he was a good man, he was wrong.

The moment I saw him, I knew *the truth*.

Those eyes hid his poisonous heart.

Those lips were vessels of deception.

That body? Made for inflicting pain.

He wasn't sent from heaven. He was sent to drag me back to hell. The hand with the scorpion tattoo—between his thumb and pointer finger—would be wrapped around my throat. The one he had on his neck wasn't as obvious, but it didn't need to be.

I knew men like him. Fast-talking New Yorkers who had some Sicilian to spare. They came to the old country to hide when they had prices on their heads.

Been there. Done that. Was still dealing with the aftereffects of *that*.

I would rather sacrifice myself to Mount Etna than to have another one of *him* in my bed.

*Him.*

None of the men he came with would say his name, and when Anna had her husband, Fabrizio, ask Uncle Tito about him, he said it didn't matter, because he would be leaving soon. He was only passing through. The money he earned for harvesting the pistachios would go for his room and board.

"Stop lying to yourself, Alcina," Anna said. "He might be trouble. But you *like* him. You *like* the way he looks. Admit it to me—or I will invite him over for dinner and prove it."

"Do it," I said, opening my arms, but secretly thrilling at the sound of my name, because it was rare when we got to use it. "You can't tell when I *like* someone."

She threw her head back and laughed. "I can! You start blinking, like this—" She started opening and closing her eyes, going as fast as she could.

"You are lying!" I laughed, not really meaning to. She looked ridiculous.

"Am not!" She laughed even harder. "You did the same thing when Ezio, the Greek god, would talk to you. Right before we left Forza d'Agrò for New York. You would write his name in your notebook, and you cried when he got married. He was eighteen, you were eight, a baby to him."

I turned to face the window again, looking out at the darkness, not able to see through it. I never could, not unless the moon was out and it shed some light on the everlasting night of my life. Even in the day, darkness cloaked me.

"He *is* beautiful, Alcina. In the way men are when they are strong and confident. And those eyes—" She sighed. "You're not the only one who has noticed. *Papà* told me Calista almost trips over her feet when he comes into the restaurant. Even *mamma* has blinked at him a few times."

I turned and she was blinking at me again, a smile lingering on her face.

"He is trouble," I said, crossing my arms over my chest. "He knows who I am."

She shrugged. "He only watched *papà* and *mamma*."

"Studying them to get to me," I said. "If the bull—Junior—" I hated to say his name, but I did it sometimes just to spite him. Other times, he was the bull.

"Uncle Tito wouldn't have brought him if he felt he was a danger. And if he is—" She made a snipping motion at me. "You still have the shears."

We stared at each other for a second before my grin matched hers, and we started laughing.

She lifted a pointer finger. "The bull—poetic justice at its finest. If you have to make this one into a eunuch, that would be such a shame. He is *so* pretty."

I shook my head at her. "I am taken, remember?"

"I remember," she said. "So is he. Uncle Tito told me he is

arranging his marriage. He will be married by the time he leaves. But." She bit her bottom lip, tilting her head a bit. "We must fight fire with water. He is not married yet, and neither are you. If he claims you..." She shrugged. "Let him fight for you."

I laughed, louder than she had. "Claim me?"

She nodded. "In a way that you have never been claimed before. The way he was looking at you today..." She nodded. "I recognized it. Most woman can't, unless another woman tells them—a woman has no idea what it means to be claimed, until *after* she is."

"I thought the woman claims the man," I said.

"True, we do, but we make them *think* they claim us first." She grinned, and it was evil. "You think you are sly, but I saw what you did. You dropped that glove on purpose, to have him pick it up for you."

My heart fluttered a bit, remembering the moment. I silenced it with thoughts from the past. "It does not matter," I said. "What is done is done."

"Nothing is *done*," she called after me as I opened the door to leave, grabbing the shears I carried with me. "Not until your final breath!"

It was something our *mamma* told us—life was not done until we were. If we were still breathing, we still had a reason.

The lights were on outside, old-style lanterns on the villa, and when I turned, I found jeweled eyes, the color of dark amber, staring back at me. He stood against the house, one shoulder against it, waiting.

"Alcina," he said, and my name sounded so beautiful from his mouth.

Even when he had stopped me earlier in the groves, when I'd dropped the glove on purpose, his voice had that same calm to it, and it was smooth. *Fucking*, as they would say in America, *deceptive*.

He didn't need to flaunt his power. It was just...his. He

owned it, like the scent in the air around him. A fine cologne that was his alone and unforgettable. It was mixed with his sweat and the dirt from working the harvest.

I turned toward him, narrowing my eyes to see him better, and then, without thinking twice, snapped the clippers in the direction of his balls. "Stay away from me, *scorpione*," I said, equally as quiet. Then I turned, the feeling of his eyes on my back refusing to leave me, even in my dreams. And even in dreams, he was never what he seemed.

# 8

# ALCINA

I needed better places to hide.

I would walk to one side of the grove. *Lo scorpione* would suddenly be there.

I would run to another. He would already be leaning against a tree. His eyes on me. A grin on his face.

I would hide in the kitchen of the factory, and as soon as my foot would hit the outside of it, he would be standing there.

I left Anna's villa. He waited outside of it.

If I moved left, he moved left. If I moved right, so did he.

We were dancing a dance I was unfamiliar with.

He was tripping me up, his moves (or motives) at odds with my safety, but my heart raced and my breath became shallow every time our eyes met and we somehow completed a step.

"Bad, bad heart," I whispered to myself, picking pistachios from a tree that was rooted on a steep mound of volcanic soil. As I picked, I kept muttering to myself, having a conversation. No one else was around but me (*lo scorpione* had been sent to help Uncle Tito do something medical with an animal), and if I could not work this out, who could?

I felt like a puppet on a string, some unknown force the master of my emotions.

How could I want a man who was so bad for me? A man who probably had his mind set on taking me back to New York and delivering me to hell?

At the same time—all of the feelings that rushed through me at the thought of him were heavenly. Sometimes when I caught him staring, I felt like I could float.

"Don't move!" The order came at me in Sicilian.

My hand stilled midway toward a branch. A lazy breeze moved through the air, touching the sweat on my skin, making me feel feverish when I registered the tone of the voice, who it belonged to, and the hiss of a serpent from below.

I wondered how close to my legs it was, but I did not want to even look. It had probably wedged itself within the crack in the rock, looking for shade. I should have checked, but I had been preoccupied.

My shears were balanced against the rock a ways away, and from my peripheral, I saw him move forward, snatching them.

The *vipera* hissed.

"Get off the rock, Alcina," he said. "*Adesso.*"

My legs were trembling. I couldn't move.

"*Adesso!*" he snapped.

I closed my eyes and jumped from the rock onto another, barely making it. I held on to another pistachio tree, trying to steady myself.

The *vipera* had been next to my ankle the entire time, while I picked the pistachios. I probably would not have known what had hit me until it was too late. It was camouflaged against the rock, trying to hide from the sun.

It coiled itself into a tight S, its tongue scenting the air, ready to strike.

*Lo scorpione* watched it with hard eyes, the shears open and ready. He had a long-sleeve shirt slung over his shoulder, and he waved it away from him. The *vipera* struck out at the fabric, and *lo scorpione* snapped the blades. The snake's head fell to the side.

I made the sign of the cross. "I did not even see it."

He nodded and came toward me, opening his arms.

"I can get down," I said.

I had walked these groves many times, certain of my footing and how it worked with the terrain, but when I went to step down, my knees gave out.

He caught me and started carrying me toward a more populated area with ease.

I stared at his face, admiring how chiseled it was. Then my eyes drifted and stuck on his lips.

He smiled, and I had to force myself to stop blinking.

"Wait!" I said, trying to wiggle out of his arms. "I have to go back!"

"The head won't stop moving until the sun goes down," he said. "Whatever you forgot, I'll go back later and get it."

"My shears!" I said, wiggling even harder.

He stopped moving. "You don't need them."

"Why not? I do! I need—"

"You don't," he said, moving again. "I'm here."

"You are," I said. "But that is not helping *me*."

He glanced at me and then looked ahead. "I'm more dangerous than shears."

"Which is why I need them. I need something to protect me from *you*. Or to help."

"Nothing stops me when I want something," he said. "Least of all a pair of rusty old shears." He stopped moving again, looking down at me. The only way I could describe his face in that moment was someone who had started to connect the dots.

"You will get tetanus if I snip you with them," I whispered.

His eyes gazed into mine, and then they roamed over my

face. His explorations stilled on my lips.

I was suddenly so hot that it was hard to take in a breath. I went to speak again, but only my lips parted. No sound came out.

Another breeze blew, rustling my dress. He situated me so that it was tight underneath his arms, but his fingers had touched my bare skin. They were rough from working every day, but the touch was the opposite.

I shivered in his arms, like I was cold.

"You're not in shock." He said it like he already knew the answer but wanted to check anyway.

"No." I shook my head.

A slow grin came to his face.

"What?" I said.

"I knew you'd end up here, but not this way."

"I do not even know your name," I said.

"You will."

"Is it a secret?" I stared up at his face as he moved us again.

"Depends," he said.

After a few minutes, I said, "On?"

"Whether or not I trust you."

I wiggled even harder, demanding he put me down. He walked a few more steps and then set me on my feet. My knees were still unsteady, but I made myself stand straight.

He was much taller than me, wider, with muscles, but I would not back down.

"You do not trust *me*?" I said, the shock in my voice apparent. "I do not trust *you*." I pointed at him.

He grinned again, stepping up to me. I held my ground and our bodies almost touched. He bent down, getting closer to my ear. "You will," he whispered.

I closed my eyes, another shiver racking my body as he moved away from me. When I opened my eyes, he had already disappeared into the field of men—a modern-day Houdini.

# 9

## ALCINA

For the tenth time since my eyes opened that morning, I almost ran into one of the men who helped me bring the boxes from the kitchen in the factory to the delivery van.

My focus felt broken and in pieces. Not only did *lo scorpione* haunt my dreams, but he still appeared where he once wasn't. It was throwing off my game.

I did not need the distraction. I had enough on my mind, and his presence only reinforced why my life was the way it was.

Through our channels, I had learned that *papà* was close to finalizing the terms of the arrangement. Even though they were dangerous men he was bargaining with, me as the chip, as they say, he refused to budge on one detail. Only one person seemed to know what it was, and that person was my *mamma*.

There were days I was thankful for this. For the time it gave me to be somewhat free. Other days I was not. I had a guillotine hanging over my head, and every second of every day I wondered if it was going to come crashing down.

After a man recovers from being castrated, an animal like

Junior... I shivered to think what his punishment would be. Even with two balls, his temperament was horrible.

"This one?" one of the guys helping asked.

I nodded. Besides making pastries for the pistachio festival, and generally helping where I was needed, I also made candles. It was something I did to free my mind when it became over-crowded with thoughts and worries. Every so often, I would take a trip to Modica and swap pistachio goods for some choco-late, which the city was known for, to use in my pastries.

The Ranieri *famiglia* had shops in different parts of Italy. The main one was in Modica. They sold their famous chocolate and other things, including candles. They ordered extra supplies for me so I could pick them up and take them back to Bronte.

The Ranieris were *famiglia* on my *mamma's* side—my *mamma's* aunt was married to Pasquale, a famous poet.

I had stayed with them for a while, to give me a different place to hide, but after Pasquale passed, I decided to be closer to my sister. I had never mentioned Fabrizio or his *famiglia* to Junior, because he was a man who did not ask many questions, only demanded to know certain things. Such as the layout of my body.

My stomach felt sick thinking of him, and I hauled the last box from the counter and turned too fast, running into the stomach of the man behind me. His arms came around the box, and mine were already there, so we stood awkwardly.

He smiled at me. "I can take this."

Even though Fabrizio's business was mostly run by *famiglia*, there were always new men from year to year. I did not get close, because I did not trust anyone.

A throat cleared from the open door. I smelled him in the air before he even entered into the room. Spice from his sweat and dust from the fields—and that cologne that no man could buy, but still had to own. Power.

The guy holding the box turned to look at *lo scorpione* a second after I did. *Lo scorpione* gave a slow, sharp nod, and immediately I knew what he wanted. For the guy to release the box and get out.

The guy was smart enough to do it.

For a man with such frightening tattoos, he was almost too beautiful to the eye. His hair was as black as a moonless night. His skin was smooth and had been kissed by the sun. His eyes were like two dark amber jewels. Cautionary tales if you could see past their hypnotic purposes.

He was wearing a thin t-shirt, khaki pants, and boots. The long-sleeved shirt he wore to keep the sun off his back was slung over his shoulder. And when his bare skin touched mine, I started to blink. More aware of it ever since Anna brought it to my attention.

I stopped blinking suddenly, like pressing the brake on a car too fast, and he grinned at me before he went to take the box. I held on and he pulled. When he realized I was doing to him what he had done to me with the glove, he smiled and my breath caught in my throat.

"What is your name?" I asked in Sicilian. My voice was low, breathy, and there was nothing I could do about it.

"Why? You gonna collect the payment on my head once I tell you?"

"Depends," I said, switching to English. "On how much your head is worth."

"Less than yours, angel eyes."

The words—*angel eyes*—sent a thrill through my blood, like hot lava flowing through my veins. I unintentionally let the box go from the burn. He took it from me, setting it on the counter, and then moved in closer.

Staring into my eyes, he lifted a piece of hair that had fallen from my scarf onto my neck, and then let it fall again. He traced the strand with his finger, over my pulse, and then down the gold chain and the cross at the end of it. The cross rested against my pounding heart, where his calloused fingers lingered.

His touch was fire against my heated skin. My blood started to boil, but a shiver felt bone-deep made me tremble all over.

My mouth parted at the same time his hand came around my neck and pulled us together, my body moving with his like fire in the wind, our lips crashing, our tongues tangling.

A moan, soft and trembling, left my mouth, and he drank the sound down.

Walls slammed against my back as we moved from spot to spot, something uncontrolled and wild forcing us together, refusing to let us part.

A frustrated noise left my mouth when he pulled away from me. It was sudden, a rip, a tear, in something with no name that demanded more of the stitching—the creating of something life-changing.

My sister cleared her throat. When I met her eyes, it seemed like she had been clearing her throat. She stood at the open door, men behind her, with her hands on her hips, blocking their entrance.

The leftover fire from that kiss seared my cheeks, and I pushed past her and the men, engulfed. She was blinking furiously when I did, trying to hide a smug grin.

"Attraction, Alcina," my *mamma* once told me, "*is desire in waiting.*"

What my *mamma* didn't tell me was that, once I gave in to it and it was set free, there was no going back to that room with four walls and no windows.

*Lo scorpione* had dragged me someplace, but it did not feel like the hell I had imagined. His hell felt more heavenly than anything I had ever touched in my life.

I LIFTED my head from the steering wheel of the van when I heard someone open the doors and place a box in the back.

*Lo scorpione.*

I groaned, but not loud enough for him to hear. I needed some time to breathe. To recover. To make sense of the senseless.

He climbed in beside me after he set the box I had forgotten with the rest.

"What are you doing?" I said in Sicilian.

He stared at me for a minute, those eyes unnerving me with their intensity. I felt like I could not take in air properly when he looked at me like that ... when he was close ... when I thought of him. I could not escape him even in dreams.

"My name is Corrado Alessandro Capitani," he said in perfect Sicilian. "I am a wanted man—by enemies and by the law."

"I know that name," I whispered, and my hand was on the door before he could put his on my arm to stop me. We stayed that way for a while, his touch blistering my skin. I looked out the window, refusing to look at him. "How much is the price on my head worth?"

"To me..." He paused. "Invaluable in worth."

"Will you hurt me?"

"No."

"Will you kill me?"

"No."

"Will you—bring me back?"

"That's the deal I made."

"You will have to hurt me or kill me to do it," I said, my voice firm and unwavering. "You should have let the *vipera* get me."

His grip on my arm turned almost painful, but I let it flow through me. Nothing could compare to the thought of living a life with the bull and his *famiglia*. "I would hurt or kill myself before I gave you up," he said.

My head turned slowly, our eyes meeting. "Why?" I whispered.

He turned away from me, nodding toward the road. He wanted me to drive. I looked in my rearview mirror and noticed a car behind me. Nicodemo was in the driver's seat, and Uncle Tito sat next to him. The two men who came with Corrado—the American who looked like a chipmunk and the Italian with the never-ending serious look on his face—were in the backseat.

"I gave myself up to you," he said, his face still forward. "That's all the assurance you need that my word is good, but if not ..." He glanced in the mirror.

I had my answer. He knew I trusted Nicodemo and Uncle Tito.

"Your sister sent them," he said.

Ah, yes, she was looking out for me. The moment I saw *lo scorpione*, my mind started floating in the clouds, not grounded by reality, and she knew that.

I started the van, and we drove in silence for over an hour. It was only two from Bronte to Modica.

"Tell me why you did it," he said.

I glanced at him. He was staring at my face. He had been doing that periodically during the drive, but since I did not meet his eyes, it did not bother me as much.

"I have done many things," I said. "Just this morning—too many to count."

"Why you cut his balls off."

My hands strangled the steering wheel. "How much do you know about me?" I said.

"Enough," he said. "But not nearly enough."

I nodded. "I was born in Forza d'Agrò, where most of my *famiglia* still live, but when I was eight and Anna was six, our *papà* took us to America to find better opportunities. He got a job with a fruit market, and we lived with his brother and wife, with a few cousins, until we were able to afford an apartment of our own. *Mamma* got a job working at the same place."

A car swerved in front of me and I lifted my hand, yelling at the driver, before I shook my head and continued.

"We lived in New York for eight years before we got a call that our *nonna* was sick. *Mamma* had been homesick for a while. She wanted to go back. We did. After *nonna* died, *papà* and *mamma* took over the restaurant. We ran it as a *famiglia*.

"One day an American man came in with some men, and he noticed me. He came every day for a week, using the little Sicilian he had to speak to me. He was nice enough, at first, but there was nothing about him that drew my eye. The more he came in, the more I kept my distance."

*Mamma* started to take his order instead, but he would get impatient and demand that I serve him. Then one day he went to *papà* and said that he knew how things were done in Italy, and he wanted to marry me. *Papà* told him no." I sighed.

"No is usually a universal word, but he could not understand it. He pushed and pushed. Then one day when I was walking home, he said that I *had* to marry him, or his *famiglia* in America would come after mine. I was young and scared and agreed to it. He did not want me to tell *papà* and *mamma* until after."

"You're still married to him," he said.

I shook my head. "I was *never* married to the bull." I ran a hand along my neck, leaving it in the crook. "He was not fluent in Sicilian or Italian, and I told the priest that he was forcing me. That his *famiglia* in America were powerful. I asked him not to truly bind me to him, as a mercy. I would have to give my body, but I refused anything else."

I glanced at *lo scorpione*, and his eyes moved me to finish.

"The bull does not ask. He steals. And he hurt me. He beat

me...when I said I was not ready for him." I swallowed down acid in my throat at the thought of him. "He behaves like an animal, so he was treated as one. The place he rented for us to live was an old farm. It had the rusty old shears. I hid them next to the bed, in case he tried to hurt me. He did. I used them."

"You've been hiding ever since."

"*Sì*." I nodded, lifting my hands from the steering wheel for a second. "The men with him were staying in another part of the villa for the night. After he screamed, I had a few seconds to run. I ran in the darkness by the light of the moon.

"A woman a few miles away hid me after I told her I was running for my life. She brought me home, and I have been on the run ever since. His men came looking for me the next day, after they found him and got him help. Then it was other men, scarier men."

"You're fortunate," he said, "that they didn't use your parents to lure you out."

"They tried," I said, reaching for the cross against my chest. "But *papà* made a deal with some men after they started threatening my *mamma* when they could not scare him. He made an arrangement with a *famiglia* that does not care for the men who come here from America."

"You're the deal."

"Not at first. It was just money. But now I am to be married by October." I shrugged. "Right before you arrived, two men came to Bronte looking for me. They found Anna. That was when I agreed to the arrangement. I will no longer have to hide, and my *famiglia* will be safe. But there is something stopping it. *Papà* will not tell anyone what it is. He will not allow the man to meet me, either, before he agrees to this condition."

I could feel his eyes on my face. "Is it worth it?"

"My life?" I said, narrowing my eyes against the glare of the sun. "I had something to live for, so *sì*, it was worth it. I was living for me—for the life my *mamma* gave me."

"You misunderstand," he said. "Is the new arrangement worth your life?"

I hesitated, but then nodded. "My *famiglia* will be safe."

We said no more as I found a place to park the van. After we stepped out and I opened the door, Corrado took the box I grabbed out of my arms, but neither of us tugged or let go. We stood that way for a minute or two until the men that came with him started to move around us, going for the boxes.

"Where do these go?" the chipmunk asked.

I pointed in the direction of the store with my chin. "There."

"Inside," Corrado said to me, nodding ahead of him, wanting me to walk. His eyes searched the crowded street. I wondered if he was looking out for himself or for me.

It did not matter. By October, he would be married, and so would I.

I WAS SURPRISED to see Mariposa—or as we called her, Mari—working behind the counter, holding her baby. Mari was Amadeo's wife. He was my cousin.

The store was busy, as usual, but when our eyes met, a smile lit up her face.

"Bringing us some gold?" she asked when I got close enough.

I made a "give me" motion with my hands, reaching out for her *bambino*, Saverio, pulling him close and kissing his little head. He smelled like heaven. "*Sì.* I also brought these two along." I nodded toward Nicodemo and Uncle Tito, who were coming up behind me.

Corrado stood off to the side with his men. He was still holding the box, as was the serious-looking Italian, but Chipmunk had already placed his down and was looking at the chocolate. He constantly had food stuffed in his puffy cheeks. If he didn't, he was looking for it.

"Here is the gold," I said, giving Saverio fat kisses on his delicious cheeks. "I also brought pistachios for the *zie*."

"They've been waiting." Mari pointed her finger behind her, about to speak, but hit a chest instead. My cousin Amadeo stood behind her, eyeing Corrado and his men. If Mari was close, so was my cousin. His cold blue eyes assessed them as he took Saverio from me, sticking the hand with the black wolf tattoo under the baby's shirt.

This made Mari and me both eye them. Amadeo had been a wanted man in America. I did not know much about why, but I did know his father and brother were bad men. His father treated his mother, Noemi, so poorly that the family felt that was why she had committed suicide.

She had suffered with mental illness most of her life, and the life she had with him eventually took its toll. Then his father tried to kill him. The mark on his hand proved what *famiglia* he had once belonged to. He claimed them no more. But that was all I knew about the situation.

Corrado stared back at Amadeo, and I did not like the look on either face. I noticed one of the men Corrado came with, the serious-looking Italian, touch the guns he kept hidden underneath his shirt. The tension pushed me to take the box out of Corrado's hands and stand between him and Amadeo.

"Where are the *zie*?" It took Amadeo a minute to answer me. I had to say his name.

"Back," he said in Sicilian.

As he said the word, Stella, Eloisa, Candelora, and Veronica came out of the room in the back of the shop, arguing with each other. The *zie* were his *mamma's* sisters. They caused enough of a fuss to disrupt the tension between the men.

The aunts were followed by a red-haired woman laughing at whatever the aunts were arguing over, and a man with a tiger tattoo on his neck and a little boy in his arms. A little girl stood close to the red-haired woman. I had met her at Mari and Amadeo's wedding, but I could not remember her name.

"Cash doesn't do sugar." The red-haired woman rolled her eyes at the man with the tiger tattoo. Cash was stuck behind the aunts and a few people shopping the store, so he didn't see that she had done it. He was busy fixing the little boy's hair anyway.

Mari popped up next to me, and she smiled at Corrado. He gave her a polite nod back. "We're going to the beach. Keely and Cash and the kids have never been. Do you want to come?"

So Keely was the red-haired woman's name. "No," I said, kissing her cheeks. "I need to get back. The harvest."

"I ordered you extra supplies," *zia* Candelora said, motioning with her hands to follow her into the back. "I figured you would want them."

I touched Corrado's hand, wanting to break the dangerous spell between him and Amadeo, hoping he would come with me.

I did not miss the look on Amadeo's face when I did. Neither had *lo scorpione*.

Amadeo nodded at Uncle Tito to follow him out.

I took the opportunity to redirect Corrado's eyes by just leaving the room.

# 10

## CORRADO

Two days after I took the ride to Modica with Alcina, Tito Sala invited a woman named Rosa to the pistachio orchard to meet me.

She spoke very little English, and as we walked, she moved her hips closer to mine, smiling shyly as she bumped me every so often. It wasn't her eyes that had mine, though. It was the angry woman who was named after a sorceress in a poem that had me looking over my shoulder every so often.

It fucking unnerved me when she was too far away. I kept my eyes on her at all times. There was still a bounty on her head, and even if I were to order Silvio to call it off, he might agree to my face but go behind my back until she was found.

Even though Silvio and I were friendly, tension ran high between us after my grandfather said he would give me his blessing to run the *famiglia*. If Silvio knew how I felt about Alcina, he might do it just to spite and weaken me.

"Your family is very powerful, I hear," Rosa said, smiling at me. She touched her neck. "You will buy me jewelry?"

"I'm a poor farmer in America," I said. "I have nothing."

That was far from the truth.

Rosa stopped walking. After a few steps, I did, too. She picked up a second later, walking beside me again, but her hips were on the opposite side of the worn path, no longer bumping me.

I nodded to Rosa and her family when we came to the central villa, where her people waited for us to return from our walk. I kept walking until I was back in the orchard, straps around my neck, ready to fill my bucket. The sun had started to make its way to the horizon. I only had an hour or two left to work.

Even after it became dark, though, there would be some light still left. Red lava spilled from Mount Etna. It shot out, like a woman spewing curses from her mouth, and then ran down the side.

A bump stronger than anything Rosa had given me made my bucket rattle. Alcina stormed passed me, and when I called her name, she turned around, walking backwards. She lifted her arms. "*Mi scusi*," she said, her tone as fired up as the fucking volcano.

The group of women she walked with turned their heads at her tone. The men kept looking between us, trying to mind their business but not.

We could have an audience. I'd taking a fucking bow once this was over.

I grabbed her by the arm when she turned her back on me. She tried to yank it out of my hold, but I held on, dragging her toward a more secluded area. We were in a manicured grove with a manmade path through the trees, which were evenly spaced. Not balanced on crooked lava rock.

As soon as I let her go, she went to storm off, cursing me in Sicilian as she did, waving her hands wildly in the air.

Before she could get far, I grabbed her by the shoulders, turning her around, her back slamming against a pistachio tree when she tried to move away from me.

Her eyes rose up to meet mine in defiance when I put both arms around her waist, locking her in. Her chest heaved like she'd run a marathon. Her breath washed over my face. Her fingers were curled into fists at her sides.

If I stared into her eyes for too long, my angel eyes, she fucking possessed me. My mouth slammed against hers, and her hands fisted into my hair, her leg coming up to wrap around mine. I ran my hand under her dress, feeling her hot skin against my palm as I cupped her ass.

All of a sudden, this woman was both the center of my world and the bane of my existence. A vice and a visceral need. She was stubborn and willful. Fucking wild, like she was made from the moon, and that madness moved through my blood like nothing ever had before.

It was one of those warring things that were total opposites but couldn't live without each other. I never wanted to have her, but I was desperate to keep her.

She moaned into my mouth, her hands fisting in my shirt, and then she pushed me away as hard as she could. She couldn't move me with physical strength alone, but when she said the word, "No!" I took a step back.

Her hand trembled as she set it over her mouth. She shook her head. "What is going on between us? I don't understand it. I don't know you, but somehow I have known you my entire life. I know you have come to drag me back to hell, and you probably will, but I do not mind the thought of going with you. Because when you kiss me, when you *touch* me, you take me to heaven, too."

She stared at me for a minute, and then she shook her head and lifted both hands. "But I cannot do this. I cannot be envious when you walk with another woman. I cannot think about you with her and want to claw her eyes out. Yours, too! The thought of you marrying that—*that* woman burns me deeper than the lava on that mountain." She flung a hand toward it.

"You are not *mine* to keep, Corrado Alessandro Capitani, but my soul tells me you are! You are *mine*. But how can I keep you, when it will start nothing but trouble? Not just for me, but for you."

She went to run away from me, but just as she could push me back with one word, I could stop her with one, too.

"Alcina," I said.

She stopped, keeping her back to me.

"*Lu murrisi per tia,*" I said in Sicilian. *I would die for you.*

"If you stay," she said, balling her hands into fists again, "you will. And so will I. It is too late for us."

She disappeared into the orchard as the sun sank completely into the horizon. The volcano came even more alive in the darkness, spitting out fire, the air filled with the smell of smoke, ashes drifting in the wind.

# 11

## ALCINA

I did not realize that I was cursing under my breath until my sister told me to stop.

"You told him to go!" She waved her hands at me.

"I did not tell him to go!" I waved my hands back. "I told him—I did not tell him to *actually* go." Which he had. He had been gone for five days. His men went with him, but Nicodemo had stayed behind.

She leaned against the counter in what I called my candle kitchen. The hidden *casa* on the property had a small kitchen for cooking, plus another one set in the back, which I used for my candles. No one knew about the *casa* but my sister and Fabrizio's *famiglia*.

It had been Fabrizio's grandfather's *casa* when he was still alive. He did not care for people, but only the company of his cats. The product of a past generation sat in the window, licking her paws, watching as my sister and I shouted at each other.

"What do you want, Alcina? Tell me. Tell me as if you are speaking to a wish maker."

I turned from my sister, wiping a hand along my forehead. It was hot with the burners going and the summer air from outside. The smell of lemon and chocolate was pungent in the small space. Especially the citrus. I made my own oils for the candles.

"I want my life to be *mine*," I said. "I want his life to be *his*."

"That is a simple wish," she said.

"How can it be?" I wiped my hand on a towel, staring out of the window. It was secluded in this area, nothing but trees and cats. "It is complicated. I am wanted for what I did to Junior, and I am to be married to a man who would start another war if he found out I have even been spending time with another man. It has been doomed from the start." I waved a hand casually, but my eyes burned.

"You are right," she said, and even though I could not see her, I knew she was nodding. "The two of you will start a war. On your side and his. It is good that he has gone. Let him marry *Rosa*, and you marry Elmo—I mean, *Eraldo*. Everyone lives unhappily ever after."

Even though it was the truth, and I needed that from her, it made me mad. "It might not be *Rosa,*" I snapped.

My sister started to laugh. I whirled on her, a candle in my hand.

She lifted hers. "It does not matter her name, does it? I hit a soft spot."

"*Sì!* I do not know how to make it go away. The jealousy."

"It will not," she said, all traces of humor gone from her face. "Because you love him, Alcina."

"Love does not happen overnight!"

"*Sì!* It does. Every second of every day, love *happens*. It just moves at its own speed. Sometimes it comes as a speeding thunderbolt. Sometimes it moves at the speed of a lazy summer breeze. It does not matter how fast or how slow. All that matters is that it moves us.

"You will never know real love, Alcina," she said, her voice taking on a pleading tone, "until you give yourself over to it. It does not matter if he marries Rosa, or if you marry Eraldo. What matters is that you give in to love. However this ends, you can always say you had today."

"I do not have today." I snatched a basket from the counter. "He is gone."

She grabbed my arm, stopping me before I rushed out the door. I usually made the candles to clear my head, to create light in my life, but I needed air. My heart and eyes burned from the ache I could not escape. The internal had overflowed to the physical.

"Wars are started for much less," she whispered to me, "than true love."

---

I TOOK a hard step out of the door, landing at an awkward angle on the step. I fell forward, right into the arms of a man. *Lo scorpione.*

"And we meet again this way," he said, looking down at me.

"How did you find me?" I said, looking up at him.

It took a minute for him to right me. When he did, he set me straight but did not let go. "Walk with me, Alcina."

I swallowed hard and nodded. I thought I would never see him again. I thought he was gone for good. The relief I felt was both physical and internal, much deeper than anything I had ever felt before.

I turned to set the basket down, but my sister took it instead. "Today, and for much less," she whispered to me in Sicilian, and then went back into the *casa*.

Corrado and I walked next to each other in silence. It took about ten minutes or so to leave this part of the land and head toward the main property, where the manicured grove was. The place where we had our last conversation.

"You were gone," I whispered, looking at him from the side of my eye.

He nodded but said nothing else.

"Have you come to say goodbye?" I asked.

He stopped walking and so did I. That's when I noticed two bikes sitting side by side.

"You can ride?"

"*Sì*," I breathed out. "Of course."

"Let's go."

My sister's voice echoed inside my head. *Today, Alcina.*

"Where are we going?" I smiled.

"Wherever you want to go."

I nodded, and after we both took our seats, we started peddling toward the exit of the property. The two men Corrado brought with him came with us. The Italian stayed in front, peddling a bike with a side seat for Uncle Tito. Corrado wanted to laugh but didn't. The chipmunk always lagged in the back. It took us longer to get to the city because he had to keep stopping.

Once we did, he demanded food. We ate in the *piazza*, and I tried not to laugh when he stuffed his puffy cheeks with pizza. When he caught me staring, his grin came slow, and so did mine.

We decided to visit *Museo del Carretto Siciliano*, or Museum of the Sicilian Cart. It did not matter where we went. It felt good to spend time with him, to be free for the day.

"*Carretto da Gara*," I pointed at an exceptionally beautiful one. It showcased how the cart and horse were dressed up for a special occasion. "Those are used for parties or weddings. The others. *Carretto da Lavoro*. Those are used for work."

"My grandparents were married in Sicily," Corrado said. "They had a cart and horse after they were married."

I nodded. "They are traditional. Tell me more about your people."

He did, but it wasn't much. It was as if he was reciting stats from a page instead of speaking of his *famiglia*. He spoke nothing of his *mamma* or his *papà*. He spoke of his *nonno* and *nonna*, but it was brief, and it felt...not as warm as a *famiglia* should be.

"Tell me something, *scorpione*," I said after we left the museum and he bought me gelato. "Your marriage is to be arranged. Why is Uncle Tito doing it?"

"Silvio and I were both groomed to take over the family if something happened to my grandfather. I did a thing that put me in a tough spot before I left. My grandfather and my uncle wanted to teach me boundaries. Or whatever the fuck the lesson is." He looked around for a second, thinking or checking our surroundings. There were a lot of people out. "The family is mine, under one condition."

"Ah," I said, licking my lips. "Marriage."

"My grandfather gave the responsibility to Tito after I got here."

"You did not want to choose for yourself?"

"Not particularly."

I thought about this on the ride back to my sister and her husband's place. I demanded to live for such a choice, but he gave his away for nothing.

"Did your grandfather take your choice away?" I said as I stepped off the bike. His arms came around my waist and I looked up at him. The lowering sun hit his amber eyes like candlelight. In this light, they were a much lighter shade than his skin.

"He didn't," he said. "That bother you?"

"*Sì.*" I nodded. "To have such a choice..." I shrugged and sighed at the same time. "It seems like such a sin to waste."

"Some people might appreciate not having to make such a big decision when love isn't involved."

"That is cowardliness," I said. "Pure and simple."

"You think love should be involved in all decisions," he said.

"Not in all." I shook my head. "But in that decision love should play a part. Even the potential to feel it." I hesitated but kept talking as we walked the groves. "That feeling of having your breath stolen when you see—" I looked at him and then turned forward "—*someone*. The madness that happens to your stomach. You cannot eat, but suddenly you taste everything. And—" I inhaled, smelling him in the air "—the smell that lingers, the one that belongs to the one you love. It is unforgettable. It *is* home."

"You're fucking wild," he said.

I threw my head back and laughed. "*Sì!* This is what my *famiglia* tells me! This is why—" I gave him a pointed look "—I am in so much trouble. I have a wild spirit, *mamma* says, one that some men would love to tame, and eyes that belong to a cat, which lure them in."

"You blink," he said.

"Not for everyone. Or so Anna says."

We became quiet for a while, evening settling around us. Then a breath left my mouth when he took me by the arm and pulled me against his body. It was like crashing into solid rock, the soft parts of me forming to fit.

"You blink for me," he said.

"*Sì*," I whispered. "I do."

His mouth was close to mine. I had to stop myself from biting his lip, and then sucking it afterward.

"Tell me, Corrado," I said, breathing out his name, "why did they send *you* to find me?" I ran my hands up his chest, over his shoulders, until my fingers found the tattoo on his neck, right over his collarbone.

"Because I always find the ones who hide."

"After you do?"

"I never fucking let them go," he said, and then his mouth claimed mine.

I was lost to anything but him, like a moth to the volcanic heat of Mount Etna.

It was not until I lay in bed that night, thinking over the day, that I realized why *today* was so hard after he had walked me to my *casa*.

*Today* would never be enough. It was forever with him or nothing. My heart only would accept one, and if it was not to be, it might just stop beating.

I pressed my hands over my heart, over the hurt that welled up at even the thought, and whispered, "*Il cielo mi aiuti.*"

*Heaven help me.*

## 12

# CORRADO

That fucking mad energy was running through my veins again, and I blamed it on the full moon. It was so bright it looked like someone was shining a light in the window when I'd been trying to sleep.

I couldn't sleep.

I couldn't relax.

I couldn't keep still.

It was hot as fuck outside. Sweat constantly beaded and fell from my temples.

"This is not a game that can last forever, *cugino*," Nicodemo said to me. "Make a move."

Nicodemo and I sat across from each other, playing chess at a table placed outside of the building we were staying in. Some of the men who worked the groves were doing the same thing we were, trying to catch the breeze, because there was no air conditioning. It felt better outside than it did inside.

Nunzio sat against the building, staring up at the sky, smoking. "A man who has no patience should not play a game that requires it," he said.

"A man who likes his tongue keeps his mouth shut," Nicodemo said.

I looked between the two men, but I didn't give a fuck why one hated the other. It was a sign of respect in our business to be hated, and by many.

Adriano had a wet towel around his neck, looking through a metal bucket filled with ice and drinks. "This heat has me fucking starving," he said. "Like after you go swimming. I'd give my left nut for some cold watermelon."

I made my move, keeping my eyes on the board. "Tell me why you're here, Nico," I said.

Whenever I called him Nico, it was the equivalent of him calling me *cugino*. I wanted honesty, but on a different level. The terms brought us back to when we were kids, when he would spend summers with my family in Sicily.

He studied the board for a minute. "Giuseppe hid me when —" he made a move, a look coming over his face that made him seem more like the killer he was "—after my parents were killed."

Nicodemo was just a kid—maybe five—when both of his parents were murdered. He was an orphan, and Tito Sala had intervened and found him a family. By the time I could remember going to Sicily every summer, Tito would bring Nicodemo and we would spend them together. I had no brothers or sisters, he was alone, so we kept each other busy.

"Ah," I said, trumping his move. "Obligation."

He made a move that beat mine. "You know me better. I am obligated to no man." He looked me in the eye. "I like the family. Good people."

"How did it get this far—with her?"

He took my meaning clear enough. Why didn't he intervene before, or have Tito involve the Fausti *famiglia*. They were known to revere women. It spoke to their romantic side—the other side was ruthless. They didn't believe in breaking something smaller than them. I tended to agree.

I also didn't say her name, because some hunters blended in with the scenery.

"I was in Israel for the last two years. You are getting slow in your old age." He grinned when he made another move that took my piece. "They did not know how to get in touch with me, and Tito has been more active than usual. Luca has a son only a few members of the family were aware of. It has been a busy time—after Marzio was killed, the Faustis have been at war from within."

He studied the board for another minute and then studied my face, trying to read my next move. "Lothario is acting as the head, as you must know, and it is harder to reach him. He does not make himself as available as Marzio did. He is more selective about who he will help. There have been complaints. He is not his father."

"No," I said. "None of us are."

"*Infatti*," he said, "but if we appoint ourselves to such a high position, we must either meet the men we respect, or exceed their power. We must become them or better."

Yeah, that was the fucking *truth* all right.

Tito came toward us, his oversized hat in his hands. He stopped next to the table, staring at it for a minute, and then gave me a narrow look. "Time waits for no man, not even you," he said, and then he knocked my winning piece over with a flick of his bony finger.

He stormed off, the smell of medicine following him. I would always associate that smell with him.

"What the fuck is wrong with Dr. Salad—I mean, Sala?" Adriano stared after him. "I wonder if he can get me some watermelon?"

I picked my winning piece up, holding it in my hand, studying it. The pieces were crystal, the board black and white.

The light of the moon went straight through it. When I looked up, Nicodemo was staring in the direction the good doctor had taken. Even though his attention was focused elsewhere, I knew he'd hear me when I spoke.

"If I had decided the information worth my death was worth sacrificing her life—"

"—this would be a one-player game," he said, turning his eyes to mine. There was no emotion there, only the reality of the life we chose to live. *Cugini* or not, it would have been a war between us, and one of us would be dead. We chose our paths, and that was that. It was what it was, however it ended.

I nodded, agreeing. I'd kill any motherfucker who came after *mine* now—Alcina Parisi. Including him, if he made the wrong move.

His grin came slow—some said it was the grin of a man who had just gotten vengeance. "What can I say? I like the ones who come out to play when the moon is full."

Yeah, he would. Crazy motherfucker.

---

EMILIA ONCE TOLD me that when I couldn't sleep, it meant that I was awake in someone else's dreams. But Emilia had wild ways, and she told me more than once that Luna had been wilder than her.

I wondered if that was why, when the moon was full, madness seem to run through my blood at a quicker speed. I would concede to that one thing, because usually when the moon was full, something more than blood seemed to draw me out, but no more.

My grandfather was practical. Businesslike. Rooted in reality. He had created the bigger parts of me, and Emilia hated to admit it.

And the other one?

Corrado Palermo.

Fuck. Him.

He never claimed me. I'd be damned if I ever claimed a piece of him. He was lower than whale shit, and there was no going any lower than that.

I refused to even think of him, or anything else belonging to that world, letting a familiar path direct my quiet footsteps. I had only been in Bronte a short time, and already this direction had burned itself into my memory. Even without the moon, I didn't need light to see by. I could find my ending destination in my sleep.

Her.

Her tiny *casa* was hidden deep in the property. Nothing else was around but cats, trees and shrubs. Mount Etna stood directly across, and it made the stone *casa* seem so little in comparison. The moon hung over the mount, perfectly round and golden.

More cats seemed to be out tonight, probably sensing the insanity in the air caused by the full moon. I would have blamed my madness on it, but I'd done this before, many times since I'd arrived—found her *casa* and sat on an overturned bucket outside of it.

Her *casa* was hidden in the trees, but there was a straight path to her place from where I sat.

The first night I'd debated on whether or not I was going to take her back with me.

I never claimed to have a devil on one shoulder and an angel on the other. Both were devils, but an angel had opened her wide eyes, stuck her hands on her hips, and then started arguing with the both of them—in Sicilian.

I grinned, thinking about her snapping those shears at me.

After that, leaving her unprotected made me think harder about who else was out there. Silvio salivated for the chance at vengeance, and he had no idea if I'd been looking for her or not, since communication between that world and mine had been slim. So it would make sense that he would still have other men looking for her, even though he knew I never let the enemy go.

This woman was no enemy to me, though. She was a fucking weapon. Something that made me even stronger as a man.

The closer I came to *la casa dei gatti*—the house of cats—I could smell her in the air. Lemon. Chocolate. And something else tonight—something I hadn't smelled before. Sandalwood. Maybe cedar. It smelled like a fucking man.

Music drifted out into the night, probably from a little radio that ran on batteries and still played cassettes. I'd seen it sitting outside once on a different night. The sound of female laughter melted in with the song.

From my place on the overturned bucket, I couldn't see a fucking thing because freshly washed laundry hung on the lines. It cut off my view.

The shadows of two women danced behind the curtains. The moon dyed the clothes golden-silver, but the shadows were black. With each reach of an arm, twirl of a body with a basket, bump of a hip, a cat circling a leg, or doubling over of a woman's body to laugh, shadow puppets formed. Only two pairs of dirty, bare feet were visible from underneath.

Alcina's laugh rang out, and it seemed to echo in the recesses of my memories, like she'd been with me my entire life. I just had to find my way back home, follow the sound of her laughter.

A cat moved around me, circling my legs, and I bent down to scratch her on the head. She had a mark there like a lightning bolt. I remembered Alcina called her Arista.

The cat purred for a second before she lay down next to me in a bunch of flowers that grew wild around the *casa*. During the day, they curled in on themselves to hide from the sun. They only opened at night.

Alcina called them moonflowers, and against the darkness and in the light of the moon, they were neon white.

I grinned again. The song was in English, but they were singing in Italian—one of them trying to. Anna could sing. Her sister couldn't. That didn't stop her from trying, though.

The show behind the curtains went on for about an hour, and when I heard footsteps coming toward me, I opened my eyes to find Anna standing in front of me, holding a basket against her hip.

She took her pointer and middle finger and pointed them at her eyes, and then stabbed them at me. "We watch you, too," she said. "You watch her. We watch you. My sister is not the only one who knows how to use shears."

"Or worse," I said, trying not to laugh at her. She was cute. "Those clothespins might take my eyes out."

It took her a second, but a slow smile came to her face. That's when I realized her cheeks were wet with tears. She sniffed. "I have not seen my sister so happy in her life. Can you believe it? Her *entire* life. You have given her a glimpse of real light in the darkness. Do not drag her further into it. Or..."

"Or," I said. Hesitation was deadly. It was like hesitating when pulling into oncoming traffic. Either fucking go or stay put, but don't brake.

"You will not see me coming, *scorpione*. I will kill you in your sleep."

A few cats ran after her when she left. I could hear her talking to them, telling them to go back home, until her voice faded and I knew I was alone with Alcina.

The radio turned lower, almost off, and I knew she was doing it so she could hear. I put my head back against the tree, closing my eyes, thinking about what Nicodemo had said to me, about the ones who came out to play in the moonlight.

I wondered if he had ever watched them dance.

An unfamiliar feeling burned me deep, and I thought about getting up and finding him—to take his eyes out with his memories. Even in those plain dresses, Alcina's body made them seem indecent.

It didn't take a man with a creative brain to imagine what was underneath. Her body was a fucking gun. Her eyes the trigger. Her love the killer.

A woman like Alcina Maria Parisi was the strongest weapon known to man, and she belonged to me.

"Judge a man by what he's willing to die for, not by what he's willing to kill for," my grandfather said to me often. "What a man dies for makes the man."

She made me.

It was fucking insane, I never saw it, or her, coming, but so was the moon, and it still took over the sky when the time was right. I was a mere man.

I must have drifted for a minute or two, comfortable in my spot, but her voice had me straightening up.

She was bent over, petting Arista, telling her how bad she was for pulling down a quilt that had been blocking my view. It was on the ground, and the cat was sitting right next to it.

That cat was getting the best fucking tuna from me. I'd been planning on moving it once Alcina fell asleep. A candle next to her bed went out when she did. Her room would glow and then go dark.

My eyes narrowed when Alcina picked the quilt up and laid it on top of one she must've brought out when my eyes were closed. She'd put it down between a patch of moonflowers. Her hair was up, as usual, and she was in the same dress she had on earlier. Her feet were dirty from going barefoot, and I could smell candle wax and fresh laundry when the wind blew.

She turned to the side, facing the moon and Mount Etna,

but she was more outlined by the darkness than brightened by the moon. She was caught in the middle of the contrast.

Her mouth moved to the music playing in the background —*I've always been in love with you*— before she released her hair from the scarf. It fell down her back like dark waves.

I'd never seen her hair down. It became a sacred thing to me then, something for me only—to admire, to touch, to pull when my cock was buried deep inside of her and she was screaming out my name.

She swayed a little, still mouthing the song, and then started to unbutton her dress with slow moving fingers.

One.

Two.

Three.

Four.

Five.

She slid one shoulder out, then another, and then she let the dress fall to the ground. She stepped out of it and then threw the dress in a basket that had been left outside. Left in only plain cotton, she became as stark as the flowers at her feet.

Her hand came up, and she placed it in the crook of her neck, moving it from one side to another, something she did to ease the strain. Her neck was graceful, and the cross that hung around it glinted gold against her skin.

The wind blew again, and she seemed to close her eyes even tighter, as I opened mine even wider. I could taste her on my tongue. Her scent was something I'd kill to keep—to claim.

She unhooked the plain bra, throwing it toward the basket. Her throw wasn't long enough. It hung on the side, halfway in, half-way out. Then she hooked a finger in each side of her underwear, just as plain as the bra, and shimmied the fabric down until she was naked. This time when she aimed for the basket, she made the shot.

A decent man would have closed his eyes. Would have walked away.

I wasn't a decent man, and I never would be. And where this woman was concerned, what she had, who she was, every breath she took, was mine. Even if she hadn't grasped the enormity of that fact yet, and what it meant.

It meant that if any man even dared to look at her wrong, they would answer to me.

Right now. She was answering to me. A call that went deeper than the sound of a voice.

Every one of my deepest desires was playing out like a fantasy in real time, and my eyes feasted on her naked body like they were gluttons.

She swayed a bit to the music, moving her hips from side to side, before her fingers made a slow trail from her neck, between her breasts, back up to her mouth. She traced her lips with a finger, smiling after. It wasn't full, but there was something rebellious about it that I recognized right away.

She lowered down to the ground after, getting comfortable on the quilt, and then lay down, like she was at the beach and the moon was the sun. The light fell on her body, and I could make out every bone highlighted by the dark shadows. Her breastbones. Her hipbones. They created the shape of her flesh.

Her fingertips stroked the sides of her body, until one hand rose up higher, circling her nipple. The other hand went lower, between her thighs, until it disappeared between her legs.

Her mouth parted as she started to move her fingers between her legs and tease her nipple even harder. Her legs parted even wider, and I could see every move she made.

How high she was becoming. How fucking turned on she was.

The inside of her thighs was coated, soaked. My dick was so hard that it was painful.

Her cheeks were red, almost like she was ashamed of the

pleasure her touch gave her. This was forbidden for a woman like her. A woman who was told self-pleasure was a sin.

"Forbidden" seemed to dare her—turn her on. It was buried down deep with that wild spirit she could never set free.

I recognized it right away. It was the reason she'd fallen so hard for me.

I was all of those things and fucking more.

It wasn't the madness from the full moon in my blood. It was this woman running through my veins.

Her breath started to hitch, quiet moans coming from her full lips, and her back arched while she pushed against her hand, fighting for the release.

I could smell her desire and her frustration in the air, like chocolate and lemon. She needed more.

The craving was there, as concentrated and as hot as the air, but not the satisfaction.

My name escaped her lips, once, twice, like a call from the wild, and I stood.

I had been playing a game all night, so I decided to play one more. One Bugsy called Italian Roulette.

# 13

## ALCINA

I had never done this before. Explored my body with my hands—not in this way. I had thought about it, craving the feeling, the release, but nothing had ever turned me on enough to give myself over to it.

I knew it was wrong, forbidden, just like the man I fell in love with, and I couldn't stop that either. So I gave myself over to it...the ache, the unyielding want. The desire.

To be touched...

His face so close in my mind. His eyes staring into mine. The fantasies of him touching me. Doing things to me that I knew were...

*Arrgh...!* A frustrated sound came from my lips as my fingers worked faster, trying to reach the highest point, but it was no substitute for the real thing.

For him.

I needed his touch more than food, more than drink, more than the breath in my lungs, which came out of my mouth in pants.

"Where are you, *scorpione?*" My voice came out breathy, almost begging. My eyes slowly opened and I blinked a few times, staring at the man watching me. My fingers stilled, but the ache continued to claw at me. I should have been embarrassed, mortified, but all I felt was great relief.

A fantasy had come to life in my darkest hour.

The golden light made him glow. The moon was the biggest candle of all.

I opened my mouth, ready to speak, when he removed his t-shirt, so bright against the darkness of his skin, and his boots and pants. A second later, he was fully naked, the moon at his back.

The breath left my mouth, and I shook my head, sitting up. "Please, *il mio amante*. I need you. Your touch. I—"

"You want me to touch you."

"*Sì.*"

"You want me to taste you."

"*Sì.*" The word trembled out.

I got to my knees when he was close enough, soaking in the rugged beauty of him—the only man I had ever called mine. If he claimed me tonight as *his*, I wondered if I was going to be able to walk in September. He was as hard as stone, and as hot as the lava that poured from the mountain. His skin radiated heat, and it circulated between the space between our bodies. A cool bead of sweat ran down my neck, and his finger came out and reversed its trail, all the way up to my mouth.

His finger tasted of salt, of me, of him, and I sucked even harder. He made a guttural noise in his throat and then pushed my head closer, until I took *him* into my mouth.

He was as salty as the finger, but much, much better. I swirled my tongue around, taking him even deeper, but I did not think I could take him all the way. He was too long, too wide, but the more I tasted, the more I wanted.

He hissed and I stopped, looking up. "Teeth," he said.

My fingers cradled his balls. "I want to keep these," I breathed, taking him inside of my mouth again. He placed his hands on my head, starting to move with me, making me take him even deeper, touching the back of my throat. When I moaned around him, he took himself completely out.

My *patatina* had a pulse that matched my heart, and so sensitive that one touch from him, and there would be nothing left for me to hold on to. I would take the fall from heaven.

He knelt in front of me, and taking me around the waist, pulled my body against his. His hands slid down my arms, taking my wrists, pulling them behind my back. His grip was painful, but it made me breathless—the strength.

"You know why hands on this body is forbidden, angel eyes? Because this body belongs to me. No one fucking touches it but me."

His mouth came against mine, and our tongues thrashed, the sounds of raw pleasure echoing around us in the night. His *cazzo* was hot and hard against the softness of my stomach, until he positioned it between my legs. One hand fisted in my hair, and the other slid between my cheeks, pushing me forward, directing me to move against him.

His hardness slid against me, my desire coating my trembling thighs and him, and it was a gorgeous rhythm. A melody between two bodies that had no words, even if the noises were raw and ugly. This was something I had craved, needed, and it did not take long for the pleasure to rise up in me at a manic speed and then overflow, making me come around him. I screamed out his name, my hands gripping his shoulders, every ounce of my energy draining with the release.

"Ah," he breathed out. "You're a screamer."

I screamed out again when he leaned back even further, taking me with him, his *cazzo* entering me fully and to the hilt. The pain made me dizzy, and my body was suddenly drenched in sweat. My nails sunk deep into his skin.

"As tight as a virgin," he said, his eyes like fire on mine.

I bit into my bottom lip, my eyes meeting his. The truth passed between us, and I nodded.

His face turned to stone.

"My choice," I said, my voice steadier than my trembling body. "You are my choice. Please. Do not stop now." And even though the pain of the breach rocked me to my core, the pleasure waited in the wings. My hands fisted in his hair, my mouth coming against his, my tongue tempting and teasing his.

We started to move together, our breaths coming in pants—my lungs took in his air, and his took in mine—and I could smell bitter iron mixed in with his scent. It surrounded me, made me feel like a queen next to her king, and even though we were close, I wanted to be even closer.

"Corrado," I whispered, my neck tilting back, my hair fanning, feeling him so deep inside of me. "*Il mio amante.*"

He sucked in a breath and then hissed it out. He kept me close to him as he switched our position, my back to the ground as he opened me up even further, moving over me. He hit a spot that sent shockwaves throughout my entire body. The first stroke of pain had faded, leaving a burning that only enhanced the feeling of pleasure.

"*Mmmm,*" I moaned out. "Never stop moving inside of me. *Mai.*"

He was going at a steady pace, and then he hit me hard. I screamed out, wrapping my legs around him, wanting to keep the feeling as close as possible. He urged me to open my mouth, and my tongue came out, tasting his, before I was lost, completely consumed.

Out of control.

Wild.

He had set me free but shackled me at the same time.

His eyes were cautionary tales, but I found safety behind them. At the thought, he closed his eyes, moving even faster, rougher. I whispered his name this time, having a hard time finding my breath. He spilled himself inside of me at the same time I came around him again.

His breath fanned over my skin as his head rested against mine, and I wrapped my arms around him to keep him close.

Why was enough never enough with him? Close never close enough? Why did I see him and still miss him? Why did it feel like he took the most vital part of me with him whenever he left?

I did not only want to feel him moving like madness in my blood, but rooted in the pit of my heart, the vines of his love keeping me prisoner for the rest of my life.

WE WERE BOTH QUIET AFTER, the night suddenly so loud in our silence.

He rested next to me, picking leaves out of my hair, and I took comfort in the fact that he didn't push too far away from me after I'd sat up.

"You smelled like another man," he said, his voice raspy.

It took me a minute to hear him, to understand what he had meant. Then I caught his meaning, and my cheeks flushed. "I made a candle earlier," I said, keeping my voice low. "I wanted to capture your scent. I put a little of the oils on my skin..." Cedarwood and sandalwood and amber. I had done it before I went outside and he had found me the way he had. The scent had turned me on more than my own touch had.

We became quiet again after, and I pulled my legs up to my chest, wrapping my arms around them, staring up at the moon. I sometimes found myself sitting in front of the moon when it was like this, reliving the night that had changed my entire life: when I'd run from the bull after he'd been turned into something lesser than what he thought he was. A man.

Sometimes I relished the life it led me to. It gave me time to live it somewhat freely.

Sometimes I resented it for the life I had, even though it was not to blame.

Corrado's fingertips touched the very end of my hair and I shivered, wanting to face him, but not. He had stormed my body, making me restless and comfortable at once. Like the storms I always enjoyed outside of my window at night.

It was hard not to look into the future and think of nights to come without him in them. Filling my heart and dreams but not my arms or my bed. That would be someone else—for the both of us.

With the man *papà* chose next to me, would I return to this place, this moment, and relish the memory of us, or resent it?

Would he do the same with the woman Uncle Tito chose? When he touched her when the moon was full, would he think of me, of us, in this moment?

The thought burned inside of me like a dark candle, hateful and vengeful, and I took a deep breath, sighing it out, trying to put out the flame.

"Alcina."

He called my name, and it was instinctual. I could not ignore him, or I would be ignoring my roots, my true home.

I turned my face toward his, but not my body.

"You didn't tell me."

I stared at him for a minute, trying to place his words. When I did, after he touched my stained thigh, I nodded. "You are my choice. I made the decision. Who. When." I would never regret it. It all led me to this moment. "I gave you a part of me no one else can steal now."

His eyes narrowed, and I turned my face away from his.

"What is your favorite color?" I asked.

"Color," he repeated.

"*Si.*" It suddenly felt so important to know everything there was to know about him. He was a man who was always in control of his emotions, his steps, and I wanted more. I wanted everything. Something another woman would never get—a small taste of his intimacy.

"You," he said.

I turned to face him for a second and then looked away. "What color am I then?"

"The color of a flame. The moon. Of all that's bright in the world."

Not meaning to, I smiled a little at that. Charm on him was a weapon. "Do you sing? Dance?"

"Neither."

His body moved closer to mine and he leaned on his elbow. I could feel his eyes on me.

I asked him a few common questions (favorite food, favorite place to visit) and then a few that were not (favorite dream, favorite thing to do at night).

The last two he answered, simply, "You."

I became quiet, thinking about the most important question before I asked it. "I am still here," I whispered. "Why didn't you take me back to New York? I know you could have found me sooner. You stayed in *Forza d'Agrò* longer than you had to."

His eyes were still on my face. After a few minutes, he turned away from me, reaching for something, and then it touched my leg. I took it from him, holding the picture up to the light to see it better.

"That," he said.

I was around eleven, kneeling in church, a *mantello* covering my hair, my eyes closed, my rosary pressed to my lips. Candles burned in the background of the black and white photo. My *mamma* kept it on a table in her *casa*.

"There is no color in that picture except for you," he said. "I could see it. The life inside of you burning to be set free."

"And you fell in love with me," I teased.

He became quiet. I looked at him, meeting his eyes this time. He lifted his little finger. The round diamond and the smaller ones that created the band glinted against his skin.

I stared at the ring and then glanced at his eyes, at the ring, and then back to his eyes again. "I don't understand," I whispered.

He took my left hand and slipped the ring on my finger. It felt perfectly. I took it off and handed it back. I grabbed a sheet from the line, covering myself. Then I stood before he could grab me, but that did not mean he could not stop me.

"Alcina," he said, settling comfortably, the calm in his voice unnerving now.

"We cannot!" I hissed, like someone could hear. "There are arrangements—for you and for me."

"I knew you'd say that," he said. "And I have an answer."

"What is it?" I asked when he did not go on.

"Fuck the arrangements. I'm not bound, and neither are you."

"I am!"

"You're not. You're bound to one man only." He pointed at his chest. "Me."

"They will kill you!"

"They won't fucking touch you," he said. "Or me."

His arrogance suddenly made me want to strangle him.

"My choice," I said. "And my answer is no."

"You have no choice when it comes to us," he said. "You know it as well as I do."

"I will not curse my only love to death," I said. "I will not!"

"You won't," he said.

"You are wrong." I went to turn when he called my name again. I stopped, holding the sheet tighter to myself.

"Have you ever heard of Italian Roulette?"

"The game?" I said, confused.

"In a casino, it's a game. In life—it's something different. It's a game of fate. Like Russian Roulette. Except it's a game played without protection."

I stood there, staring at him, staring at the moon, wondering what madness he was speaking of. Then it made sense. We were not protected. He came inside of me.

He smiled, so *fucking* cocky. "You could be pregnant."

I wanted to throttle him, but it was my fault as much as it was his. I did not ask him to put on protection. I did not stop what I knew could end that way.

*Mamma* always said it took two to tango.

"*Bastardo*," I whispered, not at him, but at the bull who had put me in this mess in the first place.

Corrado cleared his throat. "You will marry me, Alcina. Not because of what we did, or what might happen, but because you love me. If you walk away from me, from what I'm holding —" he lifted the ring "—you walk away from life. Don't say yes to me, say yes to life."

"That is smug, *scorpione*. To consider yourself as powerful as life."

He said nothing, still holding the ring up.

A tear ran down my cheek. I wanted him more than anything—more than life itself. But how could I put his life at risk for love? Love was the definition of selfless, and if I said yes, wasn't I putting life in front of love?

"Life is just as important as love," he said, reading my thoughts. "You can have both."

I wiped the tear away, taking the ring from him, smiling. When I went to bend down to sit next to him, he pulled me over his chest, making me lose my balance, kissing me madly, making my laughter echo in the night.

---

"ALCINA! ALCINA!"

It took me a minute to open my eyes. Anna shook me again, my name on her lips, making me sit up too fast. We knocked heads and then both groaned as we rubbed the spots.

"*Mamma mia!* Anna!"

"Listen to me," she hissed, rubbing the spot even faster. "Elmo—*Eraldo* is here! He came to meet you!"

"What?" I jumped out of bed, wrapping my naked body in a sheet. Corrado had slept over. He was not in the bed. Where did he go?

"Get dressed!" She waved her hands around wildly. "Put on a nice dress and fix your hair!" She narrowed her eyes at me and then plucked a leaf from the snarled strands. "You *will* explain later."

I was moving too slow for her. She waved her hands at me, telling me to *sbrigati*. *Hurry.* I could not. My body ached from a long night full of hard sex.

I jumped in the shower, quickly drying my hair after, and then put on a pretty black dress. What about the ring on my finger? I took it off, feeling uncomfortable about doing so, but then thought it was best.

What were we going to do about this—situation?

I stopped in my tracks when I stepped out of the bathroom and into my room. Corrado stood with his back against the dresser, a cup of coffee in his hand, only his pants on. His black hair was slicked back. His dark amber eyes were intense on mine.

My sister sat on the bed, one eyebrow lifted at me. I did not miss the appreciative glances she kept giving his chest though. He was built.

"Alcina," he said, his voice poised. He nodded to my hand. "Your ring."

I nodded and went and got it. My sister looked between the two of us when she saw it.

He took a sip of his coffee. "He wants to see her," he spoke to Anna.

"To meet her." She nodded. "To walk with her. Maybe get to know her."

"I should—" I turned my eyes to the door, ready to go.

"Alcina." He took another drink. "He looks at you the wrong way, his eyes are mine. He touches you, I will separate his wrist from his hand with a rusty, dull saw. He falls in love with you, his heart is mine. He'll be a dead man by the end of the day— one without eyes and hands before his heart stops beating."

A quiet groan left my mouth. If I didn't meet with Eraldo, his family might use my family as leverage. If I even walked with him, I might lose Corrado after he killed him. His family would want vengeance no matter what the cost.

"What should she do?" my sister asked the question that had slipped my mind.

"Have Nicodemo tell them Alcina left for Forza d'Agrò." He looked at me. "Finish getting ready, angel eyes, and then we're leaving."

## 14

## CORRADO

I wore a button-down shirt and a vest to meet with her father again. It wasn't as pretentious as a suit, but the clothes still showed respect.

I had worn the same when I first came to ask for his daughter's hand in marriage, sliding the ring I was to give her in front of him.

"No," he had said straightaway and then stood from the same seat he had been sitting in when he had entertained the Balistreris.

"Sit," I had told him, nodding to the chair. "Either way, your daughter will be my wife. So you have two choices. Work with me or against me. If you work against me—" I shrugged. "You will have to work with the Balistreris. Apparently they are not in agreement with one of your terms. Sit and we will discuss."

Alcina Maria Parisi was my wife, no matter if a piece of paper confirmed it or not. Officially she would be soon. That sacred blood she'd saved for me confirmed all I needed to know. She cut off a man's balls so she could choose me. I'd cut off a man's head because I chose her. I'd earn the name Mercenary in her honor.

Angela had squeezed her husband's shoulder, staring at me with a look on her face I couldn't place. I knew this was difficult for him. He felt that he was trading one devil for another to marry his daughter to.

With his back to me, he had said one word, "Why?"

"I love her," I had said in Sicilian and then nodded to the seat again.

I heard the breath leave Angela's mouth, and then she went into the kitchen. She returned with a tray of food and drinks for us to enjoy while we hashed out the terms and worked on a plan. Adriano licked his lips and went straight for the tray. Nunzio kept his eyes on all of the doors.

"Tell me," I had said, when I assured him I could deal with the Balistreris, "what is the last term of your deal with them—the one they refuse to agree to."

"Will you agree to it without question?"

I had narrowed my eyes at him. "Tell me."

"You will sing for her," he had said.

Adriano had started to choke on cheese. Nunzio had to beat him on the back, nonplussed by what Giuseppe had just said. It was a tradition in Sicily. The groom-to-be serenades his bride-to-be from underneath her balcony the night before the wedding.

"*Serenata*," Nunzio had said, nodding his head.

I had moved the vest, taking out one of my guns from the shoulder-holster hidden underneath. I placed it on the table before Giuseppe and slid it toward him, right next to the ring.

"Shoot me," I had said in all seriousness. "I will bleed for your daughter, give my life for her. That should be enough for any man."

The only one who had laughed was Adriano.

Giuseppe shook his head. "For men like *you*—" he pointed at me "—a bullet is easier than a love song."

He was fucking right.

"If you do not agree," he had said, "I will not give my blessing. I will not give my daughter to you without a fight. Even if that means she will go with the Balistreris. For them, this is a business deal, no claim of love. You claim you love my daughter, my *bambina*. Prove it."

Angela met my eye and mouthed at me, "Can you sing?" Bringing me back to the time we'd met in front of the church, when she'd said the same thing to me.

All of these fucking tests.

I'd sighed, stood, took my ring and my gun, and left. Which brought me here. Back to the same restaurant—empty of people—sitting in the same seat, Giuseppe in his, Adriano and Nunzio where they had been, and now Nicodemo. The men were placed strategically around the restaurant.

I had dropped Alcina off at her parents' *casa* after we arrived from Bronte. I told her to start planning the wedding—it would take place in four days. I even called my grandfather and invited him and my grandmother. He did not ask her name or where she was from, but I could tell he was pleased that I chose someone. The rest didn't matter to him.

I instructed him not to bring Silvio, and I also told him to stop him from going after the Sicilian girl he had been after to seek revenge for any wrongdoing to his son. She did not deserve the vengeance. We'd talk more about it at the wedding.

Tito Sala and his wife stayed with the women. Fausti men were placed around their *casa*, since Romeo Fausti had decided to join his uncle. He had some business in the area, and that meant more protection. They were romantic motherfuckers, when they flipped the ruthless side of the coin, and after Tito had told him what was happening, Romeo had agreed to lend some extra protection until I could get back to Alcina.

Giuseppe mopped his head with a handkerchief, watching the door with anticipation. He told me that the Balistreris were getting impatient and that the old man, Eraldo's father, had sent him to Bronte to meet Alcina. He wanted to remind Giuseppe that time ticked, and not in his favor. Giuseppe paid him to help keep the family safe, but once he agreed to go a step further, to marry Alcina to Eraldo, the old man was understanding of his term, for his son to *serende*, but not agreeable to it.

That was the only reason Alcina was not married to Eraldo. The old man respected Giuseppe's traditional side, and he gave Giuseppe until October to come to terms with that not happening.

The thought of *mine* married to *him* made me set my glass down harder than intended.

We were waiting for the Balistreris now. Giuseppe had called a sitdown at my request.

I knew it was only a matter of time before Eraldo wanted to meet her. Giuseppe's hesitation of their meeting, and the price on her head, would only make him more curious about her—was she ugly enough to hide, or more beautiful than he could ever imagine? If he saw her, this would no longer be about business, but something more personal. He would want her.

That eleven-year old girl in my pocket looked nothing like the woman who stood before me in the pistachio grove.

The door opened to the restaurant. All heads turned but Nicodemo's and mine. I picked up my glass, took a sip, and then set it down, fixing my vest after. I was used to a suit.

There were eleven of them. The old man and his son took the center. The muscle protected the hearts. Three of the men stood at the door, blocking our exit, and there were probably more placed around the building.

Nicodemo grinned, his teeth bright against the tan of his skin. He thrived in this atmosphere.

So did I.

I always reacted accordingly. The main thing about these

sitdowns, especially with men who were old school, was respect. Anything less wouldn't be tolerated.

Giuseppe's seat was at the middle of the table, separating the two sides—a representative of his daughter.

I nodded at the old man, addressing him only. "*Grazie*," I said, "for agreeing to this meeting today."

He nodded, picking up his drink, and took a sip. His eyes never left mine.

Nunzio stared at me, and I gave a subtle nod. He translated my words so the *famiglia* couldn't argue that something was lost in translation. The old man hated me on principal, and I could feel it, so I would make sure there were no "misunderstandings" at this *tavolo*.

"I called this meeting today because the deal between your *famiglia* and the Parisi *famiglia* has been broken. There will be no wedding between your son and my wife."

Giuseppe's mouth fell open. He looked between us, as fast as his daughter blinked when she was attracted to something.

Nunzio translated again.

The old man stared at me, his eyes even harder. He knocked on the table once, twice, three times, and then all guns pointed in our direction.

Adriano had his gun out before they did. He was as quick on the draw as he was with snatching a piece of food. That was why it was wise to never judge a book, so to speak, by its cover. There was a legitimate reason why he was sent with me. He would take four of them out before a bullet would touch him. Nunzio had his gun pointed at the old man, his main job to destroy the heart before the muscle destroyed me.

Nicodemo still had a grin on his face—the men at the door wouldn't know what had hit them. He was eager for it, already scenting the potential for bloodshed in the air.

Every word that I spoke, Nunzio translated, even if I would speak a word or two in Sicilian.

"You are a businessman," I said to the old man. "We can either do business, or—" I shrugged.

Giuseppe made the sign of the cross, kissing his fingertips, which came together after.

"We will see her," the old man spoke in Sicilian, and Nunzio translated.

To see what the fuss was about. I shook my head. "The only person you need to see is me."

The old man held my stare, which was unyielding, as I took a drink, just like he had done. The ice clanked in the glass; the amber moved and then slid down my throat like spiced honey.

One of the old man's men had an overachiever finger. He pulled the trigger, barely missing me. The sound of the blast seemed to echo in the room like a war drum.

Adriano had shot him before the bullet even made it past me. It stuck in the wall. Giuseppe turned to stare at it, shaking his head.

I set the glass down, still keeping eye contact, waiting for the moment of truce or catastrophe. I was prepared for both outcomes—if we stepped over the line of business into personal, we would all die at this *tavolo*. It would no longer be old school anymore.

Finally, the old man lifted his hand. I gave a subtle nod. All men lowered their weapons. Nicodemo stopped grinning.

"Business," the old man said in Sicilian. "What do you suggest?"

"Money," I said. "An absurd amount. For your loss, of course."

He grinned at me, and then we made the deal.

# 15

## ALCINA

"What is that noise?" I asked.

Mamma and Anna were sitting with me on my old bed, going through old photographs, drinking *chianti*, and laughing at the amount of lace and silk I'd gotten from my female cousins at my party.

Mamma and Anna glanced at each other, and then they both smiled in unison.

"Go see, *mia figlia*." Mamma shooed me toward the window leading out to the balcony.

I recognized the sound, a *mandolino*, but what I did not understand was why it was coming from below, right underneath my window.

I moved the curtains back, narrowing my eyes on the street. From the soft glow of the lamps, I could see a crowd had formed. At the center of it was Corrado Alessandro Capitani, accompanied by the *mandolinista* playing a soft tune on the instrument.

My eyes narrowed even further when I noticed *papà* standing on the other side of him, moving his arms like a conductor would. I could smell alcohol on the breeze, and I wondered how much they all had to drink.

Corrado cleared his throat when *papà* squeezed his shoulder, and then he started to...sing. To me. From beneath my balcony window.

A loud laugh escaped my lips. *Mamma* pinched me on the arm, hard enough that it felt like a wasp sting.

"Do not laugh at him, *mia figlia,*" she said. "He is doing this for you."

"I am not laughing *at* him," I said, rubbing the spot, but still a smile lit up my face. I imagined it was brighter than any moon, any flame, in the world. "I am laughing because my heart is happy, *mamma.*"

"*Shh,*" Anna shushed us both, closing her eyes.

The man could not sing, but still, his voice was the most beautiful thing I had ever heard. My favorite sound. I opened the windows and stepped out onto the balcony, needing to be closer. I leaned against the iron, placing my hand underneath my chin, closing my eyes, getting lost in the melody of the traditional song, "Serenata."

I knew *il mio amante* would rather take a bullet for me than to sing me this love song. He truly loved me.

I had a suspicion then on the term *papà* had set that neither the bull nor Eraldo would agree to. Corrado had.

The traditional song merged into another. I remembered, from my time in New York, my aunt's old records, that this song had been sung by a man with a throat made of velvet. I opened my eyes to see better, like it could help me see *him* better. The man my heart had known forever, but was so new to my eyes.

I swayed to the melody, keeping my eyes on his, and when the *canzone* came to an end, I applauded softly. I wiped a tear from my cheek and then bowed to him, as if the dance was ending.

Come tomorrow, our dance, a permanent one, was just beginning.

# 16

## ALCINA

I had dreamed of wearing this dress many times.

Even as a child I would beg *mamma* to let me wear it after she showed it to Anna and me the first time. Anna thought it looked old. I thought it had charm that most dresses these days did not.

It was vintage and had belonged to my *nonna* Evangelina. It was classic, elegant, and romantic—it was timeless. A dress that could have been worn years ago or in modern time.

Anna said that if the wedding dresses of Grace Kelly and Apollonia Vitelli—from *The Godfather*—had a child, it would be *nonna* Evangelina's.

"I take it back," Anna said, appraising me through the mirror in our parents' *casa* after *mamma* helped me into it. This was the first time I had seen myself all day. It was bad luck for the bride to look in a mirror before she put her gown on. "I have a better description. If old-world Roman Catholic had a mood, it would be this dress."

The entire gown was made of fine French lace, even the bodice and long sleeves, and it barely swept the floor, especially with the heels I wore.

Anna softly ran her hands through each side of my hair, which we had parted down the center, making sure it was *perfetto* before *mamma* set the matching scallop veil on my head. The tulle was made in Italy, but the lace matched the dress. *Mamma* pinned it on in such a way that it looked like it was made to be there. The beauty of it cascaded over my shoulders and ran along the floor. It was longer than the gown.

Anna smiled at me before she put her hands over her mouth. "The dress did not fit me," she said, shaking her head some, "but it is *perfetto* for you, Alcina. You look ethereal." She turned and looked at *mamma*, moving her hands away from her face dramatically. "Alcina!" she screamed. "Alcina!"

I laughed at how ridiculous she was being, but it was true. Corrado told me I did not have to hide any longer, that we would be getting married in the daylight for everyone to see, and here we were—about to take the walk to church without fear.

"Alcina!" *Mamma* smiled at me, her eyes crinkling with happiness. She ran her hands over my veil, right above it, not touching me. She wanted to, but it did not seem as if she wanted to mess up what she had done. "*La mia bambina.*" My baby girl.

She kissed her palms and then put them to each side of my cheeks. I closed my eyes, relaxing into her touch, and then a tear slipped when she kissed my forehead.

"You are not only effortless beauty, Alcina," she whispered. "You are bold strength. Remember that, ah?"

"I will remember," I whispered.

"*Bene.*" She kissed me again, letting her lips linger. "Because that man is going to try your patience, your devotion, your love."

I opened my eyes to meet her serious ones.

"They all do, *bambina mia*. In their own ways, *capisci*? Your man has a mind of his own. A strong mind. That is good. Once he wants something, or not, it does not change." She shrugged. "He wants you. And right now...this is all so *romanticismo*. As it should be. The villain has turned into the hero. Your knight in shining armor. But where there is light, there is always dark, ah? We have to learn how to balance both. We must be determined to love even when the romance fades."

"*Si, mamma.*" I nodded.

Anna sighed. "If he does not treat you right—"

We all looked at each other and then made a cutting motion with our fingers, a *snip, snip* noise with our mouths.

*Mamma* pulled us both in, careful of my veil, as we laughed, and told us as long as her blood pumped through our veins, she knew we would be all right.

---

THE WARMTH of the sun poured over my face as I kept it turned up to the sky.

As a girl, I had dreamed of roses and candlelight on this day. But as a woman, I wanted moonflowers and the sun.

*Papà* took my left hand and kissed my ring finger. The ring, which reminded me of a halo, dazzled as fiercely as the Mediterranean Sea. "I have never seen flowers like that before," he said.

I opened my eyes and looked down. Moonflowers. Corrado had sent over the bouquet, my rosary wrapped around the lace-covered stems. "They are night blooming." I grinned.

*Papà* sighed and turned his face forward. When he had seen me for the first time earlier, he had cried. It did not seem like he wanted to cry again.

"*Papà*," I said. "I am going to be okay."

He nodded, keeping his eyes forward. "As long as he remembers what it means to sing."

"You brought him to his knees," I whispered.

"*Amore*," *Papà* corrected me. "*Amore* brought him to his knees, so to speak." He cleared his throat. "My blessing was his then."

Anna stood ahead of us on the steps. She turned around and nodded at us before she walked into the church. A minute or two after, *papà* and I followed.

A choir sang in the background. The sun's rays pierced through the stained glass, but the colors subdued it, making the light glow instead of blind. Even with the prisms of color, the air reminded me of amber again, the smoky smell of burning candles drifting. I was brought back to that cold day in December, when I had asked for things I needed.

One look at the man waiting for me, and I knew every prayer had been answered.

He would be all I ever wanted. All I ever needed.

The amber was not to *warn* me, but to *warm* me.

With each step that I took, with every step I had always taken, I came closer and closer to him. But I had to pass through different levels of light as I did. Brightness that blinded. Darkness that made me narrow my eyes to see better. Then there were the areas that glowed from the prisms. They were absolutely heavenly, soothing in a way that was difficult to describe.

I would forever remember this day, the sound of my footsteps, of the journey, to help me balance the light and the darkness life would bring, as *mamma* had said. I would always remember that each step I took, one foot in front of the other, would always lead me to love.

One step. Another.

Corrado Alessandro Capitani stepped toward me.

We met in the glow.

I blinked up at him. He grinned at me.

"Angel eyes," he whispered.

*Papà* took my hand and placed it in Corrado's, and after

*papà* told the church he would be giving this woman to this man, we walked together, footsteps in sync, meeting *Padre* Greco at the altar.

The service was in Italian, and Corrado had practiced his vows. He spoke them perfectly, each word understood, each word loud enough that the entire congregation heard his promises.

*"Io, Corrado Alessandro Capitani, prendo te, Alcina Maria Parisi, come mia sposa e prometto di esserti fedele sempre, nella gioia e nel dolore, nella salute e nella malattia, e di amarti e onorarti tutti i giorni della mia vita."*

I did the same.

*"Io, Alcina Maria Parisi, prendo te, Corrado Alessandro Capitani, come mio sposo e prometto di esserti fedele sempre, nella gioia e nel dolore, nella salute e nella malattia, e di amarti e onorarti tutti i giorni della mia vita."*

Before *Padre* Greco announced us as husband and wife, Corrado cleared his throat. *"Ho trovato qualcosa per cui vale la pena morire."*

I stared at him, the amber in the air moving around him like smoke, and cleared my throat. *"Ho vissuto per te, anche quando non sapevo che esistessi."*

*I have found something worth dying for.*

*I lived for you, even when I didn't know you existed.*

*Padre* Greco announced us as husband and wife. Then he told Corrado that he may kiss his bride.

*Mio marito*—*my husband*—placed his hands on each side of my face, his touch warm and firm, his thumbs skimming the corner of my mouth, and leaning in, he kissed me in heaven, creating something sacred between the two of us.

THE AIR WAS STILL hot as we walked arm-in-arm toward my grandparents' *casa*. *Famiglia* and *amici* followed behind us— their laughter and animated conversations reflecting all that I felt.

I had never seen the look Corrado wore on his face before. "What are you thinking?" I whispered as he helped me down a particularly steep slope of road. Our village twisted and turned with the shape of the terrain, molded by the hands of it.

"Many things," he said, the light hitting his eyes and turning the hard amber into dark honey. "But they all revolve around one central point. You. *I miei occhi d'angelo.*" *My angel eyes.*

I smiled at him, and he kissed me. Rowdy applause broke us apart but did not steal the smile from my face. Nothing could. I laughed against his mouth and continued to laugh throughout the entire evening.

We had only had a few days to plan, but what we did in those days turned out to be spectacular. Like the dress, I wanted a sense of tradition mixed in with a dash of modernity. Our roots and our extending branches. Where Corrado and I had come from and where we were headed. Twenty-four hours that would stand the test of time.

Our reception was held at my grandparents' *casa*, but it was usually traditional for the reception to be held on the street where the bride lives. Since we needed more space than what my parents' *casa* had, and my grandparents' place was in a more rural area, we decided to have it there.

*Mamma* along with numerous members of our *famiglia* came together and cooked their famous *ragù* to serve with pasta. Tables were lined with homemade cookies and liquor. Two of my uncles played the mandolin and the *fisarmonica*. Some guests had already started to dance.

A small stage had been built in the yard, but no one would

tell me what it was for. The backdrop was the mountains and sea in the distance.

*Papà* had enlisted the help of Corrado and some of the other men to string hundreds of lights from the trees. The entire yard glowed as the sun sank into the horizon. The hundreds of candles I had brought from Bronte flickered from the centers of every table, adding to the light and softening the moonflowers woven between. I had made each and every candle by hand during my darkest hours. Now they created a light for all to see me by.

I did not care about *all*. I only cared about *him*.

He was talking with Uncle Tito and Nicodemo, and I had been having a conversation with his *nonna*, who had traveled from New York with a few other members of his *famiglia* to attend our wedding. Perhaps he felt my eyes on him, calling to him in a language only the two of us understood, because our eyes met over the hundreds of candles.

I did not need the heat from the flames to make me melt. I needed only one look from him. I remembered the night he first touched me, and a shuddering breath left my mouth.

Corrado Alessandro Capitani was one of the world's most talented magicians. He could touch me without putting a hand on me.

A band started to play and couples drifted closer to the stage. A soft but gruff voice—one of Corrado's cousins from America, Domenico (Dom) Casino, who was famous there, or so Anna told me—started to sing. It was an older song redone, but in the same romantic way—"Unchained Melody," by the Righteous Brothers.

I turned my eyes away from Corrado to the stage, realizing its purpose, and started to sway to the melody. When I turned back to my husband, his eyes were still on me, but his body moved.

It felt like he crashed into me when one arm wrapped

around me, the other fisted in my hair, and his lips came against mine in a kiss that stole my breath. I pulled his hair, trying to get even closer, and my fingers dug into his shoulder.

We moved to the song as we kissed.

Would it always be like this? The intensity of my feelings for him? What I felt *from* him? The secret thing that moved between us, that kept us moving closer and closer together until there was no him, no me, but only *us*—would *it* live as long as we did?

I breathed the lyrics around his mouth, and then I lost my breath when his mouth trailed down my neck, his teeth biting, his tongue licking, his warm breath moving like hot wax from a melting candle. When he reached my pulse, he sucked on the spot and I pulled his hair even harder. "You like it when I get rough with you."

"I do," I barely got out. "I am not made of glass."

"No," he said. "Just the fucking madness from the moon."

I laughed at that, and then he dipped me, making me lose my breath completely. A second later, he pulled me close to his body again. "Let me remember," I said, tapping my chin, pretending to think. "You do *not* sing and you do *not* dance."

"*Corretto,*" he said. "I also don't do the love thing. It's not for men like me."

"Ah." I smiled even brighter, using my thumb to caress his cheek. His cheekbones looked as if they had been chiseled, giving him a fierce look. The look of a man who had seen and done many things. I was sure most of them were not good. "But you do with me."

"*Solo tu,*" he said. *Only you.*

Even though the song was slow and romantic, we moved even slower, even closer. His breath was mine when I breathed in.

He took the fabric of the dress in his hand, almost violently, and I could feel the heat from his palm burning through the delicate lace. When he removed a strand of hair from my face, it was as tender as the breeze. "*Ti amo*, Alcina Maria Capitani."

"*Ti amo*, Corrado Alessandro Capitani," I breathed back. I closed my eyes, using his shoulders to lift myself, placing a soft kiss on his lips.

The song ended, the music changed, and more people were starting to dance, moving faster around us. Anna was making her way toward us with a few of our cousins.

Corrado grinned at me. "That's my cue," he said, giving me a firmer kiss, patting my *culo* as he did. His hand lingered as he put his mouth close to my ear. "It's all fucking mine."

I stared after him as he walked away and took a seat next to his *nonno*, his eyes finding mine after he'd settled. Even after I'd turned away, I could still feel them watching me wherever I would go.

# 17

## CORRADO

Don Emilio didn't expect my wife—who she was or what she looked like.

When I'd called him and told him the news, it was brief, very little detail, and he'd been satisfied to think Tito had arranged it all. That the sound of my voice, eager, had been more to do with expediting the process of being a mere spectator in the family business to a man who ruled the entire empire.

He didn't expect anything more.

In fact, the first time he saw her, before I had introduced them during dinner at Giuseppe's restaurant two nights before the wedding, he leaned over and whispered in Tito's ear, "She is too gorgeous."

The four words bothered me at dinner. I was quiet for most of it, thinking over the comment and its true meaning.

*She is too gorgeous.*

"Ah," Tito had said when I mentioned it. "Your grandfather and Carmine were of the same mind when it came to one term of the arrangement. That she be plain."

*That she be plain.*

Rosa made sense, though it seemed like Tito was being a little generous. She had hips that were padded enough not to bruise when she bumped me hard with them.

*She is too gorgeous. She should be plain.*

I had come to a conclusion, but I knew it was only a matter of time before my grandfather came out with the reason in a blunt explanation.

He sat on a bench by himself, looking over the party like a king. A king who ruled a major family, whose reach spanned from New York to Palermo. There was a reason why he had exiled me here. He could hide me in the mountains.

He knew this territory like the back of his hand. He grew up traversing the terrain, climbing the mountains and setting sail on the sea. This was his world, even though he had a kingdom in New York.

He was not a benevolent old man, full of acceptance and bedtime stories. I had once read a book about his life as one of the most powerful Godfathers in history. The book spanned back to his time in Palermo, when he had walked with a priest along the shore of the Mediterranean as a young man. The priest was a family friend who wanted to save his soul before it was too late.

"I walked next to the devil that day," the priest had recounted. "There was no line between good and evil, only what had to be done."

It was not hard for me to read my grandfather's thoughts. I usually knew when he was going to nod—a subtle, deadly move—a second before he did it. I was quicker than him, but we usually came to the same conclusions. I knew that the one second I had on him was the reason he wanted me married and settled. That one second could make a difference when it came to the longevity and success of the family.

That one second was the reason, as he watched my wife dance with her family, that he wondered whether I had been too hasty in my choice. Whether he should have taken matters into his own hands and picked a woman like Rosa himself.

I had surprised him, which was unusual. He couldn't predict my exact actions, but he already knew the mistakes I would make and the level of success I would achieve. He had groomed me to become him, but better.

There was always this drive inside of me to become better than him. It was the reason they all called me Scorpio. I never let go of what I wanted, once my mind was set. I would have what I wanted no matter how high the cost.

My eyes rested on her. She was worth heaven in hell.

My grandfather's eyes were on her, too, but harder with judgment. It rubbed me the wrong fucking way, but out of respect, I bit my tongue.

"I didn't expect her," he said, finally getting to the point. "Martina would have done." He was quiet for a minute, studying my wife even harder. The cross around her neck glinted against the lace in the glow of the candlelight. "You could have kept this one on the side."

Martina was the daughter of one of his men. She was the girl next door, and she could cook. Whenever we had family functions, she was the type to help bring them to order.

Simply put: wife material.

She would be the kind of wife who kept to the kitchen and didn't question why her husband smelled like blood and another woman's perfume at night.

All part of the life. The excess of it.

Besides, they liked to keep it in the family, so to speak.

The only thing the wives and the *goomahs*—mistresses—had in common: both were sworn to loyalty, both in same and different ways.

I considered all of this before the night I spent with Alcina under the moon. All of the temptations that were not temptations before I left New York, but fucks that came with no strings attached. I had decided that I would set that one rule for myself. No other women. I wouldn't hurt Alcina in that way, not after everything she'd been through. Though I was sure there were countless other ways that I would.

I'd leave my wife before it came to that, but I didn't see that happening, either. The thought of me without her, after I found her, was the first truly painful thing I'd ever felt. It proved that I had a heart under this armor. Even after the loss of Emilia, all I could feel was the need for vengeance.

"My wife is not a side dish," I said finally. "She's the center-piece—the golden platter."

"Filled with exotic fruits, none more symbolic than the grape," my grandfather muttered, almost to himself. "She's the entire focus, which is not an option. You were groomed to take my place. The *famiglia* comes first. She knows what kind of man you are—who you are.

"She's intelligent and intuitive. A smart man can sense that about her. She also has a temper. I can sense that about her, too. Which means she will not sit back and accept it all—not without a fight."

I grinned at that, watching her dance with her sister. Even though my eyes were trained on her, I knew my grandfather was watching me.

"*Famiglia e lealtà*," I said, holding out my hand for his. It took him a second, but finally, he took it. "This thing of ours... that is my oath—*family and loyalty*. My code. I won't fail you or the *famiglia*."

He squeezed my hand and then let go. "This is going to be a problem with Silvio," he said. "He is seeking justice for what happened to his son."

We had had a talk about that the night he arrived. I told him everything I knew. It fucking pissed me off that Junior had come to the old country threatening innocent women and their families with the Capitani name to get what he wanted. My grandfather and his *famiglia* were known in Sicily, and most people were aware of the empire he'd built in America. He was respected.

What made me thirst for blood, more than anything ever had before, was the picture Anna had showed me of my wife after Junior had beat her when she told him no.

Alcina had downplayed the situation—omitting two black eyes, five stitches in one eyebrow, a busted lip, and head to toe bruises—but there was no denying that she was a smart woman. She knew if he beat her that badly once, just for saying, "*I'm not ready,*" he'd beat her for the rest of her life. So she chopped his balls off and then ran away, valuing her life too much to stay.

"Junior lies to us," I said. "Silvio covers for him."

"Your wife tells her story one way," he said, and I could tell he was rubbing his chin, his pinky ring glinting in the light. "Junior tells it another."

He became quiet for a while and then made a noise that told me his mind was made up. "I will talk to him. We will come to terms on this situation." Silence settled between us once more before he cleared his throat. "The Scarpones are dead."

Four words.

The Scarpones are dead.

I didn't even turn to look at him.

"You didn't involve me," I said.

"You are in enough trouble," he said. "Both situations are being taken care of. Once they are, you will return home to take my spot. You don't need anything else standing in your way."

"I should've been there," I said.

"None of us were there," he said, his voice so calm it was like he was talking about the weather. "It happened a month or two after you left for Sicily. Someone acted before we had the chance. All signs point to the Pretty Boy Prince, Vittorio Scarpone. I knew it was only a matter of a time. My hunches are rarely wrong. The Irish—Cash Kelly, Ronan Kelly's son—helped, to a certain degree."

"He's a walking dead man," I said. "Vittorio Scarpone."

"You must really enjoy the scenery here," he said.

That was easy to translate: the more I pushed the issue, the longer he would keep me here, even after the smoke had cleared at home.

I didn't turn to look at him, keeping my eyes on my wife, who was talking to a man. Ezio, my sister-in-law had called him earlier, when she'd introduced us. Word going around was that he had just returned from Greece after his wife left him. Before he built up the courage to talk to my wife, he'd been watching the way the lace moved against her body when she danced. The way her hair fell down her back and swayed. The way her mouth moved but no words came out. The way her eyes brightened when she laughed.

"Corrado Palermo," my grandfather said, barely breaking through my concentration. "Your biological father. He got a taste of powerful blood when he came close to killing Arturo Scarpone, when he was this close to slitting his throat. After, it did something to him. It clouded his judgment. He lost it all because he couldn't see past his own arrogance. He became blinded by it. A blind man doesn't go far in war, especially on an old battlefield, where he's up against ghosts who died there."

I leaned forward some, watching her eyes when she looked up into the man's.

My grandfather made a noise in his throat. He was put off by my lack of focus, but not surprised by it. But if he thought I wouldn't recover at some point, he would have said so. "I am proud of the man you've become, Corrado," he said. "That is why I give you the gift of this woman, of clearing her debt with one of my closest men."

"Is that my wedding gift?" It was the closest thing to a wish from a genie in our world. Whatever his children or grandchildren asked for on their wedding days, he gave it to them.

"No." He sighed. "You still get your choice of a gift."

"I want Junior dead. There's no room for the both of us in this world." I would have done it myself, but I had no idea when my exile to Italy would be over. I couldn't risk defying my grandfather, and I refused to risk Alcina's safety. No one could protect her like I could.

"It's her word against his," my grandfather said.

"She tells the truth."

"You would put your balls on a chopping block for her word?"

"Both of them," I said. "Even my heart."

He became quiet for a minute or two, stroking his chin. Finally, he cleared his throat. "It will be my pleasure to bestow this gift upon you on your wedding day."

"I want his face unrecognizable," I said. "I want him to run, to feel real fear."

"No," he said. "This I cannot do. His father is one of my best men, my most trusted men."

"They lied," I said, reiterating the point.

He moved around some and then placed a key in my hand, signaling the end of that conversation. "This is from your grandmother and me—something more personal. A gift for you and your wife. A private plane will take you there tonight. Nunzio has the information. I'm sending more men with him, since it's a little further than I'm comfortable with."

"*Grazie*," I said. After I stood, I kissed him on each cheek, and then turned to go.

# 18

## ALCINA

The post wedding high was still surging after we left my grandparents' *casa*. We were headed toward Catania—that's as much as Corrado would tell me. Once there, we boarded a private plane. The men who filled the cabin were unknown to me, except for Nunzio, the serious Italian, and Adriano, the Chipmunk. I'd finally learned their names during our reception. I did not think Corrado would be introducing me to anyone else.

He had been quiet on the drive from Forza d'Agrò to Catania, and he was still quiet an hour into the flight. Though right after the plane took off, when he must have sensed my unease —it had been years since my flight from America back to Italy —he opened his arms for me, and I found peace there.

"*Grazie, mio marito*," I whispered and then looked down at the dress. *Mamma* and Anna had helped me change into it before I left.

Corrado had given it to me as a gift. It came in an elaborately wrapped box, stamped with a luxury brand name. Inside was a gorgeous cream silk dress. It was the most beautiful dress I had ever worn, apart from my wedding gown. The material was thin and soft, it had no sleeves, and it came in at the waist. It showed a good portion of my back but fell below my knees. It came with a pair of heels to match, with silk bows at my ankles.

His fingers stroked the bare skin on my back. The soft touch and his steady heartbeat lulled me to sleep, and when I woke up an hour—or two?—later, we were bouncing on the runway as we touched down. I went to get up once the plane came to a complete stop, noticing the jacket from his suit over my arms, but he kept me in place. A second later, he picked me up.

"It's customary," he said, "for a man to carry his wife over the threshold."

I grinned, but I could tell that the mood that had followed him from Forza d'Agrò had caught up, or never left. It started after he had a conversation with his *nonno*.

He carried me to a waiting car. It was too dark to see anything but the immediate area around us. Corrado pulled out a long strip of black silk and told me to turn around in my seat. I did, and he secured it over my eyes.

"This is overkill," I said, but smiled. "I cannot see in the dark."

"You might figure it out on the ride, or if you see our next mode of transportation."

All I could tell was that our next mode of transportation was a boat. I could smell water in the air and feel the sway of it beneath his feet. He still refused to let me walk.

It did not take us long to get to wherever we were going, but we did not disembark right away. The men from the plane were whispering to each other, and as soon as Nunzio told Corrado all was okay, he lifted me up and started walking. This part seemed to take time, because he was being careful of his steps.

Finally, he set me down on my feet, and I had to secure the jacket over my shoulders before it fell to the floor. I lifted the collar closer to my face, inhaling, my heart rising and my stomach dropping at his scent. A second later he took it from me, and I stuck my hands in the pockets of the dress, not sure what to do with them.

Even though I could not see him, I felt him moving around me, as if he were appraising me.

"You are so beautiful," he said to me in Sicilian, his voice coming from behind. I craved the heat of his body. My head fell back, letting the weight of it settle against his chest. His fingertips barely traced the cross around my neck and then brushed my bare arms, my back as he moved toward the zipper of the dress.

"That's one of my favorite sounds," he said. "Me undressing you." The dress made no noise as it hit the floor, but my body was instantly aware of his heat. No barriers, except for the lace lingerie.

His arms came around me, pulling me closer. Already his *cazzo* was hard enough to strain against his pants.

I hissed out a breath when his hands searched my body, and then sucked it back in when he pulled me against him roughly, his *cazzo* to my behind. His hand fisted underneath my hair, tugging, and I gave him access to my neck, the frantic pulse there.

"You're a fucking weapon, Alcina," he said. "Either your love or this—" his hand slid, roaming over the cream lace, until he touched me in *the* spot, the one that made me moan "—is going to kill me."

"*Bang*," I whispered.

He had started to suck over my pulse, but at that, he grinned against my skin.

He removed the silk from around my eyes, and I blinked against the soft light, the new place. He had turned me toward what would probably be the most stunning views come morning.

An arched doorway, much taller than me, taller than him, stretched from the floor to the ceiling. There were no lights to see by, but I could make out the outlines. There was a lake, or some kind of body of water, and mountains beyond it.

"Where are we?" I whispered, straining to put the lines together and form clearer shapes.

"Menaggio," he said.

"Como," I said and then whirled to face him. "Lake Como."

He nodded. "This is ours."

I narrowed my eyes at him, and not because he had already stepped out of his shoes. I wondered just how wealthy he was. I had no idea...

"My grandparents wanted us to have something special." He shrugged. "He's been holding on to it for a while. He bought it years ago, along with another property not too far from here. He thought you would enjoy it."

I was not sure what to say. It seemed like his grandfather liked looking at me, but he did not *like* me. Anna told me I was being foolish, but I wondered if he approved of me. It did not seem like I was the kind of woman he expected for his grandson. I overheard him tell Corrado the night I met him that I was "shiny." Maybe like a fucking toy.

"He built an empire," Corrado said, his eyes roaming over the details of the room. "The construction years in New York were good to him."

"It is beautiful," I said, not even needing to see the rest of the house to speak those words in truth. "Beyond beautiful. I will have to thank him."

His eyes came back to mine. Our stares seemed to crash like the waves rushing into shore outside. There had been something on his mind ever since we left. His mood felt...dark, almost dangerous.

He took a step toward me. I took a step back. We did this until he had me pinned against the glass door, his body much bigger and stronger than mine. He made me feel like a woman.

I looked up at him, and in the reflection of his eyes I noticed that I was blinking. He took my hand in his and lifted it against the glass, pinning it there. The black silk slid between our palms. His other hand came around my throat, *lo scorpione* against my windpipe. One squeeze and he would crush it. The pressure was enough to almost make me gasp for air.

"I might have sung and danced for you," he said, his voice in total control, but there was something underneath the surface that was as dangerous as his mood. "But I'm not your fucking puppet, Alcina. I'm your husband. Your mind, body, soul, wants are mine. You get hungry. I feed you. You get thirsty. I pour the wine down your fucking throat. You need to get off. I fuck you. Every inch of you belongs to me."

My head swam in dizziness. My eyes could barely focus. My lungs burned. Not enough air. But I was so wet that the lace between my legs was cool from being soaked. My nipples were painfully stiff, and I was so turned on that a whimper left my mouth.

He applied a little more pressure and I lifted my neck, trying to take in just a little more air, or maybe I would pass out. "You even think about taking another man to bed—" he came in closer, his lips a mere kiss from mine "—I will kill you. Then I will die. *Capisci?*"

He was not doing this to be sexual. The threat in his voice, along with the pressure on my neck, was real. I could see it in his hardened dark-amber eyes. The color was no longer a warning, or warming, but to keep me in his grip for the rest of my life.

I reached down with my free hand and grabbed a handful of his cock and balls, almost squeezing, giving him a warning in return. "*Sì, Scorpione*," I barely got out.

He grinned at me, but it was wicked. He applied a little more pressure, and I had the insane urge to claw at his fingers, to dislodge them from my throat. But I waited him out, defying him by keeping my eyes hard on his. I meant it when I had told him I was not made of glass. I did not shatter when the bull beat me. *He* had, after I disconnected him from his manhood.

No man would ever put his hands on me that way and not expect to be seriously wounded, if I could help it.

This man. He would never hurt me, unless I hurt him in that way first. He was claiming what was his. I knew the difference between what my husband was doing and what the bull tried to do. I also understood what Anna had meant in that moment when she said sometimes a woman could not understand it until it happens to her—to be claimed down to her soul.

"Who am I to you, Alcina?" The pressure lightened a little, but not by much. "That's what you call me."

"*Mio marito*," I rasped out.

"*Ti amo, i miei occhi d'angela,*" he said.

Removing *lo scorpione* from my throat, I inhaled, almost gasping for breath, but he did not give me any breathing room.

His mouth came against mine, and I stole his breath for my own. My hands fisted in his hair, needing him even closer. My leg ran up his, and he locked it in place. His mouth moved lower, devouring my neck, his lips almost gentle. It was the opposite sensation of his rough hand.

"I'm going to fuck you until you scream so hard, I'll have to gag you so none of my men hear. No one hears you but me. Your pleasure is all mine."

I pushed his mouth even lower, trying to feed the ache. *You get hungry. I feed you.*

He bit my nipple through the fabric. My thighs trembled so hard that it reflected out of my mouth in a long, shaking moan. His tongue licked from my neck back to my mouth and then he kissed me again. I thirsted for more. *You get thirsty. I pour the wine down your fucking throat.*

I ripped his shirt, sending the buttons flying to the floor.

Then I unbuckled his pants, using my leg and foot to push them down. He stepped out, undressing the rest of the way.

I decided that *cazzo* was not a good description of his cock, but *lo scorpione* was. I licked my lips, and as I lowered down, I used my hands to caress his sides.

His hands slid in my hair and pulled me closer, making me take him all the way. I swirled my tongue around him, careful not to use my teeth, from base to tip.

He groaned as he seemed to get even harder, and before I could start to move faster, he started to fuck me like he did the first night. He hit the back of my throat, making tears come to my eyes, but I moaned around him. I felt the tremble move through him as he spilled himself.

His neck was back, throat exposed, and he growled in his throat at the release. A second later, he lifted me up by my arms, turning me, my hands against the glass door, facing out.

"Spread your legs for me, Alcina," he said.

I did. My ragged breath fogged the window when I breathed out. The black silk was wrapped around his palm. His hands moved over my sides, slowly inching closer to the back-less lace bra, and then he removed it, throwing it to the side. He caressed my skin with a touch that was barely there, but I could feel callouses on his fingers from working in the groves. The contrast was as delicious as he was.

The more he explored—his touch became a mixture of caresses and a deep tissue massage—the more I trembled.

"Do you like my touch, angel eyes?"

"*Sì, mio marito,*" I whispered, hardly able to talk.

His hands came around my breasts, and he teased my nipples as his tongue started to lick my skin. He took the route from my neck all the way down, licking harder in the indention between my lower back and behind. His teeth bit into the lace of my panties, shimmying them down until I stepped out.

I could feel his warm breath between my legs as he inserted

his finger inside of me at the same time his tongue licked over my behind, meeting his finger.

"Ah!" I screamed out. I lost all balance, my nipples pressing hard against the cold glass. The pressure was too much. I started to pant, hardly able to catch my breath. My hands were pressed against the pane, but my fingers ached to claw, to sink into his skin.

It did not take long before I screamed out his name. I came around him in an explosion.

"Fucking *delizioso*," he murmured, his tongue swirling around his lips. He stood, his front to my back, and turned me to face him.

My cheeks burned, but not from embarrassment. I wanted more. He read the look in my eyes.

"You want me to fuck you, Alcina," he said, his voice gruff.

I looked down at his hand, the silk, and then at his glistening cock. I licked my lips, bit my lip, not sure what I wanted —to have him in my mouth again or inside of me.

He grinned. Wiping *lo scorpione* off with the black silk, he tied it around my mouth. I salivated at the taste of him.

He ran his fingertip down my face. I tried to bite him but couldn't. His grin melted and his eyes hardened. He lifted me up, my legs going around him instinctually, and walked me through the villa until we came to a bedroom.

I was barely aware that the chandelier was lit, but it looked like melting candles, their wicks on fire, instead of actual lights.

He set me down in the middle of a wide bed on my knees and then knelt down behind me, using his knees to nudge my legs apart. "Pretty *patatina*," he murmured. "Too bad I'm about to fucking destroy it."

His fingers ran over my *culo* again, until he started to tease my *patatina*. I tried to scream, to moan so loud that I would wake the entire villa, but the gag stopped me.

It kept me from letting out another scream when he

slapped me between the legs, the sting of it ringing out in the room.

While the sting was still burning, he placed himself at my opening, slowly entering me, but then pulling out before he was fully buried deep inside of me. A frustrated, garbled sound came from my mouth. I squeezed the sheets, my knuckles turning white. My mouth was not working, but my body was. He was at the tip, and then I was slammed back, screaming out when he hit me deep inside.

He started to fuck me like he had never fucked me before. He had my hair and the gag around his fist, and every time he impaled me, a pain from scalp to uterus soared through me, followed by pure pleasure.

Even though my screams were muffled, they seemed to shatter the quiet in the villa, echoing inside of the empty walls. The sound of his balls slapping against me was even louder, and so were his groans. Sweat dripped from our bodies. We slid against each other like two oiled machines. The smell of our sex was an aphrodisiac.

"Fuck, Alcina," he said. He stopped moving, and then he slammed into me so hard that I felt him in my stomach. "Come. Come with me. Now."

His order was my undoing. I shattered around him as he spilled into me. That highest point was almost violent, a crash, an explosion, followed by a maddening surge of pleasure that was the equivalent of touching heaven—a moment when my heart stopped beating and then started pounding when I began to fall.

His head fell against my back. He placed a firm kiss between my shoulder blades. "*Bang,*" he said. Then he flipped me over and placed my hand over his racing heart.

THE MASTER BEDROOM of the villa was on the second floor. It had numerous arched doors that led out onto a long terrace. The room itself was pleasing to the eye, especially this early in the morning: soft colors on the walls, redone floors that still held the stamp of time, and furnishings—there were not many —that were lush. The chandelier was a nice touch. It was created to resemble floating candles, wax dripping from their bodies.

The bathroom. I sighed. The floor reminded me of pearls set in marble, and it was not the nicest feature of the space.

Nothing in the villa compared to the view.

I stood in the bedroom Corrado had brought us to the night before, staring out the window. The lake spread out as far as the eye could see. The water was clear blue with pockets of green that together made teal, and the gold from the rising sun shimmered along the surface. Jade-colored Alps towered in the distance over the small, picturesque villages tucked into the foothills. Clouds seemed to hover like smoke in between the mountains and water. Villas were placed along the mountainsides, some wedged into the crevices, some facing the water. Others were closer to the shore.

Our villa was closer to the water, but it sat back far enough to have a garden area between. Flowers bloomed everywhere. Some I recognized—bright bougainvillea that clung to every surface it touched, blue moon wisteria, and topiaries in different shapes—and some I did not.

It felt as if I had woken up inside of a painting.

I opened the doors, stepping out into the direct rays of the sun, feeling the warm, humid air move over my body. I had found a gold silk robe in the bathroom, and I decided to wear it instead of one of my dresses I had brought from home.

I moved further out onto the balcony, leaning against it, looking down.

I smiled to myself. Corrado was swimming naked in the

pool that overlooked the lake. The muscles in his back worked
as his arms moved him from one side of the pool to another,
time and time again.

Leaving the doors open, I went in search of a way down.
The villa was humungous, and I started to wonder if I was
going the right way until I met men roaming the house. They
did not look at me. I did not look twice at any of them. Until I
found Adriano in the kitchen.

"Corrado," I said.

"Out swimming," he said around a mouthful of food. He
shrugged. "He swims after his workouts." He swallowed the
bite, or stuffed some in his cheeks for later, and showed me
how to get outside.

The grass was soft beneath my bare feet, and the sun was
hot on my face already.

"What's wrong?" Adriano said, narrowing his eyes against
the glare as he stared at me. "Why are you movin' so slow? You
got a cramp or somethin'?" He used his tongue to clean a piece
of food from his front tooth.

I tried not to laugh, but all I could manage was a grin. I was
moving slow because last night was *my* exercise, and I was
feeling it in my bones. He must have thought I was grinning at
him, and slowly, his puffy cheeks inflated even more when he
smiled at me.

"Come on." He nodded toward the garden. "I talk to you too
long and he might dump me in the lake and use me as fish
food."

"Why is that?"

He shrugged. "He either has an arm around a woman to
keep her close, or it's around a man's throat. It's either love or
hate for him. Not that he's ever been in love before you..."

I followed behind him, wrinkling my nose when the wind
blew. His cologne was something that could only be described

as unpleasant, and it usually made me sneeze in confined areas. It was like pepper.

He stopped a few feet away from the pool and then went back the way we came. I set my hand over my eyes, watching him so I would know where to go.

"Mrs. Capitani."

I turned to find Corrado hanging on to the side of the pool, his skin glistening in the sun. His hair was slicked back, making his chiseled features seem even sharper. His eyes were a shade or two lighter than his skin, which made him look almost wicked.

Corrado pointed to his lips. I walked over to him and bent over, about to kiss him good morning. Instead, I hit the water and went under. I came up spluttering, wiping the hair from my face.

As soon as my eyes would focus, they focused on him. He was smiling at me.

*Bastardo!* He had pulled me in.

I hit him in the face with water.

He came after me, and I tried to get away. His arm came around my waist, pulling me hard into his chest. My legs were useless. They floated.

"*Bruto*," I said, splashing him in the face again.

He laughed some, kissing me behind the ear. "You like when I'm a brute," he said, sucking on my earlobe.

I closed my eyes, placing my hands over his wrists, letting him float me around the pool. My eyes opened when he set me against the wall and undid the tie of the robe. It floated off a second later, and he brought me close again, nothing between us but the water. I wrapped my arms around his neck, my legs around his hips, leaning my forehead against his.

"What if the men see?" I whispered.

"They know better," he said. "I doubt any of them want to go blind. My men watch the areas they're ordered to, or they watch other men under them. Only a few watch me. Nothing slips past me." He lifted my chin, examining my neck. He placed a firm kiss on a spot that was a little bruised from the night before. "This hurt?"

"No." I shook my head. "Just a little tender. My *culo*..." I made a face. "That hurts."

I opened my eyes to judge his expression. He had none either way, but there was more to it.

It took me a minute to figure it out, but after he had left me alone this morning, I thought about what had happened before we left my grandparents' *casa*. He had been watching me talk to Ezio, who had returned from Greece a single man. I could tell by the look in Corrado's eyes that he did not like it. At first, I thought his mood was because of his grandfather, but after what he had said and what he had done the night before, I connected the dots. He was jealous.

"It'll be my pleasure to kiss that, too."

I smiled. "You did. It did not help."

"The water will."

"It is nice," I sighed, leaning my head back, turning my face up to the sun, while his mouth worked over my throat. "Where do we go from here?"

"I'm going to spoil you, angel eyes," he said, weighing my breasts in his hands as they floated close to the surface of the water. He caressed my nipples with his thumbs. "After breakfast, we'll do some shopping. I've already arranged it. You need clothes, and the house needs furniture."

I forced myself to focus on him and not what he was doing to my body again. "I mean in the future. Your grandfather. What he meant about you going home and taking his place. When?"

After his grandfather had said it, I heard Adriano call Corrado the future Don Capitani. Corrado had told me he had enemies in New York, and I was no fool to his business, but I wanted to know what was going to happen now that we were married. Would it take years or months for his problems in America to be resolved? Or was our future in Italy just as uncertain as anything else?

His hands moved to my back, and he swam us around for a while before he answered me. "It depends."

I nodded. "You will be Don Capitani after we get to New York," I said, staring into his eyes.

He nodded once.

"You are so...young," I said.

"Age is just a number." Then he said something about not being the youngest in history.

"What about the bul—Junior?"

He studied my face for a second. "He won't be a problem."

I grinned at him, but it was weak. It bothered me that he did not trust me with this part of his life. Not fully. "Nothing is a problem for *Don* Capitani," I said.

"Not a fucking thing," he said, his answer quick and solid.

I looked away from him, staring into the distance at the mountains, wondering how that was going to work. I was not afraid of the bull, but I did not want to see him either. The bull's *patri* seemed even more eager to make me pay than his son.

Corrado turned my face toward his, his grip firm, staring into my eyes for a second before he tilted his head. "Tell me you trust me, Alcina."

"I trust you." It was *them* that I did not trust.

He shook his head. "You trust me *what*?" He turned his ear closer to my face.

"I trust you, *Don* Capitani," I breathed in his ear.

"That mouth is going to get you into fucking trouble, *mia moglie*." *My wife.* Then he dunked me under the water. I could hear him laughing as I started to resurface, the sound of it deep and raspy.

# 19

## ALCINA

Corrado had a car waiting to take us to Milan after our morning swim. I asked him what kind of car it was. He said it was an Aston Martin Vantage. It was not sleek, but strong and sporty.

It sounded like an animal on the hunt as it raced against the twisting and turning roads that led us closer to the city. Since it only had two seats, Nunzio and Adriano stayed close behind in a fast car of their own. More men followed behind them in a van.

"I have never seen you without them," I said.

"My grandfather ordered them to stay with me," he said. "Extra protection."

"These men, these enemies—they really want you dead."

He wore sunglasses, but I could tell he glanced at me from the side of his eye.

"I am not made of glass, remember?" I reminded him.

"No, you proved that last night."

I lifted a finger. "This morning, too."

A slow grin came to his face before he answered me. "They do. My cousin Bugsy figured out that a man who was working for him was using his casino in Vegas to auction women. We don't fucking stand for that."

"So you killed him."

"Them," he corrected. "But yeah, that's the short version of how things went down."

"I have time for the long version."

He reached across the seat and took my chin in his hand, stroking the side of my jaw. I wrapped my hands around his fingers, stopping him. "I am your wife," I said in Sicilian. "I am sworn to the same secrets you are. I am bound by this life. I am here to be your highest council."

He squeezed my fingers, bringing them to his mouth, placing a long, warm kiss on my wedding rings. He stared out of the window for a few minutes, taking the turns as if he were a born racer. He cleared his throat. "*Sì.*" He nodded. "You are my wife. My secret keeper," he said, answering me in the same language. "You are all the things the closest man in my family could never be to me."

He switched to English after, maybe not having the appropriate words. "Time and place, Alcina. There will come a time when life will revolve around my family, my business, and I will need your council then. More than I need it now. What's done is done." He paused. "Right now I'll enjoy my wife, getting to know her, to spoil her on our honeymoon."

"I like the getting to know me part," I said. Then I looked down at myself, at one of the nicest dresses I owned, which meant that it hadn't first belonged to my *mamma*. "But I am fine with what I came with."

"Not the point," he said. "You need new things. I'm your husband. It's my job to provide you with everything. Or would you rather insult me?"

"When you are being so *romantico*?" I laughed. "I would not dare!"

"If I was acting like a bastard?"

"Then I would reconsider."

"Yeah," he said, a smile coming to his face. "Thought so."

We talked the entire time he drove about what we were going to do.

Villages in Como that were worth sightseeing.

Places worth eating.

He told me he could drive a *Vaporina*, the kind of boats they used on the lake, and would teach me. We even discussed going across the border into Switzerland, since I had never been.

A slow song came on in the background, the radio on low, and I asked him what kind of music he liked. He mentioned a few bands and artists I had never heard of. I told him I enjoyed the older stuff.

"Like that song you were listening to the night—"

"*Sì*," I said, remembering the night we had under the moon. When he found me touching myself, and he came out of the darkness like a fantasy come to life. "To me, they don't make music like that anymore."

"That's what my grandfather says," he said. "Bugsy agrees. He listens to Roy Orbison—music like that."

I reminded him of the song he sang to me the night he serenaded me under my balcony. That was old, too.

"Yeah," he said. "That's a classic. So is the song we danced to the night of our wedding."

"That is my favorite song," I said. "It will always be special to me."

He kissed my hand and then pressed a button on the dash. A second later the song came on. I understood then why *mamma* cried when a song she had danced to with *papà* came on. I had always thought it made her sad because she missed those times, but the music gave her the power to relive them.

"Remind me to thank Bugsy," he said.

"*Per*?"

"For teaching Dom the classics." He turned it up some.

"When we get back to New York, we'll listen to it in my old Cadillac."

There was so much about him that I did not know. "Tell me something about yourself that will shock me," I said.

"You first."

"That is not fair!"

"Agree or not." He grinned. It was mischievous to its core.

"Let me think." I tapped at my chin. "I am so boring. All I did before you was hide and make candles."

"And touch yourself."

"No!" I laughed. It sounded wild in the car. "I thought about it a few times, to find the release, but I did not go through with it. Not until the night of the moon—*ah!* That is it. I go a little... wild...when the moon is full. It does something to me."

"That doesn't shock me," he said.

"That is all I've got. Now tell me yours."

"You show me yours, and I'll show you mine." He laughed. "I enjoy the opera."

I thought about that for a moment. "I can see that about you," I said. "The opera is...how do I want to say this?" I arranged the words in my mind for another moment. "It is refined, romantic, but there is something about the music that is...ruthless, at times. It is an emotional ride. You do not shy away from any of that."

"You ever been?"

"No. I have not done much. But I remember watching it on the television with my *zia* once."

"My mother—" It was the first time I ever heard him hesitate, but he went over it so smoothly that, if I had not been paying attention, maybe I would have missed it. "Emilia, she's the one who used to bring me. She said it was a date, and one day, I'd bring the girls there to make them fall in love with me."

"Did it work?"

He shrugged. "I never brought a date."

"Ah." I smiled. "You did not need to bring them there. One look at you and...*bang*. Any girl would fall at your feet."

"You didn't."

"I did." I blinked at him, wondering if we were living in separate times when I had first set eyes on him.

"You didn't fall at my feet, Alcina." He kissed my hand again. "You stepped up to my side."

"I can dodge a few bullets." I grinned. "Tell me more about your *mamma*." The only thing I knew was her name and that she had died right before Corrado came to Italy.

"Emilia wasn't my mother," he said. "She was, but she was actually my aunt. My biological mother—Luna—died when I was just a few months old. Emilia stepped in and became my mother. I didn't know until recently. Or who my father was."

Did he think him enjoying the opera was more shocking than this?

"How did you find out?" The question came out as a whisper.

His jaw was tense. The muscles in his neck strained. "Emilia was murdered by the Scarpones. They were looking for my little sister, Marietta. They thought Emilia knew where she was, or was hiding her. Marietta and I share the same father—Corrado—but different mothers.

"The Scarpone family killed our father and her mother. Their bodies were found, but my little sister was never heard of again. For some reason, the Scarpones still think she's close and want her found. Or they did, before someone took them out."

*Scarpone. Scarpone. Scarpone.* Why did the name sound so familiar?

"You recognize the name?"

It took me a minute to look at him. "No." I shook my head. He was so intuitive that it was almost unnerving. "I thought... no." It did sound familiar, though, but where had I heard it?

"Why would I? I know the names here. I am assuming this is a *famiglia* in America."

He nodded but said nothing else. His mood slipped into the car. There was that danger again. It was coming out at the speed we were traveling at. He seemed to have an excess of it. It came out in creative ways when he wanted to burn some of it off.

"The opera," I said, squeezing his hand. "Tell me more about it. Which was your favorite? The most memorable?"

"I haven't been to that one yet."

"No?"

"No." He checked his mirror and then switched lanes. We were entering Milan. "The most memorable will be the one where you sit next to me. Not as a girl out on a date with a man, but a woman out on a date with her husband."

"I look forward to that," I breathed out, and then kissed his hand.

***

COMPARING myself to the rest of the world made me feel the time I spent in hiding, though I did not feel like I had missed much.

Milan was busier than what I was used to. I stood in the midst of the crowded galleria, watching as hundreds of people passed without noticing me. They were too busy taking pictures in front of the many boutiques with famous names.

"Look," Adriano said, nodding down.

The floor mosaic was created to pay homage to Rome, Florence, Turin, and Milan. Four coats of armor were created. Adriano nodded toward the bull representing Turin.

"According to legend, you have to keep the heel of your right foot on the bull's balls while spinning counterclockwise. It brings good luck."

"I think I have plenty of that," I said and smiled at him.

He started laughing, his cheeks puffing out. "Savage," he said, shaking his head.

I turned to see if Corrado was still on the phone. After we had arrived, he said he had a call to make. His eyes were on me as he spoke to whoever. He nodded toward the boutique across from where we stood.

"Come on," Adriano said. "He'll meet us inside. It'll give you a chance to look around."

I sighed, not sure if I was prepared for this. Mostly, I was a simple woman. I enjoyed being outside, or making my candles. Fancy clothes were not something I indulged in. That was why my wedding gown felt so special. It was an occasion to dress up, to appreciate the feel of the fine lace and silk against my body, to feel like the most beautiful woman in the world when my husband looked at me.

All of this—I looked around once more before I entered the shop—seemed like excess.

Adriano held the door for me before I could open it.

"*Grazie*," I said, entering in before him.

The shop was empty except for a few women who loafed around the boutique, straightening shoes and rearranging jewelry in glass cases. As if in a sci-fi movie, their heads popped up all at once.

They said nothing to me. I said nothing to them. I moved around the displays and then laughed nervously when I noticed a price tag on one of the shirts.

"This cannot be," I said, narrowing my eyes. There were too many zeros for such a plain top.

"It is," Adriano said, sticking close to me. "Get used to it. Corrado doesn't usually flaunt, but he has expensive tastes."

"Can I help you?"

Adriano and I looked at the saleswoman who decided to leave her station and offer help.

I opened my mouth to speak but then closed it when I noticed the other women staring at me, too.

Adriano was dressed plainly, and so was Corrado. I had a feeling they usually wore suits, but maybe for my benefit—since my clothes were vintage and plain—they decided to dress down. The women eyed us with judgment.

A wild laugh built up in my throat when I thought about the American movie Anna and I used to watch. *Pretty Woman.* It was the same scenario. The poor girl goes in for nice clothes and she gets judged for it. I had to fight the urge to lift pretend bags in their faces and say, "*Big mistake. HUGE mistake.*"

Anna would have probably done it, but since my temper was starting to heat, I kept my mouth shut. It was sometimes easier to be quiet then to get started. It was hard to calm me once I was ready to fight.

The door opened again, and again, every salesgirl turned at the sound of it. This time, except for the woman who stared at me, maybe thinking I was going to steal the overpriced shirt, everyone hurried to help him.

He was dressed in a t-shirt and jeans, and they could sense something about him.

Power.

He commanded every room he walked into.

"*Signor,*" one of them almost purred at him. "How can we help you?"

He ignored her and looked for me. I waved at him.

"My people called ahead," he said. He gave a last name that I did not recognize. "The store is ours for an hour."

My mouth dropped. Then I snapped it shut. He had reserved the entire store?

Corrado placed a hand on my lower back when he was close enough.

The woman who had been judging me stood straighter, her cheeks turning red.

"Of course," she said. "Allow me—"

"No." I shook my head. "I do not want to shop here."

I looked at her when I said it. Her lips pursed even tighter. Corrado looked between the two of us and nodded. "I have somewhere else in mind then." He applied pressure to my lower back, ushering me toward the door. When I got there, I decided to do it.

I lifted the pretend bags and said, *"Big mistake. HUGE mistake."* I grinned at the look on their faces as the door closed. On the way back to the car, I told him to bring me to a store that was not as fancy.

"Nonsense," he said. "Only the best for my wife. Fuck them and the commission they just missed out on."

The best, in his opinion, was the same designer label that had made the dress he had given me as a gift. Even though the atmosphere was completely different, it was still lush.

Seeing that I was having trouble deciding, Corrado ordered the women to start bringing me outfits into the dressing room, which looked more like a five-star hotel, or nicer.

I tried on clothes of all different styles, in all different fabrics and colors, but he seemed to like me in gold and black the best.

"That one," he said to an all-lace dress that lifted my breasts close to my chin. Usually all he did was nod, and I knew he wanted me to have it. One nod for him spoke a thousand words.

"I like this one, too." I smiled at him.

He grinned at me, and then his phone rang. I did not hear him speak to Adriano on his way out of the room, but again, silence for him was not uncommon when he was giving the men orders.

*"Mi scusi."* I stopped one of the girls who were helping pile the clothes up. Corrado had told them that I would need a special gown. "The gown...I would like to try something in gold."

"*Sì.*" She nodded, looking me over once more. "I have the perfect one."

I hurried and tried it on before he returned. It was stunning, and it would look perfect next to him. I told the girl to add it to the bill but not let him see.

He came back into the dressing room right after she had taken it to be wrapped. Through the many mirrors in the room, he eyed me with a hungry look. I had stuffed myself into a black lace bustier and was busy attaching the black stockings with little bows onto the garters.

"Those heels." He nodded toward a high black pair in the corner. "Put them on."

I did, moving slowly on purpose. My palms felt ultra-sensitive, as if I were looking down from an absurd height, my stomach dropping at the thought of the fall, when he moved a little closer.

"Turn around," he said in Sicilian, and when I did, he murmured, "Close your eyes."

A second later, cool metal touched my neck. I lifted my hand, feeling smooth and uneven textures beneath my fingers. Three necklaces seemed to be stacked one on top of each other.

His breath fanned against the skin behind my ear as he said, "Open your eyes, Alcina."

The mirror reflected both of us as his finger traced the necklaces against my throat and my chest. They were three different lengths. The one around my throat had a filigree pattern. It was intricate, almost like lace. The other one was a little longer with the same pattern. The third one came between my breasts, and at the end was a diamond that reminded me of a golden moon. My tiny gold cross was hidden behind it.

My eyes rose to meet his while my hand touched the cool gold strands. His eyes bored into mine, but his hands roamed. Each stroke of his skin against mine made me hotter and hotter.

When his finger started to caress my *culo*, along the thin fabric, a low, rocking moan left my lips.

He pulled against the tightest necklace, and it dug into my throat some. "No one hears you but me," he said. Then he pumped a finger inside of my *patatina* and I bit my lip, keeping my moans quiet and deep. I placed my palms flat against the mirror, needing to steady myself.

I could see what he was doing to me from all angles. It turned me on beyond anything we had done before.

He reached around and pulled the bodice halfway down, exposing only half of my breasts. My nipples strained against the fabric, and the harder he pumped into me, the more the satin and lace would rub.

"What do you want, Alcina?"

My head rolled before it fell forward against the glass. "You."

"How?"

"Buried." I hissed out a breath when I glanced in the mirror and saw the way he was looking at me. "Deep inside of me."

"What do you want buried deep inside of you?"

Opening my eyes and focusing on him, I said, "Your cock. *Lo scorpione*."

He grinned at me, pulling my hair back, my neck twisting toward his at an angle that gave him access to my mouth. He kissed me deep, hard, and so long that I started to get dizzy. When the kiss ended, I panted for breath. My skin was slick with sweat.

"The moment I saw you," he said, undoing his pants and pulling himself out. He was rock hard, and he stroked it before he rubbed himself against me. "I knew you were the sorceress. Those eyes have me fucking obsessed." Then he rammed into me so hard that I had to bite my lip to keep from screaming.

The necklace bit into my throat, but I could not keep my eyes off of him, of what he was doing to me. He was fucking me like he needed me to breathe, his grunts deep and quiet, and it was beautiful but cruel to watch. My *patatina* was taking a beating, each stroke on display as he buried himself deep inside and then pulled out. He had a firm, almost painful grip on my hips. But his eyes...they stole my breath.

"You feel so fucking good," he said, his voice gruff. He started moving faster, even harder, and I wondered if my hands were going to shatter the glass from the intensity. "Your body is mine to pleasure," he said in Sicilian, his fingers biting even harder into my hips. "But other times, I am going to make you beg for mercy."

The sound of our bodies slapping echoed around the room. I wanted to scream out at the maddening pain, at the insane pleasure, but I kept it locked inside, waiting for the right time to unleash every ounce of desire he had freed inside of me.

AFTER THE TRIP, we spent our days between Milan and Como.

Corrado wanted the house furnished, so we spent time choosing pieces that seemed to fit us as a couple in the city.

In Menaggio, we spent time on the Vaporina, exploring the lake by boat. We visited all of the quaint villages set around the water. We spent hours hiking up the mountains, finding obscure old churches and other places that took some breath and muscle to find. During these times, we became familiar with restaurants and the staff, finding that we had "our" places while we were there.

Corrado even taught me how to drive the Vaporina, and even though I caught on right away, sometimes I pretended not to know what he was talking about. He would put his arms around me and help me steer whenever I did.

I loved watching him drive the most. Especially in the evenings when the sun was starting to sink into the water and the world around us turned shades that were hard to describe in words. I would wrap my arms around him, setting my head on his shoulder, and we would watch together as the stars came out. He would kiss my head, letting his lips linger, and it was one of the most intimate things I had ever felt.

I found that my husband could be as romantic as he was ruthless.

"*Your body is mine to pleasure,*" he had said in the shop. "*But other times, I am going to make you beg for mercy.*"

No truer words had ever been spoken from his mouth, and I turned to the side, staring at my reflection in the mirror, wondering which version of me he would get tonight. The woman who inspired his romantic side or the one who teased his wild side?

The necklaces he bought me in Milan complimented the dress I had hoped to surprise him with. I slid my fingers against the one around my throat, remembering how it had bit into my skin when he was fucking me against the mirror.

I sighed, straightening, admiring how gorgeous the gold fabric was against my skin. The dress showed off my shoulders, and the sequins danced under the soft lights in our bathroom. I had put my hair up because he liked to take it down.

Movement from the corner of my eye made me jump a little. Then I put my hand over my throat, smiling, but my heart raced. Not from the scare, but from him. His tux was black and his tie gold—it enhanced the color of his eyes. They glowed dark amber against his black hair and tan skin.

He was careful that he did not step on the hem of the dress as he came closer to me, slipping his hands over my hips. "You finally bought something on your own," he said.

I smiled. "The day we went to Milan. I wanted to surprise you." I fixed his tie, even though it was straight. "*Grazie, mio marito.*"

"What are you thanking me for?"

"For all of this—" I gestured with a hand around the bathroom, even though I meant the entire house. "For the clothes. For *you*. For everything."

"I'm actually a selfish bastard," he said. "I didn't buy the clothes for you. I bought them for me."

I looked up at him, confused.

He grinned. "So I can see you in them."

"And take them off?"

"Guaranteed," he said.

I tapped at his tie. "Will you tell me where we are going now?"

"You'll see soon enough." He offered me his arm and I took it.

A car I had never seen before was waiting for us. It was all black, even the windows, and it had the name Bugatti on the back. Adriano stood close by, keeping guard.

Corrado opened my door and helped me in.

A second later he took off, and I looked behind us. "The other men are not coming?" Usually it was a cavalcade.

"No. Only Adriano and Nunzio tonight. The place we're going has enough security. The Faustis will be there."

"Ah," I breathed out, and then looked out of the window. I was familiar with the Fausti *famiglia*.

Amadeo was close to them, and usually, whenever he was around, so were they. After Amadeo's grandfather's funeral, Rocco Fausti was one of the reasons I had decided to leave. He was married to the famed opera singer Rosaria Caffi, but they had an arrangement. They fooled around with other people. Rocco made me an offer, and I turned him down. It was not something I was comfortable with.

I could have told Rocco about Junior, but I did not want to involve them. I did not want to owe them. Anything.

It did not feel like we were in the car long before we pulled up to La Scala.

I turned in my seat. "The opera?" I should have known. We were listening to opera music on the ride.

Corrado nodded. "It's a special night. There's a certain dress code—women in gowns and men in tuxedos. The proceeds from ticket sales go to a charity."

That made sense. The Fausti *famiglia* were big on charitable events. The fancier, the better.

Corrado left the car running as he got out, and Adriano came from behind and slid into the driver's seat. Corrado only trusted Adriano and Nunzio to watch or park his cars.

"This is something out of a dream," I said as we walked hand in hand into the theater. The air was cool, and I could smell the history floating in it. It was like opening a very old book in a chilled room. I wondered what story it would be telling tonight.

"*L'Europa Riconosciuta*," Corrado answered after I had asked. "It was the premiere performance when the house first opened in 1778."

We were running late, so we took our seats right away. Nunzio sat on Corrado's side; Adriano sat on mine. No one could get close to us.

My eyes took in the boxes along the walls. They were lined in red velvet, and the details on the outside were done in gold. I narrowed my eyes some. In the box directly across from the stage, I thought I recognized Rocco and Rosaria, along with Uncle Tito and his wife, Lola.

I glanced down at my program. Rosaria's younger sister, who was also a soprano, was starring in the show. They were one of Italy's finest opera families. I thought maybe the couple next to them was Brando, Rocco's older brother, and his wife, Scarlett. She was a famous ballerina. They had a picture of her in the hallway on the way to the theater.

I looked around just before the lights went dim and the

show started. I wondered how many of these men were like my husband.

I did not think on it long, not when the music seemed to steal my attention. At the sound of her voice, I grew cold, but inside, I felt warmed. The entire production was nothing like I had ever experienced before.

My eyes were glued to the stage.

My husband's eyes were on me.

Every once in a while, he would take my hand and place a warm kiss over my wedding rings. Especially when one touching scene made me cry.

Before long, it was time for intermission. The halls were packed with people, but at least there was not a wait in the bathroom. Rosaria stood next to Scarlett, fixing her makeup, but I did not stop to make conversation. I had enjoyed talking to Scarlett once or twice, but Rosaria had never grown on me.

I stood outside of the bathroom for a second, looking for Adriano. He usually stayed close to me when Corrado was not. I tried to stand on my toes, even in heels, looking for him, but I did not see him in the crowd. I did not see Corrado, either.

As I searched the many different faces, my eyes crashed with a man's who was standing across from me. He was dressed in a suit. It seemed like he was waiting for someone, but he never moved from his spot. He kept staring at me.

My heart started to race, and I gripped the dress in my hands, my knuckles straining.

Where was Corrado? Adriano? Nunzio?

A group of women leaving the bathroom together were walking close, but not close enough that they would notice me if I slipped close to them. I glanced over my shoulder as we walked, weaving around more foot traffic, and the man followed.

I picked up the pace. So did he.

I was walking so fast that it could have been considered a

slow jog. He was not far behind. He weaved in and out of people.

"Ah!" I slammed into a chest. Two strong hands gripped my arms, and I almost flung them off until I realized who it was. "Rocco."

"Alcina," he said. "What are you doing here?" he asked in Sicilian. I did not miss how his eyes took in my face and my dress. His eyes were a green made from the sea, and his skin as tan as the sand. His hair was as black as my husband's, and just like my husband, the contrast was almost shocking.

My chest heaved up and down, and his eyes moved to the pulse in my neck, where he could probably see it beating like a drum from the panic. I had nothing to defend myself with.

"I am waiting for my husband," I said.

He narrowed his eyes at me. "I heard the news. Congratulations."

I nodded. "*Grazie.*"

"Where is he?"

I looked around.

The relief I felt when I saw him made me crumple in Rocco's hands. Rocco noticed and nodded when he saw him, too.

Corrado's eyes were frantic, though his face was stoic. He was looking for me. When he took me from Rocco's hands, pulling me close, I looked around for the man who had been following me. He had disappeared in the crowd, but I could still feel his eyes on me.

Rocco and Corrado made small talk for a minute before Uncle Tito and his wife joined the conversation.

Even though Corrado acted as if nothing had happened, his body had become more rigid after we walked away, heading back to our seats. "Why did you walk away from Adriano?" he said, his tone sharp.

"I could not find him," I said.

"He was standing next to the bathroom. He said one minute you were there and the next you were gone."

"Where were you?" I asked.

"Not far from him. I was talking to Nicodemo."

"Why is he here?"

"He had some news from my grandfather."

"Good news, I hope?"

"The bull is dead," he said.

I stopped walking, and Corrado did, too.

"Wh—" I swallowed hard. "When?"

"Last night."

I looked around and only saw a few people rushing toward their seats. Adriano and Nunzio appeared among them. Adriano looked at me and his eyes showed nothing but remorse. I noticed a pack of nuts sticking out of his pocket.

"Yeah, the motherfucker was eating," Corrado said. "He dropped the bag and bent down to pick it up, and that's when he lost you." He took me by the arm and started ushering me back toward our seats. "Tell me what happened, Alcina."

"Nothing," I said, trying to catch my breath. He had broken the news so smoothly, as though he was telling me that the rodent problem we had at home had been taken care of. Like the only reason it mattered was because it mattered to me.

"Don't fucking lie to me."

"A man," I said. "I thought—he was following me. But if the bull is dead..." I took a deep breath. "Maybe I was imagining it."

"No," he said. "Silvio might still have people looking for you, which means they're looking for me, too."

"What does that mean?" I looked at him, at the set of his face, and there was nothing showing there but a man determined to get back to his seat before the show began again.

"It means that if Silvio decides he wants me dead because I ordered his son dead, we will not agree to disagree."

"We should leave?"

We took our seats again. This time it seemed like Adriano and Nunzio were on higher alert. Nicodemo took the seat directly in the back of me.

"No." Corrado fixed his suit after he sat, taking my hand again. "My wife will enjoy the rest of the show. My grandfather exiled me to Italy for his own reasons, but when it comes to *il mio cuore*, I'll die before another man puts his hands on you."

He looked at my arms, where Rocco had touched me, his eyes hard. After a minute, he turned in his seat, his face as solid as the amber in his eyes.

The lights dimmed, the music started, and the curtain lifted. Conversation over.

# 20

## CORRADO

I watched my wife as she took her bag and followed the land down toward the boat slip. I told her to stay close. She took a seat in a grassy area not too far away.

Her back faced me, her hair pulled up and a scarf around it, her sunglasses on, but her face was set toward the fading sun. It was going to kiss the water soon—that was something she said —and she always wanted to be there for it.

Adriano stayed close to her, more eager than usual after the fuckup from the night before. It was the first time I'd ever had an issue with his eating. It usually didn't stop him from doing his job. He claimed to have not eaten much the entire day. His blood sugar was low, so he needed protein to keep from passing out.

"*Cugino*," Nicodemo said.

He sat across from me under the pergola.

"You're still here," I said. "Tell me what's going on."

Nicodemo was like smoke. The only time you really saw him was when there was a fire. He wasn't a motherfucker you wanted to draw close, because unlike the animals who prowled in the night and were afraid of the flames, he wasn't.

"I found the man. He was waiting outside of the theatre—as I would have been. He was sent by Silvio. To kill you both."

I rubbed my chin. "Silvio knew where to find us."

"To be the men we are, we must think like the men we are." He tapped his temple once. "He knows most of the places Don Capitani is connected to. A patient and wise man goes over the list more than once. People are drawn to what is familiar. Silvio knows this."

I grinned at him, but it wasn't friendly. I knew this—this was how I knew sooner or later Alcina would return to her parents' *casa*. But after I'd found the picture of her, I became curious, which changed the entire game.

I wanted to know her village, her people, her parents, and in the end, her. I wanted to know her story. My world was usually colored black, white, and red—hers was in a colorful Sicilian print.

Then I looked into her eyes, and that strange fucking madness that entered my blood when the moon was full took over all logical thinking. She was my madness and my sanity.

Where was my focus? I looked at Nicodemo again. Truly looked at him.

"He also knows about your marriage to the woman who castrated his son. He goes to sleep every night dreaming of her head on a platter. Now that you married her, vowed to protect her, and ordered his son's murder, it is the both of you in a burning building he dreams of."

I nodded. "We'll go back to Sicily then. There are more places there we can go that he knows nothing about."

"There are more people willing to protect you there."

"Yeah," I said. "I agree."

Nicodemo looked over his shoulder at Alcina, who had just stood and dusted off her skirt. It flowed down to her feet and wrapped around her bathing suit. She started toward the Vaporina, slinging her bag over her shoulder. Adriano stood back, watching her.

Nicodemo grinned. "You did not stand a chance," he said in Sicilian. "The old goat knew it."

I stood and then he stood, and I clasped him on the shoulder. "Fate has no purpose where Tito Sala is concerned." I laughed. "He was leading me to her all along."

"Without a fucking doubt," Nicodemo said.

We met up with Adriano as Alcina stepped onto the dock leading to the boat slip. She stopped for a minute, turning around, waving at us.

Another boat came around a turn, going slow, and two men stared at us as they passed. It only took a second for Nicodemo to hit me, for Adriano to scream out her name, and for me to start running.

A *click, click, click*, like the sound of the irreversible hands of time, echoed around us.

The second my body collided with hers, the force from the explosion rocked us at a sideways angle as we were in mid-air, and a second later, we hit the water and it took us under.

Debris splashed against the surface as embers touched down in slow drifts, and dark smoke drifted over the water like rain clouds.

Alcina was pressed up against me, but her mouth was open, her arms floating. She was unconscious and taking in too much water.

I broke the surface, bringing her up first. Nicodemo was waiting by the shore—the dock completely destroyed by the blast—with his hand ready. His shirt had gaping holes where the heat from the blast had burned through, and his skin was blistering already, along with his face.

I took a tight hold of his hand, and he pulled us out of the water. I turned Alcina on her back and started to do CPR. We were not under long, but I had no idea if the blast had done something else to her. Her bathing suit had holes, and so did the skirt. But my main priority was to get the water from her lungs.

"Come on, Alcina," I said, as I listened for her breathing. "Come on, angel eyes, look at me."

I did another round of chest compressions, two more breaths, and then she started to cough, water coming out of her mouth. The sound of her breathing sent air into my lungs. I pulled her tight into my chest, falling back onto my ass in the grass with her between my legs.

The men were in a frenzy around the villa, all doing what they could to make sure the rest of the place wasn't going to blow, or we weren't going to get attacked while we were vulnerable.

Nunzio knelt on the ground next to Adriano. He was sprawled on the lawn, either unconscious or dead.

Nicodemo nudged me, wanting me to look toward the stairs that led down to the yard. Tito Sala and a few other people hurried toward us. He had his doctor's bag. He always kept it close.

Nicodemo's phone rang. A second after he picked it up, he handed it to me.

"Corrado," Uncle Carmine said, hearing my breath. "You must come home. Your grandfather is dead."

My eyes focused on a spot in the water, where a board floated, Alcina's bag next to it. I wasn't sure when Nicodemo took the phone back, or what anyone said after that.

All I could hear was the words *your grandfather is dead*. I watched as something silver drifted closer to the shore, away from the bag that clung to the wood like a life preserver.

EVEN THOUGH MY wife was adamant that she was all right, I demanded that she be taken to the hospital to get checked out. She had flesh wounds, like Nicodemo and me, but I wanted to make sure that when I had hit her, I hadn't broken her in a place I couldn't see.

They had already rushed Adriano to get help, since his wounds seemed more serious, though Tito thought he was going to be fine.

He did not take us to a regular hospital. He took us to a makeshift *ospedale* close to Milan. The Fausti *famiglia* used it whenever one of them, or a group of them, was hurt in the underground wars they fought. I knew they had them throughout New York—we had access to them—but I had no clue about Italy.

The places we used in New York were assigned by our territories, and we had to pay a fee to access them. Tito had an on-call staff that was sworn to secrecy—no one talked. It was in their best interests not to.

A female doctor that Tito said he trusted, Dr. Abbruzzese, was in there with my wife. Tito wanted to speak to me alone.

"I didn't realize you had these places in Italy," I said.

He took a seat on a rolling chair in his office, a folder in his hand. I wanted to know if my wife's name was on it, but then again, I didn't. If this had to do with her—

"Traditionally, no. I could go to any hospital, in any area, whenever I wanted. Things are a bit dicey right now. You have met Brando Fausti and his wife, Scarlett?"

I nodded. "I met Brando. Briefly. I heard things about his wife."

I actually heard things about the both of them, but I didn't want to get into a lengthy conversation about it. Brando Fausti was Rocco's older brother. He hadn't claimed the family as his until he met them in Italy.

The general idea was that Brando Fausti was as fucking

ruthless as his father, Luca, but there were some issues where his wife was concerned. Some big names in the international game wanted her for their own reasons, and it was a constant battle to keep her.

Tito adjusted his glasses and tilted his head, like he wanted me to continue, but I didn't have the time or the energy to deal with the Faustis.

"I heard that she's a famous ballerina—and that she's caused some trouble." I left it at that.

"Trouble." He grinned. "Which is the exact reason I decided to bring the idea of having these places here from New York." He lifted the folder. "This is not about your wife, but your grandfather."

For the second time that day, I knew what it felt like to have my breath stolen and then miraculously given back.

He handed me the file and said one word, "*Prova.*"

*Proof.*

Uncle Carmine could have been just telling me that my grandfather had been killed to get me home, and then ambush me when I got there.

I opened the folder. Photographs were stacked one behind the other. The first one set the tone for the rest. My grandfather sprawled on the cement in New York, his mouth open, a salvo of bullet wounds through his chest in many different spots.

The photographs were taken from many different angles. Some of his men were beside him in death. One draped over the car. Another one on the cement, his head separated into two parts.

One of his underbosses, who also doubled as a bodyguard, should have been with him—and it wasn't me.

I lifted the folder and only then realized that Tito had his hand on my shoulder, squeezing. "His life was not meant to end this way," he said. "I always assumed it would be in the penitentiary, if anything, but not this."

I nodded, bringing the folder down. I opened it up again, removing a photograph. I didn't recognize the place. "Where?"

Tito cleared his throat. "Macchiavello's."

I searched my memory of all of the places I knew in the city, and remembered. It was a haunt for some high-powered officials, rich housewives, and made men. In between them, regular folks who wanted to try what the entire city, it seemed like, raved about. The steak and the fancy booze. I wasn't a man who ate out often. No one cooked like my *Nonna*, and now, my wife.

I cleared my throat. "It was a setup."

Tito shook his head. "As far as I am concerned, it was a legitimate meeting. I set it up myself. He was ambushed on the way out. I had no idea."

"The commission," I said.

The commission was the ruling body of the organization, so to speak. It was set up so that the organization would have rules to follow. Some rules had harsher punishment than others if broken.

If four out the five bosses did not agree to have a boss killed, the idea was vetoed. If someone didn't listen, and still had that boss killed, it was punishable by death.

I had a hard time believing the other four bosses voted to have my grandfather killed. This was not a life where friends were valued—a friend today, a man you made into a corpse tomorrow—but two of the other bosses considered my grandfather a man worth looking up to.

Tito shook his head. "They did not agree to this. The commission is discussing how to go about dealing with what happened. It was unsanctioned."

"Silvio is going to lie," I said. "He did it, and he wouldn't have made a move unless he felt some people out before he did. Made sure he had some backing."

Tito fixed his glasses and crossed his legs. I could tell he was thinking. "Rumors spread quickly after something like this happens. It has been whispered that Silvio ordered it, but he will not admit to it. Not unless he has a death wish." He studied me for a moment.

"The *famiglia* voted in your absence. It is the general consensus among his men that you did not earn this position. That your grandfather gave it to you. It's not enough, though. The majority of the men voted you in. Which means, if the vote does not eat at him, jealousy will."

Both factions were Silvio's now, but the entire family belonged to me.

"Carmine is speaking to each boss," Tito said. "He is briefing them on the conversation the four of us had in your grandfather's office on the day of your cousin's wedding. Just to make the situation clear. Though it really does not matter. You earned the vote."

I nodded. My grandfather wanted to make his wishes clear. Not only did he invite his own *consigliere* into the meeting that day, but one of the most well-known advisors in history.

Tito Sala. He was the *consigliere* to one of the most infamous bosses of bosses Italy had ever seen. Marzio Fausti.

Tito was married to Marzio's sister, Lola, and as such, was Marzio's closest council. It was usually someone in the family, or a close friend, who was chosen for these roles.

It was almost an unspoken rule that a *consigliere* be Sicilian, or at least Italian. It was important to choose someone trusted.

There was no one as trusted as Tito Sala. He gave his honest, unbiased opinion, whether accepted or not.

"You will have to return to New York," Tito continued. "To claim what is rightfully yours. I also think it wise to have a sit-down with Silvio. There are men who voted for him to become boss in your absence. If the commission decides not to act, since he is denying the attack, then it might become a war amongst you and some of your men, Don Corrado."

"It will be," I said, noticing how he had used a formal title to address me. "This is unforgivable."

He stared at me for a long minute. "I knew your grandfather a long time," he said. "He was my friend. Personally, I take this to heart. But. You must weigh the outcome with the price of war. You will win, but at what cost?"

"I will consider it." I lifted the folder. "Tell me more about Macchiavello's. Who was my grandfather going to see."

"There is much more to the story, but all I can tell you is this—the man's name is Mac Macchiavello. He owns the restaurant."

I watched him for a minute. He was unassuming by looks alone, but when pressed, his eyes became hard, and there was no budging him. Even though he didn't shy away from recommending war, he was also a peacekeeper. He had boundaries. We all respected them.

"He spoke to my grandfather?"

"*Sì*," he said, and it was clear he would say no more.

"Tell me one thing, old man," I said in Sicilian. "Did the meeting have to do with the Scarpones?"

"*Sì*," he said, and then made a motion with his hand, as if to say, *no more questions*. His silence on the matter spoke volumes. Why didn't they want me to know more?

He changed the subject. "I believe this is a reason why the commission is not acting as they usually would. After the death of Arturo Scarpone, his son, and his sons, they are missing a boss right now."

A knock came at the door, and Dr. Valentina Abbruzzese stuck her head in. "*Signor* Capitani," she said. "Your wife would like to see you."

I nodded, giving Tito the folder back so my wife couldn't see. Though she put up a strong front, she didn't belong in this life. She wasn't fucking expendable, not like most of the men considered the *goomahs*.

She was the one I'd sacrifice it all for. She was the one I'd die for.

---

THE ROOM WAS DARK, the lights dimmed. There were no windows, and for good reason: the enemy couldn't blast through the glass if they were on the hunt for retribution.

I took the seat next to her bed, noticing her rosary placed across her stomach, and then took her hand. She had burn marks in numerous places, bruises coming up in purple and black patches, and four stitches above her right eyebrow.

She tried to get more comfortable in the bed, to face me, and her breath hissed out after she moved too fast.

"Don't move," I said squeezing her hand. "I can see you."

She grinned, but it was weak. "I cannot see you. Not like I want." She moved slower this time, and then finally, she released a slow breath. We faced each other.

She ran her hand up my arm to the row of stitches I had. Her mouth moved like it did when she sang, silently, no words coming out, just her lips moving. She was counting my stitches. Seven.

"Corrado—"

"It was close, Alcina," I said. "Too fucking close."

She nodded. "It happened so fast," she whispered.

I watched her face until her eyes met mine. "Tell me to leave," I said. "Tell me I'm no good for you. Tell me you're going to get hurt because of me. Tell me all the fucking things you should have said to me the first time you saw me."

"This wasn't your fault," she said, her tone turning bitter.

"It was. I should have kept you in Sicily, where you were safer."

She shook her head. "They were looking for me, too. They have always been looking for me."

"I should have killed Silvio and Junior myself. I should have gone back to New York and taken care of it."

She studied my face for the longest minute of my life. "Then you would have died," she said. "And what about me?"

"You would be safe."

"I will never be safe—with you or without you," she said. "You are my life, Corrado Alessandro Capitani. No matter what happens, my life belongs to you, but my death has been set before I was even born. I refuse to allow you to take responsibility for something that has never been yours, and will never be, unless you kill me with your own hands. And that would mean I did you wrong—with another man—and I *will* never."

"I'm fucking selfish by nature," I said. "I wanted you no matter what the cost, not realizing that there was no cost. There was never a cost. Not when it comes to you."

"Are you leaving me?" she whispered.

"I should. I should make sure you're safe, and will be, and then leave."

"Go then," she said, trying to point to the door, her hand tugging at the IV, at mine, but I refused to let go. "Go and never look back."

I sat there, not moving, and she moved her lips, silently daring me: *go.*

"I refuse," I said, squeezing her hand even harder.

"That's because I will never let *you* go," she said, her voice hard. "No matter what you do, I will always be there with you. Even if you can't see or touch me. It will be much worse, because you will be in love with a ghost that refuses to leave your side. I will haunt you while we both still breathe."

"You're the strongest fucking force I've ever known."

"I know," she said. "Because you love me. That's what love is. *Una forza da non sottovalutare.*" *A force to be reckoned with.*

I brought her hand up to my lips, kissing her cold fingers.

"Even if you would have tried to leave, I could have stopped you," she said.

"How?"

"Have you ever heard of the game Italian Roulette?" She made sure to pronounce the last two words correctly.

I looked into her eyes as she smiled at me. They crinkled on the sides. It brought me back to my time in Forza d'Agrò, when her *mamma* asked me if I could sing.

She reached for something that was tucked into the side of the bed. After she had it, she shook the silver thing at me. It was a baby's rattle. Her bag hung on the edge of the seat I had taken next to her bed—she had demanded that Nunzio get it before we left, or she was *not* leaving—and he must have stuck it inside of the bag when he noticed it floating toward the shore.

"Game over," she said, laughing some. "The house wins. You are going to be a *papà*."

# 21

## ALCINA

T he doors to the plane opened. Corrado stepped out first, giving me a hand down the stairs.

I was thankful that I had chosen to wear one of the designer dresses we had bought in Milan. It was a classic long-sleeved dress with a red rose print set against black velvet fabric. It ended above my knees, and I wore a pair of black knee-high boots with it. My hair was done in a center-part chignon, and I wore a pair of dangling cross earrings to match the dress.

I wore the dress because it had some stretch around the waist. Even though I wasn't showing, I wanted to be comfortable. In this instance, though, I was thankful for comfort and style. The dress matched the color of Corrado's suit. Black with a blood red tie. He said it was his grandfather's favorite color.

It was fitting for a dark king about to return to his bloody throne.

The men who waited for Corrado all wore suits. They judged me behind dark sunglasses that they thought hid their eyes as we made our way closer. I did not need to see their eyes to feel the weight of their stares. Like his grandfather, they were all sizing me up to see if I was worth the title.

The new Don's wife.

It had nothing to do with attraction. It seemed to have more to do with this life, how I would withstand it next to my husband.

Also like Corrado's grandfather, it did not seem like these men were expecting me.

I lifted my chin, my eyes appraising them from behind the over-sized designer glasses I wore. I could size them up, too.

"Don Corrado," one of the men said, stepping up.

Corrado released my hand as the man offered his and they shook. The man kissed each of his cheeks and offered condolences for the loss of his grandfather. Corrado nodded and thanked him. As we made our way to a waiting car, each man did the same.

Another man stepped out of a waiting black Cadillac, leaving the door open. He was older, perhaps around Uncle Tito's age, with the same pure silver hair, but this man had ice-blue eyes.

He greeted Corrado by squeezing his shoulder. They both turned to look at me.

"Uncle Carmine," Corrado said, pulling me closer to his side. "This is my wife, Alcina Capitani. Alcina, this is Uncle Carmine."

"It's a pleasure to meet you finally," he said, taking my hand in a gentle way. "The family will be thrilled, since we didn't attend the wedding."

"The pleasure is all mine," I said.

He nodded and then released my hand. He gestured toward the waiting car. "We will talk on the way."

The conversation was general on the way to Corrado's grandfather's house. We would be attending the funeral the next day, even though it was reported to be the day after. The family did not want the press coverage.

"Tito arranged the—" Uncle Carmine looked at me and then cleared his throat "—meeting with Silvio on the day the funeral is supposed to be held."

Corrado squeezed my hand at this. I had not realized that my palms had gone cold until he did.

Uncle Carmine pulled something out of his suit pocket. A smallish box. He handed it to Corrado from across the car. Corrado opened it. It was a ring made for the little finger, with a "C" stamped into the gold.

Corrado stared at it, not removing it from the box.

"Your grandfather was going to give you that," he said. "As you know, it was his. Something special to him."

Uncle Carmine watched as Corrado slipped it on. Something about it satisfied the old man. He did not say the words, maybe because I was in the car, but I could hear them as if he had spoken them out loud.

*"Welcome home, Don Capitani."*

It was the only official act I'd probably ever see.

Corrado took my hand, and none of us spoke again as we made our way deeper into the city that never sleeps.

―――――――

BLACK IRON GATES opened after the car pulled into the drive. A second after we were through, they closed automatically. I had a burning urge to turn around and look, to see if there was a way out once in. I held my face straight, though, my eyes rising to meet the towering mansion that grew bigger the closer we came to it.

In this affluent area of Staten Island, it seemed a place by itself, with hardly any other "houses" around. The land was protected on all sides, leaving this mansion to stand on its own.

The driver took the turn around a horseshoe driveway, Corrado's side facing the front door, and parked.

Corrado kept my hand tightly in his as we made our way inside.

The furniture and the decorations were all something that reminded me of my *nonna's* house, except the feeling in this... mansion...was completely different. I did not feel warm, but almost chilled to the bone. I used my free hand to rub my arm, thankful for the long sleeves.

The lights were dim, candles burned in numerous areas, and I could hear whimpers, but I could not tell where they were coming from.

Corrado led us to the kitchen, where his *nonna* sat, wearing all black, dabbing her eyes with a tissue. When her eyes met his, she whispered, "They killed him in cold blood."

I stood back when he went to her, and I was faced with an entire kitchen full of women who stared at me harder than the men who had come to welcome their new Don home. One in particular, a plain-looking woman who tried too hard not to be, stared at me with red-rimmed eyes that were more evil than sorrowful.

As I did with the men, I looked at each one of them, letting them know that I was not intimidated.

"Alcina."

Then and only then, when Corrado's *nonna* called my name, did I look away.

She wiped her eyes and then stood to embrace me. She and I had gotten along when I had met her for our wedding. She seemed like a decent woman with a good heart.

"Alcina." She patted my cheeks, her hands cold. "I'm so glad you came." She glanced at Corrado, but her eyes quickly returned to mine.

I took her hand in mine, trying to warm it up some. "I am so sorry about your husband," I whispered.

Her eyes filled with tears. She nodded at me. "Thank you," she said. Then, with a few women following her, she left the kitchen. I could hear their footsteps moving up the stairs.

Corrado took my hand again, his face hard, and we followed the women.

A picture at the top of the stairs stopped me from going any further. It was a picture done in oil of three girls. I ran a finger along the elegant gold rim and then looked up. Corrado was staring down at me from the top of the stairs.

"My aunts," he said, his voice gruff. "My mother."

He did not point out who his *mamma* was, or who were the aunts. I wondered if it did not matter to him anymore. My heart hurt at the thought. He had been deceived his entire life, and then, after the woman he thought was his *mamma* had been killed, was left to deal with the truth of his birth.

I ran my finger up higher to a girl who seemed like the youngest. Another girl had her hand on her shoulder. "This one," I said. "She is your *mamma*." There was something wild in her eyes, something that the others did not have. Corrado had it, too.

"*Mamma*," he said, copying my accent. "Or aunt. They are interchangeable for me now."

"This is Luna?" I knew that was his *mamma's* name, but the woman who raised him as her own was Emilia. I suspected she was the one with her hand on Luna's shoulder. There was a connection between them that I could feel through the painting, like the artist had captured it.

It reminded me of the connection I had with Anna. She would have died to see me safe. There was no question of my love and loyalty to her—I would have done the same if our positions had been reversed.

He nodded but said nothing else.

"Your father," I said, letting my hand fall. "Who is he?"

"I have no father," he said. "There's only the man who created me. Corrado Palermo."

I narrowed my eyes at the name. Why would she name her son after the man who left them?

"Come, Alcina," he said, holding out his hand. "You need to get used to this house."

I took his hand and he led me down a long hallway. There must have been over twenty rooms, at least. "Will we be staying here long?"

"For a while. Until I get things settled."

"Settled?"

"My place doesn't have the security this one does." He stopped at a door in a section of the house that seemed more secluded than the others, opened it, and then waited for me to enter first.

The furniture matched the rest of the house in style. Old world. All of our bags were placed around a vintage armoire that was big enough to hold a few bodies. A matching vanity held my cosmetic bags. An en suite bathroom was bigger than the *casa* I had occupied in Bronte.

"This is our space," he said, his breath fanning over my neck. I felt chilled as he moved away from me, draping his jacket over a chair. "No one will bother us back here."

"No one to hear me scream," I said, smiling a little, but my heart raced.

His fingers trailed down my arm until he took my hand again, leading me toward a fireplace. It was brick and so wide that I could step inside of it. A gold mirror with a filigree design hung over the mantelpiece.

Corrado reached into the mouth of the fireplace, up behind the opening, and pulled out a skeleton key. He lifted it up so I could see. Then he told me to come forward and look at what he was doing. He inserted the key in a hole that was in the wall of the fireplace itself.

It looked like a decorative addition—there were eight of them.

He put the key into the fourth one. After the key clicked, he took it out and moved back. The wall rotated and opened up halfway.

He gestured for me to step inside. I was mindful of my head, but once through, it opened up to a room that looked almost identical to the one on the other side, except it did not have as much furniture.

A bed, a chair, and along the walls, weapons of all different kinds hung behind glass doors. It also had first-aid kits and a cabinet full of food and drink.

"Alcina."

"Hm?" I turned to look at Corrado.

"Watch carefully." He inserted the key back into the door, and it closed the entire way, leaving the key entry on our side. "Always put the key back here." He placed the key in the same spot he had taken it from on the other side.

I stepped next to him, looking through a two-way mirror. I could see into the other room. I could not see into this room from the other side.

"This room is soundproof and bulletproof. If you ever find yourself in trouble, you hide in here, understood? There are keys in rooms that have gold doorknobs. The ones with crystal doorknobs don't have them. Remember—you can't see through gold. Crystal you can. The keys are always in the same place.

"You have to put your hand underneath the lip of the fireplace to find them. Slip the key toward you, or it will just feel like a metal lining. The key always goes into the fourth lock, on either side. Once the door closes on the safe side, the key stays with you and there is no opening on the other side."

"*Sì*," I said, and our eyes connected from across the room.

"My grandfather had these put in when he first built this

house, years ago. It's an extra level of security that no one knows about, except for a few."

"But the builders," I said.

"Not anymore," he said, taking a seat on the bed, loosening his tie and kicking off his shoes.

"They have all died by now?"

"Yeah," he said. "Something like that."

*Ah.* After they built the house, his grandfather had them killed so no one could tell.

"What if they told their families?" I said, thinking it through.

"Couldn't. My grandfather gave specific orders that whoever was working on the house—the ones in charge of building these rooms—had to live on the property. There's a pool house out back, and that's where they stayed while they worked here, along with the architect who designed them. They couldn't leave. My grandfather sequestered the men until it was done. He offered them enough money that none of them refused his offer."

"I doubt they would have anyway," I said, thinking about how he was like his grandfather in that way. He had a way about him that made it impossible to say no to him.

He shrugged. "The day they were finished, the van driving them home blew up—something to do with a mechanical issue."

Sometimes it was hard to accept how their minds worked, how cruel they could be.

"My grandfather took care of their families," he said, as if he could read my mind.

He said it so simply, like his grandfather had put a sticky bandage on a gaping wound, and that was enough.

"It is still cruel," I said. What was worse than murder? Not much, and they were immune to it. In fact, it was a way of life for them, and business was business, no matter how it was dealt with. If it became personal? I refused to think about it. Death was the end game, but getting there was hell on earth.

"So are you," he said. "Standing that far away when you look like that." He grinned. "You're blinking at me, angel eyes."

I stopped after he pointed it out. I stepped closer to him, and when I was close enough, he grabbed me around the waist, pulling me between his legs. My breath caught, and it shuddered out when his hands started to caress my legs. He unzipped one boot and then the other. I stepped out of both.

His hands roamed up my back, and at the top, slowly unzipped the dress. I removed my arms from the sleeves and let it fall, moving it to the side.

His eyes took in my body greedily, the black lace I had worn, and his hands fisted under the chignon, pulling my head back. His tongue licked from between my breasts, up my throat, until he came to my mouth. Then, removing the pins I had in place, he released my hair. It fanned down my back, and he groaned deep in his throat as it did.

"No one can you hear you scream in here," he said.

I moaned at the look in his eyes. His mouth came over mine, hard and rough, as his hand fisted harder into my hair. Our tongues moved in the same rhythm, but then became a melody of hard and then soft. He kissed me this way until I felt the desire go from pooling to a mad rush between my legs.

I unbuttoned his shirt, moving my hands against his skin, as his mouth moved lower and he started to suck his way down my neck. He was marking me. I wanted him to. I wanted him to mark me forever. He bit the lace bra, bringing it down, and I cried out when his mouth closed over my nipple. He sucked even harder and then bit me.

"So loud," he murmured against my sensitive skin. "You're not made of glass, but let's see if we can fucking make you break it." His hand lingered over my *culo* and then came between my legs, moving the underwear to the side.

He sucked my nipple even harder, and when he put his finger inside of me, pumping in and out, I screamed even louder. It was the first time I had ever had the freedom to.

"You want more, Alcina?"

"*Sì.*" I moaned so long and so loud that he growled in his throat at the sound. "Harder."

"Fuck," he said, slamming into me. "You're so wet."

I came around his hand, not able to control the feeling, my entire body convulsing from the pleasure. At my scream, he pulled me into him, kissing me as hard as his finger had been rocking me. We tangoed on the bed, rolling around, and after he was as naked as I was, I took him in my mouth.

He hissed out a breath, fisting my hair in his hands, pushing me to take him even deeper.

"You taste so good," I said, as I slid my tongue up and down, looking at him from underneath my lashes.

"On top," he said, and it was an order.

I situated myself around him, close to coming again just by the look in his eyes. I was still so tender, so sensitive, and when I placed myself over him and came down, my nails dug into his sides. I could barely catch my breath.

"Move, Alcina," he said.

He felt so good that I did not even realize I had stopped. He was so big that he filled me completely, and it took my body a moment to stretch, to accommodate him.

He directed my hips, and after I came up, about to come down, his hips came forward and slammed into me.

"*Ah!*" I screamed out. "Fuck!"

"That's it, angel eyes," he said. "Get fucking loud. Show me how much you want me."

Our bodies started to move in sync. The noises we made were loud, ugly, and raw. He growled and I shouted. I clawed his skin, and he bruised my hips and *culo* with his almost violent touch. His hands came up, twisting my nipples, and I started to move faster, harder.

He took my face and turned it to the left some. My eyes connected with Adriano's. He was looking through the mirror on the other side, fixing his hair with the one good arm he had. The other was in a sling.

Panic that he could hear us started to cool my fire, but Corrado shook his head. He impaled me so hard again that I could not stop the scream that exploded from my mouth.

Adriano kept looking in the mirror, still trying to fix his hair.

"No one sees you like this but me," he said. "I'm the only man with the right to touch this body—*e`mio*. The right to be the only one to hear you—*e`mio*." His hands slid up my arms and he sat up some, reaching my mouth, our tongues touching before he rammed his into my mouth. Then he licked my cheek up to the corner of my eye where a tear had started to fall.

"If you weren't already pregnant," he said, "I'd fuck you until you were."

He slammed into me again and I lost my breath, starting to move like I had been before. He flipped me a second later, his body over mine, and fucked me until I could not hold back any longer. I screamed out his name, giving myself over to him. A second later, he spilled himself inside of me, his head back, his throat exposed.

I closed my eyes, trying to catch my breath. His lips moved against my body again, this time not as hard. He stopped at my stomach, his hands cradling my hips.

"I needed this," he said, his breath warm against my skin. "I needed you."

"Keep me with you forever," I whispered.

He said three words that I was willing to bet my life he would die to see through.

"Consider it done."

# 22

# CORRADO

Rain hit the windows of Macchiavello's and ran down the panes in fast-moving lines. My grandfather had risked his life to have the steak, so I decided to check it out after his funeral.

The man who owned it, Mac Macchiavello, had my attention.

It could have been something as simple as my grandfather had ties to the restaurant. Maybe one of his men made a lot of money through it, and he wanted to try the famed steak.

It wasn't that simple. I was aware of all of our dealings.

My grandfather was no recluse, but the older he got, the more he enjoyed being at home when he wasn't at the Primo Club. Outings were rare for him. It took some pull to get him there.

Tito had told me he had arranged the meeting, which meant Mac Macchiavello had enough pull with one of the biggest crime families in history to get my grandfather to dinner. Even Emilio Capitani had a boss.

It wasn't a usual steak and potato place, but then again, it was. The smell of meat and starch meandered through the air, but so did high-quality booze from the opposite side of the restaurant, where people could get a pricey drink and listen to live music. The bar was old time, prohibition-influenced. It was already starting to get crowded.

I recognized a few men right away. They usually traveled in packs, and this place accommodated them.

Alcina squeezed my hand. "It smells good in here," she said. "Familiar."

"You used to steak and potatoes?" I said.

"No." She shook her head. "You can't smell it? It smells Italian."

I purposely went a little deeper when I inhaled. I nodded. "Yeah. It does." After she pointed it out, I could smell garlic and tomatoes lingering underneath the heavy scent of red meat. It was almost on every plate.

"I would try the Italian dishes," she said, "but I do not want to be disappointed."

I laughed at her sour face. "Spoken like a true Italian," I said. "No one's cooking is as good as yours—or like your *mamma* or *nonna* makes."

We passed a table where a woman had some kind of pasta dish. Alcina narrowed her eyes, studying the woman's plate as if she was rating it mentally.

"What's the verdict?"

"Hm?"

"The verdict on the pasta dish." I nodded toward it. The woman gave us a hard look before she set her fork down, refusing to eat while two strangers stared at her.

"Ah. It looks pretty good." She smiled. "Actually, *sorprendente*."

"Since it looks *amazing*," I said, "we'll get a few things to try."

We met the men who had gone in ahead of us to get a table. A man dressed in a suit, who introduced himself as Sylvester, told us to follow him. He led us to a room that was set off of the restaurant itself. It looked like it was used for parties. A table that fit no less than fifty sat in the center. A two-way glass was built in the wall.

"Compliments of Mr. Macchiavello," Sylvester said, placing our menus down on the table.

I narrowed my eyes. "I'd like to speak to him."

Sylvester nodded. "I will let him know." He gestured to the table. "Enjoy your dinner, Mr. and Mrs. Capitani." Then he left Alcina and me alone.

My men waited outside the door, since this was an outing with my wife. I wouldn't mix business with pleasure, even though I could feel it starting to spill over in this fucking place.

"You want the door closed, boss?" Baggio asked, sticking his head in the room. He had been in Adriano's crew before Adriano went to Sicily. He'd been promoted in Adriano's absence.

I looked to my left a little, where Adriano stood. I made eye contact with him. Adriano told Baggio something, and instead of closing the door the entire way, he left a small crack open and then stood in front of it. Nunzio stood right next to him. I had asked him to come to New York for a while, to keep an eye on Alcina.

I pulled out Alcina's chair, and she fixed her dress before she took a seat. I took the one next to her at the head of the table.

She looked over her shoulder. "That is interesting."

"Yeah," I said, watching as a woman stopped to check her lipstick as she passed. The mirror was on the other side. "You don't see that often."

We both checked out the menu, but I wasn't really there for the food. A few minutes later, Sylvester came back in and took our orders.

I grinned when Alcina ordered three different items. I

figured I'd have the steak, since it was my grandfather's last meal.

"Good choices," Sylvester said in Italian. "It will not be a long wait."

As soon as he disappeared, a woman came with our drinks. Alcina took a sip of her water with lemon. She had been quiet ever since we left the burial.

I took her hand. "Tell me."

"Tell you...?" She tilted her head, studying me.

"What's on your mind."

She sighed. "Something feels familiar about this place...the smell." She inhaled. "Chocolate and lemon. It reminds me of Modica. The chocolate shop there."

She was intuitive. I hadn't even realized it, but it did. The day we went to drop off the pistachios and pick up her supplies, the shop had had that same unique smell. It was more condensed in this room, where there were only the two of us and not that many plates.

It brought me back to the guy with the tiger tattoo on his neck—Cash Kelly. I planned on paying him a visit soon. I recognized him. He was the son of one of the most infamous Irish bosses Hell's Kitchen had ever seen. After Cash got out of prison, he started a war to get his streets back.

"Besides that," I said.

She took a drink and then started to speak. "You have not cried over your grandfather. I know what kind of man you are, what you are accustomed to, but you have been conditioned to be so...unfeeling about death. Even to those closest to you."

I had no fucking clue what she was talking about.

"He was my grandfather," I said. "I'll miss him. But life moves us all toward death. We accept it and keep moving."

She was right. It was a fact of this life. We were conditioned to accept our fates. No one wanted it, and most men tried their best to avoid making stupid mistakes that would cost them, but

in the end, it was what it was. We were all going to end up in
the same place someday anyway.

"I understand that notion," she said. "Still. The loss hurts.
It's okay to cry, to grieve. Those emotions make us human."

"Emotions make us weak," I said.

"I am not weak," she snapped. "And I feel everything. That's
what makes me strong. I grow after I go through it." She leaned
back in her seat. "*Grazie*," she said to the waiters who set her
plates down.

Sylvester set mine in front of me, and Alcina licked her lips,
her eyes growing big. "That smells good," she said.

I grinned, cutting her a piece. I put it to her lips and she
closed her eyes, opening her mouth. "How is it?"

She put her hand up to her mouth, signaling that she was
still chewing, and then said, "So good."

Alcina had always enjoyed eating, but ever since she found
out she was pregnant, she was on an entirely new level.

"Shouldn't you be sick right now?" I cut off another piece
and took a bite. The steak was damn good.

She laughed, twirling the pasta around her fork like a
fucking pro. "All pregnancies are different. Some women get
sick." She shrugged. "Others do not. I do get a little bothered by
smells—raw chicken. But nothing severe, or you would know."
She twirled more, but this time she fed it to me.

I nodded. "Good, but not as good as yours."

"My *zie* in Modica make a pasta like this." She smiled.
"Paired with the smells, it brings me home."

We didn't talk much after that. We enjoyed our meals in
companionable silence, swapping bites and a little conversation
every so often. We were sharing three plates of desserts when
Adriano stuck his head in the room.

I could tell he was trying to inhale the food through his
nose; his nostrils flared. "Company."

I dropped my napkin on my empty plate, meeting his eyes.

"Silvio and some of the men."

The sit-down wasn't scheduled until tomorrow. I guess he got the feeling he was going to get walked into a room but never walked back out. He was fucking right. Why go ten rounds with a guy when I could knock him out in one? It was that fucking simple.

What wasn't simple was having my wife with me.

Sylvester stepped back into the room and cleared his throat. "There is another room," he said, pointing to the left. "Mrs. Capitani is more than welcome to wait for you in there, until business is over."

I nodded at Nunzio and he nodded back.

"I guess you are sending me away," she said.

"Just for a minute."

She huffed and stood. When she was almost to the door, Silvio stepped in front of her. She stopped like she had run into a wall. Her eyes moved up to his and hardened. He couldn't hide the shock in his eyes—he wasn't expecting her. What she looked like.

"In a different league than Junior," I said, forcing his eyes on me. "Makes sense now. Why he had to force her into something she didn't want."

Her lips moved without sound again, and I wondered if she was cursing him as Nunzio escorted her into the next room. If Silvio believed in what the old folks said, he should have cupped his balls to ward off the *malocchio*. He had so much heat coming for him, though, that even cupping his balls wouldn't have saved him from the evil eye.

"Sit," I said, after she had gone. "Let's talk."

He moved deeper into the room, a few guys following behind him. They took their seats, and so did my men. Vito, the guy Silvio had appointed his underboss, as if the position was his even after I'd been inaugurated, refused to move his eyes from my face. He was Junior's godfather.

I took a drink and set it down. "Our meeting is tomorrow. You're a day early."

"This is a personal meeting," he said. "We'll deal with business tomorrow."

"Let's get down to it."

"I owe you for finding Junior's wife."

"No payment needed. I found *my* wife. The only record of marriage you'll find for Alcina Maria Parisi is to me. Their sham of a marriage was never legal, nor was it consummated. It was forced, which means it's void in the eyes of the church —and me."

He narrowed his eyes at me. "You have proof of this."

Silvio thought he was slick. Part of the code was that we didn't mess around with other member's wives. We didn't look at them the wrong way. We were never alone with them. We couldn't even mess around playfully with wives, sisters, or claimed women unless we had honorable intentions.

Silvio thought he had me there, and even if he did—my grandfather would come back to haunt me for this—I would have broken the code for Alcina. The day I told her I would die for her in that pistachio grove, I meant it literally.

I grinned into my glass. "The proof was the loss of your son's balls. He wanted her. She had a difference of opinion. When he forced the matter, after he beat her, she settled it. The only thing she did wrong was not going for his jugular instead of his balls."

"No wonder the Scarpones wanted to rid the earth of the Palermos," he said. "The only thing the Scarpones did wrong was not killing him before he had the chance to procreate. Luna was so in love with him. Stupidly so. I remember." He touched his temple. "I didn't know it was him at the time, but I know now. He left her for Maria, a girl from the old country." He nodded toward the door. "A girl like that one."

He grinned at me a second later. "Your grandfather didn't

want you looking for the Scarpones because he knew Vittorio Scarpone is still alive."

Just because you were the smartest man in the room didn't mean you had to flaunt it. Sometimes it was wise to pretend you were the dumbest. In this instance, it was wise to pretend I was the smartest.

I opened and closed my hands, as if to say, go on.

"You're still looking for him. Looking to rid the world of all Scarpone blood. And if you're looking for him, he's waiting for you." He shrugged. "He'll take care of you and make things easier for me. You don't stand a chance against a ghost."

I matched his grin. "Bitterness doesn't suit you, Silvio. What's done is done. The family voted."

"The family might have voted, but you'll have to work to get me into a room with four walls and no way out."

"I look forward to it," I said.

He stood, and so did his men. I watched Vito carefully as they made their way toward the door. He walked behind Silvio, and as they reached the door, he did two things at once: he reached inside of his jacket, and he touched Silvio on the shoulder. Before Silvio could react and turn around, Vito put the gun he pulled from underneath his jacket to his best friend's head and pulled the trigger. It had a silencer, but it couldn't hide the bloodshed all over the wall and the floor.

Vito tucked the gun back inside of his jacket and turned to me. He took out a handkerchief from his pocket and wiped his face. Our eyes met and held.

He would pay for this. The commission had ruled that it would be done on our terms, not his. Instead of following orders, Vito was telling me that even if he had to do it, he was going to do it his way. Except he did it in a public place, which meant that it could cause trouble for my men and myself. I was the boss of my family, and without a head, the body fails. If this wasn't a place that catered to men like me, I might have truly considered the implications. However, this wasn't about the act, but about the blatant disrespect.

Vito and I had a problem.

Vito turned around and stepped over his best friend a second later, rushing out of the restaurant.

Sylvester appeared as soon as Vito disappeared, closing the door behind him. He had a card in his hand. He slipped it on the table. "Dinner is on the house," he said. "Mr. Macchiavello will be in touch. Do not worry about this." He nodded toward where Silvio bled out.

Dishes clanked next to me. Adriano had pulled Alcina's plate closer, removing the plate he must have put on top of it so the blood wouldn't splatter onto it, and was finishing her dessert. "I'm starving," he said, shrugging. "The doc has me on steroids and I can't get enough to eat."

---

"ARE YOU SURE ABOUT THIS, *cugino?*"Adriano sat next to Baggio in the front of the car, narrowing his eyes against the windshield, trying to see past the rain coming down harder than it had two days ago.

"If I wasn't—" I fixed my tie "—we wouldn't be going."

I took out the card Macchiavello had passed on to me through Sylvester, flipping it around with my fingers. Something shady was going on with him. He ran one of the most successful restaurants in New York. He owned one of the biggest nightclubs in New York. The Club. And none of these places were on any of the books.

He could have been a legitimate business owner, but he catered to too many high profiles. There was a certain kind of honey that was put out for men like us. Once we started hovering, we became comfortable, patronizing places we knew.

*Some* men got comfortable.

I never created patterns in my life. It was too easy to figure out people who did. One thing I learned in this life—we were all capable of the same amount of damage, so none of us feared each other. What was important was to be able to outsmart the next guy.

Mac Macchiavello was smart.

I was, too.

I had an uncanny ability to read every man in the room, his intentions, and to approach him in a way that would turn the situation in my favor. If not, I acted accordingly. Rarely did I lose my cool, though, because there was no need.

It was either to be or not to be. What was there to get upset about?

"You don't get mad, Corrado," my grandfather used to say. "You don't even get even. You strive to rise above, no matter what it takes to get there. If the door refuses to open, go through a window. It's as simple as that."

My grandfather taught me early on what it meant to be a man worthy of this life.

What it meant to have respect, not only for men, but for women.

What it meant to be loyal. To respect a code put in place for a reason.

What it meant to carry on traditions. To honor our old ways and welcome new ones that would only make us stronger as a family.

What it meant to love as fiercely as we hated.

He was a product of that life.

So was I.

I wore the fucking suit.

Alcina felt that I was cold, even callous, and I was. I was a gangster, a mobster, a racketeer—a rare breed in this life, my grandfather used to say—and the boss of one of the largest and most powerful families in New York. I wasn't even forty years old yet. I had started at the bottom just like everyone else, and I made my way up to the top with no problem. I was smart, and I rarely made mistakes.

Yet, despite who I was, I loved that woman more than a poet loved romantic words. Even more than the night sky loved the moon.

My grandfather used to say, "You can't have a heart, Corrado. They're too expensive."

Alcina Maria Capitani was out of my price range then. Because I had a heart. It was that woman. And I'd never be able to afford her. I'd owe for the rest of my life and beyond for her love.

Of course, my grandfather wasn't referring to a woman, but to this life of ours. The only feelings you were allowed to have was for yourself. If you didn't take care of the situation, the situation took care of you. But when my wife would say something to me, point out how callous I was, how cold, sometimes I could see the contrast between her world and mine.

I couldn't truly see the darkness of the night without the moon's light.

I took out the picture of Emilia from my suit pocket, sticking it in front of Macchiavello's card. I flipped it over and over between my fingers, the dim light making her picture seem black and white.

Emilia had wanted me to marry someone like Alcina. Someone good and beautiful. Someone with heart and passion, but also a woman that took no shit. Wasn't afraid to speak her mind.

She wanted me to go to school, graduate, get a 9-5 like the rest of the schmucks earning an honest dollar—a dollar that came from billion-dollar corporations, who were the most ruthless gangsters on the block, apart from the government. FBI—we all knew it stood for Forever Bothering the Italians.

It was never in my future to be the guy who got suckered.

From the moment I knew what it was all about, I worked for the suit.

I stared out of the window, fat droplets moving like amoebas down the pane. The Cadillac shimmied when Baggio made a turn, making them move faster.

"So I says to him, 'You fucking bum, my ma will out-cook your ma any day. Any. *Fucking*. Day.' It's as simple as that, ya know? Who da fuck does this guy think he is? Telling me *his* ma cooks better."

"What kind of stuff does your ma cook?" Adriano said, turning to face him. "I could be the judge, if he decides to agree."

These fucking guys.

I sighed, slipping Emilia's picture along with Mac's card back in my pocket. We were in Hell's Kitchen, and I could see the building coming up.

Baggio smoothly parked the Cadillac in front.

"You wait out here," I told Baggio. I nodded to Adriano, and he nodded back.

Baggio stepped out to smoke in the rain. Adriano and I walked up to the building.

"He's not right," Adriano said tapping at his temple as we made our way closer to the door of the warehouse. It had Kelly Enterprises painted in green on the side, with a tiger emblem. "Baggio, I mean. He's the closest thing to a sociopath I'd ever met." He grinned. "But he's a lot of fucking fun.

"Listen to this: He goes home to a fish every night named Gilberts, and he talks to the motherfucker like he's a dog. *Here Gilberts, Gilberts, Gilberts.*" Adriano said it in a monotone that sounded like *here fishy, fishy, fishy,* while he acted like he was sprinkling food over a bowl.

He laughed. "So much fucking fun." He opened the door and cool air blasted against my face. It smelled fresh, like new paint, wood, and metal.

I fixed my suit jacket and tie before I went to the counter where a guy, maybe around my age, looked down at something. At the sound of our footsteps, he looked up, narrowing his eyes.

"I'd like to see Mr. Kelly," I said. "I heard he was in."

I'd also seen Cash Kelly eating at Macchiavello's the day after I'd eaten there with Alcina. I went back to talk to Sylvester, who was nowhere to be found. Kelly was with the same red-haired woman that I saw him with in Modica.

Even if no one was willing to talk about Mac, or he wasn't willing to talk to me, I assumed he had something to hide. A man like Cash Kelly didn't eat at just any place on the street.

"Mr. Kelly sees people by appointment only," the guy said.

"Your name?"

He narrowed his eyes at me. He was probably calling me Pinky Ring in his head. It was no secret that the connected Irish thought we were too flashy with our expensive suits and cars and jewelry.

"Harrison Ryan," he said. "I'm Mr. Kelly's legal counsel. We're short a person at the desk. So you'll have to come back, Mr...?"

I set my hand on the counter, so the gold ring on my little finger would glint a little. "Corrado. Corrado Scorpio." News hadn't spread yet, outside of the families, of my new role. For the moment, I wanted to keep it that way. "I'll wait if he's busy. As long as it takes."

He eyed Adriano behind me and then watched him follow as I took a seat in the waiting area. I picked up a magazine about my grandfather that was left out as reading material.

Harrison Ryan cleared his throat a minute later. "Mr. Kelly will see you now." He looked at Adriano. "Only you."

I stood, removing my jacket, proving that I wasn't packing any heat. I lifted my shirt, turned around, and then lifted both pant legs.

"We can skip the shake down," I said. "If this is sufficient."

Harrison Ryan nodded. "Follow me."

I tucked my shirt back in, slipped my jacket back on, and nodded once to Adriano. He nodded back, touching the gun underneath his jacket in a subtle way.

Cash Kelly started an assessment on me the moment I walked into his office. In the brief second it took for him to stand, for us to shake hands, his mind worked out three things: who I was, what I was about, and what I wanted. After that, he'd decide if he would be willing to help me with the latter.

I doubted it.

He worked with select families. The Irish and Italians sometimes worked together, but it was never close. We had our own thing; they had theirs.

He checked out the scorpion on my hand, and I checked out the tiger on his neck. His old man was a legend around here. He was following in his footsteps.

I respected Cash Kelly's stance on drugs, how hard he fought to keep them off his streets. It spoke to the tradition in me. My grandfather never allowed it, and neither would I. There were too many other opportunities to make money if a mind was creative enough.

I also knew that Kelly was more willing to trust a man who had spent some time in jail. Maybe he would sense that about me. Maybe he wouldn't. Either way, though, my message would get back to its intended target through him.

He nodded to the seat across from him. I took it.

"I'm going to be brief," I said. "Word on the street is that you know a man that goes by Mac Macchiavello."

"Know him," he said, studying me harder. "Or can get close to him."

"I don't need you to get close to him," I said, sitting up some, fixing my suit, before I relaxed again. "I'm here to confirm that you know him."

"That he exists."

I waved a hand. We could play this game all day long. I pulled out a picture of Emilia and slid it across the desk toward him. I wanted him to know there was more to this situation than just me looking for him.

His eyes moved over her face, studying her, trying to place her. He released a breath when he did. "My condolences." He slid the picture back. "But I can't help."

"Can't." I grinned. "Or won't."

He waved his hand—either way, it was a hard no.

I shrugged. "I'll find him, regardless." I took the picture, slipping it back inside of my pocket, and then I stood.

He stood and offered me his hand. We shook once more. I stopped when I was at the door. "You didn't ask why I wanted to find him."

"Why?"

"Because when I do, I'm going to fucking kill him."

My gut told me Mac Macchiavello was Vittorio Scarpone— the Pretty Boy Prince. Even back in the day, he was a smart motherfucker. Machiavellian to the highest degree. Men used to talk about how he was the only one who was capable of getting out of the life without help—help meaning, either in a body bag or by becoming a stool pigeon.

His old man saw to it by trying to get rid of him in a body bag. I'd seen it before. Father and son. Brothers. Best friends. If it was time to go, it was time to go. Vittorio Scarpone did a stupid thing by not killing the entire Palermo family, and stupid things had punishments.

Deep down I was thankful that he spared my sister. I wasn't a fucking monster. Besides, killing children was against our code. If anything, Arturo Scarpone should have gotten whacked because he even ordered such a thing. But I wouldn't give Vittorio Scarpone a pass for doing it. The Scarpones had no feelings for the woman I called mother—and they all needed to be destroyed.

I actually wanted to applaud this motherfucker Kelly for helping take out Arturo and his sons. The commission had been considering taking out Arturo for a while, and since his underboss happened to be his son, all of the men who could rise in ranks had been destroyed at once. It was about time.

If Mac Macchiavello was Vittorio Scarpone, Cash Kelly would tell him I was here. Hopefully he'd get the message: where his old man had failed, I'd fucking succeed.

# 23

# ALCINA

His hands slid around my waist as he helped me walk from the Cadillac to...wherever he was leading me.

"Are you bringing me somewhere quiet?" He had tied a silk scarf around my head again, hiding my eyes from the surprise he had for me.

He kissed me behind the ear. "We have a place where you can scream as loud as you want."

I smiled. "The last time you blindfolded me..." Cool air rushed over my face, and familiar scents almost made me take the scarf from around my eyes. I could tell we had moved from the busy street to a quiet area. "We are not in a library?" I whispered. I wondered if he was going to take me there like a dare— see if he could keep me quiet enough to get away with it.

"Even with something in your mouth, you'd draw attention in a library." He roared with laughter.

"Apparently not as loud as *you*," I said, searching for him. He had moved away from me. His heat had become something reassuring to me. Something I was drawn to. Addicted to. I could not sleep without him by my side now.

He hands found mine, and I intertwined our fingers

together, holding on tight. I leaned in, and he knew what I wanted. He kissed me. As he did, he untied the blindfold. Even though I could open my eyes, I didn't. Not until the kiss ended.

"Where are we?" We were inside of a store, that much was clear, and it was Sicilian-inspired. It brought me home with the tiles and textures of Palermo. Vintage looking wooden shelves lined the walls. They were all empty. There was a checkout area with no one behind it.

I stepped away from Corrado, narrowing my eyes against two painted ceramic heads that were the focal point of one wall. Her brown hair was pulled back, a crown atop of her head. Lemons were woven into her side-parted hair, but the inside fruit looked like the inside of figs. The man next to her was clearly a king. Red chili peppers and the same lemons with figs weaved around his crown.

"This place is perfect," I said, reaching out to stroke the king's face. "What do they sell here?"

After a minute or two went by, I turned to look for Corrado. He stood next to a shelf, a few of my candles lining them. He lit them one by one with a lighter from his pocket.

"Candles," he said. "Yours."

I stared at him, not truly understanding.

"I called Anna and had her send some of your candles from Bronte. The ones that you had ready to sell before we left." He looked around the store. "I invest in men every day. In business that I know won't fail." He looked at me. "You, Alcina Maria Capitani, invested in me. Not the other way around."

I smiled a little. "Let me understand. If you fail me—"

"I fail at life."

Our eyes connected from across the room.

"I'm going to fuck up, angel eyes," he said. "But I'll always redeem myself with you—understand?"

I touched the necklace around my neck, the cross, and then my throat. I nodded. "*Sì*. Love does not come naturally to you."

"It came naturally for you, but not how to react to it." He grinned. "I understand it in these terms. Plain and simple—I can't afford to lose. I can't afford not to pay my debt back. Because make no mistake. I'll never be able to pay you back. We'll never be square. There is no price on your love."

"Instead of roses or jewelry, you buy me a...candle shop?"

"Bella Luna Candles by Alcina Capitani." He pointed at his chest. "My wife."

Anna had encouraged me to do something special with my candles when I lived in Bronte. The furthest I got was choosing a name for a business I never thought I'd have. Bella Luna Candles.

I smiled a little but then stood up straighter. I walked around him, my hands behind my back, eyeing him from head to toe. "This business will be legitimate, yes?"

"*Assolutamente*," he said, watching me move around him from the side of his eye.

"I will name a candle after my husband."

"That depends."

"On?" I stopped in front of him.

He reached out and pulled me toward his body. I lost my breath when I crashed into him. He looked down at me, moving a strand of hair from my face.

"The name."

I grinned. "*Lo scorpione.*"

He threw back his head and roared with laughter again. "I fucking like it," he said.

"I *fucking* like it," I said.

He put his fist up to my chin, like he was going to give me a punch, but instead, he brought my face closer so his lips could claim mine.

"That mouth on you," he said after he'd pulled away. "I fucking love that." He turned and blew out all of the candles he'd lit. Then he swept me off my feet, carrying me toward the door of the shop. He stopped before he stepped out of it. We stared at what was starting to become something special.

"This is all you, angel eyes," he said. "This is your thing."

"It is," I whispered. "And this—" I put his hand against my stomach. "This is *ours.*"

"*Il nostro sangue in un cuore,*" he said. *Our blood in one heart.*

I kissed the pulse in his neck. "It is an honor to carry a piece of you within me," I said in Sicilian. In that moment, I could not remember a time when I did not love him.

*L'ho amato per sempre. Lo amerei per sempre.*

*I loved him forever. I would love him for always.*

He had been warning me of the hurt he could cause. I accepted the warning. All things in life worth bleeding for are worth living *and* dying for.

# 24

## ALCINA

P ulsing music blared from inside of The Club. I felt it rattling the cement underneath my heels as we made our way to the door from the car. Corrado put his arm around my neck, pulling me closer.

A line wrapped around the building, hundreds of people waiting to get in.

I looked at Corrado as we passed the crowd. He kept his face forward, his arm tight around my neck, ushering me past.

Some of his men were ahead of us, a couple on each side of us, and a few behind us. The men working the security at the door allowed us in without even looking at us. They wore head-pieces, and I heard one speaking in Italian. "He has arrived."

Corrado wasn't flashy, but he was stylish, and the papers were reporting that he had started a new era of bosses. He was an ode to days long gone, when men wore suits to be respectful of the job. They said he was bringing back the Golden Days of Capone.

*He is quiet about his dealings,* one paper said, *like his grandfather.* Even though they knew what he was, they couldn't prove it. He was exactly what had gone missing in this modern society—he didn't exist even though people knew he did.

His *nonna*, Teresa, made sure the news was on whenever I went into the kitchen. She'd leave me newspapers and articles to find.

I kept to myself in the house, because the women who spent most of their time with her did not like me.

The feeling was mutual.

There was one—the one with the evil eyes—who cursed me every time I walked into the kitchen. Her name was Martina.

She was one of the reasons why I was with Corrado tonight. He spent a lot of his time doing business, and even though he had the pool house converted into a place for me to work on my candles, the mansion felt suffocating.

I needed to breathe. To live outside of the confines of the baroque gates.

It did not seem as if the wives usually came with the men to places like this. Corrado did not say as much, but this was not a social visit. He was here for a different reason, one that was not entirely business-related, either. He had told me he was looking for a man who had something to do with his past, with his father, Corrado Palermo.

I had never been to a place like this, and when I told Anna I was going, she demanded that I send her proof or it did not happen. I slipped the phone out of my pocket, taking pictures of the people, of the stage, of the entire setup as we made our way to a private table.

The music, the lights, the smells…it all started to move through my bloodstream. I had the urge to dance.

We stopped at a booth tucked away in one of the darkest corners. The seats were blue velvet and plush.

"No." Corrado helped me slip off my dress coat. "No dancing." He set it over the crook of his arm, gesturing for me to sit.

He eyed me up and down before I did, looking over my dress again.

It was a shorter version of the one I wore to the opera. The rich gold fabric hugged all of my curves, even the small swell of my belly. He had gotten me out of it before we left. The look in his eyes told me he wanted to do it again.

It must have been written across my forehead that I wanted to dance, though, since he mentioned it. "Have you ever been to a place like this?"

"Yeah," he said. "But not to dance."

A candle burned in the middle of the table. I put my hand over it, feeling the heat beneath my palm. I inhaled when some of the smoke lingered in the air. Chocolate. I wondered...no. It could not be, even though they smelled the same.

My family in Modica was not the only ones who made candles that smelled of lemon and chocolate. I even asked Anna about it. She said she was not aware that the *zie* shipped their candles to America.

"The same man who owns the restaurant owns this place?" I asked.

Corrado stared ahead, his eyes turned up to the second level of The Club. It was made of glass. It seemed like he was trying to see through it.

I touched him on the arm. It took him a minute, but he looked at me. He took my hand and kissed my fingers. "You thirsty, angel eyes?"

"Yes," I said. When we walked in the air was cool, but back here where people crowded around the stage, it felt like a sauna.

Nunzio turned around and Corrado nodded at him. That was all it took for them to move. A woman working the club came back with a tray with two drinks and a bottle. After she had gone, Nunzio set everything in front of us.

Corrado had ordered Amaro del Capo. The glass was

frosted to keep it cold. As he drank, I could smell mint, anise seed, and licorice floating in the air.

My mouth watered as I imagined how it would taste on his tongue. I picked my glass up to take a sip of water with lemon, but he set his hand against my neck and pulled my mouth to his.

"You make me do things I shouldn't while out in public," he said against my mouth before he kissed me again. He tasted like the drink, and I did not want him to stop. He did, though, when he must have sensed one of the men wanting his attention.

Nunzio cleared his throat. "Mariposa and Keely are here to see your wife."

I went to get up when the name made it to my ear. Mariposa. Mari. I had not seen her since Modica. I remembered then that she and Amadeo lived in New York most of the time.

Hearing her name was like catching my breath.

Corrado put his hand on my arm to stop me. He nodded at Nunzio to let them through. She stepped through the men as if it were an everyday occurrence to have to bypass a muscle wall to get to someone. Keely, her red-haired friend, was beside her. Keely sat next to me, and Mari hugged me from across the table before she took a seat next to Corrado.

He studied her face, a little harder than he had in Modica.

"Corrado," I said, "this is my *cugina*, Mariposa. Mariposa, this is *mio marito*, Corrado."

She held out her hand and he took it, but she did not let go right away.

"It's nice to meet you," she said, staring at him in the glow of the flame.

He cleared his throat and took his hand back. He only nodded. I looked between the two of them. After a second, she looked back at me, a smile on her face. She introduced us to Keely, but Keely only waved. She was staring at Corrado, too.

We exchanged small talk. Mari asked about the wedding. I asked about Saverio. Then I asked her where Amadeo was. I could not see Mari here without him. If Corrado was...possessive, I knew Amadeo to be the same.

"Work," Mari said, but her eyes were on Corrado again. "He's not far, though."

"Amadeo," Corrado said, taking a drink. "He the man with you at the store in Modica?"

"Yeah," Mari said. "My husband."

"My husband was the other guy." Keely pointed to her neck. "The one with the tiger tattoo."

"Yeah," Corrado said. "I'm familiar."

Keely grinned. "Seems it's a small world."

"Too small," Corrado muttered into his glass. He pointed to the area in front of our booth where the men stood. "If you'll excuse me, ladies, I have business to attend to."

Mari moved out so he could. There was a moment in time when they were standing in front of each other. She looked up at him and he looked down at her. He nodded at her and went to stand with the men.

Mari slipped back into the booth. She nudged me. "Tell me all about married life."

"He giving you silvers yet?" Keely laughed into her glass. "Hairs, I mean."

I opened my mouth to speak, but it seemed like people were trying to move out of the way of oncoming traffic.

"Rocco and Romeo are here," Mari said, peeking through the wall of men.

Romeo stopped to shake Corrado's hand. Rocco stood on the other side of him. Rocco looked between the men and our eyes connected. I looked at Mari after a second, not because I was too weak to keep contact. Corrado was watching.

I downed almost the entire glass of water before I set it down.

"Have you tried the drinks here?" Mari said.

"No." I smiled and touched my stomach. "I don't think the baby would like it."

It took a second, but Mari grabbed my hand, squeezing. "I'm so happy for you! Saverio will have a new cousin to play with. Do you have a number? We can make plans to get together more often."

I squeezed her hand. She had no idea how much that would mean to me. I would not have to be stuck with the women in that house all of the time. We exchanged numbers.

"I need a bathroom break," Keely said, lifting her hair and fanning her neck. "Who wants to come?"

"Yeah, all of these men in fine suits are crimping my style," Mari said, sliding out of the booth after Keely did, laughing a little. "Come with us, Alcina. We can talk some more."

I nodded, stepping out of the booth. Corrado slipped a hand around my waist before I could get past him.

"Where the fuck do you think you're going?" he whispered in my ear.

I put my mouth close to his ear and whispered back, "Bathroom."

His grip on me didn't lighten, even when I started to walk away. The heat of his touch still felt like it was burning through the fabric even when his hand wasn't touching me.

Keely glanced behind her. Corrado was still watching me walk away, another glass of Amaro in his hand. "That was intense. Who's the guy following us?"

"Nunzio," I said. "He goes where I go."

We turned the corner. Three guys dressed in nice clothes were coming too fast. The one in the middle grabbed me by the arms when I ran into his chest. I went to step back, but he held on.

He whistled. "You just getting here or leaving, sweetheart?"

Nunzio stepped closer. He looked at the man's hands on my arms.

The two men next to the guy holding my arms put their hands inside of their jackets, like they were reaching for something. Nunzio grinned at them and did the same.

A second later, the two reaching for something inside of their jackets put their hands up. The one holding me dropped his hands.

I looked behind, and Corrado stood between a few of his men. He was eyeing the three around me. Just looking at them —it was cold enough to make goosebumps appear on my skin.

"I meant no disrespect, Don Capitani," the man said. "I didn't realize the woman was with you."

"My wife," he said.

All three of the men's faces paled.

The tension seemed to grow with every second that stretched. People were no longer moving toward the bathroom, but trying to go in the other direction. Corrado looked at Nunzio. Nunzio nodded in the direction of the bathroom. He wanted me to move. He rarely spoke a word to me.

"Come on, Alcina," Mari said, taking me by the arm.

After we were done in the bathroom, we promised to keep in touch, because it seemed we both knew my night was over.

The three men were gone after we stepped out. Mari kissed my cheeks, so did Keely, and then they went in a different direction. It was the same direction Corrado was facing.

I turned to look, but like a ghost whose shadow moved along a dark wall, whoever he was staring at was gone—a second after Mari and Keely disappeared behind a door leading to the second level of The Club.

# 25

# ALCINA

New York was changing. Leaves were starting to turn different shades from the weather turning crisper—a palette of dull browns, vibrant reds, and yellows that were a throwback to summer.

I was changing, too.

I turned my eyes from the window of the car and looked down at my stomach, tracing the small round bump. From the side, it looked bigger than it did from the front. At my last appointment, the doctor told me that the baby was the size of a lime, and that everything looked *bene*.

Everything did not feel fine, except for the happiness I felt whenever I thought about the baby, about our future—because I was looking ahead to a different time. A time when things would be different.

After the night at The Club, something in my husband's eyes changed.

I had never seen it before. It was as if he had gotten an idea tattooed in his head, and he could not separate from it, like he couldn't separate from his scorpions.

The man he was searching for was the one who had given him the tattoo.

I knew even if he found him, it would not bring back what he lost, or cure the world of anything. Corrado would never be satisfied until he accepted what had happened.

He tried to deny it was about the man killing his father. He said it was about men having respect, and I was sure some of that was true, but the man had spared his little sister. How could he not spare him? It went deeper, and he did not want to face it.

"*Rispetto*," I muttered.

If Corrado was anything, he was a man of great honor and respect. He gave it, and he demanded it in return.

That night in The Club had changed more than his obsession with finding the man who had played a role in changing his life.

The morning after, I had walked into the kitchen first, preparing to have breakfast with Corrado before he left for the day. Martina was there spending time with his *nonna*.

She usually cursed me. This time she called me a *goomah*. What we called *cummare* in Italian, which sounded like *goomah*. A mistress. She started to laugh, but it faded when Corrado walked in right as she said it.

"Jealousy is a bitch," I said to her. "And so are you." It was the first time I'd ever responded to her low remarks. Anna told me I needed to put her in her place, or she would never stop. It was the first time she had ever disrespected me in front of Corrado, and that seemed even worse.

"At least I don't act like a tramp," she said.

I opened my mouth to speak, but Corrado cleared his throat. "Get out," he said to her. "Get out and never step foot in my home again. If you disrespect my wife, you disrespect me."

Martina looked at Teresa. She turned her face away. Martina started to cry, but she took her purse and left.

I stared at Corrado while he sipped on his coffee. He had been distant after we left The Club, but my instincts told me it was more than just what happened with the man he couldn't find. It had to do with what had happened with the three men.

They had called me "the woman," and it made sense after Martina had called me *cummare*. Those men must have thought I was Corrado's mistress. The dress I had on. Where I was at such a late hour.

The *good* wives were home taking care of the house.

One thing I had learned from spending time in this mansion—these women enjoyed gossiping. It was not the first time I had heard about a woman who was not respectable.

"My daughter would not be out acting like a *puttana*," Martina had said about a family member's daughter who was out in a bar acting too freely. A man from the family had to send her home.

Even though this was modern day, to be respectable meant something to these men. They viewed the wives much differently than they viewed the mistresses.

The thought of my husband touching another woman made my blood boil. My *mamma* always said that jealousy had a shape, and it comes in the form of a *vipera*. But the poison only destroys the heart hosting it. I was full of deadly poison, but it did not feel dangerous to me—it was him I wanted to hurt when I thought of him hurting *me* in that way.

"I will kill you," I said to him. It was plain and simple. In a language he understood better than English. The thought of him having a *cummare* made me start to burn, like I had never burned before. It was not something I had truly considered, until that moment.

He took another sip of coffee. Then asked his *nonna* for some privacy. She looked between us before she headed out of the door to her garden, a few women trailing behind her.

He looked up at me. "You'll get some new clothes today.

Most of the ones from Italy are perfect. The gold one—and ones like it—only go on in the bedroom from now on."

"I will kill you," I said again, but this time in Sicilian. My voice matched his, nonchalant, but inside, I trembled.

He grinned at me.

I had to squeeze the counter to keep my fingers busy. I was going to throw my coffee cup at his head.

He brought his dishes to the sink, which was next to me, running water on the plate and into the cup. He shut the faucet off. Then he caged me in, one arm on each side of my hip. "Why do you think I married you, angel eyes?"

I refused to answer him until he acknowledged what I had said.

"I married you because you are a respectable woman, and because you are the most beautiful woman I have ever seen. More beautiful than any *goomah* a man could have. Every fucking fantasy I've ever had plays out in our bedroom every night—and every fantasy I'll ever have will have you in it.

"You are the best of both fucking worlds. A man asks for more than that?" He shrugged. "He's fucking gluttonous." He kissed me once on my forehead, once on my nose, and once on my lips. "I married you because I love you, Alcina."

I refused to respond.

He turned to go, but before he did, I said his name, stopping him. "I will kill you."

"I'll give you the knife to carve my heart out," he said, his tone as serious as mine. "Go shopping and take Brooklyn with you. She'll be with you and Nunzio from now on."

*I'll give you the knife to carve my heart out.*

Since he would be carving mine out if he were unfaithful to me. Maybe there was such a thing as loving someone too much. His soul tattooed itself on mine the first time he looked into my eyes. It went beyond what the eye could see. It went beyond flesh, blood, and bone.

My *mamma* always told me that marriage was a merger between two people who had to learn how to create one life together. Give and take being a big part of it. As long as both partners understood that, it would work. I knew how much respect and honor meant to Corrado. So I went shopping. I bought clothes that were a mixture of my life back in Italy and my new life in New York.

I blinked at the brightness of the day and all of the colors, the memory of that morning in the kitchen fading as Nunzio drove us to Bella Luna. Instead of staring out of the window of the car, lost to my thoughts, or at my stomach, even more lost to my thoughts, I looked over at Brooklyn, who was one of Corrado's cousins and sighed.

She had just graduated from college with a degree in art. Instead of going out into the world, she was stuck with me. Brooklyn came with me wherever I went. She was to make sure Nunzio and I were never alone. At least she told me Corrado paid her well. More than any other job had offered her. The experience would be lacking, but she seemed happy enough.

She flipped through my sketchbook, a smile on her face. "I like this one. *A lot.*" She held up a rough sketch of a mosaic-tile design I had done for a candleholder.

I smiled at her. I actually liked her company. "*Grazie,*" I said. "You like them all."

"I think they're going to be a big hit! *HUGE!* I brought some of your sample candles to my friends and they *totally* love them." She looked up, her eyes connecting with Nunzio's in the mirror. Her cheeks flushed and she looked down, a curtain of black hair falling around her face.

I hid my grin, but she kept stealing glances of him. He had noticed. Every so often their eyes would meet in the mirror.

"This is our stop," she said, reaching for the door handle.

I put a hand on her arm to stop her. The car had not stopped moving yet.

"Ah!" She squeezed my arm as we made our way to the door of Bella Luna. She leaned in closer. "He *is* fine. I can't think around him!"

"Always think when the car is moving," I said. "Or you will fall out of it."

We laughed as I opened the door to the shop. Brooklyn went in ahead of me and turned on all of the lights.

She spun around. "I love it here! I can't wait for opening day!"

"Me, too," I said, looking around. It was a dream come true. I couldn't wait for the shelves to be stocked and the store to be full of people.

"I'll go check the backroom. We've had some deliveries. I want to check them off my list." She lifted her phone, waving it at me, before she left me alone.

I sighed. I wanted to keep paper records. I did not trust technology. If it all died today, what would the world do? Be lost. But I would still have my paper trails. I set my jacket over the counter, my sunglasses on my head, and went to the two heads on the wall again. The heads were one of my favorite aspects of the store.

"Alcina?"

"Hm?"

"This is George," Brooklyn said. "George Halifax. He owns the candy store next door."

George Halifax stepped forward and we shook hands. "Alcina Capitani," I said.

"I actually own the company," he said. "We're a chain store that strives to be one of a kind. Like this place." He grinned at me as he stuck his hand in the pocket of his designer jeans. "I'm based in London."

"This place is one of a kind," I said. "There are no others like it."

His grin grew into an easy smile. "You got me there. But I

doubt it'll stay that way for long. I can tell you're going to have something special here." Then his eyes narrowed on something behind me.

I almost jumped when I noticed Nunzio. He had stepped into the store and was standing with his back to the wall, watching.

"Well," George said. "I can see you're busy, Ms. Capitani. I just wanted to introduce myself. It's always good to know your neighbors." He handed me a card from his pocket. "If you have a sweet tooth...drop in sometime. I'm in town for a while. I'm in and out of the store quite a bit lately."

I lifted the card. "I appreciate it."

"Does that include her employees?" Brooklyn asked as he walked toward the back entrance again. It did not seem like he wanted to cross Nunzio.

I tried not to grin again when Nunzio moved past me, closer to the back. He was trying to see them—to hear their conversation.

He seemed to relax when there were no more murmurs, but then he slipped into soldier mode when a scream to shatter glass echoed around the store. He ordered me to come with him, one hand on my arm, as we both bolted toward the back room.

He released me when we made it to the door. I stood back, trying to avoid the mess—a hundred or more scorpions, scrambling all over the floor, going in all different directions. They had escaped from the box Brooklyn had just opened.

"Do not move," Nunzio said to Brooklyn. "These are highly venomous."

Her eyes were closed tight and she was trying not to breathe.

Nunzio scooped me up and threw me over his shoulder, setting me down on the counter. A few seconds later, he had Brooklyn over his shoulder, but he laid her down.

"Did one of them bite her?" I was scrambling to look at her feet, at her legs.

"She told me no," he said in Sicilian. "She fainted after."

I did not see any sting marks. Did they leave sting marks? I wasn't sure, but I thought...I was starting to panic.

"I think we should call an ambulance," I said.

He nodded, his phone already out. Before he could dial, his phone rang. He did not say a word, only listened to whoever was on the other side of the line.

Brooklyn started to stir, her eyes opening. She groaned. "Did one of them get me?"

"I do not think so," I said. "Are you burning anywhere?"

"Only my face," she said, wrapping her arms over her eyes. "I passed out. That's so embarrassing."

"We need to go," Nunzio said, hanging up, sticking his phone back in his pocket. He looked at the floor, where I could see a few of them crawling around. "Stay there," he told Brooklyn. "I will be back for you."

She made a shoo motion with her hands, which were still over her eyes. "Trust. I'm *not* going anywhere."

He lifted me from the counter, but then he hesitated. He told me to hold on to his back, and after I did, he picked Brooklyn up from the counter, surprising her. He carried the two of us outside at the same time.

"We need to get her to—"

"We are going to a place now," he said. "Your husband has been shot."

---

I WONDERED if the sound of my flats clacking against the floor would stay with me forever. Each footstep that brought me closer to him made me wonder if the next would be the one that would change the entire course of my life.

Nunzio did not have specifics, only that Corrado had been shot and where we were to go.

We were in a plain-looking building from the outside, but inside, it reminded me of the place I was taken to in Milan. It was equipped with rooms to help men, even if it was not a real hospital.

Nunzio carried Brooklyn next to me. When Uncle Tito met us, he pointed to a room a few doors down. "Dr. Carter will see to her," he said.

Nunzio nodded and took her into the room.

Uncle Tito took one look at my face and grabbed my hand. "He is fine. You can see him in a minute. We will speak first, ah?"

I went into the room he pointed to. He told me he would be right with me.

There were a few folders out on the counter. One was open. I glanced at it and could not stop staring. Photos of Corrado's grandfather—dead in the street.

Uncle Tito came in and noticed it. He slammed it shut, pushing it behind him as he took a seat with wheels. He pushed himself closer to me, taking my hands. "Your godfather would not tell you lies," he said. "It was a near miss, but he is doing fine. Only a flesh wound to the head."

"To the head," I whispered.

He nodded, studying my face from underneath his glasses. "How is our little baby?"

"Fine," I said, but words were not coming easily. I kept imagining Corrado in the same place as his grandfather, dead on the street.

"Alcina."

I met Uncle Tito's kind eyes.

"I cannot promise you that your husband will be safe in this life. There are no such promises in anyone's life, but you are one of the strongest women I know. You have more strength than most of the men I deal with."

"Did the man Corrado has been looking for do this?"

"No. A man within the family." He waved a hand. "However. I do want you to speak to him about the man he is looking for. Perhaps where my advice has fallen on deaf ears, yours will fall on an open heart, ah? It is not worth his time to pursue dead ends. There is no honor in it. Things are as they are supposed to be now. Maybe even better. Time will only tell."

I nodded. "I would like to see my husband now." I squeezed Uncle Tito's hand and we both stood.

He led me to Corrado's room. He was sitting up in bed, a bandage around his head, one spot soaked with blood.

Nunzio stopped talking when I entered the room. He nodded at Corrado and then shut the door on his way out. I stood with my back against the door, staring at him. He had a card in his hand, twirling it between his fingers.

"You gonna say something to me?" he said.

"A minute," I said. I was trying to catch my breath. Trying to moderate my irrational anger at him for getting ambushed and the hate I had for the men who'd tried to do it. Then there was the fear, the worry, the uncertainty, matching the pulse of my blood.

He stopped twirling the card, staring at it before he started doing it again. "This is nothing," he said, and I knew he was referring to his wound.

I marched across the room and lifted my hand to slap him across the face for being so smug—so disrespectful—in the face of death. Like him leaving me did not matter.

He grabbed my wrist, pulling me into him, and I fell awkwardly against his body. "They can't kill me that easily, angel eyes," he whispered in my ear as I held on to him tighter. "I've had worse is what I meant."

I took a deep breath in, inhaling the scent of him. "But you did not *have* me," I said. "You told me you would die for me. What gives worth to the things you will die for, if you are not willing to live for them, too?"

He grabbed my shoulders, moving me away some so he could see my face. He looked into my eyes. "I am who I am."

I nodded. "Me, too."

"What do you want from me then?"

"Your life more than your death."

"You already have it," he said, touching my stomach. He kissed me on the forehead and then pushed me away a little more. "Let's go. I hate these fucking places."

# 26

# CORRADO

"It feels like old times," Uncle Carmine said, getting comfortable in the seat he had held for many years.

We were in my grandfather's office in his home. I kept my finger up to the lace curtains, holding them back. My wife was out in the garden with my *nonna* and Brooklyn. Her dress showed the swell of her stomach. Her hands were underneath the smallish ball, and every so often, she would trace the shape with a finger.

"It does," I said, but I refused to look away from her. I didn't like the fucking way her light seemed to be dimming. It concerned me in a way that I had never understood before.

Uncle Carmine came to stand next to me. As my grandfather's *consigliere* for many years, he was a man I had great respect for. He was wise, and even though my chosen *consigliere*, Francesco Di Pisa, was just as good, it was still wise to consult with the old timers who were left. Uncle Carmine knew what I was trying to bring back, the code as it used to be, and he supported me in doing it in accordance to the old ways.

"Your grandfather was worried about you marrying her," he said. "He thought you'd lose your focus."

"Only when she's around," I said. "I don't bring my personal life into this life."

"It's just that she's so beau—"

I looked at him and he closed his mouth. It was no secret that we were expected to marry the girl next door, ones we grew up with even, like Martina. Back in the day, virgins. My wife was fucking gorgeous, but she was a woman of great respect, and in any social situation, superior to any woman I'd ever known. It was the same in the bedroom.

I was a rarity in this life—a man who could be a gangster and a businessman—and so was she.

He sighed and took his seat again. "How long do we have?"

I stuck the curtain behind the holder, keeping it open, and checked my watch. "Fifteen minutes."

"Fucking Silvio," he said, growling. "He started this entire mess because of jealousy. Rules are like bones. We have them for a reason. If one man breaks them, it gives another man the right to do the same. Then what do we have? No body."

I nodded. "It's been a long time since our family has been at war from within."

It took him a moment to answer. "Would you call this war?"

I thought about it for a minute. "Yeah, I would. Vito tried to take me out. He has men who back him. Any bloodshed is considered an act of war."

"At least your men don't have to go to the mattresses." He took a sip of his drink and set it down. I heard the glass hit the table. "I'll never forget my first time. I was a young man, and I'd never heard of such a thing."

Yeah, in his day, going to the mattresses meant that all of the men had to stand together or risk getting caught alone. Nothing was worth leaving your crew for because alone, it was easier for the enemy to pick you off.

"I won't allow it to get that far. Vito and his crew will be done for in a week."

After Silvio's underboss had tried to have me killed, the commission ruled that, again, it was unsanctioned, and he had no backing whatsoever. They had given Vito a pass after Silvio, but now he had run out of his nine lives. I was taking his men out one by one, until I got to him.

If anyone would go to the mattresses, it would be Vito and his crew. But they hadn't. They had scattered like pigeons and were hiding out like the cowards they were.

"We'll get to that in a few minutes," I said. "But I want you to tell me about Vittorio Scarpone."

"Skilled in warfare, and that's all you need to know."

"You're telling me he was smart in life. So you're also telling me he'd be smart in death."

"Whatever you're thinking, let it die, Corrado. Your grandfather wanted you to leave it alone. Why can't you?"

"You know as well as I do that the Scarpones never belonged in this life. They were fucking brutal, but that's all they were. They were left in power too long because the commission decided not to touch them. The commission voted against my grandfather when he wanted Arturo removed. The Scarpones made money but let their men starve. They put family second. They wanted all of the money for themselves and the bloodshed for everyone else."

"I agree," Uncle Carmine said. "But what's done is done." He rubbed his hands together, like he was wiping them clean. "The commission voted, and Emilio listened. What else can you do in this life, Corrado? Rules. Rules. Rules. Are like bones, *capisci?* You break them and you weaken this thing of ours.

"That's why Vito is where he is. You're no better than him, Corrado. No one is better in this life, only smarter. I knew your grandfather for years. I've known you your entire life. You're cagey, just as good as the old timers, and you're too smart to waste it all on a ghost." He paused. "Off the record. A ghost who deserves revenge."

"What's so fucking special about this bum?" Why did everyone like the motherfucker?

"Other than he probably lived years as a ghost in his own town?"

Yeah, I'd give him that. If it were true, which I tended to believe, he had pulled off something massive.

I'd seen parts of the motherfucker twice. Once at The Club, when he opened the door for the girl Mariposa and her friend, Kelly's wife, and I saw his hand. A wolf tattoo on it. He closed the door right after. I would have been stupid to believe he left it open for me. I was a smart man, so I didn't even try.

As I was leaving his restaurant, and the fuckers tried to lay me out like they had my grandfather—poetic justice and all that shit—a shooter took out one of the guys who had aimed for me. Then all hell broke loose with my men.

I'd gotten a glimpse of the extra shooter, though. That Machiavellian motherfucker with the wolf tattoo on his hand again. The Scarpones had them. It was their thing.

A knock came at the door, and I told the men to come in. My underboss came in first, Calcedonio Badalamenti, followed by Adriano and Baggio. The rest filed in after.

"So I says, 'He's like a fucking dog! He comes when I call him,' and the motherfucker says, 'Prove it!' First the thing with my ma and her cooking. Now this?" Baggio was saying.

"I bet Gilberts comes when you put food out. That's why I'd come," Adriano said as they all shook my hand and Uncle Carmine's, and then took a seat.

"It's more than that," Baggio said. "I'm tellin' ya. He's a fuckin' genius fish."

"Yeah, but does he like worms or flakes better?" Adriano said.

This fucking guy. I had considered making him my underboss, but after spending time with him in Sicily, I decided on Calcedonio. He was less food-motivated and more money-minded. And he was respected, which also meant he was feared.

But fuck me, no one was better with a gun than Adriano Lima. The men respected him, too. He just had to quit his obsessive relationship with food. Some of the men had recently started calling him Adriano Lima Bean.

The men all quieted down as I became quiet. Then we got to business. We discussed small matters first.

"Sammy Bravata." Sal said. "He got picked up on some charges."

"Take care of his family while he's in," I said. "Keep an eye on his businesses until he gets out."

A few more of these went around. Then we got to one of the main points.

"Vito," I said to Calcedonio. "Where are we?"

"He can't make a fucking move without us knowing about it. He's hiding out with his current *goomah*."

I sat back in the chair, steepled my fingers, and set them over my mouth. "Baggio," I said.

He nodded. "You got it, boss."

"Get with Calcedonio on his location. It's not going to be as easy as you think, but since he's alone now, we only need him."

"I'll have more than one plan in play, Don Corrado," Baggio said.

I nodded.

This wasn't going to be an ordinary hit. I wanted Vito's head on a stick and scorpions stuck in his eyes and mouth. Since he cared enough to send them to my wife as a warning, and put my family—my wife and baby, my little cousin—in danger, I'd care enough to give them back to him.

"Nunzio," I said, taking a card out of my desk. I flipped it around my fingers, thinking about the fuck who offered my wife candy. I had asked one of my younger guys if "candy" was code for sex these days. If it had been, Halifax would have been buried underneath his building, not leaving it. "How's the situation?"

"Gone back to England. The store will be closed in a week." Nunzio grinned at me. "I made him an offer he could not refuse. We will have sweets for a long time."

"I'll take it off your hands," Adriano said.

"Get outta here," I said, waving my hand. They all started to leave and I stopped Nunzio. "Adriano doesn't go near that shop."

"He needs an intervention," Nunzio said, lifting his fist, and then he shut the door behind him.

An intervention to Nunzio would be breaking Adriano's jaw so he couldn't eat. He'd suggested it in Italy.

Uncle Carmine remained with me, since he was staying for dinner. I went back to the window and found my wife again. She was in the same spot, staring toward the sky, the sun falling on her face. She could have been sitting in the dark, for as blank as her expression was. I didn't fucking like it.

"Uncle Carmine," I said.

"Yeah?"

"Get Tito on the phone."

It was time to make some plans.

# 27

# ALCINA

**W**inter had been brutal, but spring was blooming all around us. I could barely get up without help these days, but to get out of the house, and to do something different than make candles, I spent time with Corrado's grandmother out in her garden.

She grew *frangipani* on one side. Her husband had the other side of the garden when he was alive. He only grew tomatoes. They were all dead. I had asked her if she wanted me to help her replant when it was time. She told me no, they had died with her husband.

The wind swept the ground, and the sweet but spicy scent of the flowers drifted in the air. The scent of vanilla, cinnamon, and roses all mixed together in the breeze. They were a common flower in Sicilian gardens. Some even grew them on balconies.

The smell brought me home. I held my rosary tighter, thinking of my *famiglia*.

I missed Anna's big mouth. The way we would fight and then laugh over nothing.

I missed *mamma* chasing us with wooden spoons. Her

words of wisdom. The smell of her cooking. The way *papà* would be grumpy until we made him laugh.

I missed Sicily. The colors. The smells. The sounds.

My eyes moved to the big house. My heart twisted with pain at the sight of it. It was more like a prison than a fortress.

"My *nonna* gave me this plant the day I was married," Teresa said, pointing to the *frangipani* with her trowel. She moved the wide-brim hat from her face so she could see me better.

Her hair was pure silver, always pulled back into a chignon, and her eyes were warm brown. She was short and plump, and her eyes matched her face—warm. I had seen a picture of her on her wedding day. She had been a pretty woman, and some of that youth came through her smile, when she used it.

"To bring to your new home." I smiled.

It was an old tradition for Sicilian women to plant the flower and then give it to their daughters or granddaughters after they were married.

She smiled, too, maybe remembering. "I decided to plant it here. I was close with my *nonna*." She had started to dig around the flower when we first came out, and I did not realize until then that she had probably gone deeper than the roots. She stopped for a second, looking up at the window. "My grandson is watching you again."

I looked up and met his eyes. We did not turn away from each other. That was not the problem—no. *Problems.* He had become obsessed with my safety after the scorpion incident, especially since the man who had sent them had not been found. He had become obsessed with the man without a name, too. And it seemed like each day he moved into places that I could not follow without a bright light.

He was always watching me, though. *Per sempre.* Maybe waiting for another full moon so he could find me again.

I looked away from him and back at his grandmother. "Did your husband watch you from the same window?"

"No," she said, going back to digging. "He did not watch me at all. He saw his wife. The mother of his children. But he did not see me."

I braced my hands against the bench, sitting up some. She did not look at me, but I knew she could feel me watching.

"This life of theirs becomes ours, too, " she said. "It's not business for them, it's a way of life. When you choose this life, there is no other. We live on the outskirts of real life, even though we can see it happening right in front of us. We socialize with other wives—their children become like our own. We throw parties for our family—Christmas, New Year's, Easter, Fourth of July, weddings, baptisms. It all looks so glamorous. It looks like we live *the* life.

"You're a smart girl. I don't have to lecture you on the realities. The constant scrutiny from the government. The constant hovering around your house. The *other* women—we go to some places, and they go to others. They can have a *goomah,* but they can't disrespect us by bringing the woman, or women, to the same places. It's expected that they have them. How can a man that powerful only have one woman? What would that make him?"

"A man," I said. In this life, it would be harder to stand up to that particular expectation than bowing to it.

She stopped digging for a minute and grinned. "You are full of heat," she said, and then she sighed. "Then the day comes when you have sons. And you ask your husband to spare them from this life. *Yes, yes,* they tell you. *I will try my best.* But it gets to them. It gets to sons, cousins, uncles. It even gets to the girls. They usually marry a son or a cousin. They become us."

"You," I said. "They become you."

"You carry the Capitani name. You carry on the legacy. You carry many women who have sat where you are now—" she nodded to the bench "—with you. You are the Don's wife. You are who I used to be. No matter how different we look."

"It's not the way we look," I said. "It's the way we react."

She grinned again, and this time, it seemed out of pity. "Did Corrado tell you about my daughters?"

"Some," I said.

She dug a little harder. Then she stopped after another minute, wiping the sweat from her brow. "I knew who his father was."

"I thought—"

"They have their secrets. We have ours." She looked at me then. Her eyes were dull, flat, even in the sunshine. "Luna fell in love with Corrado Palermo before she left home. That's why she left, and Emilia went with her. We did not want her to leave, but she knew her father would never allow it. Corrado belonged to a different family, and at the time, there was a war going on.

"It would have caused even more strife if Emilio had found out. Luna was terrified that if he did, he would have him killed. At that time, Corrado Palermo was making a name for himself. Even I didn't want her associated with him." She touched her temple, leaving a dirt smear. "An idea made it here. To his head. It didn't leave unless it was tired or done.

"My daughter was the same. So she left home and went to Vegas. She knew he would come after her no matter where she went, and her father would disown her when she did. Emilio did, Corrado Palermo followed, and she got pregnant not long after. But things were happening here, bad things, and since Corrado Palermo was like a son to Arturo Scarpone, he sent him to Italy to lay low for a while."

"Corrado Palermo had a contract on his head. When things were safe here, he came back and broke it off with Luna. He had gotten married while he was in Palermo."

She went back to digging, sighing. "He didn't want anything to do with the baby or with Luna. She made us swear on each other, Emilia and me, that we would never tell. I have never spoke a word of this until today. My girls are gone."

"Why are you telling me?" I whispered.

She brought her shoulders up to her ears and then let them fall. "I see that same obsession in my grandson. It worries me. History repeats itself, especially when it's in the blood."

"He is not his father," I said. "He is not his grandfather either."

"I agree." She lifted the trowel and then started digging again. "But he has been raised in this life his entire life. He never had a chance to be anything different." She looked me in the eye.

"My husband slept sound every night. All the things he did, and not once did he stir in his sleep, unless he ate something that bothered his esophagus. All of the things he did—where was his conscience? Tell me. Does my grandson, your husband, sleep sound?"

"Maybe his conscience *was* his esophagus," I said.

She grinned, but she knew I was avoiding the question she already had the answer to. Corrado slept sound whenever he slept, except for one time. When the boat in Lake Como had been blown up. He stayed up all night staring at me.

"I love him," she said. "My grandson. More than my own life. But he chose this path." She hit something in her garden. A metallic sound rang out.

She set the trowel to the side, took her gloves off, and then pulled out an old metal box from the ground. She dusted it off. The square box was clearly old, worn down even more by the mud that it had been packed in for what seemed like years.

It didn't take her as long to pack the mud over the hole. She clipped a few flowers after, and then, tucking the box underneath her arm, rose from the ground without any help. "Walk with me," she said, nodding toward the door that led into the house.

I looked up at the window. There he was again, watching me. I walked next to her, and he watched until he could no longer see us anymore. The lace curtains fluttered when he closed them.

She turned to me when she knew he could not see and gave me the box with the flowers. She took my hands in hers, squeezing. "I learned to hate him," she said. "My husband. I loved him. I loved him the moment I saw him. It came so naturally. To love. But over the years—the life, always coming second to it—I learned how to hate.

"It was not an easy emotion for me. I wrestled with it. But after time, so much time, *things*, the loss of my children, the loss of a life I expected, the hate came, and it has never left me. I *hate* him. I had always thought the best day of my life would be my wedding day. It was the day we put him in the ground."

She squeezed my hands even harder. The metal box, my wedding rings, and the rosary bit into my skin. "My *nonna* gave me this tin. She told me there are two things a woman should always have: a garden and a money tree to bury. It should grow over the years, given to the next generation, so if they need it, it'll be there." She shrugged. "They have their secrets. We have ours. One thing we have in common, we all bury them, *capisci*?"

She looked into my eyes and then took a deep breath, releasing it slowly. "If you love my grandson, *go*, or one day, you will be me. You will have so much hate in your heart for someone you once couldn't imagine living without. Preserve what you have. Don't let this life kill that, too. This life always comes first. Everything else comes second.

"Give your baby a chance. A chance to...choose life. Not this one, but a good one. Give this tin to your daughter, or your son, empty. The two of you build it up together again." She released my hands and went into the house.

Men were around, but behind the gates, they browsed more

than they watched. I cracked the tin, and inside, rolls of money filled it. She wanted me to take the money and leave.

"We're digging up buried treasure now," he said.

I shut the tin quietly and then looked into my husband's eyes. He could be as quiet as a ghost when he wanted to be.

I sighed, lifting the tin and the flowers. "Your grandmother gave me a family heirloom," I said. "When the baby is old enough, we will bury this tin after using the *frangipani* seeds inside for a garden. A family tradition."

He put his arm around my neck and kissed my temple. "Don't fucking lie to me, Alcina," he said. "I can smell the old money in that tin."

We stopped walking.

"It's a secret," I said. "Between two women. Why do you have to know about it? You do not tell me everything."

He studied my face. "You want to leave me."

"If I did?"

"Yes or no," he said.

I did not say anything. After a minute, he put his lips closer to my ear, pulling me even closer. "If that's a yes, tell me before you do, and I'll give you the knife to carve my heart out."

"You have been offering a knife to me a lot lately."

"You're the only person I would allow to kill me," he said. "Without you, I'm dead anyway." He said the words so nonchalantly, but with so much weight, I suddenly felt tired to the bone.

We stepped into the house, and after he walked me to the dining room and pulled my chair out, he cleared his throat. "What I told you the night of our wedding—" He paused. "It stands the test of time. I'm the only man in your life, whether you're beside me or not. I'll kill any man who even tries to get close to you."

Then he left.

# 28

## ALCINA

He looked at her like she hung the moon.

That was why he named our daughter Eleonora Lucia Capitani—the night she was born, the moon was full and bright enough to see by. Like the night he came to me in Bronte, he was moved by something bigger than the life that ruled him.

Eleonora means "shining light." Lucia means "graceful light."

Her dark hair was hardly enough to brush through, and her skin was like fine porcelain. Her eyes were brown, but I had a feeling they were going to lighten to dark amber. She would share the color with her *papà*. Or maybe even hazel. A mixture between his and mine—amber and brown.

He could hold her with one hand, and she ruled his world.

He slept very little after Eleonora was born, and something about it satisfied me.

After the conversation with Teresa, I watched him at night while he slept. Towards the end of my pregnancy, I could not sleep anyway. He never stirred in his sleep, and he looked more peaceful than he did awake, but when one of us needed him the most, he kept guard.

I'd decided that consciences came in all different ways and in different forms. His happened to speak the loudest when he could see the difference between his world and ours, and how far he was away when he could compare the distance.

I knew who my husband was. I knew it the moment I looked at him. The moment I fell in love with him. The moment I married him—the moment of moments—and promised him forever.

I knew who my husband was.

That was why I fought a battle he could not see. If he became lost in a dangerous obsession that he could not let go of, I knew I would lose him to it.

He had enough wars to fight. The one with the mysterious man bothered me the most.

It was not about business, but something personal. I could see it in his eyes when he was alone for long periods of time, with too much time to think. How he could not let the idea of it go, especially since the man seemed to be playing games with him.

Corrado Capitani was not used to losing.

Neither was I.

I'd be damned if I lost him to anything other than natural causes when he was old and tired.

I was capable of doing all of the things my husband did on the streets. The difference between us: I would only do them for love. He did them for *the* family and obligations. It was almost instilled in him. He was a product of *the life*, as they called it.

Love is not a weakness; it is the greatest weapon of all. I reached inside of the pocket of my dress and touched the rosary there, knowing just how strong I was. What I would risk for love.

The life I had fought so hard to have—this was it. It was my husband and my daughter. *La mia famiglia.*

A soft, warm hand touched my shoulder, and I smiled, putting my hand over hers. "She's a good sleeper," *mamma* whispered.

Corrado had arranged for *mamma* and Anna to be here when Eleonora was born. We were going to take her to meet her *nonno* at the end of summer, when we flew back with *mamma* and Anna.

"Like me," Anna said, peeking over my shoulder. "She is exactly like me."

The three of us hovered around her door, watching Corrado hold her while she slept. She had a bed in our room, but sometimes he brought her to her room to rock her to sleep after her bath.

"What is it about that kind of man holding a baby that is so sexy?" Anna whispered.

I grinned. "It is."

*Mamma* pinched Anna and she laughed quietly. "It is, *mamma!*"

"I am not disagreeing, but don't give her—" she nodded at me "—any ideas. She has to give Ele some time to be the baby. Look at her. She's bedazzled."

Anna and I looked at each other and started laughing, trying to keep our voices down.

"*Mamma mia!*" Anna shook her head. "It's *dazzled*. Not *bedazzled.*"

"What is the difference, smarty pants?"

"Dazzled is when you are bewitched. Bedazzled is what you do to clothes." Anna started to walk toward the stairs. "Who is up for cards tonight? Since the hot man has the adorable baby."

At home, sometimes we would stay up all night and play cards. We would put on a pot of coffee and some music, eat sweets, and laugh. Sometimes Anna and I would play with a few cousins, and *mamma* would sit and listen to us while she crocheted.

"You need a dictionary, Anna," *mamma* said, kissing me on the cheek. "Bedazzled is correct." Then she waved her hand. "I'm tired. We can play tomorrow."

"Same for me," I said.

Anna touched her nose and then pulled her finger away, like her nose was growing. "*Bugiarda,*" she mouthed at me. *Liar.* "There are so many people in this *castello,* I am sure I can make some easy money. They won't see me coming. I'm so sweet looking."

Corrado looked at me when I opened the door the entire way and shut it behind me. Ele's head was against his chest, her mouth open. I ran my hand through her hair, the little she had of it.

"I bedazzle you," he said, meeting my eye when I stood after kissing her delicious cheek.

I smiled. "Since the moment I saw you."

He touched his nose and then pulled his finger away, doing the exact thing Anna had done.

I narrowed my eyes. "Are you calling me a *bugiarda,* too?"

He shrugged. "You're happier now."

"Ele's here—"

He shook his head. "You've always been happy about Eleonora. You haven't been happy with me."

It was the first time he brought it up since we got to New York, and my heart swelled. He was in that space and time where he could feel the distance. He wanted to bridge the gap.

"Not with you," I whispered.

He kissed Ele on her head and took her over to her bed, laying her down. He took the chair again and touched his leg. I curled up in his embrace and took a deep, deep, breath. It felt as if I had been holding my breath, waiting for this moment. I could finally breathe again.

It had been wonderful having Ele. Our time was spent surrounding her, enjoying her, loving her. But this was what I had needed from him, one lover to another.

"I love you more than life, Corrado," I whispered. "But I get lonely."

"You've been spending time with some of the wives."

I tried. I couldn't. They were different. They talked about shopping, and cars, and places to go for spa days. Our conversations had no real substance, or any real depth, or any true feeling—when they laughed, it wasn't true.

I was thankful for Mari. She had called me a few times, and I had called her. She even invited me to girl's nights with the Fausti wives, but I didn't go.

Corrado did not like Rocco, and that was a problem. If things got tense between them...I did not want to think about what would happen. It wasn't worth the trouble. And then Mari and Amadeo had gone back to Modica for a while. We made plans to connect when they returned.

So it had been rough until *mamma* and Anna arrived. But.

"I still feel alone," I said. "This house." I looked up at him. "It has everything, but nothing. It's not warm. There's hardly any laughter. It feels like a prison."

"You traded one for another."

"No," I said. "You freed me, but without you here most of the time, nothing ever feels like enough. There's excess all around me, but not the kind that matters."

"It's me," he said. "I'm doing this to you."

He was one of the smartest men I had ever known in many different ways. But in love he was lost.

"Your grandmother told you of our conversation," I said.

"No, she lies to me. Just like she lied to my grandfather. It was the nature of their relationship."

"It's not the nature of ours," I said, sitting up, taking his face in my hands. "This is not about you, or about me, but about *us*.

I miss you. I haven't seen you this way since we left Italy." I searched his eyes. "You do not look at me. Not like this. Not enough."

"How am I looking at you, angel eyes?" he whispered.

My heart raced and my breath caught, like the very first time he looked at me this way. "Like you miss me, too, even though I'm next to you." I put my head against his, breathing him in.

He tucked his finger under my chin, lifting my mouth to his. He kissed me slowly, deeply, and then with the same roughness that made me feel claimed.

He broke the kiss and ran his hands over my head, then pulled ours together. "What do you want from me, woman?"

"Everything," I said.

"That's the fucking trouble," he said. "I can't deny you anything."

"What's done is done," I whispered. "Forgive the past."

He seemed caught off guard that I had asked that of him. "I can't do that, either," he said, and then sighed. He picked me up and carried me to our room, setting me in the bed before he brought Ele to hers.

He wrapped me in his arms and fell asleep not long after. But I could not sleep. My conscience was at peace, but my mind kept me up.

What had he been expecting me to ask of him? To leave his life behind and start a new one with me?

Never.

That was the stuff fairytales were made of. In this life, there was no such thing.

# 29

## ALCINA

"I am leaving with your closet!" Anna said, lying down on the soft rug on the floor, making a snow angel with the fake fur.

I touched her with my toe. "You must have drank too much prune juice as a child and shit all of your common sense out."

She rolled around even harder, laughing even louder. "I have not heard that since...*bisnonno*! He used to tell that to the men who would try to swindle him out of money for his fruit, remember?"

"How can I forget? *Mamma mia*! My ass still stings."

Our *bisnonno, great grandfather,* was a fruit peddler, and when men used to try to lowball him on the price of his fruit, he used to tell them that. I did not realize it was wrong to say as a child. I repeated it to my teacher when she gave me a bad grade. I got my behind whipped by my *mamma*. *Papà* tried not to laugh when he found out what I'd said, and then *mamma* hit him with a broom. She grinned the entire time.

"Can you imagine Ele saying that to her teacher?" My sister sighed, wiping her eyes. "Such a ladylike thing to say, Alcina!"

I grinned and turned to the jewelry box, choosing a watch

and a few gold bangle bracelets to wear. We were going to Bella Luna and then meeting Mari at Macchiavello's for lunch.

"I will need to have all of these clothes tailored for me though." Anna sat up, looking around at all of the clothes and shoes. "You were lucky enough to get a nice *culo*. Mine is *flat*."

I stuck it out and she slapped it.

"*Puttana*," she said, laughing.

I stuck my tongue out at her.

She grinned. Then she became quiet, watching me slip my shoes on and then spraying perfume. She was already wearing the dress she chose and was ready to go.

"You look different, Alcina," she whispered.

"I gained some weight," I said, shrugging. "It has only been three months since Ele was—"

"No," she said, her voice suddenly hard, making me narrow my eyes. "You are beautiful. As beautiful as ever. Physically— you are perfect. This is deeper."

I turned from her, going back to the jewelry box. I threw her a few bracelets that would match her dress. She caught them and slipped them on, but she refused to stop giving me a look that meant she wanted me to answer.

I sighed, running my fingers over the gold cross earrings with amber gems Corrado had given me in Milan. "I reach him, and then I cannot," I said in Sicilian, being honest.

It had been two months since our talk in Ele's room, and for another month, I thought maybe he was going to let the past go. I hoped his willingness to be more present in our lives would have lasted longer. I had not seen him much this month, and even when he was around, his mind was not with us. He even postponed the trip to Forza d'Agrò to see my father. We were going to baptize Ele in the church we were married in.

"It's not as bad when you and *mamma* are here, because I do not feel as lonely, as homesick, but..." I caressed the metal, the feel of it comforting to me, like a rosary. "I am worried, Anna.

Truly worried about him. He eats, sleeps, breathes revenge for something that happened years ago. Something that can no longer be fixed."

"Have you told him this?"

"*Sì*," I said, trying to take a deep breath, but it felt shallow, like I could not catch it. "He sees only one way. I see something different. I see the train coming, and I do not think I can pull him out of the way in time. Uncle Tito told me to change his direction, his path, but I am not strong enough. If I lose him to this, Anna, it will ruin me. I don't even know who this man is who has possessed him, but it feels different."

Anna lifted herself from the floor and came to stand beside me. She put her hand on my shoulder. "You knew this was his life, Alcina."

I shook my head. "This is different. He can separate himself from the business. He cannot separate himself from this. It is like a dark seed has taken root, and no amount of light can make him see the truth."

"Did you say those exact words to him?"

"Not exactly," I said, sighing.

She studied my face for a moment. "Would you rather him not be who he is?"

"I am bound to him by love," I said. "It does not matter who he is."

"When I said that you looked different, I did not mean physically. When I asked you if you would rather him not be who he is—I meant his title in this life."

"I knew from the beginning." I shrugged. "I have no right to feel differently now."

"Maybe not," she said. "But do you?"

I went to turn away from her, but she took me by the shoulders, turning me toward her, forcing me to look her in the eye.

"Listen to me," she almost hissed. "This is your life. What do you want from it?"

What did I want? What did I need? What was I really asking for?

*Him.*

I had always wanted him and our life—our little family. The specifics got lost in translation.

"Life will rule you, sister," she said in Sicilian, "if you do not rule it. Fucking rule it like the Sicilian queen you are. Your clothes do not matter. This house does not matter. Nothing matters but how you react. You decide what you want, what is best for your family." She lifted her finger. "When you do, you find a way to get it. You are bound by love. So is he. I remember two people standing at that altar vowing: *I will live for thee. I will lay down my life for thee. We are bound by one flesh.* Two people sharing one life, Alcina. *Sharing.*"

Anna and I both became still—we had not been using hand gestures like usual, but our conversations always felt almost physical, even when we were not.

Corrado cleared his throat from behind me.

Anna let me go, turning toward the jewelry box, tinkering around.

Corrado slipped his hands around my waist, pulling me close, giving me a kiss. He always did before he left. It was a strange sort of place to be—not close, but still close. It felt a lot like the day I first saw him, when he returned my glove. I went to take it, but he pulled it back.

"The day we met," he said, like he could read my mind.

I nodded. "You returned my glove to me," I said.

"You actually returned something to me," he said, and then he studied my face before he went on. "Romeo Fausti has this thing. Whenever he sees a guy chasing after a woman, he says the guy is chasing after his rib."

"A dog after a bone," I said. I knew the Faustis well, and this was something I could see one of them saying. For ruthless killers, they were also known to be very romantic in an archaic kind of way.

He grinned and then shrugged. "That could be true. He's referring to Adam and Eve in the garden, though. '*The man gave names to all the livestock, to the birds in the air, and to every beast in the field. But for Adam no suitable helper was found.*' Not until he was made to fall into a deep sleep, and when he woke up, he was missing a rib. A piece of him, but in its place, the woman was brought to him. His."

"Do you want your rib back?" I grinned, running my hands up his sides, settling on his ribs. I loved his entire body, but that was one of my favorite spots. I loved to run my fingertips up and down them at night.

"Already got it," he said, kissing me once more. "The day in that pistachio grove. I woke up and found you."

He said the words plainly, like they were simply the truth. Like they wouldn't leave my heart stuttering in the closet when he walked out of it.

Anna wrapped her arm around mine, yanking me into her. "I am amazed at how different men can be. My husband is an honest worker—he does not do the things your husband does. But he does not...talk to me like that. He does not arrange for my family to be there when I need them the most. Fabrizio is wonderful in his own ways, he is wonderful to the world, but your husband is to *you*. He is cruel to the rest of the world, but you are his exception. He has found a way to love through you."

We walked out behind him, going to say goodbye to *mamma* and Ele before we left. *Mamma* had her out in the sun, taking her for a walk in the stroller around the property. I refused to leave her with anyone else in the house.

Corrado got to them before we did. He smiled at her and picked her up, and she started to cry. He hadn't been home much during the day. The time he spent with her was at night when she was asleep.

He turned around and handed her to me. She calmed right away when I spoke to her, kissing her on her wet cheeks.

"She just does not recognize you," I whispered.

He fixed his suit, nodded, and then left with his men.

---

BELLA LUNA WAS PACKED. The line was out the door. We'd completely run out of *Lo Scorpione*. It was one of the most popular candles in the shop.

Nunzio followed Anna, Brooklyn, and I out as we left.

*"Accidenti!"* Anna said, smiling. *Damn.* "You are a hit, Alcina!"

"Not me," I said. "The candles."

She stopped before we got to the car, looking at the empty shop next door. "What happened? It looks like a nice place. Like a candy shop. It's sweet looking."

Nunzio opened the door to the car and I slid in first, followed by Brooklyn and then Anna.

"He was not there long," I said. "He came to introduce himself and then not long after, the shop closed."

Brooklyn started to laugh. "You seriously don't know what happened to him, Alcina?"

"No," I said. "Why would I?"

She shook her head and sighed as Nunzio started the car and pulled out into traffic. "Two words. Your husband."

I narrowed my eyes at her. "He ran him off?"

"I'd bet my date on it," she said. "He runs this town. No one talks to his woman and gets away with it. Well." She bit her lip. "That's what I'm betting happened. I saw Halifax on his way out, and he wouldn't even look at me." She pulled her phone out and pressed the side button. "Speaking of sweet...here's the cutest baby in the world." She showed us her screen saver. It was Ele. She was smiling.

I missed her instantly, and then my heart felt heavy when I remembered how she had cried when her *papà* had picked her up.

Anna nudged me. "*Mamma* has this. Enjoy your day. You rarely leave." She smiled at Brooklyn. "Tell us about your date."

Brooklyn's face lit up, but it fell when the car came to an abrupt stop. We all flew forward, the seat belt biting into my neck. There was traffic, but nothing that would have caused Nunzio to slam on the brake. He refused to meet my eye through the mirror, but he looked more sour than usual.

"Oh!" Brooklyn tucked her hair behind her ears after it fell into her face from the jerk. "He's a chef at one of the nicest restaurants in town. His name is Michele Sorrentino. My mom introduced me to him. She works at the restaurant."

Anna started egging her on, telling her to borrow a black lace dress I had for her date, since Michele was taking her to his cousin's fancy wedding.

"My..." Brooklyn made a motion over her breasts. "Are not big enough!" Then she looked at mine. She and Anna started to laugh.

I smiled, but I was watching Nunzio through the mirror. He had both hands on the wheel. He was squeezing the life out of it. I touched Brooklyn on the leg, nodding toward him, lifting my eyebrows.

"I will tell you about it later," she mouthed.

There was a line for Macchiavello's, and after Nunzio pulled the car up, he got out to open our door. Before he did, Adriano said something to him from the street, and he stood there talking to him.

"Tell us!" Anna said, rushing the words out.

"He...likes me, I think. But I can't see him. Not like that. My dad was the same thing...well, he was like Corrado used to be, you know? Not that high up in ranking like Corrado is now. I'm not sure exactly *what* my dad did, but he was hardly ever around. My mom was miserable. And then he got killed." She shrugged.

"I never really knew him, my dad, but my mom would go crazy if she knew I even...liked Nunzio. Because I do. I like him a lot. But it would never work. She told me she would rather die than see me marry a man like my dad. And by 'a man like my dad,' she means a man in that life."

"Your life was hard?"

She shrugged. "My mom refused to take a penny from the Capitanis, even though she let me see them. The only reason she did is because one of my best friends is my cousin. She's about to marry a made guy. My mom has been obsessing over it —in *the* worst way. She says if you dance at one of their weddings, you might as well dance at their funerals. But I digress.

"After my dad was killed, she started working a lot. Sometimes two jobs, seven days a week, to keep us going. She said she didn't want a penny of their blood money. I've had a good life, but she's bitter, and I never got to know my dad. Even when he was around, he was never around, if that makes sense. There are no happily-ever-afters in that life, that's what my mom always says."

Brooklyn became quiet when Nunzio opened the door and offered her his hand. She stepped out, and I noticed when she tried to let go of him, he held on a second longer than he should have.

"That is depressing," Anna said. Then she stepped out.

The restaurant was packed, but we were seated right away. No matter where we went, we were always seated without a reservation. Not that we went out a lot, not after the scorpions, but when we did, it was almost like the red carpet was rolled out.

Mari was waiting for us when we entered the same room Corrado and I had been seated in the first time we came.

"I love it here," I said to Anna, even though my attention was elsewhere. Brooklyn had reinforced the scene with Ele this morning, and it weighed heavily on my heart. "The food is really good."

She did the nose thing, like I was lying.

"You will see," I said. "It tastes familiar. That's why I thought you would enjoy it."

Anna and I took turns hugging Mari. I knew her a little better since I had lived with her in-laws in Modica for a while, and she would visit with Amadeo. Then we introduced her to Brooklyn. We all took our seats, looking over the menu, and then we ordered.

Conversation flowed as Anna and Brooklyn got to know Mari better. We chatted about Saverio, Ele, the aunts, the chocolate shop, Bella Luna, and then Brooklyn's date again. Before any of us realized, we were finished eating.

"The food is so good," Anna said, patting her stomach. "I think even *mamma* would approve of this place. I am stuffed! Anyone want to take a look at the bar area with me? I need to walk."

"I will!" Brooklyn stood. "I've always wanted to see it up close."

I sighed after they left, setting my fork down. I looked up and found Mari staring at me.

"This life is romanticized a lot," she whispered. "But it's a little different when you're the one in the story, am I right?"

"How did you know?"

She shrugged. "I hear things. I know things." She toyed with her napkin for a second before she looked me in the eye. "My dad was...connected to that life, at one time. I was only five, so I don't remember much, but he worked for the Scarpones. He tried to kill his boss. From what I've learned, Arturo Scarpone was greedy, and he was barely paying the men, even though he was making a lot."

She waved her hand. "Anyway. My dad would get ideas in his head, or so I was told, and once they got stuck, he couldn't get them out. He was so focused on killing Arturo that he basically ran us into the ground. My entire life up until I met Amadeo was spent in hiding." She sighed. "So I understand, whatever you're going through, more than you know."

We both became quiet. She had her thoughts and I had mine.

"Alcina..." She hesitated. "Did Amadeo tell you that about me?"

"No," I said. "He does not talk much."

We both grinned.

"He doesn't," she said.

"It's familiar, though. I have heard similar stories. One as fresh as just a few minutes ago."

"Ah," she said. "Brooklyn."

I nodded.

"There's no room for family in that life," she said. "Only *the* family, and basically nothing else. It splits actual families apart."

"Your *mamma*...she left?"

"Yeah." She took a sip of her water with lemon and then set it down. "Arturo had her killed."

I grabbed her hand and squeezed. She squeezed back.

A knock came at the door. We both turned to look when it opened. I sat up straighter in my chair when Rocco walked in.

"Mari." He nodded. "Alcina." His eyes lingered. Then he cleared his throat when he looked at Mari again. "Would you mind giving Alcina and I a moment alone?"

Mari nodded. "I'll check on the girls at the bar."

I wanted to look at her, to narrow my eyes and shake my head, because I did not want to be alone with him, but I did not want to make it obvious. I was not afraid to be alone with him —I had been before in Modica—but I did not think it was appropriate. However. What the Faustis wanted, the Faustis got. I suspected that was why Nunzio had not stepped into the room.

The door closed, and instead of taking Mari's seat, he took one on the edge of the table, one leg dangling. "You look beautiful, Alcina," he said. "Marriage and motherhood suits you."

"*Grazie*," I said, picking my glass up, taking a sip, trying not to look at him too long. But again, trying not to make it obvious.

These men, like my husband, were not ordinary. Subtlety was an art form to them. If our eyes lingered for too long, he would think I was interested or challenging him. If I blatantly looked away from him, he would either think I was being rude or I was interested again but did not want to show it. Either way, it was a fine line.

"What is your daughter's name?"

"I thought you would know," I said. "You seem to know everything."

"I do," he said. "I want you to tell me."

"Eleonora Lucia Capitani," I said.

He repeated her name, without her last, pronouncing it perfectly. "I am sure she is as gorgeous as her *mamma*."

"Listen," I said, this time looking him in the eye. "I do not have much time. What did you want to speak to me about?"

"I wanted to make sure you were happy," he said in Sicilian. "I have always cared about you."

"I am," I said. "So even though your concern is appreciated, it is wasted."

We stared at each other, before I slowly broke eye contact and took another drink of water. Some of the women in Modica said that the color of his eyes was stolen from the Sicilian sea, right when the sun starts to sink into the horizon. But he was looking for his great love. He would not find it in me. I did not have it to give to him. Never had.

He laughed, and it was raspy and quiet. "You've always bitten back," he said.

I looked up and he winked at me. He stood from the table and started making his way toward the door. He stopped when he got there. "Have you seen Amadeo since you arrived in New York?"

I shook my head, reaching for my glass again. "No."

He stared at me, but in a different way this time. It was like he was thinking before he spoke. Usually the words just rolled off his tongue, each and every word perfectly executed.

"I will tell the aunts you enjoyed their food," he said, nodding to the plate. "Amadeo had them create the menu." He fixed his suit. "It was good to see you, Alcina. If you ever need me, you know how to find me."

The glass fell out of my hands, clattering to the plate, the remaining water, lemon, and ice spilling onto the gorgeous arrangement. A piece of glass had fallen into my lap. I hissed when I picked it up and it cut my finger. Blood ran down, but I did not even bother to clean it up when Mari stepped back into the room.

She eyed me uneasily, like she was unsure.

"Why didn't you tell me?" I whispered.

She nodded to my hand. "You're bleeding."

"Fuck the blood." I hit the table. "Amadeo owns this restaurant. The man Corrado has been looking for."

She sighed and took a seat. She refused to look at the cut on my hand. Her face was pale. "He does. He owns this place. The Club, too."

"He's Vittorio Scarpone." It came to me then. The last time I had probably heard his real name was when I was a child. We had always called him Amadeo for as long as I could remember. Anna used to joke that he was so important that he did not need a last name.

"Correct," Mari said. "It's...funny how that works out. You're looking right at something, all signs pointing, but you don't see. Not until it's meant to make sense."

"That means..." The tightness in my throat was a warning that my food was about to come back up.

"That means." She sighed again. "Vittorio killed my mom and my dad—or that man, as I call him. Corrado Palermo was his name. But Vittorio saved me and then hid me."

"*Mio Dio.*" I made the sign of the cross, reaching in my pocket for my rosary, bringing it out.

Her breathing picked up when she saw it. It was as if she was looking at a ghost, or something she had seen before, and it made her anxious.

"Vittorio," I whispered, clutching the beads. "His throat."

She nodded. "Arturo—that other man—did that to him because he refused to kill me."

"If you are Corrado Palermo's daughter..." I could not even finish.

Mari nodded. "That's right. Corrado—your Corrado—is my brother. Uncle Tito told me. He thought I had a right to know. It's been tense between him and Amadeo ever since."

My heart pumped so hard that the blood gushed out of my finger. "We need to talk," I said.

"Desperately." She lifted a finger. "But first. You need to cover that up. I don't feel so well." Then she passed out.

# 30

# CORRADO

I t didn't matter what time of the day I went to Macchiavello's, or how late I showed up at The Club, that Machiavellian motherfucker always seemed ready for me.

I'd get the best table in either place.

I was used to that, but when he did it, I knew he did it to fuck with me.

The music pounded in The Club. The lights swirled. Every night was ladies' night. There were five women for every guy. I'd already identified a few men in my family with their ·goomahs. It was no surprise. It had some of the best alcohol in the city and some of the most expensive talent on the stage.

However. I set my cup of Amaro down, my eyes rising to the second floor, where I knew he was watching me. Even though he reserved the best tables on this level for me, he never invited me into the hidden world he created above.

This time I didn't come to wait for Mac Macchiavello to make an appearance. I came because I wanted to meet with Rocco Fausti.

It usually took a while to arrange a meeting with one of

them, but since he requested a meeting with my wife, alone, I knew he was in town.

I set my glass down harder than intended.

Calcedonio looked at me but said nothing. Nunzio took the bottle and poured himself another glass. He came instead of Adriano, who had vertigo and kept running into walls when he moved too fast. There was no such thing as a sick day in this life, but what good was a man who'd shoot left when he had to shoot right?

From my visits, I'd learned that the Faustis frequented Macchiavello's and The Club, so I knew they were familiar with Mac Macchiavello. That meant he meant something to them. Time was precious to the higher-ups in Fausti *famiglia*. They only spent it on people they thought worthy.

It was Romeo Fausti who agreed to set up a sit-down between his brother and me. The thing about the Faustis, though, was that someone higher had to sit in. That high up, it was usually an uncle or an older cousin.

The Faustis had a different setup than we did. Even if we had men who were blood-related in each family, our families were not all related. The higher a man went up in the Fausti *famiglia*, the most likely they were to be blood-related.

They were the secret society of secret societies.

We had the commission. The entire world had them.

Another man had tried to be the middle guy back in the day, between them and us, but that guy didn't last long.

In all truth, the Faustis never messed around with the families unless there was a problem that couldn't be solved by the commission. They were an honorable bunch of men, bred to live and die by their family motto—*my word is as good as my blood*. Truth meant something to them.

It was hard to come by these days, that kind of honor, but their family still proved it could work. That was the old way I wanted to bring back. The golden age. The Faustis had never left it. Though, in fairness, they never had the scrutiny we had either, as far as the government.

That being said, I requested Romeo bring someone who outranked Rocco to the sit-down. Romeo was younger. Brando was older, but he was in and out of the life. I could never get a good read on that fucking guy, but as long as he was decent to me, I'd show him the same respect.

Romeo said he had someone and it wouldn't be a problem, though.

A bunch of women walked up to our booth. Calcedonio looked each girl up and down, his eyes hungry. Nunzio looked at them but then poured himself another drink.

"You seem thirsty," I said.

He drank it down without really tasting it.

"Ladies," Calcedonio said, "if you'd wait over at the bar, the drinks will keep coming. On me. But if you don't mind..." He made a shoo motion with his hand.

They smiled at him, and his eyes lingered on one longer than the others. He sent one of our men to keep an eye on them at the bar.

Nunzio poured another glass. He held it in his hand. "I want Michele Sorrentino." He downed the glass.

I narrowed my eyes, trying to recall the name.

"The chef?" Calcedonio said, scratching his head. "What the fuck did he do? Give you shrimp instead of steak? I ate there last week with Adriano and Baggio, and it was off the charts."

"He is on a date with your cousin," he said, looking at me. "Brooklyn."

"That's it?" I said.

"Yes," he said. "That is it. But I do not trust him. He looks like a fucking Lothario."

"What's a Lothario?" Calcedonio said, sliding his hands through his hair, trying to tame the sides down.

"Not what. Who." I slid the bottle closer to Nunzio.

"Lothario is a name. It means an unscrupulous seducer of women."

Calcedonio and I looked at each other and grinned. But that still didn't take away from the fact that Nunzio wanted to kill a man who was not a part of this life and had done nothing wrong.

"You know the rules," I said. "No."

Calcedonio squeezed his shoulder. "Stay away from her. She's a real nice girl, but her ma got burned, and she'd set you up if you even tried to get close to her daughter. That woman has the longest fucking memory in history."

Nunzio grumbled something into his glass and then downed it.

I checked my watch. Two minutes. Even though I'd been visiting The Club often, it wasn't my fucking scene. But I went where Macchiavello's business took him, and Romeo suggested it for the meeting place.

The three of us stood when Romeo started to make his way toward us. The crowd parted to let him through.

He held out his hand when he was close enough. We shook and then pulled each other in. Romeo and I enjoyed each other's company. We occasionally shared drinks and cigars and some conversation.

Calcedonio and Nunzio shook his hand. Then he leaned in closer and told me how to get to a room in the building. Second floor. He'd meet us there in a minute.

One of the guards opened the door for us before we were even there. It could only be opened from the inside, and when the door closed, it shut flush with the wall. Unless someone opened it, it didn't exist.

We were led to a floor with less people. A more exclusive area. The music was subdued. The furniture was richer. The men sitting around smoked expensive cigars and drank fine liquor. I recognized a few famous athletes and some politicians.

The guard opened a door off a hallway, and Rocco Fausti stood at the one-way mirrored wall, looking out over the dance floor.

"Take your seats, gentlemen," he said. "My *fratello* will be here shortly."

We were offered cigars and an assortment of liquor that back in the day would have only been offered to dignitaries and gentlemen of substance.

I declined the drink but accepted the cigar. The three of us took seats on regal chairs at a table fit for a king. The guard delivered the cigars and the drinks Calcedonio and Nunzio had ordered. He set down a bottle of Amaro and a chilled cup for me.

Yeah, Macchiavello was fucking with me.

I'd drink to that. I was fucking with him, too. I raised my glass and grinned. *Saluti, motherfucker.* Then I downed the drink.

My eyes met Rocco's when I set the glass down. He was eyeing me through the mirror. I wasn't looking away. We'd stare at each other until the world fucking ended.

The door opened and Tito Sala walked in, breaking the reflection into three.

"Why this place?" Tito was complaining. "Every time I come here, two women decide to make me into a T*ito* sandwich, nephew!"

Romeo's laughter was raspy. "That is because you are an old gangster. An original." He squeezed Tito on the shoulder. "The *donne* see a man dressed as nice as you. Such style." He whistled. "They all want a piece of you."

Tito fixed his collar. "I do have a certain charm," he said. Then he cleared his throat. "That is beside the point! It is late and I have other obligations."

"Such as staying at home with *zia* and watching *I Love Lucy* reruns?" Romeo laughed again and took a seat closer to where

Rocco would sit. Even though we were tight, he still had a side. I had my family, and he had his.

Tito slapped him behind his head. "I will be watching when you are my age from above, and I will be laughing." He gave a fake laugh. "I outmatch all of you in energy now, and I was born long before all of you *ragazzi* knew how to use a pot!"

He took a seat in the middle of the table—the old gangster would be judge and jury for this sit-down.

He fixed his glasses and then looked at the three of us. "*Ragazzi.*" *Boys.* He nodded. "Do you have anything to add to this conversation?"

"Tito." I nodded back and lifted my hands. "Not at the moment."

"*Bene,*" he said. "Let's get started."

Rocco looked at this watch, and at the same time, Guido Fausti came in the room. Once he took his seat, the meeting would begin.

Our formations were the same. Rocco on one side—a man on each side of him. I was at the other—a man on each side of me. Tito sat in the middle.

"Let us be sure the reason for this meeting is clear before we get started," Tito said, sitting forward some, steepling his fingers. "Corrado, you requested this sit-down tonight because you feel as if Rocco has disrespected you."

"He has," I said, keeping my eyes on the accused. "Rocco sent my man here—" I nodded toward Nunzio "—away when my wife was out to eat with friends and family at Macchiavello's. My men are never alone with my wife. My rules." I tapped on the table once. "So tell me this. Is Rocco Fausti above the rules I set for my own family? And this is not even business. This is personal. My wife is *my* wife." I touched my chest.

I didn't bring the issue up with her because she hadn't mentioned it. It ate at me like fucking acid that she hadn't, but my real problem was with him. I knew that look in his eye because I had seen it before. When Rocco Fausti wanted a woman, he made it his mission to have her.

He had women all over the world and one at home. Though their relationship was open. He didn't care if his wife fucked other men, as long as he didn't know names. Bugsy had, and I told him he was fucking nuts. It was one thing if she took schmucks to bed, but another to take a man from this life. Word spreads.

Word was also that Rocco had wanted my wife before I entered the picture. Yeah, it was my right to call her my wife even before she was. The day we got married was not the day her life belonged to me. It had always belonged to me. It was just sealed that day.

I'd seen it that night at the opera with my own eyes. The way Rocco looked at her, like he was a hungry fucking lion on the prowl for a juicy piece of meat. Again when he'd seen her out with me at The Club.

Rocco cleared his throat. "We were at a restaurant," he said, opening and closing his hands. "It is not an intimate place."

"The place doesn't matter," I said. "Conversation can be inappropriate or intimate anywhere. Especially when no one is around."

"You believe your wife to be that way," he said.

I had to keep a lock on the urge to put a bullet in his chest for even insinuating that my wife was that kind of woman. The three fuckers who had treated her that way in this club had paid for it. One with his tongue and the other two with an eye. One spoke while the other two watched, so it was symbolic for a tongue and two eyes to go toward the debt. They lost one head; they were fucking lucky they didn't lose all three.

"I believe that about you," I said.

His face changed completely. I had called him out on his bullshit, and essentially said that he was the equivalent of a whore. He wanted to kill me, too.

Good. Let the slaughter fucking begin.

This thing of ours had a long memory; so did I. Even if we were square after this, I'd never forget it.

"Did your wife claim that I spoke to her indecently or touched her in the same manner?"

Point for him. My wife never spoke a word about it to me. He probably knew that. He knew Nunzio had told me. He wanted him to. The object of this meeting was to make a point while being respectable about it. I'd fucking lose if I outright called him the words on my tongue. Fucking bastard.

"If she had," I said, "permission or not from her, you wouldn't be sitting there. *Capisci?*"

He stood and I stood, followed by our men.

"Sit down," Tito said. His voice came out cool, collected, and we all obeyed him. He didn't look at any of us after we did. He kept his face forward, staring at the wall for a few minutes. Then he cleared his throat. "If it were your wife, Rocco, would you have called Corrado here to this sit-down?"

He grinned but said nothing. He didn't call men to a sit-down for his wife. He only killed them if he had a name. But I understood where Tito was going with this. He did, too.

"Between us," Rocco said, using his hand to motion between him and I.

Tito went to open his mouth, but Rocco lifted a hand. "*Dammi questo, zio.*" *Give me this, uncle.*

Tito looked at me. I nodded.

Rocco cleared his throat. "This will save time. Tell me what will happen if I speak to your wife again—alone."

I looked him straight in the eye and said the words easily, "*Ti ucciderò.*" *I will kill you.* "Fausti *famiglia* or not."

This was about more than him being alone with her. This was about respect for another man in this life and his wife. If boundaries were not set, and enforced, he would walk all over them. There was nothing some men wanted more than what another man had. It was the equivalent of a virus in this life of ours. It ran rampant.

The Fausti *famiglia* were a step above the rest. They had more power and money than all of the five families put together, and it only grew over the years.

Rocco Fausti had wanted Alcina before me. He didn't get her. After I did, he was going to fight even harder to have her. "No" wasn't a deterrent to some men; it was a word that triggered them to work harder for what they wanted.

When it came to my wife, fuck that. Fuck him and his name. He set one more foot over my personal boundaries, and all civilities were off. The only reason I did this was because of the respect I had for Tito and Romeo, and in general, the Fausti *famiglia*.

He nodded and then stood. We all stood.

Tito nodded. "We all agree then," he said.

Rocco nodded and then I did. He fixed his suit and walked over to me, Romeo and then Guido behind him. He offered me his hand and we shook.

"Alcina is a special woman," he said. "I respect your boundaries, and I respect you more for having them. You will take good care of her."

I didn't respond. It was none of his business what I did or didn't do with my wife. *You will take good care of her* was not a casual comment. It was an order. I didn't fucking need that from him.

He grinned, because make no mistake, he was an intuitive bastard. You had to be in this life. "It will not matter much after your death anyway, since you keep fucking with the wrong man," he said, moving past me toward the door. "I will still be here."

Yeah, to fucking take care of my wife.

I turned and spoke to his back. "Fucking bastard," I said, finally getting it off my chest.

He stopped, and after a minute, he finally turned around. We faced each other.

Tito rushed toward us, coming in between us again.

"We have an agreement," he said, pushing his glasses further up his nose. He was much smaller than us, shorter and thinner, but he was more respected than all of us put together in this room. To stand next to him was like standing next to an immovable, impenetrable wall. You didn't fuck with him.

"For now," Rocco said, fixing his suit again. "Rules are void when a man is not alive to enforce them."

"If it's the last thing I do on my deathbed," I said. "These rules will stick."

He knew how serious I was being then.

"There are worse men than me for a woman," he said, and then left.

Romeo squeezed my shoulder before he followed his brother. Guido looked at me and shook his head.

Tito stood in front of me, forcing my eyes on him. "It makes you think, does it not? If you keep up this foolishness, chasing after old ghosts, who will be here to take care of your family if something happens to you?"

I narrowed my eyes on him. "That's our life," I said. "The fucker in this club or the fucker on the corner who pulls the trigger—the bullet goes in the same way, and I don't come out alive."

He studied my face. "The product of this life, through and through," he said. "I treat grown men who are dying daily. I see and hear all types. Some men cry for their *mammas*. Some men are angry, because anger hides true fear. But you—men like you—you wake up with acceptance.

"'If it is not *this* knife in my back, it will be *this* bullet in my heart.' However. You are in a position that is not like the rest. You have earned the right not to constantly have a dagger over your head, or a gun pointed at your heart. Why waste it on what happened years ago?"

I didn't answer.

He sighed and shook his head. "What Corrado Palermo did was against the rules," he said. "He tried to kill his boss without permission. He failed. It kills me to even say his name, but Arturo had every right to seek retribution for what Corrado Palermo had tried to do—but only on Corrado Palermo, not his family. It was his right as a boss. Just as it is yours. You of all people should understand the rules. You practice them every day, and now, you enforce them."

"Why do you care?" I said. "What does this have to do with you?"

"There is so much to lose here," he said, shaking his head. "And even more to gain, if you would only stop focusing on the past and look toward the future." He hesitated for a minute or two. "Your sister. The one they never found. What about her? Why haven't you looked for her?"

I shrugged. "He took that away from me, too. The chance to get to know her. To have someone who shared my blood. But it doesn't matter. If she's still alive, she's better off not being involved in this life. She escaped once. She should count her blessings."

"If he saved her life? What then?"

I had considered that from the beginning. My answer was still the same. "Doesn't change a fucking thing. That entire family needs to go. You give 'em an inch and they take a mile." If he had sons, I'd find them when they were older and take care of them, too.

Tito became quiet for a minute. Then he opened his mouth to say something but closed it on a snap.

"Speak your mind," I said. "It's not like you to hold back."

"A waste of my time," he said, straightening up. "It would not change anything if I did." He waved me off. "Tell your wife that Lola and I will be by to see her and the baby soon. Lola is complaining pictures are not enough."

He walked out then, but with a different energy than he had when he had come in. He seemed almost defeated.

I took out my phone and pressed a button. Once in, I scrolled through my pictures, a grin coming to my face.

He was right about one thing. Just like her *mamma*, pictures did not do my Eleonora justice, but instead of smiling at me like her *mamma* did when I came home, she cried.

# 31

## ALCINA

**M**amma stared at me while I did the dishes. I scrubbed a little and then loaded. She stood next to me, like she was going to help, but instead she watched my face. Anna danced around the kitchen with Ele before bed.

"*Cosa c'è, mamma?*" I whispered. I had no idea why she kept staring at me.

She acted like I had not said a word when Corrado came into the kitchen and kissed her and then me on the cheek. He thanked us for a wonderful dinner. Then he said he had some business to attend to.

He had been cold to me ever since the morning Ele had cried when he'd picked her up. He said very little to me, and when he fucked me, it was hard and ruthless, like he could reach me through his anger and change something. Even the kiss he gave me was hard.

I did not know what he wanted me to change. If he wanted Ele to stop crying when he picked her up, I suggested that he be there with her sometimes during the day. I could tell her how wonderful her father was when she started to grow. I could show her by the way I looked at him, but someday, *he* would have to prove it to her. That he loved her. That he would always be there for her. I could not do that for him.

He playfully touched her chin and then kissed her cheek. She turned her face, and then he left. She started to giggle at Anna right after, when she started to kiss her cheeks and dance even more.

Even though the house was empty—Corrado's *nonna* had gone to spend time with her sister's daughter—except for the men watching it, it felt fuller than it ever had, but not complete. It felt complete when my husband was here, even for a few hours every day.

*Mamma* started to take the dishes from me. "The hardest years of marriage are the second and third," she said. "The first year the flesh is more than happy, but it takes time to build the bones. How all of the arms and legs will work together, ah? This one goes this way, while the other tries to go another."

"It is like a *really* long version of that game," Anna said. "The one where one person's leg is tied to another's. You have to figure out how to win together. You will fall a couple of times, but it is the getting up that counts." She blew against Ele's cheeks, and she giggled so loud that we all laughed.

If our life was only that simple. If only trying to figure out how we worked together was a fun game. If we fell in this life, it was not as simple as just getting back on our feet and trying again. Mistakes were debts owed in blood.

*Mamma* and Anna had no idea that Corrado wanted to kill our own blood and his sister's husband either.

Ele started to cry, so I dried my hands and took her from Anna while she helped *mamma* with the dishes. She was a healthy eater, with little rolls, and I lost myself in her while I watched her eat and then fall asleep. I knew she would probably be more comfortable in her bed, but I decided to hold her while Anna started to get the card game ready.

Even after the game was over and we went upstairs to watch a movie, I felt more secure with her in the room with me.

*Mamma* and Anna both fell asleep in our bed. I laughed quietly, noticing that *mamma* had stuck a gummy candy to Anna's forehead. She had fallen asleep first.

My laughter did not last long. Soon, the quietness of the house closed in, and the heaviness in my heart weighed on my mind. I turned away from *mamma* and Anna, staring at the candle beside the bed. I put my palm over it, watching the flame waver when I moved it back and forth.

My eyes must have closed for a minute or two, and my heart raced when I realized I had left the candle lit.

A shadow moved across the wall, stealing my attention, the soft light highlighting the shape of a person.

"*Mamma*?" I whispered.

I put my hand behind me. She was still there, between Anna and me. I sat up some, checking on Ele, who was at the foot of the bed in her own bed. I looked to my right. Anna was still asleep. Her hand was on her forehead, the candy squished between.

My heart sped up even more, and it felt like it had lodged in my throat as I went to rush to the bottom of the bed to grab my baby. A hand wrapped around my mouth and flung my head back. It hit the pillow, but my entire body went to move forward again, to fight him off.

Whoever it was stunk like garbage. His eyes were wide in the glow of the candle. "I'm not here to hurt you," he said, pressing a gun to my temple. "I want your husband. If you be quiet, I'll take my hand from your mouth."

I said nothing, staring at him. After a few seconds had gone by, he released my mouth tentatively, to see if I was going to scream. I didn't make a sound.

"Good girl," he whispered. He tucked the gun behind his back. "Now tell me where your husband—"

Before he could finish his sentence, I took the candle from beside the bed and flung the hot wax in his face. He put his hands up to shield himself, but it was too late. He growled when the wax clung and stuck.

"What is—"

"*Correre, Mamma!*"

It only took her a second, but she got to the end of the bed and snatched Ele, while Anna, out of nowhere, flung herself on his back. He slammed her against the wall, pinning her against it, and the crack of it made me stop. I was making sure *mamma* and Ele got into the safe room. Corrado had showed them the same thing he had showed me. They each had a room of their own.

"Help her!" *Mamma* shouted, while she ducked into the fireplace.

"Close it!" I screamed. Ele started to wail, and my breasts tightened and started to leak.

*Mamma* didn't know what to do.

"Close it!" I said again, this time more forcefully.

She nodded and the door closed. The crying stopped immediately and all went quiet.

I took slow steps toward the fireplace, my eyes darting to my sister, who was on the floor. A dark pool of blood started to form around her head, spreading on the wood.

"Why did you have to go and do that?" He took his gun out, pointing it at me. His face was covered in hardened wax. "I told you. I want your husband, not you." He shot past me, a whizzing sound coming from the gun, hitting the mirror behind my head. It shattered all over the floor. "Stop right where you are. I've heard stories about you, woman. You're a fucking witch. You'll make a man's balls disappear."

I cleared my throat, hoping it would come out even when I spoke. "My husband is not home," I said.

He waved the gun. "Put your hands up. I want to see them at all times."

I did, and took a small step back.

He narrowed his eyes. "I didn't come here to hurt you, but I fucking will. I said *don't* move."

I did not trust a word coming out of his mouth. If he had the balls to come into this house, he was not going to waste the opportunity and leave empty-handed, if my husband was not home.

As if he could read my mind, he grinned and pulled a rope from his back pocket. "I taught your husband that. Never waste an opportunity." He stared to unroll the rope from its lasso. "He started his life with me, did he tell you that?"

I shook my head, stealing another glance at Anna. I could smell the blood in the room. It was making me anxious to get to her. I had to keep calm, though, keep my eyes on him, because something told me he was much smarter than he looked.

"He did. He was just a kid when he started out in my crew. It didn't take him long to move up. Your husband, he's a smart motherfucker, I'll give him that much. He made the family some money, but then again, he had an in. Silvio and me, we worked for this family since we were young. Years and years, and this is what we get? That position belonged to Silvio. And if not Silvio, me." He stabbed a finger at his chest. "So, it's either kill your husband or hide for the rest of my life."

He laughed some, and I stopped trying to take small steps backwards when he suddenly stopped.

"This life is so political. You bust your ass—take the rap, rough the guy up, *kill* the guy, fucking burn down a building for the insurance—and where does it get you? Hiding out in someone's fucking trash like a rat, ready for the right time to make your move on the—" he made air quotes, still holding the gun and the rope "—boss. You married the rich grandfather's grandson, is all you did, witchy lady."

"Get the fuck out of my house," I snapped.

"You makin' demands on me?" He pointed to his chest, the rope dangling. He lifted the gun, pointing it at me. "Who's got the gun?"

"You fucking rat bastard," I said, my voice starting to shake when Anna moaned.

He laughed. "He must have the men staying far away from this room. That's why they haven't riddled me with bullets. Martina was right. He's fucking worried you'll find a new him and leave. What a pussy. I heard he stopped fucking all the girls, too. You really must be a witch. You got some voodoo going." He tucked the gun in again.

"By the way, after this, I'd stay away from Martina. She told me how to get in this place, and that you'd be all alone tonight. The family left with the old lady. Now if you'll just play nice with me for a little while, while we get the fuck outta here—"

He started to advance on me, and I started to move back as fast I could, until my back slammed against the mantle of the fireplace. I went to turn around and he grabbed me by the hair, yanking my head back. The hair tie slipped out of his grip, and I was able to reach under the mantle again, my fingers clawing the wood to get my hands on the hidden gun underneath. He yanked me back again, before I could get to it. They slipped and I lost my grip.

"I'm not dying over you, lady," he said, hitting me so hard with the gun across my face that my head spun. The gun was pointed at Anna when my eyes focused. "You or your sister. Make your choice."

It wasn't in me to surrender to the enemy. I never surrendered to the bull, not fully, and my mind worked a million miles a minute trying to decide what to do.

He lifted the gun. I turned my body some, preparing for the hit again.

Instead, he snatched my arms, securing them behind my

back with the rope. He went around once, and on the second, a force knocked us both to the floor. My shoulder slammed against the wood when I hit.

It happened so fast that all I could register was noises. Two men grunting on the floor, fighting like animals.

I got to my feet, ran to the mantle, and snatched the gun. Corrado was on the floor, the man on top of him, a knife close to his face. It glinted silver.

I did all of the things Corrado taught me how to do, and when the gun was ready, I hit the man in the shoulder first. When he went over, I was prepared to hit him in the chest.

"I am not dying for you either," I said, keeping the gun pointed at him. "You could not kill me before. I will be damned if I let you kill me now. Or anyone that *I* love."

Two shots whistled through the air, but it did not come from my gun. The force of the bullets made his body jump as two holes appeared in his chest.

"Alcina."

It took me a minute to realize that Corrado was talking to me. That he had taken the gun from me. That his hand was on my head and he was trying to get me to pay attention.

"Eleonora," he said, his phone to his ear, tucking his gun and the one I had behind his back when I looked at him.

I pointed behind me. He pulled me close, kissing my head, and then he started to talk to Uncle Tito. As he did, he dropped to the floor beside Anna, checking her pulse. I followed him. I took her hand, holding it close to my heart. The breath left me in a rush when Corrado ran his hand through her hair and she hissed.

He spoke a few more words. Hung up. Dialed again. Spoke a few more words. Men started to flood the room. Corrado stared at me again. Got up and went to the fireplace. He did something and it opened. He brought me Eleonora, and I held her close to my heart, kissing her head over and over. *Mamma* sat beside me, taking care of Anna until Uncle Tito arrived and checked her over.

Corrado stared at me again, studying me.

*I will be damned if I let you kill me. Or anyone that I love.*

Those were the same words I had spoken to Junior after he almost beat me to death. After he told me he would have my entire family killed. Right before I cut his balls off.

I took a deep breath, released it, and then kissed Eleonora on her head. I stood, just like I had done after Junior had tried to snuff me out, and started to get my fire back.

My life was my own.

I had something to live for—something I always knew would be mine someday. Life and the freedom to live it with my family. I had risked it all for this moment, no matter how dark it was.

I would be damned if I let this steal my light now.

## 32

# CORRADO

I was living proof that devils didn't only creep in the night. They claimed in broad daylight and then hid their prizes in the darkness.

My wife was trying to fight the demons Vito had brought to light again.

*"You could not kill me before. I will be damned if I let you kill me now. Or anyone that I love."*

Those words burned me to my fucking core. I could tell when she had been looking at Vito—the rat that had been hiding in our trash—she had been remembering Junior, reliving what had happened to her.

Every so often, I'd pull out the picture Anna had taken of her after Junior had beaten her in Italy, so I'd feel the fire of what he'd done to her in my bones. I would trace the silver scars left on her face from his fist some nights. Each one was a reflection of what could be seen in the picture.

She would only speak about what Junior had done to her when I brought it up.

I had an uncle who would only speak of war when asked.

He'd give few details, and after, it was over. He didn't want to talk about it anymore.

Alcina gave off those same vibes whenever I mentioned it.

If I could go back and kill both of the fuckers again, I would, but since it was impossible to die twice—for most of us—there was nothing I could do but watch her. Watch her to make sure she was not slipping too far away from me.

We were at the park with Eleonora. Alcina wanted to get her out of the house, and since I'd been paranoid ever since Vito, I hadn't let either one of them out of my sight.

It was the only time I didn't think about that Machiavellian motherfucker and getting rid of him. Though at night, Vittorio Scarpone's blood haunted me like a ghost. It taunted and teased me.

I couldn't even find a picture of the man he once was. Which was fucking strange in itself. We lived in an age when information was readily available at the tap of a key, but there was nothing on the former Prince of New York?

Yeah, I wasn't fucking buying it. So I got in touch with one of my associates. His kid was on house arrest for hacking into one of the most popular social media platforms. He took down pictures of all the government officials and replaced them with cartoon characters. He got caught because he told a girl he wanted to impress—who happened to be the daughter of an elected official he made into Goofy—that he'd done it.

I checked my watch. He was meeting me at the park in an hour. He said he could meet me without a problem. The ankle bracelet was only an irritant.

I sighed as I relaxed on the bench, making sure the men were around but staying back. I was fairly certain Alcina and Eleonora were going to be safe in this life that I lived now. Most men didn't fuck with women—the wives and the children. Occasionally we had rogues like Silvio and Vito, and the Scarpones, but usually, we kept it amongst ourselves. If anything, we watched out for each other's families.

The sun hit me in the eye and I sat up some, grinning as I watched Anna dance around with her camera, trying to make Eleonora smile while Alcina held her.

After what happened, Alcina's *mamma* and Anna refused to leave. I could see her *mamma* was more paranoid, her eyes more watchful of her daughters and granddaughter.

Since Anna refused to leave, too, her husband had showed up.

Fabrizio Pappalardo was not about this life. Not even in Italy. His family did a certain thing—they grew pistachios— and that's all he was ever expected to do, but when his wife called him and told him she didn't know when she was coming home, he came to me once he arrived in New York.

"Make me one of you," he'd said.

I'd sat back in my chair and shook my head without even thinking twice. "No."

There was more to it than just being made into what we were, but that was beside the point.

He blinked at me for a second before he narrowed his eyes. "Any guy on the street can do it," he said.

"True," I said. "But a lot of those guys die for stupid mistakes. You'd have to become something I can sense you're not."

"My wife was hurt," he said. I could see the fire in his eyes, and my level of respect for him went up a notch.

I nodded. "I take responsibility for that," I said. "I gave my men specific orders, and it was because of that they didn't know he got in. The alarm didn't go off. My grandmother gave the code to someone she thought she could trust. It won't happen again."

"I will be here for a while," he said.

"You'll enjoy New York," I said. "Spend time with your wife.

Take her to the opera. To catch a show on Broadway. You'll do things. Keep busy."

"I am not a man to ask twice," he said. "I can do this."

"Listen," I said, sitting forward. "You're angry. I understand. You have every right to be. But if I take you into this life—" I lifted my finger. "One, the fucker is dead, so there will be no revenge." I lifted my middle finger. "Two, my wife will never forgive me, because if something happens to you, it'll come back on me. Your wife will want me dead. My wife will take her side. And that is fucking that. *Finito.*" *Finished.*

I relaxed in my seat. "And if you haven't noticed, my wife has it in for me for something else. And no matter who I am in this life, I might not be able to help you if you do something stupid that will cost you your life. Rules are rules. It's that simple."

He thought about this and then nodded. "I noticed you do not get along with too many people," he said.

*I noticed you do not get along with too many people.* I had one —one—incident when I worked for him where I knocked a guy upside his head with my bucket because he told me I was working too slow. And I couldn't get along with people? I was a people-ing motherfucker, as long as you didn't fuck me over.

"I will have to convince Anna to come home," he said.

"She will," I said. "I'm working on Angela, because Giuseppe is giving me hell, too."

You sing, and suddenly everyone thinks they can fucking push you around. That's why I always said my cousin Dom was a pussy. He had "handlers" who all thought they could turn him into a singing puppet. He let them.

Fabrizio brought me back to real time when he started making funny faces at my Eleonora. She laughed at him, but she cried for me. That hit a fucking nerve. If he weren't a man I considered family, I'd probably kill him out of envy. He had something I wanted—a smile from my daughter.

Alcina's smile grew wider when she noticed the girl from Modica, the same one from The Club, Mariposa, coming up with the boy I had seen with her in Italy. Her son. Her husband hadn't liked me from the moment he set eyes on me, but who the fuck was he? If I was good enough for his cousin to marry, I was good enough for him to accept.

The little boy in Mariposa's arms reached out and touched the top of Eleonora's head. She smiled for him, too. Everyone but me.

It was all so idealistic looking. The mothers. The aunt. The grandmother. The cousin (Brooklyn). The friends. The kids playing in the park.

For the first time in a long time, I realized how far on the outskirts I was of this life, and how deep I was in my other. It was times like these that something hit me worse than jealousy, or even envy, both emotions that Alcina had introduced me to. In that second, I was experiencing something else. I couldn't put a fucking name to it because I wasn't sure what it was.

It was what Alcina had explained to me one night. *"Like you miss me, too, even though I'm next to you."*

The word "miss" was wrong. That seemed like such a simple, uncomplicated word to describe the mayhem I felt in the center of my chest.

To sum it up. I felt like I had spent an entire lifetime with these people, and every bad thing I ever did they held me accountable for, but loved me despite of them. Then suddenly, I found myself in a separate world, but I could still see them. I was on the inside looking out. It sent a rush of something I had never felt before through me. Panic—maybe. That I might never get to them.

I had never had my heart race. Not even when death was at my door. So maybe panic was the wrong word. Maybe it wasn't strong enough. Or maybe it was. I didn't fucking know because this was an entirely new world for me.

One thing was certain, though. The times when I reached them were fleeting. Over too fucking fast. Then my mind went in a different direction, my body following the orders, and the feeling would recede and nothing else registered but the life.

"Hey."

I leaned forward some, narrowing my eyes at the girl walking out of the sunlight toward me with her son. She took a seat next to me on the bench, like she had known me forever.

I was a people person to a certain extent—I wasn't fucking lying about that—but not too many people chose to sit next to me. It was usually done for a reason in my world.

The boy sat between us, playing with a toy. For a kid, he had a serious face.

I sat back so I could see her face better. She wasn't a plain woman, but she wasn't extraordinary either. It was hard to describe what was attractive about her, and not in a sexual way. She was somewhat regal looking. It was her nose. The way it curved. It gave her something special. Character that I didn't see every day.

"Mariposa." I nodded.

"It's actually Mari," she said. "My husband is the only one who calls me Mariposa."

Maybe I was reading too much into it, but it was like she was telling me that for a reason. Like she wanted me to know that about her. Maybe she just wanted anyone to know.

"Your husband. The man in Modica. My wife's cousin."

"Yeah," she said. "That's him."

"So that makes Eleonora and—" I looked at the kid.

"Saverio," she said.

I nodded. "Saverio—"

"Cousins," she finished for me. "It does."

"It'll be nice for Alcina to have family so close. Once her *mamma* and sister go back home."

She nodded, tucking a strand of hair behind her ear. "It will be. They can grow up together." She fussed over her kid's hair. He had a ton of it. "I didn't have any family growing up. I was alone most of my life."

My eyes had roamed over to Alcina again, and at this, I looked at the woman again. Did she need a friend? Because that was something to discuss with my wife, not me.

"I have a ton of family," I said. "You can have one of them." I grinned, trying to make a joke, but she didn't.

She shrugged. "It would have been nice, you know, to just... share something with someone. Something familiar."

"You mean like blood," I said.

"Yeah." She stopped fussing with the kid's hair and really looked at me. Almost studying me. "Someone with a similar feature or two. Someone who is supposed to be there no matter what." She nodded toward Alcina and Anna, who were squishing Eleonora between them, before Fabrizio took the picture. "You have a beautiful family."

I tapped the kid on the head. "I'd say you do, too."

She grinned this time. "I do." She hesitated a minute. "Do you have any brothers or sisters?"

I sighed. "No."

"Oh. You said you had a big family, so I assumed." She shrugged. "I guess you're pretty much alone then, too."

"Define alone."

"I get it," she said, smiling this time. "You probably have a lot of cousins. Like Saverio and Eleonora."

"Ele," I said. "Everyone else calls her Ele but me."

Mari's smile grew even wider. "Ele and I have that in common then. We both have someone special to say our names." She looked down at her jean shorts, picking at something there. "It's nice to have a parent that does that. Calls you something special."

She said the words quietly, but I heard her. She scooped her son up and held him close to her chest, kissing his head.

Alcina came over to us with Eleonora. She sat between Mari and me. She handed me Eleonora. Even though she didn't cry this time, she stared at her *mamma* with wide eyes, wanting her. I stroked her head, settling the small tufts of hair she had, while putting my arm behind Alcina's back. She leaned into me, getting comfortable.

"It is such a beautiful day," Alcina said, sighing.

I stared at her face. Maybe she believed it, but there was always something underneath the surface lately. She said the words, like she was forcing herself to believe them, even if she didn't feel they were true. She was battling the demons to get to the place where she could believe and feel it.

"You can't escape me!" Anna pointed at me. "I know you don't like pictures, but just this once. I want to get you all together."

Alcina pulled even closer to me, taking Eleonora's hand, and then she reached out for Mari.

"Closer!" Anna said, keeping her eye to the camera, using her hand to direct Mari. "He does not stink. I would say he doesn't bite, but he does."

Mari looked at me and then settled her son on her lap before she moved closer to Alcina.

"On the count of three!"

On three, I looked to my right when I noticed the kid I was supposed to meet. He was waiting at our agreed spot. After eye contact, he'd go to another secluded area in the park.

"You were looking away!" Anna said, looking at the picture on the screen.

"Good enough," I said. I kissed Eleonora on the head, handed her back to Alcina, kissed her, and then went for a walk around the park.

ADRIANO CAME with me to meet the kid.

He huffed as he tried to keep up with me.

"I smell the pastrami on you," I said. "You're fucking sweating it out."

He looked like he wanted to respond, but he didn't want to waste his breath. Either way, he would have been. He either took responsibility for his situation or he knew I'd start calling him "Excuses" until he got his shit together.

There was only did or didn't. Yes or no. Anytime there was a "but" attached, it was a fucking excuse.

"Is that the kid?" Adriano narrowed his eyes, stuck a hand over his eyebrows, and then blew out a hot breath.

I followed the line of his sight. "Yeah, that's him. He said he'd be wearing a black turtleneck."

"In this fucking heat?" He scrunched his face up, narrowing his eyes even more. "He looks like a mini version of Roy Orbison. Even down to the glasses and the fucking hair."

"You going to run out of breath if you keep talking and walking," I said.

"I'm easily susceptible to things," he said. "That's why I have to take steroids sometimes."

"More of a reason to take care of yourself then," I said.

"I still can't get over this guy," he said, staring at the kid again. "He's Roy Orbison the remake. CRYING!" he started to sing. "I'm CRYING."

This fucking guy. I shook my head.

"I bet Bugsy would love to meet 'im." Adriano wiped sweat from his forehead.

I grinned because Adriano was right. Bugsy would. The fucking kid didn't even need a costume for Halloween. He channeled Roy Orbison from wherever he had gone.

"You think Alcina is going to wonder why we're going to meet this kid?"

We were close to meeting up with him. Calcedonio had set

it up with his old man, and he was waiting in the exact spot in the park we had agreed on. It was far enough from my wife and family that they wouldn't come looking for me or overhear anything.

"No," I said. But after I'd gotten up, so had she, holding Eleonora as she watched me walk away until she couldn't anymore.

"Dum dum dum," Adriano sang as we got even closer. "Only the lonely..."

I shot him a look. He made a motion against his lips, like he was turning a key, and as we passed a trash can, he threw it away.

The kid held his hand out when we got close enough. "Gene Champollion, at your service."

I held my hand up. "We're good." I could tell his hand was clammy from wearing a fucking sweater in the heat.

He looked at Adriano and just nodded. Adriano nodded back. "You look just like Roy Orbison," he said. "I had to tell you that."

Gene nodded. "I get that a lot."

"'Cause it's the fucking truth," Adriano said.

"Give me what you have," I said, stopping any further conversation. There was no telling what the fuck Adriano was taking, and it was making him chatty. Usually my men took care of things like this. But this wasn't business. This was personal.

Gene stood up straighter. "To tell you the truth, sir, nothing."

"Your old man said you're the best," I said. "His exact words to my man were, 'there's nothing he can't find.'"

"In my entire fifteen years, there's nothing I haven't found when I looked. Even the government wants me. This is a first."

I narrowed my eyes at him, and he visibly started sweating even more. He wasn't hot. He was scared shitless.

"The thing is," he said, sighing, "I'm pretty sure someone was fucking with me the entire time. I found a few things—a picture, easy shit like that—but when I'd go back, they'd be gone. *Poof.* Like they never existed in the first place."

"You couldn't find one thing on Vittorio Scarpone."

"Two." He lifted two fingers. "He was the son of Arturo Scarpone, and his father allegedly had him killed. The second article was about the slayings of the Scarpone family at a restaurant named Dolce. There were actually a bunch of those, but only one or two actually mentioned Vittorio."

"No pictures," I said.

He twisted his cheek and shook his head. "Again, only one. Then it was gone."

"Describe him."

"Blue eyes. Black hair. Sharp features. Probably Italian, like you. Real handsome."

"Your take on this?"

He scratched his head, dusted some dandruff into the air, and then made a face when it sprinkled around him like salt. "I'd say whoever it is knew I was looking. He or she was letting me know he or she knew. I'd get into specifics, but it can get pretty wordy."

So the Machiavellian son of bitch was a fucking gangster nerd.

It was starting to feel like I was actually up against a ghost. A fucking ghost that was whispering, "*Boo, motherfucker, here I am*," every time I got close, and then he'd disappear.

"Oh! I will say this," Gene said, his voice screeching a little. "I knew of one of his—" He closed his eyes, his mouth moving, but no sound came out. "He would have been one of his neph-ews. His brother's son. He was extremely knowledgeable about the same things I am. If you catch my drift." He winked at me and then made a face, like he couldn't believe he just did that. "Bad move, Gene," he whispered to himself. "*Bad* move."

Adriano took a few steps away from him.

"I'm not following," I said.

"He was smart. Like...extremely *smart*." He said the word slowly. "So his uncle probably is, too."

No shit, I was going to say, but he was already looking at me like he was prepared to speak slowly again. He didn't even say anything technical. He thought he was the smartest guy around, but he was forgetting that he got one-upped by a gangster. Our specialty was the streets, not usually sitting behind a computer. But Vittorio Scarpone had lived an entirely different life for years. It made sense that he would develop skills to help him stay hidden.

Back in the day, it was easier to disappear. Everything wasn't digital in the old days.

"You got something else to say to me?"

He was staring at me, hard, like he was debating. "You didn't ask for this," he rushed out. "But." He pulled out an envelope from his back pocket, handing it to me. "The second article. It mentioned a little girl. Apparently there was some speculation about what happened to her. Vittorio killed her parents, but no one knew what had happened to her. Her name is or was Marietta Bettina Palermo. Your half-sister." He shrugged. "Some information is listed for her. Birthday. Blood type. Thought you might want it."

"How'd you fucking find that?"

"I find everything." He shrugged. "Even when someone doesn't want to be found. The guy you're looking for, it's not that he doesn't want to be found. Simply put: he doesn't exist anymore."

"What about her?" I said.

He shrugged. "He doesn't exist and neither does she, except for what I gave you. Or maybe I didn't give it to you at all. Maybe he let me find it to give to you."

He was controlling this fucking conversation, too. Everything he gave, he gave for his own reasons.

"Keep looking," I said.

His eyes narrowed, but after I raised my eyebrow at him, he nodded.

"Yeah, okay, but I don't think—"

"You're right," I said. "That's exactly what he's doing. He's only giving you what he wants me to have."

Sooner or later, when he was ready for me to find him, he would get in touch with me. Sooner or later, this kid was going to get a message from a ghost, and *boo, motherfucker,* it was going to be on. He was going to be there when I got close enough. Close enough to touch. Close enough to fucking kill.

# 33

## ALCINA

W e had spent the day driving around the city in his old Cadillac. Even though his grandparents' place was big enough, with excess to spare, I felt as if we were repeating history to stay there.

I did not tell Corrado this, but he seemed to sense it. Or perhaps he wanted out for his own reasons. I could sense that, too.

It was hard to put into words, but the house almost felt like a part of the family, but not ours. The other one. It was built to protect secrets, to protect them, but it was not made to keep a family close.

Corrado wanted me to get a feel for the different areas of New York, even though he mentioned staying close to where we were. Instead of buying something already there, he decided that we should build.

"So we can put in hidden rooms?" I turned to face him in the car.

He didn't respond, so I called his name. He still did not look at me. He was in his own world, and it was only getting worse.

"*Don Corrado*," I said with force.

He looked at me then, narrowing his eyes before he turned back to the road. Of course he would respond to that. It was all he was lately.

He nodded. "I feel it's necessary."

"You heard me?" I crossed my arms over my chest.

"I hear everything."

I cursed in Sicilian.

"That's why I didn't answer," he said. "I don't want to argue with you. I know where the conversation is going. And I'll do what I have to do to keep my family safe."

I shook my head. "My walls will not be stained with the blood of men who had no idea they signed up for a death sentence!" I understood the concept of it, but I refused to live with ghosts. We had enough of them roaming around. "What about Dario Fausti? He's an architect. He understands this life. He would be trustworthy enough to do it."

The mention of the Faustis made him visibly change. He became harder, more difficult to read. I knew he had a problem with Rocco, but Dario, his middle brother, was different.

Corrado had a problem with one, and he blamed all. I could trace the vein of it in my mind, like I could reach out and trace one on his arm. It was the same vein where vengeance for my cousin lived—he blamed one man for an entire family's wrongdoing, not able to see that my cousin had more than one side. Our side was good people.

I sighed, looking out of the window. "If we must have the rooms, and you'd prefer him not to do it, I'd rather stay where we are. That sacrifice was enough."

He said nothing as he turned the car around and headed back toward his grandparents' place.

It was hard to think about anything else, though, when I started to think about the situation between my husband and my cousin. Now was not the time tell Corrado that his sister was alive, because once I did, I would have to tell him that she married the man he desperately wanted to kill. His son, when he was old enough, too. His nephew.

I sighed again, clutching my purse. "Tell me one thing," I whispered.

"Anything," he said.

"Why? Why do you want to kill him? The real reason?"

He didn't even question who. He already knew. It was all he thought about when he wasn't dealing with family business. "That entire family needs to go. They never followed the rules. Killing kids is not a part of our business. It will never be, as long as I'm alive."

"What about Corrado Palermo?" I said. "He did not follow the rules."

"He didn't."

"I understand about your sister. There are no words for that. But why do this for him, too? Why avenge a man who knew the rules and broke them anyway?"

"I'm not doing this to avenge him," he said. "Other than ridding the earth of the Scarpones, I'm doing this because I want to kill him."

"You're angry that—that man killed Corrado Palermo first?"

He nodded. "Angry is not the right word for it."

"This is not about avenging Corrado Palermo," I said, suddenly understanding. "You hate him so much that you want to kill him, but you can't."

He became quiet for a while. "Maybe if I could kill him, I could rid myself of him," he said quietly. "I can't get rid of him, angel eyes. He's too much a part of me. He's in my blood. I hate myself for it."

All of his life he had been programmed to get rid of a problem, and then move on. He could not get rid of this. There was no one to touch, to strangle, to kill. He was dealing with two ghosts. Vittorio Scarpone and Corrado Palermo. Both phantoms of the past.

I took his hand and brought it to my heart. "You can't kill a ghost, *il mio amore*. A ghost is already gone. You bring them to you by calling them, by giving them *your* life to cling to. It is you who won't allow them to go." I squeezed his hand even tighter, hoping to get through to him on his side of this life we shared. "If you hate yourself for what's in your blood—how do you think Vittorio Scarpone feels?"

He took his hand away. "I don't give a fuck how he feels," he said. "I loathe him for doing this to me. For not giving me the chance to rid myself of that man who never claimed me. For hiding my sister from me. For being who he is."

"If you kill him it is over," I said. "If he has to live with these same feelings—wouldn't that be worse?"

"If he fought to stay alive this long," he said, "he feels right with life."

"You will kill him," I said, my voice betraying me. It was that scene over and over again—the one in the pistachio grove. Where he went to hand me the glove but held on. "And just get another ghost."

"At this point in my life," he said, turning into the drive, "I've lost count. One more will not kill me."

"No," I whispered. "Just destroy you even more."

------

A CAR PULLED up behind us as the gates opened. Corrado stopped the car, but after realizing it was Brooklyn, he pulled all the way in.

"You're with me today," he said.

I nodded. I had no plans on going to Bella Luna, so he did not call Nunzio in. He only came along when Corrado would not be there. And when Nunzio was there, so was Brooklyn.

Sometimes Brooklyn would come over and spend time even when we did not go to Bella Luna. It seemed like she liked to be around *mamma*, Anna, Eleonora and me. Corrado probably did not realize she spent so much time here, since he was always doing other things. Even when he was in the house, sometimes it was like he was not there.

He stared at my face after he put the car in park. "It would be a mistake for you to think I don't know what the fuck is going on in my own house," he said. "I know every move you make." He reached out and touched my chin.

"I am not your house," I said.

"Yeah," he said. "You are. You're my home. I know everything that happens inside and outside of it—at all times." He reached out and slid me toward him. When we connected, it had the same effect as a pump between a body and a heart.

My hands fisted in his hair, and I wanted to yank it out by the roots, while his mouth did things to mine that caused me to moan.

*This.* This was what happened when he finally let the glove go and we came together. *Perfezione completa.*

*Complete perfection.*

"It's time to play a game of Italian Roulette," he said, his mouth roaming from my lips, to my chin, to my throat, then to the pulse in my neck. He sucked so hard I knew it was going to leave a mark. "I'm going to bury my cock in you so fucking deep that there's no way you won't get pregnant again."

I hissed when his mouth moved lower and he kept sucking. He sucked all the way down to my breasts, and through the shirt, the heat from his mouth burned through.

A knock came at the trunk. I stilled. Corrado bit my nipple and then grinned. He sat up and fixed himself before Brooklyn came to my side of the car.

The window was down, and she sniffed before she wiped her red eyes. "We need to talk to you both."

"We?" Corrado said.

She nodded. "Nunzio and me."

"Meet us inside," Corrado said.

She nodded, and when she got close to the front door, Nunzio met her, putting his hand on her lower back.

"Where did he come from?" I said.

He grinned, probably at the confused look on my face. "He was driving her car."

Corrado got out first and then came to open my door. We walked into the house hand in hand, meeting Brooklyn and Nunzio in the kitchen. He stood with his back against the counter. She sat at the table, her head in her hands.

From the window behind Nunzio, I could see Anna holding Eleonora, and Fabrizio making faces at her. *Mamma* sat on the bench, crocheting, smiling, while she listened to them laugh. It sent a strong longing through me, to see them that way, so carefree with her, but I ignored it.

"What is going on?" I said, looking at Brooklyn instead.

"We got married!" she blurted. "I told my mom and she pulled a knife on Nunzio and he's bleeding and then she was screaming and...*Oh God*! I don't know what to do."

I looked at Nunzio and noticed for the first time that he had blood dripping down his arm.

He shrugged.

"You're old enough," Corrado said to Brooklyn. "You can marry whoever you want."

She looked up at him, her eyes red, her nose swollen, tears flowing down her cheeks. "But she's my mom, and I love her, too. I want her to accept him, to accept us."

"Did you try talking to her?" I asked Nunzio.

He lifted his arm to show me. Even though I knew he meant he had tried, I still wondered...I couldn't remember a time when he had spoken to me casually.

"Talking is not going to change her mind," Corrado said, looking at Nunzio. "It's going to take time."

"How did this happen?" I said, sitting down next to

Brooklyn and taking her hand. I moved the hair from her face, trying to dry some of her tears.

"I told you I liked Nunzio. I actually love him, but I was too ashamed to admit it. I mean, who falls in love with the first guy they really like? It's like picking the first wedding dress you try on. How often does that happen?" She sniffed. "Then my mom...she wanted me to like the chef. The night I went out on a date with him, Nunzio showed up at my apartment after I got home. He told me how he felt. He told me that if I didn't marry him, he was going to kill Michele."

Corrado narrowed his eyes at Nunzio. For the first time, I saw something on Nunzio's face that I never had before. Not shame, but something close to it. I did not think it was for what he had done, though, but for something else.

"You forced her into it!" I shouted.

Nunzio shook his head. "Explain better," he said to his wife.

She waved a hand. "I mean, that came after a few things...it wasn't like he said, 'Marry me or I kill the chef,'" she said, making her voice sound like his. "Well, kind of. But I don't want to get into what happened before that, okay? It's personal. But the point is...I've been disowned! I thought...I thought if we were married ma would have to accept it."

I took her chin and made her look at me. "She will. Corrado is right. Give her time."

She shook her head. "You don't understand. You didn't see her face. I knew she would have a hard time accepting it, but *never*, never did I think she would stab someone."

"You must not know your ma," Corrado said. "She's a wild card."

I shot him a look. He was not helping.

One of the guys cleared his throat at the entrance of the kitchen. "Adriana," he said.

Corrado nodded. The man left and came back with a woman a minute or two later. Brooklyn shot up from her seat and stepped in front of her husband, trying to use her body as a shield. Nunzio moved her so she was beside him, so they were standing side by side.

The woman, Adriana, was attractive. She was tall, thin, with long, blonde, wavy hair. I could see, though, that life had taken a toll on her. She looked haggard in a way that made me feel as if her soul was tired.

"Ma," Brooklyn whispered.

"Don't." She held up a hand. "Don't even call me that. I'm nothing to you. You chose this life over me."

"I didn't!" Brooklyn screamed. "Daddy did! Not me! I chose love!"

"Love." Adriana laughed, actually cackled like a witch. "You'll see what you're going to get in a few years. Love—there's no such thing in this life. Do you think she—" she nodded toward me "—is going to get real love? Do you think her daughter will? You know how it feels! You were ignored, always coming after this life, and then he left! Like I figured out he would. One way or another."

"You knew that when you married him!" Brooklyn said. "You made your choice. *Please.* Let me make mine. Things will be different for me."

"Ha! What a fucking joke. You think things will be different? That's what they make you believe when you turn them away. *You're different.* He'll say the right words and do all the right things. Make you feel like you're the only woman in the world. This one—" she nodded at Nunzio "—probably did something to make you feel like the world revolved around you and only you." She shook her head, almost in disbelief.

"Women who are not in this life look at us and think, '*They know what they're getting into!*' Yeah, some of us do from the start, but some of us don't. But even when we do, not many women stand a chance against them. When they want something, they'll have it. So let's use some common sense. If men like them don't stand a chance against each other half of the time, what makes those bitches think we can? You're no better than them for doing the same thing to me. Judging me for doing the best I could. And you still didn't learn."

"But I love him!"

The words were like a slap in the face. Adriana visibly flinched. "Love him today. Hate him tomorrow. Mark my words." She looked at Corrado. "Undo this. *Please.*"

Corrado stared at Nunzio for a minute. He shook his head. "Nunzio is not a part of my family, not officially."

"He's not...one of you?" Adriana sounded almost hopeful.

Corrado shook his head. "He's from Sicily," was all he said.

I narrowed my eyes at Corrado. There was something he was not saying. Nunzio was not a part of his family, but he still did whatever Corrado told him to. Then again...I wondered if Corrado was doing this for him because he had agreed to protect me here. A favor for a favor.

*A life for a life,* judging by the look on Adriana's face.

"No!" She shook her head. Then she went after Nunzio again with a knife she pulled from the pocket of her jacket. The man who stood at the door wrapped his arm around her waist, pulling her back just as she went to slash him again. She was stabbing the air, kicking her legs, screaming, "NO! My baby! You won't take her from me! You won't kill her spirit like he killed mine!"

Then she started to wail as if someone had died when she realized she couldn't get to him. What was done was done.

"Let her go," Corrado said to his man holding her.

The man did not hesitate. He let her go, but he took the knife from her hand. She did not even notice. She crumpled to the floor, on her knees, crying at the top of her lungs. Begging. Pleading. Bleeding out on the floor of a house that did not care for her tears or her loss.

I pulled the rosary from my pocket, worrying the beads between my fingers.

Maybe Corrado called my name when I rushed out of the kitchen, heading toward the garden. Maybe he did not. I could not hear over the sound of the wailing. I could not hear over the sound of another mother's pain.

It seemed like Adriana had made one mistake in this life. She cared at one time.

Once out in the garden, I took Eleonora from Anna, holding her so close that I hoped to absorb her into my skin and keep her there forever.

# 34

# CORRADO

I didn't come to my grandfather's social club, Primo, often. When he was alive, I frequented, but after he died, it lost its appeal.

Most things he left behind had.

Except for one thing that had nothing to do with him directly, though it all stemmed from the life.

Macchiavello.

My wife tried to tell me I was channeling all of the things I couldn't control into my hate for him. The more out of control things felt—the dullness behind my wife's eyes, the smile I couldn't get from my daughter—the more I wanted to kill him.

Maybe I was fixated on destroying him.

The thought of him was destroying me. Everything he stood for and had stolen from me was like acid to my mind.

It was why they called me Scorpio. I had poison inside of me, and once I received an order, or my mind was made up about something, I refused to let go until it was over. Just like I refused to let the enemy go.

It had been two months since I met the kid in the park. Two months since Adriana's dramatic performance in the kitchen.

Two months since the light in my wife's eyes seemed to dim even darker, mostly when she was thinking, not noticing that I watched her. Two months of my daughter growing and rejecting me.

"Self-imposed misery," I said to the man in the picture, repeating something he had said to me once.

It hung across from what had been his desk. The men hung it up after he was murdered: Emilio Capitani when he had first arrived in New York. His profile was mine, but other than that, it was hard to find the family resemblance. My eyes and features belonged to Corrado Palermo.

I'd seen a picture of him walking out of the courthouse, after the Scarpones had gotten him off some charge he was probably guilty of.

Self-imposed misery was what Emilio had once told me made men did to themselves. There was nothing to be miserable about in this life of ours. The world was at our feet. Men like us were untouchable, unless we did something stupid and broke the rules. At the time, I thought he had meant physically. But the words came at me differently this time, because I was at a different time in my life.

We were untouchable when it came to feelings, not just flesh and bones.

We did what we did, and that was that. We felt what we felt, and then we moved on. That ideology carried over to home life.

It took me up until this second of my life to realize I had them. Feelings. Not for all but for two.

A knock came at the door, and I didn't break eye contact with the man staring at me from across the room. Another ghost.

"You hear any more from the kid Lima Bean calls 'Roy'?" Calcedonio said, standing to answer the knock.

I shook my head. "Not a fucking thing."

"Maybe he really is a ghost," he said before he opened the door. Baggio came in first, followed by Adriano.

"He says to me, 'Pigeons are the way of the future.' And I say to him, 'No, go with a fuckin' fish. I'm telling you. They're intelligent.' You know what he tells me?" Baggio said, taking a seat. "He says, 'You don't say what to go with. *I* say what to go with.' And I tell him, 'Go with a fuckin' horny toad for all I care. Your entire place is going to smell like bird shit.'"

"Fuhgedaboudit," Adriano said, plopping down in the seat next to Baggio. "He hasn't seen what Gilberts can do. Though I do think fish delivering messages to a person would be difficult. The message wouldn't last. And how would he get there?"

"Yeah, birds have an advantage, but that's not taking away the thinking capacity of a fish."

Men started to come in while this fucking conversation went on.

"Between chicken and fish..." Adriano scrunched up his face. "I really enjoy both. Both are lean, depending on the way you fix them, but I think eating fish might be better. Brain food, with the oils and stuff."

"Fuck-exactly!" Baggio said, crossing his arms over his chest. "Though I'd really fuckin' hate to eat Gilberts. Only if I had to."

These fucking guys.

After all of the men arrived, we discussed the usual business.

Calcedonio mentioned redoing the Primo Club, maybe making it look like a real gentlemen's club. It needed to be different, he said. It was about time.

I liked the plain look of it. The tables scattered wherever with cards on them. The old bar with countless scuff marks. Even the floors gave it a touch of nostalgia. They had been there since my grandfather had owned it. Ceramic tile with red rose patterns. Some of the roses looked like bloodstains. The floor had cracks that I could see when I closed my eyes. They'd been there since I was a kid.

Another man brought up the Scorpio Lounge—most people just called it Scorpio—a known business that made good money, and said that Dario Fausti had redone it.

"Moving on," I said.

Toward the end of the meeting, Tito walked in. Calcedonio forfeited his chair so he could sit. The guy next to Calcedonio stood so he could set his bag down. A dozen or so red roses stuck out of it.

Tito stared at me, crossing his arms over his chest.

"You come here to show me how your glasses can fog from your fuming?" I said when all of the men left and Calcedonio had shut the door, leaving us alone.

He took them off and cleaned them with his shirt. His eyes looked beady when he didn't have them on. "I went to visit your wife," he said. "At Bella Luna. I wanted to buy Lola a gift."

She was there later than usual. "Nunzio is with her," I said. "She's going over her inventory with Brooklyn."

"I know this," he snapped. "I was there."

I sighed. "Say what's on your mind." If he had something to say, and you didn't acknowledge it, he had a way of causing havoc without speaking a word.

He adjusted his glasses on his nose. Now he was staring at me like I was a specimen. "I feel responsible for this."

I waited for a minute or two.

"For giving her to you," he said.

"Ah," I said. "You come to lecture me on being a good husband."

He shook his head. "I am godfather to many children. I have even walked some down the aisle when their fathers were not able to, or were not fit. And I have always made a promise to them. I would always take care of them. I did the same when I became godfather to your wife." He became quiet for a minute, thinking. "I would have never brought the two of you together if I did not think you could be a good husband. If I would have even suspected you would have tried to bring her here to face Silvio and his son for any price, but especially for the price of a sham."

I narrowed my eyes against his, demanding the truth. The price of a sham?

"Silvio told your grandfather that you had disobeyed him. That he had asked you to find Alcina in return for the information he had on the Scarpones, and you had agreed. Emilio did not want you involved in the situation with Vittorio Scarpone. You knew that. So did Silvio. So you both disobeyed him. But Emilio felt what Silvio did was worse.

"Silvio was setting you up—he never had the information on Vittorio that you were looking for. So Silvio did not kill Emilio because he wanted the family. That was just a bonus. Silvio killed Emilio because he knew Emilio was going to kill him first. As for Vittorio Scarpone? Whatever your grandfather knew about Vittorio Scarpone, he took to the grave."

"Tell me what you know about the man."

"*Listen to* me," he almost hissed. "I not only hear, but I listen. I not only look, but I see. I not only have thoughts, but I think them through." He touched his temple. "I knew you were looking for Alcina long before you did. In more ways than one. I also knew that she needed you." He dug in his doctor's bag, bringing out a picture from our wedding day, slipping it toward me.

I was looking down at her and she was smiling up at me. That light, it was so fucking bright, like she carried the moon in her eyes. The one that drew me out and made me feel almost insane.

"I have been in the room when a heart is transplanted into another body," he said, but I didn't look at him. I stared at the picture. "I have heard the first beat when the connection was made. I have seen it give life to the almost dead." He knocked on the desk, once, twice, making it sound like the beat of a heart.

"That was why I sent *you* to *her*. You needed each other. The *body* and the *heart*. I stood as the hands, the *medico*, that made the connection. I heard the first beat of it when your eyes met. And the two shall become one." He slapped his hands together.

I looked at him.

"You are rejecting your heart," he said. "The second chance you have at life. You do not get them every day, Corrado. We are both men who know that. For the first time in your entire life, I saw something other than the acceptance of death when you looked at her. I saw the life in you. Something other than this." He looked around.

"Mark my words. You keep rejecting your heart, Corrado, and you will lose it. I see it in her. She is being strong because she feels she has chosen this life. She chose you. But didn't you choose her, as well? I am not saying that you have to give this up. Or even change completely. But you have to decide—is an old ghost worth losing your life over?"

"What does my wife have to do with this? Tell me what you know."

"You see," he snapped at me. "But you are not looking! Your mind will not allow you to see what you are doing—to your family, to yourself. I knew a man like you once. A man who could not give up a thought even at the detriment to his family. Your father, Corrado. Corrado Palermo. He sacrificed his wife for an idea." He stabbed his temple with a finger. "An idea that he was owed something he did not deserve."

I stared at him for a minute. "You know who my sister is. Where she is." He said Corrado sacrificed his wife for an idea, but nothing about the little girl.

"*Sì.*" He sat back in the chair. His temper had fizzled some. "I have known for a while."

"Does she know about me?"

"*Sì*. She found out about you when you discovered her." He lifted a finger. "Your relationship with her will depend on your relationship with the man you intend to kill."

"Ah," I said, sitting back. "She respects him for saving her life."

Tito stood, picking up his bag, preparing to head toward the door. "See. Hear. *Think*." He touched his temple. "You are a smart man, Corrado. I have always said that about you. Except for this. You are being anything but smart. So take my advice, ah? Use your brain and remember your heart."

"Tito," I said, stopping him before he left.

He stood close to the door.

"Tell me one thing," I said. "Where was she all of this time?"

"Not far from you," he said. "On Staten Island."

Fuck me.

I COULD HAVE CALLED GENE, the genius, and asked him to search for records of children on Staten Island when she would have been there, but I didn't. It was a waste of my time. What I hadn't mentioned to Calcedonio was that Gene's computers had been confiscated the day after we met in the park.

"I think he *told* on me," he had whispered. "The only reason I'm not in big, *big* trouble is because the government wants me. B-A-D," he'd spelled the word out.

In our world, that was called fucking *ratting*, but it just meant that Macchiavello had turned the tables on me once again. I thought he'd be in touch through Gene, but apparently, he had other plans for our first meeting.

I stood from my seat, shaking my head, going to stop Tito before he left the building. A few of the guys looked up to him, because he was old school, and that time in history was golden for men like us. They always stopped him and asked him for a few stories.

Before he got too carried away, I made eye contact with him and he came back into my office. I closed the door behind him, though neither of us sat.

"My wife," I said. "I've noticed subtle changes. I see her. I listen to her." I touched my temple. "I think about her and consider everything she does and doesn't do."

He nodded, urging me to go on after a minute.

"I looked up a few things." I shrugged. "We left Italy when we found out about Eleonora. It's been hard for her to leave her family, her home, and adjust to this new life. After she had Eleonora—" I struggled to find the words.

She had accepted this life, but whatever the fucking reason, she refused to accept my deal with Macchiavello. Over the last couple of months, it had gotten worse. I had pinpointed it to the exact day. The day she spoke to Rocco Fausti alone.

Another shot of acid ripped through me when I thought of it. She still hadn't brought it up. I held resentment not only for him, but also toward her.

My wife having a secret with him ate at me like the thought of Macchiavello. She'd see it in my eyes sometimes when she'd look at me and catch me thinking of them together, though she probably associated it with something else.

Tito nodded, a solemn look on his face. "It has been a difficult transition for her. What has happened over the last few months would take its toll on a person who has nothing else going on, but a woman experiencing changes in hormones—" He shrugged. "It can be harder to get a grip on the things we feel are out of our control when we are feeling so many things we have no control over."

"Postpartum depression." I blurted the words.

He studied my face. "Love redeems," he said in Italian and then adjusted his bag. "I have been watching her. She does not have postpartum depression. However. I've known Alcina all of her life. She takes and takes and takes. She gives her problems over when she goes to church, when she worries her rosary instead of her mind, whenever she lights a candle to brighten the darkness of her world. But when she breaks—she breaks hard."

"You've seen it?"

He nodded. "After Junior sent the first man after her. She told me she did not feel as if her life was her own. It took some talking to her to make her realize that all would be okay, but she came back stronger than before. She always does. She always will. Don't underestimate her."

"Not from the moment I saw her," I said.

"Ah." He grinned. "She snap her shears at you?"

"Yeah," I said.

"The moment you fell *innamorato*." Tito turned toward the door, ready to get home to his wife. I could smell the roses and one of Alcina's candles in his bag. It was one of her romantic ones. The old gangster was going home to seduce.

I opened the door, squeezing his shoulder, deciding to walk him out. No one would stop him then. He looked relieved. He was still spry for his age, but I could tell the life was wearing him down some. Especially with the unrest in the Fausti *famiglia* on the rise. He was always front and center when it came to them, and they were keeping him busy.

Calcedonio, Baggio, and Adriano noticed that I was leaving, and they all stood up, preparing to walk me out. A bunch of the men followed, and we gathered outside, preparing to go our separate ways. Except for Calcedonio and Adriano, who were riding with me.

A few men were walking toward us—I recognized them from Baggio's crew. They were with women. Probably from Scorpio.

"Hi, Corrado," one girl said when they stopped. I couldn't

remember her name, but I'd met her at Scorpio a few times. She leaned in and put her arms around me, her lips coming close to my ear, about to whisper something.

Before I could tell her to move along with her assumed familiarity, screaming made all of the men turn.

Sicilian curses filled the air before my wife barreled through the crowd, coming straight toward the woman and me.

"If you know what's good for you," I said to the woman, reading the look on Alcina's face, "you'll get the fuck outta here. *Subito.*" *Immediately.*

The woman only had time to narrow her eyes, to realize the volcano coming for her, before she went to take off. She was too late. Alcina grabbed her by the hair, yanking her back, and then proceeded to beat the woman, screaming insults at her in Sicilian as she did.

*Bitch! Whore! I should take your panties off and stick them in your mouth! My husband! Disrespect! Make a fool of me!*

My wife was not slapping the woman, either, she was punching her.

I said her name once, but I knew there was no getting through to her with words alone. I took a step forward, ready to end the situation, but before I did, Baggio stepped up and grabbed Alcina around the waist. He yanked her back so hard that her mouth opened. He had made her lose her breath.

Baggio was a beast on the streets, but I knew it wasn't going to be long before he burned out. Men who only had violence and no thought behind it never lasted in this life. The day before, I'd been told that he had done something violent to another woman, but the woman had yet to be found. Then there was the issue with Vito. He had let him slip past, which gave him the opportunity to get to my wife and family.

As soon as he put his hands on my wife, our eyes connected, and he dropped her immediately. She fell to the ground, wheezing for breath. The woman she had been beating slapped her across the face. She went to do it again, when I stepped in between them.

"Your face," I said. "I better never see it again."

She took off running. I didn't bother watching her disappear. I turned around and picked my wife up from the ground. She slapped at me, trying to curse while catching her breath.

I looked at Tito, who watched with a narrowed eye, Baggio, and then Adriano.

Nunzio stepped up, Brooklyn next to him. "We were passing by when your wife saw you," he said. "She jumped out of the car before we could stop her."

I nodded, walking toward where Nunzio had parked. A stream of traffic lined up. Either the cars went around or they waited. Most people in this area were familiar with who we were.

Brooklyn got in first, followed by Tito. I sat Alcina down next to him. She turned her face up, tears slipping from the sides of her eyes, rolling down her cheeks. She wasn't crying because she was upset. She was crying because she was pissed.

Tito sighed. "I will check her."

I shut the door and tapped on the roof once. The car pulled into traffic and I went back to Primo. Calcedonio was the only man standing outside.

He nodded at me. "Baggio and Adriano are inside."

"Go home," I said. "I'll see you tomorrow."

I shut the door behind me once I was inside, locking it.

Adriano sat at the bar, his back to me. Baggio stood as soon as he heard me enter.

"Boss, I—"

I held a hand up. "Get me a beer," I said.

He nodded. "Yeah, okay. We can discuss this."

He went to the fridge and grabbed me a beer. When he turned around, I shot him twice in the stomach. His eyes grew wide, his mouth opened, wheezing for breath like a fish out of water. He fell to his knees before he crumpled to the floor.

I stood over him, watching him gasp for breath. "No one touches my wife," I said. "You'll suffer for however long it takes. No help. You'll touch hell before you get there."

I had seen his face when he yanked my wife back. He got off on pain and suffering. As soon as he heard her breath catch, he got a fucking hard on for more pain. He was fucking limp now —his entire body.

Adriano sat at the bar, drinking a beer.

I nodded at him and he nodded back.

He'd take care of the rest.

"I guess I get Gilberts," he said before I shut the door to Primo. "I can't stand to see anything starve."

# 35

# ALCINA

Bruises were starting to form on my stomach, but I did not feel them.

The *vipere* were coiling deep in the pit of my heart, and my hands were ready to strike, to hurt him as much as that scene hurt me.

I couldn't see anything else.

Her hands on him.

Her mouth close to his ear.

The things they were doing behind my back.

I had never felt rage so hot before.

I was fixated on it.

I could not stop seeing it, imagining it.

His hands on her.

His mouth on her.

His face when he was buried deep inside of her.

*"Love—there's no such thing in this life. Do you think she—" she* nodded toward me *"—is going to get real love?"*

My hands balled into fists at my sides.

The moment I saw him, I knew *the truth*.

Those eyes hid his poisonous heart.

Those lips were vessels of deception.

That body? Made for inflicting pain.

I did not listen to myself. I did not go with my instincts. I went with love.

Love couldn't exist in this world.

My hand stilled on the kitchen drawer as I heard Uncle Tito and *lo scorpione* talking right outside of the kitchen.

"The break, Corrado," Uncle Tito said. "It's deep this time. She can't see past whatever she is going through."

I almost threw back my head and howled with laughter.

They thought I was losing my mind? Had either one of them spent time with my husband lately? If they wanted to see a loss of a mind, all they had to do was look at *him*.

Maybe he was rubbing off on me.

Corrado took his voice down, and a minute later, he came into the kitchen.

"Turn around," he said. "Look at me."

I refused to. He grabbed me by the shoulders, forcing me to face him, but I wouldn't look him in the eye.

"Look at me, Alcina," he said.

I refused, keeping my arms up to my chest so I wouldn't even accidentally touch him. I could smell her perfume on his body. I could smell roses and spice and something else... something I couldn't place. The unknown scent did not matter. The rest, I could smell, and they were poking the *vipere*.

His eyes were hard on my face, but I did not move. He released me suddenly, almost violently, and lifted my shirt up.

I let him.

His breath picked up when he noticed the bruises. I felt his warm breath fan against my skin in faster waves. My shirt fell as he took a step back.

He stared at me from across the room. Then in a burst of fury, he picked up one of the chairs and flung it through the window behind me. It went clear through, the glass ricocheting in a hundred different directions.

I did not even flinch.

Not even when the alarms blared.

"Boss—" one of the men said, coming to stand in the doorway.

"Turn it off," he said, not even looking at the man. He stared at me. I refused to look at him.

The man moved like a shadow in the darkness. Then another shadow appeared.

Uncle Tito cleared his throat. "I told Angela not to worry. All was okay with the alarm." He pointed his bag towards the door and then left without another word.

"Look at me, Alcina," *lo scorpione* said once more.

I refused to.

"All right," he said. He turned and put his fist through the wall before he left me alone in the kitchen.

His violence seemed to echo in the quiet while my rage seemed to scream over it.

I listened for him for a while before I turned and opened the drawer again, taking out a knife. I stuck it behind my back, moving through the house as quietly as possible.

"Alcina."

*Mamma's* voice stopped me. Anna and Fabrizio had gone back to Italy, but *mamma* refused to leave.

"Go back to sleep," I whispered.

"What is going on?" she said, her voice taking on a demanding tone.

"A little argument," I said. "We will work it out."

"Alcina," she said as I moved further away from her. "Do not do something you will regret!"

I smiled in the darkness. If anyone regretted anything, it would be him. That fucking scorpion.

He had taken a shower and was in bed. He had lit the

candles in the fireplace, and the light from the flames haloed his naked body. He could sleep even if the world was ending.

I tucked the knife in the bathroom drawer. I undressed, catching sight of the bruises on my skin before I jumped into the shower. I did not dress after and left my hair wet. I took out the knife and then walked into our room. I slipped in beside him and then moved on top of him.

His eyes slowly opened.

I pressed the knife to his throat a little harder, watching as the blood bubbled. "I told you," I said, my voice coming out hard, but with a slight tremble I could not control. "I told you I would kill you."

He stuck his neck up some. "I told you I would allow you to." He moved my hand down further, to his heart. "Do it, Alcina. If you're going to kill me, do it. Fucking do it." He pressed it harder against him, and more blood started to run from his skin.

"You killed my trust," I whispered. "My faith in you."

"No," he said, reaching up to tuck his hand deep into my hair. His thumb stroked my chin. "I swear on Eleonora."

I narrowed my eyes. "Why would you allow me to kill you then?"

"I'm killing you anyway," he said. "My life. Me. I'd rather die than see you this way."

My hand started to tremble, and something rushed through me, something so powerful that a sob rocked me to my core, even though I did not shed a tear.

What was wrong with me? I blinked at him, trying to bring him into focus, my mind sharpening. The poisons from the *vipere* started to recede, and I realized, the only damage was inside of me.

Before I could move, Corrado flipped me on my back. Instead of letting the knife go, I went to catch it before it slipped out of my hand. It cut my palm. He took it from me, throwing it toward the fireplace, and then pinned me down beneath him.

His hands were like steel bars around my wrists. "I should have known," he said, his voice sharp. "Your eyes don't belong to an angel. They belong to a witch. You put me under a fucking spell."

I tried to push against his hold, but he was too strong. "Go to hell," I hissed at him, matching his fury with my own.

He let one of my wrists go, his hand reaching around my throat, the pressure worse than it was the night in Como. "What did I tell you?" he whispered. "I would kill *you*."

"I have always been faithful to you," I barely got out.

"Have you?" He tilted his head. Blood rushed from the cuts. His heart must have been pumping faster. "I don't know what the fuck was said in that room between you and Rocco Fausti."

I lifted my chin, giving him better access. "He was worried about me. That I was unhappy."

The pressure increased. "You agreed with him."

"No," I rasped out. "I'm only unhappy because I can see you are dying inside. You are...going places I can't follow, and I cannot save you!"

His eyes were hard before he released me. Before I could even catch my breath, his mouth was on mine, giving me the breath I could not seem to find.

I cried out and then moaned, months of frustration and hurt and longing, all coming out in those two sounds. He parted my legs, and on a thrust that was so intense it made me put a hand behind my head to stop from hitting the headboard, he took my free hand, moved it above my head, and squeezed. His blood and mine entwined and stained our palms red.

It smeared between our bodies as we moved together.

"This," he said. "This is what I live and die for." His neck arched back, exposing his throat, the blood dripping down in a steady stream.

I reached up and wiped it with my hand, applying pressure to stop the overflow of it.

"Corrado," I moaned out, a truly crazed sound. The madness had gotten inside of our hearts and rushed through our bloodstreams. This one man could drive me out of my mind but make me feel sane in the same breath.

He started to move slower, reaching me even deeper than flesh, blood, and bone. I could not remove him if I tried. Not even with a sharp knife.

His eyes were on mine as he moved, and even though his body demanded mine to bow to his, his eyes were servants to mine. They were lowered, almost closed. As warm as honey in the glow of the firelight as he gazed at me.

"Come back to me," I whispered. "Be one with me again."

He hit me even harder, starting to move faster, and I knew it was going to be hard for me to walk after. This was his response, his yes, a reminder that he went deeper than what the eye could see.

We came together in a rush that made me dizzy. I closed my eyes, trying to steady my tilting world. He kept me with him as he turned us.

It hit me again, harder this time.

What I had done.

I opened my eyes and he was staring at me. I started to kiss him—all over his face, his chin, where I had cut him.

"*Mi dispiace, amore mio.*" I kissed him, saying these things, hoping to heal the wounds I had caused.

His body shook, and I stopped kissing him, realizing that he was laughing.

I narrowed my eyes at him.

He laughed even harder—his laughter was as deep as his voice.

"What is so funny? You are bleeding!"

He lifted my hand, bringing it to his mouth. "So are you."

After he reminded me, I felt it. The burning. I had felt nothing before but the burn of jealousy.

"You are not right!" I tapped at his head.

He continued to laugh, pulling me into him. "You telling me I'm not right? Who brought the knife to our bed, Alcina?"

"I had a reason," I said. "I really believed—what I saw. I snapped." I looked down at his chest, where the knife had cut him there, over his heart.

"You believed what this life has taught you to believe." He wrapped his arm around my back, pulling me even closer. "I know what you saw, but it was nothing. Just bad timing."

I looked him in the eye. "I know what I said, that I would kill you, but I did not really think I could."

"Not until you believed what you thought you saw."

I nodded, waving my hand, hating to admit to the weak moment.

He caught it and kissed the cut. "*Ti amo,*" he said, kissing me on the lips. His mouth moved even lower, to my chin, to my neck, to my breasts, to the spot where the bruises had started to turn. His eyes turned a darker shade of amber when his head had moved lower, adjusting to the flickering light.

"I love you more," I whispered in Sicilian, running my hands through his hair. "If only my mouth could heal the pain I've caused."

He took his dick in his hand and slid it up and down my body. "It can."

Our eyes met.

"You are turned on because I cut you?"

"Because you claimed me," he said.

I grinned a little. "I am the moon, and you are madness."

His eyes became intense. "Heart and body, angel eyes. You gave my body your heart. You have the power to stop me from breathing if you reject me," he said. "My life is done without you. No one has ever had that power but you. No matter where

I go here." He took my finger and touched his temple with it. "You're always here." He put my hand over his heart.

I put my lips to his, my fingers trailing over his body, hoping to heal the hurt I had caused by bringing my heart closer to his body.

A BREEZE FILTERED in through the missing window. Corrado wrapped his arms around Ele and me, and I smiled.

"It is open," I said. "Plenty of fresh air now."

He grinned against my neck. "I can make it happen all over the house."

I laughed even louder, shaking Ele a bit. She looked at me and smiled, trying to put her little toy giraffe in her mouth. Mari had given it to her.

My heart dropped into my stomach when I thought about it. She had teared up when she held Ele. She knew she was holding her niece. I stroked Ele's hair and kissed her cheeks, thinking how nice it would be for her to have two aunts.

Corrado set his hand over mine. "Her hair is getting thicker," he said.

"It is like thick fuzz." I made a funny face at her, and she giggled so loud that Corrado smiled.

"Give her to me," he said, reaching out. "You can finish making the coffee."

I nodded and went to hand her over, but she turned away from him. He went to turn away but I refused to let him.

"Take her," I said. "Play with her. She'll want to stay with you."

He took her and she started to cry, but to his credit, he took a seat at the table, handing her one of her spoons. She immediately put it in her mouth, crying a little now and again.

"See?" I said, getting the coffee ready. "The more time you spend with her, the better it will be."

*Mamma* came into the kitchen. She looked Corrado over. Her eyes narrowed on the cut on his neck. She pinched me on the arm, nodding her head back. She was trying to be subtle, but it was apparent she was calling me out.

Corrado started laughing, and Ele started to cry even louder. I was torn between going to get her and leaving him to make her feel more comfortable.

She needed that from him.

He got up from the table, bouncing her a bit, but then he handed her to *mamma*.

"I'm going to take a shower." He kissed me on the cheek and then left.

I sighed. He was pulling back again.

"What did you do to him?" *Mamma* hissed at me.

I shrugged. "We worked it out."

"He has a cut on his neck!"

"On his heart, too," I said.

"Ah! *Mamma mia!*" She put her palm to her head. Ele started to giggle and then they both started laughing. "What am I going to do with your parents, ah?" She gave her big, fat kisses on her cheeks. "Come with *nonna*. I will save you from these people with no sense after you eat."

I laughed while I made Ele her morning cereal and pureed pear. She ate it up, and then *mamma* took her upstairs to get dressed. They spent mornings together. After I fed Ele, *mamma* would change her and then take her outside for a walk. I knew *mamma* would be leaving soon, and I couldn't think about that either.

I had one main issue to focus on.

If there ever was a time to talk to Corrado about my cousin and his sister, it was now. The night before had changed things between us, and maybe if I acted, things could continue to change for the better.

If he would only hear me out.

I narrowed my eyes when he came into the kitchen dressed in a suit. After last night, I thought we would spend the day together. We would say things that needed to be said.

He put his hand on his tie before he leaned in and kissed my lips. He went to the coffee pot after and poured himself a cup. He stood by the open window, staring out at *mamma* singing to Ele in Italian as she walked around the garden with her.

"Someone will fix this today," he said, nodding toward the gaping hole.

I did not respond. I was sure he would see to it.

He took a drink of coffee, still staring out, and I stared at him.

Ele laughing. The family taking pictures. Playing at the park. Singing in the kitchen or during her baths. Going for walks.

All of these things he watched from wherever he happened to be, but never did he put himself there with us. He couldn't seem to find a way to get to where we were. He always kept himself at arm's length.

His eyes would consume the scene, as if he was starved to be there, to be present, but his body kept him rooted to wherever he was. Which was too far from us. His family.

I breathed the Sicilian word for longing. Then I spoke it out loud. He didn't hear, not paying attention to me, but to our daughter laughing. She loved music.

"Corrado," I said.

He took another drink of his coffee, stared for another minute longer, and then turned to face me.

"Longing," I said.

"What about it?"

"Longing," I repeated the word. "A yearning desire. Pining. Craving. Ache. Burning. Hunger. Thirst." He stared at me with a blank expression. I sighed. My hands moved as I continued. "You feel all of those things when you look at us. When you watch us. I see it in your eyes. You want to be close to us, but something is stopping you."

"Is that what it is?" He almost seemed relieved. Like he had thought of it before, but could not put a name to it. "All of those things. I feel them here." He pointed to the center of his chest.

"Yes," I said, trying to keep my voice steady. "It's longing."

"I want to kill it," he said.

"Why do you have to feel it? When we are right here?" I stood up, and reaching out, took his hand. I placed it against my chest. "You can touch me whenever you want. You can go outside and take your daughter for a walk whenever you want. You can put her to bed each night. We can spend time together. All day, every day, for the rest of our lives. Why? Why do you have to long for us? We're here. You can have this life *and* us."

He shrugged. "You know who I am. What comes first."

I searched his eyes. "You're at war within yourself," I said.

He nodded. "One obligation doesn't leave room for what I had no idea I needed."

"We pull you one way and the life pulls you another."

"You and Eleonora don't do it intentionally. It's just the way it is. One part of me wants one thing. The other part needs something else."

"What part of you needs?" I said.

"The part that has a tattoo of you and my daughter on its soul."

I almost collapsed in relief. To want something was one thing. To need something was another.

"You can have both," I said. "We're not going anywhere. We will figure this out. How to balance."

He grinned at me. "Why do you think I never considered getting married before?"

"You hadn't found me?"

He put his fist to my chin and moved it, like he was giving me a punch, but it was playful. Something he did from time to time. "You changed everything," he said. "I never wanted this before you. I didn't need it until it became mine without permission. Love complicates things in this world, and rarely does it win. "

I turned away from him, going to sit at the table. He took a seat across from me.

"One thing at a time," I said, mostly to myself. "We need to talk about my cousin." My heart beat painfully in my chest, but we could not go on this way.

At some point in time, the truth had to be set free. Mari agreed, and that was why she had come to see me at Bella Luna the night before. She felt it was time to tell him. She knew who Corrado was, but he had no idea about her. The rest would just have to come and be dealt with.

"You have many," he said. "You'll have to remind me which one."

"You will remember him," I said. "He was in Modica with Mariposa."

"Mari," he said, correcting me. "Her husband, your cousin, only calls her Mariposa."

I nodded. "We call him Amadeo."

He nodded.

"But only we call him that." I took a deep breath. "This world calls him Mac Macchiavello."

He stared at me blank-faced for what felt like forever, but was probably only a few minutes. "Your cousin is Vittorio Scarpone."

"*Sì*," I said. "I did not know they called him that here. Not until the day I went to eat with Mari at his restaurant. Most of his life, he has kept himself hidden from the world. After what his father did to him for not doing the same to your sister."

He narrowed his eyes at me. "Rocco Fausti told you."

"No." I shook my head. "Amadeo's wife told me."

"His wife."

Then he became quiet. I could see the gears turning behind his eyes, working it all out. "She's my sister. He married my sister. The girl sitting next to me on the bench."

"She wanted to talk to you. Get to know you. She was hoping that you would—"

He stood from his seat, placing both hands on the table. "Accept him?"

"Accept her son," I said. "Her family."

"She was only five when he stole her!" he roared.

"No, no!" I stood, waving my hands. "There is more to it. He saved her and then he hid her. A family, a daughter and father, took her in." I explained to him what happened after that. How Amadeo had left her with money, changed her name, erased her identity, and years later, they met again. "When she was old enough."

"You expect me to believe that?" he said. "That he waited until she was old enough?"

"Yes," I said. "My cousin would not lie to me. I believe them both. It wasn't done on purpose. Fate brought them back together."

"He's a Scarpone," he said. "I don't believe a fucking thing that comes out of his mouth."

"He's more than a Scarpone!" I yelled. "He has more than one side. He's a good man and he loves your sister. He almost died for her."

"So what are you saying? That I don't love you as much because I didn't almost die for you?"

I almost stumbled back. What was he talking about? He had to be in shock. I could see the surprise he tried to hide. His sister had been sitting next to him and he had no idea, and he was a man who made it his business to know everything. "I did not say that!"

"You didn't have to," he said. "You think he's a hero for what he did. It doesn't take a hero to not kill a child. Even a somewhat decent human being wouldn't do it. Anything less is a rabid animal. Like the rest of his fucking family."

"He does not want thanks for it," I said. "But they still tried to kill him for it! In many ways they did. And again, I am *his* family, too! We share the same blood."

"How was her life?" He stood to his full height. "That girl on the bench. Mariposa. Mari. Marietta Bettina Palermo. Fucking Scarpone."

"Macchiavello," I said.

He waved it off. "I could tell she had a hard life. I could tell she wanted family. She needed me to acknowledge her. To see her."

"Right!" I slapped the table. "If you do this, you will take away the life she has fought so hard to have. You do not understand, Corrado. He loves her like you love me! She is worried that her husband will kill her brother, or her brother will kill her husband. That one day you will go looking for her son. Your nephew. Then I am certain *she* will kill *you.*"

He stood still, and I walked over to him, putting my hands on his arms. "You are not a mercenary," I said. "You are Don Corrado. You know the rules. You live by them. That is why you are where you are in this life. If you do this, though, you are breaking the most sacred rule of all. One that is not set by any family, but by a greater law. If you do this, you will not only destroy your sister's family, but your own."

# 36

# CORRADO

I t wasn't her I came to see at Macchiavello's, but it didn't surprise me that she came in his place. She was curious about me, which answered so many questions about the day in the park.

My sister took a seat next to me at the table. "That's one of my favorite dishes, too," she said, nodding toward my plate. "I still can't get enough of it. Though I love the pasta and crab dish more. I get it whenever I can."

I finished my piece of steak and then took a drink. I nodded. "The food here is good."

She grinned at me. "That must have hurt coming out, huh? A compliment."

"Not at all," I said, offering her a plate of asparagus. Green foods weren't usually my thing. "The truth is the truth. I don't sugar coat it, and I don't shy away from it. I expect the truth, so I give the truth. Rarely is it anything personal." To experience emotions meant that care had to be involved. I reserved that for special circumstances. Most things were this or that. Nothing more.

She pushed the plate between us. "I like salads, but green foods are not my favorite either." Her grin turned into a smile. "We look nothing alike."

"No," I said. "We don't."

"I look more like my *mamma*," she said. She studied my face openly, without worrying about if she was going to tip me off to the secret we once had between us. "My son has your features. Your eyes. Even the color of them."

"Saverio." I nodded. "I didn't realize it at the time."

"I noticed it right away," she said. "Now I can say he resembles my brother, not that—"

"Man," I finished for her.

"Yeah," she breathed. "I don't have good feelings toward him."

"You remember him?"

"One or two things." She shrugged. "It's not so much what I remember about him specifically, but what I know he did to our family. My *mamma*. I don't have one because of what he did."

That was true. Corrado Palermo had set all of their fates in motion when he attempted to kill the boss of his family. I wondered if she realized that her husband had killed her *mamma*, though, when he could have spared her.

One look at her and I knew she was going to defend him if I brought it up. She was going to tell me that Arturo would have never stopped. Neither would have Achille. That was true, too. The son was worse than his father. He was the one who had killed Emilia.

Sylvester came into the room, bringing her a glass of water with lemon. He sat a plate in front of her. Then he brought me another beer.

"*Grazie*," she said to him.

He nodded and left.

She smiled. "I ordered the steak, too." She stared at it for a minute before she cut off a small piece. She ate like she appreciated every bite. "How much do you know about me?"

I found myself staring at her. I cleared my throat. "Nothing. Other than we share the same father but different mothers."

She nodded, taking a sip of her water.

"Is that all you know about me?" I said.

She cut another piece. "A little more, which is plenty, but nothing too specific. Like. Do you get angry in traffic? Do you like music? What's your favorite thing to do? Do you read? Take naps? Are you a world traveler?"

"No to the first," I said. "It is what it is. I do enjoy music. The opera, too. I do read, but not as much as I should. And no, I don't take naps. Not in New York anyway. I sleep hard at night." I took a pull of my beer. "I've been a few places, but my life limits me. Answer those things for me."

"Okay," she said, setting her fork and knife down, getting more comfortable in her seat. She rubbed her hands together.

I almost grinned. She became more animated, like she couldn't wait to tell me.

"I hate traffic," she said. "Though I don't usually get angry. Unless someone cuts me off. Then I can get testy."

"Which happens every second in New York." This time I grinned.

She stared at me for a minute, like she was dazed, and then she shook her head. "Where was I? Oh. I love music. I love to cook. I do read—lately, law books. Naps are a hard no for me. At this point in my life. I wake up not sure what century I'm in and then I get irritable. Then I can't sleep at night, which irritates me even more, unless..." She waved a hand.

"It ruins my entire day, usually. And I am now. A world traveler." She dug in her purse and pulled out her passport, showing it to me. She had some stamps. "One of my favorite places to visit is Greece." She took her passport from me after I'd looked it over and stuck it back in her purse. Almost protectively. She got back to work on her steak. "I love to eat, too."

"I can tell." I pushed my plate closer to hers. "You want mine?"

She threw back her head and laughed. "No! I'll finish this one, but not much else." She patted her stomach. "Good portions."

I decided then that she had character. She was charming. Someone a man like me didn't meet every day. She had to get that from her *mamma*. I assumed all the bad things came from him, which was why I was who I was. It came from both sides.

"Tell me about your life," I said.

She finished her bite, set her fork down easily, and then took another drink of water. She set her cup down so quietly that it didn't even make a sound. She wiped her mouth. She cleared her throat. "It was hard." Her eyes focused on a piece of lemon floating in her glass. She used her nail to trace the shape of it.

"I'm not going to sugar-coat the truth. We have that in common. I had no parents, but I did have two people who loved me. Two people who took me in and treated me like a daughter and a granddaughter. But it didn't last long. My adoptive grandfather died, and then my adoptive mother not long after. I became a system kid after that. Some homes were good. Some were terrible." She looked at me. "I'm going to leave it at that."

"We were close," I said. "In distance."

"Yeah." She nodded. "Both on Staten Island, but worlds apart somehow."

"I agree. To a certain extent."

"I get it. We had a bridge because of who that man was," she said. "He connected us, and not only to each other, but to this life."

She was smart. Perceptive.

"However." She sighed, and then she looked at me, really looked at me. "I have no regrets. I'm where I'm supposed to be. This is my place in the world. I've been seen. I know who I belong to."

"You were just a kid," I said. "He took advantage—"

"You don't know anything," she said, "about anything. You don't know him. I do."

"Yeah," I said, taking another long pull of my beer. "I don't know him. No one knows him. He's a ghost."

She smiled, but it wasn't as friendly as before. "Vittorio Scarpone is a ghost. *That* family took his life."

I could hear the bitterness on her tongue, the anger, and it simmered in her eyes. His pain was worth more to her than her own.

She took the last bite of her steak, finished the potatoes she had, and then drank the water until the last drop. She surprised me by taking my hand. "You have a beautiful family, Corrado. I love Alcina. I've loved her since the moment I met her in Modica. And I love Ele."

She took a deep breath. "To hold my son changed my life, and to hold my niece...it's hard for me to put into words how much that day meant to me." She squeezed my hand. "I love you, and I don't even know you. But I see. I see him in you. In the way you think. You get an idea, and it haunts you like a ghost."

"Your husband," I said. "He's a ghost."

"To you," she said. "But I don't care what he is to the world. I know who he is *to me*." She released the pressure on my hand. "I know that you have this idea in your head, an idea that you refuse to let go of. It might be different from the one Corrado Palermo had, but the ending is the same. He killed his family because he couldn't let go of how things were supposed to be.

"The funny thing is, you are exactly where he *wanted* to be. He wanted to be who you are in this life. He died for it. He sacrificed his entire family for it, including you." She pointed at me. "What are you going to sacrifice for this idea of yours? Your family?"

She shook her head. "I refuse to allow you to sacrifice my family—for anything. I don't abide by your rules, Corrado. I never have. I never will. So make no mistake. I know who I belong to, but I also know who belongs *to me.*" She pointed at her chest. "If you even look at my son, ever, with anything other than affection, *I'll* kill you."

I fell in love with her then. Her strength. Her character. Her unwavering principles.

It was too fucking bad mine were unwavering, too. We had that in common.

I stood from my seat, fixing my suit. I took measured steps, stopping when I was right behind her. I put my hands on her shoulders, and leaning down, placed a kiss on her head. "No matter what happens," I said, "I'll always be your brother. I'll always be here for you, even if you don't want me to."

She reached out for me, putting her hands where mine had been, but I was already gone.

───────

I took a card out of my suit pocket and handed it to Sylvester on my way out of the restaurant.

He lifted it up, questioning it.

I nodded to it. "My home address is on the back. I'm inviting your boss over for dinner. Make sure he gets that."

"Yes, sir," he said, tucking the card in his pocket. "Does he need any other information?"

"Such as?"

"Date and time."

"We're family," I said, giving him a mocking smile. "He really doesn't need an invite. He's welcome anytime. But if he needs something more formal, tell him day after tomorrow." I shrugged. "After dark."

After all, ghosts couldn't be seen during the day—their time to fucking play was at night.

## 37

# ALCINA

Something had changed.

The day after Corrado had gone to Macchiavello's, after he had lunch with his sister, I could sense a shift in him. No longer was he obsessed with a thought, but he seemed to have accepted the outcome of it.

He made no plans.

He told me I was with him, which meant that the entire day, he wanted us to be together.

He woke up before me, bringing Ele to our bed. He watched her face as she ate. He carried her to the kitchen after, and even when she cried a little, he tried to make funny faces at her.

He fed her.

He dressed her.

He took her outside.

He was more present.

She did not smile at him, but she kept lifting her eyebrow, like she was trying to decide what his motives were before she gave him what he wanted.

*Papà* had flown in the night before, upset that *mamma* had not come home, and he wanted to see his granddaughter for the first time.

Ele had taken one look at him, at the face he made, and giggled.

"If it's the last thing I ever do," Corrado had said, watching them, "I'll get her to smile for me."

"You're almost there," I said, grinning at him. "But she is going to make you work for it."

I had grinned to cover up what I truly felt. His words made me uneasy.

*If it's the last thing I ever do.* I wanted it to be the first thing he ever did to set us in a different direction. But he did not give me time to dwell on it. He had told me earlier that morning that he was taking me out on a date.

After we put Ele to bed, I started to get dressed.

He'd dressed in a black suit and a gold tie. He adjusted it in the mirror while I fixed my hair.

I took note of his hands. How big they were. How strong. How I could trace the veins underneath his tan skin with a finger. Even his wrists were strong, a part of him that I found erotic.

I memorized the sharp lines of his face. How his eyes looked in reflection to the candles around the bathroom when he looked at me. I dressed in the color that I knew pleased him. The same color as his eyes.

I had committed to memory how he moved with such command and power, but he did so with such ease, there was no doubt that it was just a natural part of who he was. He placed the baroque earrings in my ear and the layered necklaces around my neck.

I absorbed the heat of his touch while it branded my skin, closing my eyes to anything but him and this moment.

His fingers trailed along my collarbone, then traced the cool metal around my neck, moving to my ears, sinking his fingers into my hair. "*Ti amo,* angel eyes," he said.

"*Ti amo, mio marito,*" I said, leaning into him, placing a soft kiss on his lips. But that was not who he was. His lips claimed mine with wrath-like intensity, but to me, it felt like unfiltered passion rushing through my blood. His fingers were greedy as they moved underneath the dress and he slipped one inside of me.

My eyes rolled, my head tilted back, and my mouth parted. His tongue licked down my throat and back up before it found mine again.

Kissing him was always more than kissing. It always felt like the love between us was stealing my soul. The very breath of my existence.

Our eyes connected, and that wild thing moved, possessed, as we crashed into each other without touching. He turned me toward the mirror, my hands planted against the counter, lifting my dress over my *culo,* moving the thin strip of underwear to the side. His hand massaged, caressed, his finger slipping in and out, while he undid his pants.

"Keep your hands steady," he said.

It was not my hands that needed to keep steady. It was my heart. My breathing. The floor beneath my feet.

He entered me in a thrust so hard from behind that it made me scream out.

He pulled my hair, tilting my head back. "Open your eyes," he said. "Look at me. Give me what I need."

I lifted my eyes to meet his. He slammed into me over and over, driving me higher and higher, until my body surrendered to the demands of his.

"Corrado!" I screamed out, so fucking close.

He pumped into me even harder, the wildest noises I ever heard coming from his mouth. They echoed around the bathroom, along with the sounds of our bodies slapping, pounding, crashing.

"So beautiful," he said, his eyes lowered, his body demanding even more from mine. "My wife. *Mine.*"

I wanted to lower my eyes, my head, concentrate on giving him this, on holding back, but my body was giving in. The pleasure burned from the inside out—it was always like nothing I'd ever experienced before. But I'd always imagined it to be the same for the candle the moment its wick starts to burn.

"You're ready," he said. He was in me, all around me, no relief unless I gave in. "Now you'll be satisfied."

"Not after a hundred lifetimes with you," I said, my voice breathless, but strong.

My body gave in and then his. He poured himself inside of me, and I memorized how raw it was. How deep. How I would never forget the things he not only did to my body, but to my heart.

I stood there, breathing heavily, while he cleaned us up. His touch was gentle, and I indulged in the contrasting ways he touched me. Sometimes it was with bruising fingers, and other times, with a caress that made me shiver.

He fixed my dress and then offered me his arm.

"A hundred lifetimes wouldn't be enough," he said after he started the car and pulled out of the drive.

I shook my head. "Not with you," I said. "When I promised forever, I meant it. In this life and all others."

The lights from the oncoming cars brightened the dark amber of his eyes to honey, which contrasted with the hard look on his face.

"What did I say?" I whispered.

"Nothing," he said. "Not a thing."

"Your face. It changed." I looked out of the window for a second and then turned to face him. "What would be a perfect ending to you, Corrado?"

"At one time—going with my suit on."

Ah. Dying as he was. Who he was.

"Has that changed?"

"Some." He glanced in the rearview mirror. "Sometimes I see the pistachio groves."

"In the evenings," I said. "The weather warm. The sun going down. The world amber. On fire. Burning through the rest of the day to have a fresh start."

"Morning," he said. "The beginning of another day. Not the ending of it. Still gold but in a fresher way. Cooler."

He took my hand as he continued to drive, and we became quiet. He took me to the Met, the opera—La Bohème—and instead of watching the stage, I watched him. His eyes flicked to mine every so often, and that mysterious pull between us had us reaching out—a slide of a hand, a touch of a fingertip, the feel of a warm kiss against cool skin in the darkened theater.

He was even quieter on the way home, but his hold on my hand was tighter.

My heart beat faster. My stomach felt hollow. I felt weak deep inside, but the same on the outside.

What was he thinking?

"Do you know why I ran for so long?" I said.

"Tell me."

I sighed. "To have this. To have you. To have the ending in the grove. Or anywhere, as long as you and Ele are with me." I brought his hand up to my mouth, kissing his fingers. "We all deserve that, Corrado," I whispered. "That is what we work to achieve in life. No matter what life tries to do, we must rise above it and fight for the ending we want. Once the years go, they go. There is no getting them back. But that is why we have the future. To look forward to. A new day, each day, so that we are ready for the evenings when they come."

The house came into view. We pulled up. Got out. Walked hand in hand. My cool one against his warm one. We checked on Ele once inside. We smiled at how she was sleeping. Her mouth open. Little hands with beautiful fingers next to her head.

We showered together, and after, he slipped on a pair of sweatpants and told me he would meet me in the bedroom.

I did the usual things, and before I finished, I heard the radio playing. The same song we danced to after our wedding.

He pulled me into his arms when I asked him what he was up to. No answer came. None had to.

We moved like we did that night. We kissed like we did that night.

He took me to bed after, his eyes intense on mine, the look in them hard to describe. *Consuming* was the only word that seemed to make sense. His palms slid against mine, our fingers interweaved, and he took his time, moving slow. A tear dripped from my eye, and he leaned down and used his tongue to dry it. His lips kissed down to my mouth, kissing me in the same rhythm he had created between us. There was nothing rough about what he was doing to me, yet he was ripping away everything that had ever belonged to me only—mind, body, heart, and soul.

After, I placed my body as close as possible to his. My hands searched his skin, memorizing every line, every dip, every indention. Then I stuck my claws in, refusing to forget each and every one.

I wondered how his childhood was. I wondered how many hugs and kisses he got. I wondered what it was like growing up in the shadow of one of the greatest Dons that ever lived, according to anyone that ever spoke of Emilio Capitani. I wondered how it felt to know that your grandfather would not stop a man from killing you if you made a mistake. Because rules were rules. I wondered how it felt to learn secret after secret about a family that was destroyed by them.

I wondered how it felt to be my husband.

I wondered if he would ever tell me what it meant to be him.

I wondered if I would ever get the chance to ask, and to have him answer me without the binds that tied him to his name, to his obligations. To the code that rooted his life.

I stared at his face as he stared at the ceiling, wondering all of these things and more.

He did not sleep the entire night. Neither did I. I took out my rosary, holding tight to it with one hand. The other was on him.

# 38

# CORRADO

Either way, if I fell or he did, this would end tonight.

Either way, if I fell or he did, I was going to ruin her life.

She kept glancing at me as she packed her things. I had arranged for my wife and her family to take a vacation in the Catskills. I wanted her far enough away, but not too far.

"You will meet us tomorrow?"

"Yeah," I said, leaning against the doorframe of the bathroom, watching her. "Tomorrow."

"Then we will go to Forza d'Agrò? My parents need to be home. *Mamma* does well, but *papà*...." She shook her head. "The older he gets, the more comfortable he is at home. He complains too much." She waved a hand.

She added another shirt to her suitcase, folding it neatly. Then she looked up at me. "You gave me your word that Ele would be baptized in the church we were married in. It is special to me." Her voice came out sharp, accusing.

I nodded. "I gave you my word, and it's going to get done."

Eleonora was already baptized here. Alcina and her family didn't want to bring her out until she was. So we compromised.

Eleonora was baptized in New York, and she would be baptized in Italy.

"Keep packing," I said. "I want you on the road before it gets too late."

That wasn't because of my deal, either. It worried me to have them on the road so late. Giuseppe was driving and Angela would be there to help, but it still made me uneasy. It was safer to travel during the day, unless I was with them.

I had decided not to send men. They didn't need them. Instead, I set Nunzio and Brooklyn up with a room of their own. Just to be close, but still family-oriented.

Nunzio met me out in the hallway before I got to my daughter's room. "They are all set?"

"Not yet," I said.

"We will follow in the car." He ran a hand through his hair. "Brooklyn is trying with her *mamma* again."

"She trying to convince her to go?"

"*Sì.*" He shrugged. "We might be a little late following."

"An hour," I said. "Tops."

His eyes lost focus for a second, and then he blinked and looked at me. "*Sì.*" He nodded.

I left him standing in the hall, still debating on how he was going to get his wife to leave on time.

He would—he had orders—but it wasn't going to be easy. Adriana hadn't warmed up to the idea of him, and his wife hadn't warmed up to not having her *mamma*'s approval.

Giuseppe was going up and down the stairs, not sure what to do with himself. He forgot his coffee cup. His phone, which he really just screamed at. He didn't know how to work it.

"What did you forget now?" I said to him when he started to head down the steps again with a book.

He waved me off, muttering complaints in Sicilian.

I grinned. I enjoyed having them in the house. They were

different from my family. Even though we were big, most of us were not as close as they were. We had too many secrets.

Angela's voice drifted out into the hall. She held Eleonora in her lap on the rocking chair, reading her a book.

She looked up at me when she heard me step into the room. Eleonora slapped at the book, talking to herself as Angela stood up and handed her to me.

"You should come with us," she said, tapping my cheek. "It would do you some good to get away from here for a while."

"I have things to take care of first," I said.

"Always business!" She waved a hand. "Do you know why Italians live so long? We work to live, not live to work."

"I thought it was all of the olive oil."

She laughed, squeezing Eleonora's cheeks. "You cannot forget the wine," she said. "A glass of red a day is good for your heart."

"*Angela!*"

"Ah!" She slapped her forehead. "*Mamma mia!* When the Italian women goes before her husband, it is because she could not take it anymore."

"*Angela!*"

"When the Italian man goes before the wife, it is because she strangled him!" She brought her hands up, mimicking the act. "I am coming! *You old grouch.*" Her voice echoed as she left the room.

I held Eleonora closer while I picked the book up from the rocking chair and then sat down. One of her hands hit the page while the other reached for her foot. I finished reading the book to her and then set it back down, turning her around to face me.

She lifted one eyebrow, as if to say, *What do you want with me? I don't trust you.* She was going to have hazel eyes, like my sister. Every day they changed in color.

"At least you're not crying," I said. "That's a good start."

"Ya, ya, ya." She made some sounds, the eyebrow still lifted.

I lifted her up, kissing her cheeks, and then set her in the same position as before, stroking her head.

"You're like me in that way," I said. "You're not going to trust easily. Which is good. Don't smile for men like me. Ever. Even if they tell you a million pretty things. Promise you the world. Nothing is ever free, remember that, Eleonora. If something seems too good to be true, it usually is. There's always small print."

I fixed a strand of her hair that stuck straight up. That, paired with the eyebrow lift, made me grin. "But don't let the small print stop you from loving. Everything has a price. Even love, even though they say it's free. Free to give, but it still should be earned." I sighed. "I'm glad you're more like me in that way. Your *mamma* gave her love to me too freely. She should have held out for someone better."

I kissed her again.

"But I wouldn't have allowed it. Your *mamma* is mine. So are you. No one, no other man in this world, will ever love you and *mamma* the way that I do. Even though I have a hell of a way of showing it."

"Ya, ya, ya."

"That's all you got to say to me, princess?"

"Ya, ya, yaaaa."

"Smile for me once," I whispered, touching her chin. "Smile for *papà,* Eleonora."

She blinked at me and then yawned, her head falling toward my chest. I brought her even closer and she fell asleep in my arms.

"Corrado?" Alcina stood at the entrance to the door. "We are all ready to go."

I nodded. "I'll walk you out."

I carried Eleonora outside, kissing her head once I strapped her in. I double-checked that all of the bags were as they should be. I waved to my mother and father-in-law.

My wife waited outside of the car.

"Tell me what's on your mind, angel eyes."

"Tomorrow," she said. "All I can think about is tomorrow." She kissed her palm and held it up for me, and then got in the car and left.

---

I WENT about the rest of my day as usual, except that I made sure my wife and family were doing okay on the road and that they had checked into the resort.

I called my sister-in-law in Italy, making sure the plans I had in place were all secure. In case something should happen to me, I sent her letters and arrangements for all of the money.

I sent all of the men home. Turned off all of the alarms in the house.

This was between us, and he wasn't going to ring the doorbell.

I sat down and ate a meal fit for a king at a table hand-carved for one. My wife and mother-in-law had cooked for me before they left.

Pasta alla Norma.

Caponata.

Arancini.

Blood orange salad.

And a few other specialties.

I finished the meal off with cannoli. My wife was known for them back home. She left an assortment, but my favorite was pistachio.

It brought me back to my time in Bronte. The groves. The volcano. Her. Every day a new day with my angel eyes. Not one that kept continuously turning—same shit, different day. That was my life up until the day I met her.

I sighed, pouring myself a cup of Amaro del Capo.

Night fell, a full moon rising, and I went to the window of the dining room.

Maybe he'd be out howling like the fucking dog he was.

The Scarpone family had wolf tattoos, which made me think back to that day in Modica. He had slipped his hand underneath his son's shirt, keeping it hidden.

"Yeah," I said, taking a sip of my drink. "That's about right."

I took a seat at the table, checking my watch. It was acceptable to be fashionably late, but this was getting fucking ridiculous.

Maybe he had decided not to come.

Maybe he decided this would be set on his terms, not mine.

Or maybe the fucker would ambush me in my sleep and not face me like a man.

I couldn't see that about him. Not because he was too low to stoop to such a level, but because he wanted to see my face. He wanted to air out our grievances before one of us fatally wounded the other.

I wasn't afraid of ghosts. They were already dead.

I cleared the table. Rolled up my sleeves and did the dishes. My grandmother had been spending more time with other family members lately, but still—her kitchen was always spotless. She detested any dirty dishes sitting in the sink overnight.

It was done out of respect for her. She didn't get much of that over the years, in other ways, so I felt it was important to do it even if she couldn't see it.

To be Machiavellian meant that one had to present him or herself to the world in one way, while behind closed doors, unscrupulous practices took place.

That was the way of our world. The root of it.

My main problem with Vittorio Scarpone was that he

presented himself one way to the world, a ghost, but deep down, he was still a Scarpone at heart. And that heart had a beat.

He stole chances from me.

He kept my sister from me—make no mistake, he knew about me longer than Tito had.

His blood killed the woman I called mother.

The more I thought about it, the more I needed something to reach out and touch, to snatch, to strangle, to kill. The constant beat in my ear, the never-ending pulse in my mind—it needed to end.

I checked my watch and sighed. "Fuck it," I said, standing from the table. I didn't wait on him. He waited on me.

I turned the lights off in the dining room and went back into the kitchen. I sent Alcina a quick text.

A minute.

Five.

Ten.

She didn't answer me.

I checked the clock on the wall. Maybe she was sleeping.

Doubtful.

Even though it was late, I knew she wouldn't sleep until I was next to her. She was anxious before she left. Eager for me to meet her.

I considered calling her, but if she was sleeping, I didn't want to wake her.

On my way to the second level, I noticed the lights turned on in the dining room.

It was empty.

I smiled a little, knowing he was fucking with me.

I left the lights on and went upstairs, double-checking that things were the same as I had left them.

All was normal.

The lights were turned out in the dining room again when I

made it back to the first floor. A line of taper candles had been lit along the table. The bronze holders glinted gold in the soft light. The shapes of items in the room created shadows along the wall.

I took a seat at the head of the table, getting comfortable, my eyes adjusting.

If I had blinked, I would have missed the movement. A second later, he came forward out of the darkness, the candles bringing him to life. All I could see was the blue of his eyes at first, until his features took shape and created the man. He sat at the other head.

"Boo, motherfucker," he said, setting his gun on the table. "You wanted to see me."

I set mine across from his. "For a while."

He nodded. "This would have happened sooner, but my wife asked me not to."

"So she could meet me."

It made sense then. Why he had helped stop the men ambushing me on the way out of his restaurant. My sister wanted the chance to meet me. Because of that, he could kill me when he was ready, but if he was around, no one else could touch me.

*Famiglia.*

Blood could talk about blood, do to blood, but let anyone else talk or do?

It was fucking on.

He had that going for him, but nothing else.

"I was sorry to hear about Emilia," he said. "My condolences."

I narrowed my eyes. "She knew that you knew about me."

"She and I had a talk years ago. Emilia is the reason I never said anything to you or Mariposa about each other. She knew if you found out who your father was, you would go looking for trouble. You'd find it in the form of the Scarpones. Once they found out who you were, it would cause a war." He shrugged. "Then there was the issue of who Corrado Palermo was. She didn't want you trying to fill the shadow he left."

"We don't fit." I grinned. "His legacy is too small."

"We were not made to fill other people's shadows," he said. "We were made to leave solid marks. Shadows fade."

"Emilia knew about my sister," I said.

"No one knew about my wife but me, and certain people I trusted with my life. Once the Scarpones had been wiped out, it was safe enough for you to know who she was. If I felt in any way you could cause her, meaning me, trouble, she would still only be a woman named Mari to you. Nothing else."

There was no mistaking the possessive tone he used when he said, *"No one knew about my wife but me."* He was letting me know that she was my sister, but she belonged to him.

"What's the fucking deal?" I said. "You let her live and then you fall in love with her?"

"Whatever you're thinking," he said, sitting back, settling in more comfortably. "Wipe it fucking clean. Unless you consider falling in love with your wife something dirty. It happened the same way for us—between two adults."

He was fucking reading between the lines—it seemed far-fetched that he had left her alone all of those years, but my gut told me he was telling me the truth. At least on that.

It still didn't change who he was and who I was.

"I appreciate you taking care of her," I said. "Not killing her after her *mamma*."

His eyes seemed to grow darker when the light flickered, and then they were ice-cold. "She was a child," he said. Like that meant anything to his people.

I shrugged. "I knew your father and your brother."

He gave a short laugh, almost cocky. It was rough, gritty. "You don't know me."

"I know enough," I said.

"I know everything," he said. "I even knew your father, when you'd never laid eyes on him before a picture I let you have."

Our eyes connected from across the table. In less than a second, we were both standing, our guns pointed at each other.

"I've been here before," he said. "It didn't end well for the other side of the table."

"That other side of the table wasn't me," I said.

He moved. I moved.

I moved. He moved.

We circled.

"You think killing me is going to kill the ghost. You're fucking wrong. You can't kill a ghost," he said. "You exorcise them out. And even then, from experience, you wrestle with them time and time again. Nothing ends here."

"It has to," I said. "There is no other way. Our blood can't exist together in harmony."

"It does," he said. "Through my son."

"You don't want to kill me," I said.

"I do," he said. "But again. I'm exorcising the demons. The only reason we're standing around this table, and not sitting at it, is because of you."

"It doesn't matter what you fucking exorcise," I said. "You're still a Scarpone. That's why you're standing there."

"And that's why you're about to fall, Palermo," he said.

I knew it was just a matter of seconds. The winner determined by who was quick enough to get the draw.

One.

Two.

Three breaths.

My hand was steady, my finger about to pull the trigger.

A light hit my eyes, so bright that I blinked from the shock of it. The entire dining room was flooded with it. It brought

Scarpone into focus, and for the first time, I saw the entire man he was in this room.

He was a tall and wide motherfucker, a similar build to my own. The tattoo on his hand was a reflection of him, like the scorpion was an echo of me.

He blinked at me, doing the same.

Our guns held steady, neither of us trusting the other enough to put down our weapons. Whoever had hit the lights was of no importance. A flash of gold-colored silk moved in my periphery. I ignored it.

The moment between us held steady, ready to decide the victor. It wouldn't be Vittorio. My finger was magnetized to the trigger. One pull and his life was mine.

His eyes narrowed, but before I could process what it meant, the cold barrel of a gun touched me behind the head.

"You don't get along with anyone, do you?" My sister's voice came from behind me. She pressed the gun harder to my head. "Drop your gun, Corrado."

"You, too," my wife said, holding a gun behind Scarpone's head. She was wearing a gold silk shirt.

Scarpone and I looked at each other, narrowing our eyes even further.

This fucking complicated things.

How were we supposed to shoot at each other with them in the room?

Still. He held his gun, and I held mine.

"This is what you have done to us," Alcina said, looking at me. "You have forced our hands. If we kill you both, then one of us will not be forced to hate the other for the rest of her life. One of us will not be left without our other half, while the other goes on to be whole."

"Fucking ridiculous," Mari said. "Trying to send us away so you both could do this."

Alcina's eyes moved from mine to the woman standing

behind me. In a move that seemed synchronized, they stepped away from us, pointing their guns at each other.

"Put the fucking gun down—" Scarpone's voice and mine melted together when we both sent out the same order, except he said his wife's name and I said mine.

We were no longer looking at each other, but at them. They were staring at each other, guns raised, determination etched in their features.

They were both dressed up, like they had prepared themselves for a funeral.

"Fitting, yes?" Alcina said, staring at Mari. "You both came dressed and prepared in suits. We will go in our finest clothes, too."

"Maybe we should have worn our wedding dresses," Mari said. "Real poetic."

I moved my gun slightly. Mari pulled the trigger of her gun, the bullet slicing through the fabric of my wife's shirt. Blood started to spill right after, turning the gold purple.

My wife's hands started to shake, but she didn't lower them. The bullet must have just grazed her skin. It stuck behind her in the wall.

"Put your fucking guns down!" Mari shouted.

"Or both of us die!" Alcina screamed.

"One," Mari said.

"Two," Alcina said.

Scarpone and I both set our guns on the table, our hands forced, and stepped away from it.

*"If we kill you both, then one of us will not be forced to hate the other for the rest of her life. One of us will not be left without our other half, while the other goes on to be whole."*

*If we kill you both.*

They were going to kill each other.

"Fuck me," I muttered.

I could see it on Scarpone's face. He never saw this coming either.

"We want your words," Alcina said, keeping the gun steady.

"Swear on Saverio and Eleonora," Mari said, doing the same. "You don't have to love each other, even like each other, but you have to pretend, for the sake of the kids."

"I swear it—"

We both started to talk at the same time and then stopped.

"Really?" Mari said, shaking her head. "Capo, you go first. *Only* because you're older." She rolled her eyes at me.

He cleared his throat, looking at his wife. "I swear it on my son. This ends here."

"Corrado," Alcina said.

"I swear it on my daughter," I said, meeting her eye. "This ends here."

Both guns dropped, and the breath moved easily in my chest. I went to Alcina, looking at her arm. She moved it out of my hold, giving me a look that could have killed.

She slapped me behind the head and then started cursing in Sicilian. I stared at her, not truly understanding. Sometimes when she got that way, I couldn't make out a word of it.

"You made your point," I said, finally getting a word in.

She set her hands on her hips, fuming at me, and then she threw herself into my arms. I caught her and brought her close.

"Stop crying," I said, the urge to whip her ass and comfort her at war. I wasn't sure how to feel about all of this yet. It was hard to process what just happened. I almost lost my wife, my entire family, in one night.

"It keeps bleeding," Mari said, pointing at Alcina's arm.

Blood stained my hands. The smell of salt and iron was thick in the air, mixing in with the perfume of the candles still burning on the table.

Amadeo—Vittorio Scarpone—Mac Macchiavello—my sister's husband—Capo—whoever the fuck he was—had his hand on Mari's neck. He took one look at her face and grabbed her before her knees gave out.

"Tito," he said, holding his wife's limp body in his arms.

I nodded, looking at Alcina's arm. My jaw clenched. She needed stitches. "We'll meet him at one of the places."

We both went for our guns, and Alcina made a noise deep in her throat.

"It's not for us," I said. "It's to hold Tito back when he finds out what we've done."

It was the first time I saw a true smile on her face in months, brightening her eyes.

# 39

# CORRADO

ONE YEAR LATER

"Take a seat." I offered Mac a seat across from me, at my grandfather's desk. My men took a seat around us. Tito did, as well.

The women were right. We didn't love each other. We didn't even like each other. But it was what it was. We tolerated. Fought our demons for the greater good of this family that somehow connected us.

That scene with my wife and sister haunted me. Taught me a great lesson. Never underestimate a woman when she needed something.

It made sense.

If they could give birth, they could do anything.

"Some things are coming down the wire," he said, getting right to it.

"Charges," I said.

He nodded. "Your grandfather heard some things. Came to see me at the restaurant. He wasn't too surprised to see me. He knew what I was capable of. I respected Emilio. That's why I never fucked with him directly, when I was toying with the rest of the families." He cleared his throat. The scar made it hard for him to keep his voice level at times.

"The day we met at the restaurant, before he was ambushed, he wanted to discuss me leaving you alone. He said some men wanted to see you fail. He asked me to stay the ghost everyone believed me to be. Then he asked me to help squash some trouble you had gotten into a while back with the law. In Vegas. He said he would owe me one."

"They left it alone," I said.

"Until now. It's not about that anymore, but about other things. Things your men have done. Things you have ordered to be done. Things they can trace back to you." He looked at Calcedonio, then back at me. "It's too many counts. Wiping won't help. They're not forgetting this time. It'll just come back. They're hitting all of the families at once. History repeating itself."

"I gave them something to go hard at," I said. I had worked at changing what this life of ours had become and what we needed it to be. Bringing the life back to the golden age again, and was successful, for the most part.

"By changing the game again, giving this life a second chance at the golden age, they're doing the same thing they did back then. Going at it the same way. All five bosses will get the worst of it. They're coming soon with charges."

"What am I looking at?" I said.

"A hundred years."

Calcedonio stood with his back to the wall, his arms crossed, shaking his head. Francesco looked at Tito and Uncle Carmine, who both stared at the wall.

"Terrible, terrible food," Adriano said. "A hundred years-worth. I'm looking at ten and dreading it. I have Gilberts to think of, too."

They were coming after Adriano with ten, unless he talked. One thing about him. He only opened his mouth for food. If they changed the menu, who the fuck knew what he'd do. And then he was in love with a fish.

"Leave us alone," Mac said.

The men all nodded and left, shutting the door on the way out.

He leaned forward a little. "Even though you made the game harder for them, a little more exciting, it's not you they're focused on. Not like the others."

"Drugs," I said. My family didn't fuck with them.

He nodded and then stood. "All you have to do is say the word," he said. "Corrado Capitani won't exist."

"I've been exiled before," I said. "I refuse to hide."

"You can be sitting in the same chair you've always claimed, but if you don't exist, they don't see you. Even when you're sitting right in front of them. And if that doesn't convince you—there's no such thing as loyalty in this life anymore, unless you're a Fausti. And even they have weak links now. Your men will turn. They've already started to. Be loyal to those who are loyal to you."

I stared at the wall after the door shut.

A hundred years.

My entire life.

I'd die behind bars.

The door to the office opened, and Alcina came in, holding Eleonora's hand. She was due any day with our second child.

"Someone die?" my wife whispered. "The men—"

I pulled her to me, making her lose her breath. It wasn't hard these days, but it was from the strength of my embrace.

Eleonora hopped on a chair across from us, her little legs dangling. She lifted her brow at me, still refusing to smile.

"Corrado," Alcina said, touching my face. "Tell me, or I will think it is worse than it is."

"I'm looking at a hundred years," I said.

She stared into my eyes, not understanding, until she did. She shook her head. "We will fight."

"We will," I said. "But I've seen it before. Even if I get parole, I'll probably serve no less than sixty. It just depends on how many years I get. That's what I'm preparing for."

She tried to push away from me, but I held her close. She stared at me before she looked at Eleonora and then at her stomach.

"What can we do?" she whispered. "I refuse to accept this."

"This is my life," I said. "I go down with this family."

"Your suit still on," she hissed at me. "To the very end."

I nodded.

This time she pushed away from me. "Not a gentleman's suit, an orange *jumpsuit*," she said, crossing her arms over her stomach.

One hard knuckle knock came at the door. Rocco Fausti stuck his head in. "Tito forgot his hat."

He must have come with Mac. They were as close as two thieves.

He strode into the room, picking the hat up. He stuck it on Eleonora's head, making her laugh when she knocked it off. He touched her chin after, and she smiled and giggled at him. He nodded at my wife.

She turned her face toward mine, narrowing her eyes when she noticed how I was looking at her. I'd been watching her eyes to see if she'd blink at him.

He shut the door, but his expensive fucking cologne lingered in the room.

Alcina took my chin in her hand. "He does not matter. Nothing else matters. But us. This moment."

"You going to stay faithful to me for a hundred years?" I said to her. "When I'm locked behind bars and men like him are hovering around you constantly?"

"I will stay faithful to you until the day I die," she said, squeezing my chin, coming down and giving me a kiss that was even more solidifying than a blood vow. "You have me forever, Corrado."

"For every sunrise," I said.

"For every sunset, too. You are my night, and I am your moon," she said in Sicilian. "Something to live for. Something to die for. You are my body, and I am your heart. For as long as there is a breath in me."

# EPILOGUE

ALCINA

**Seven Years Later**

"Orlando!" I screamed across the groves. "Bring me your bucket."

"Let him go," Rocco said, smiling at me as he passed. "He is just being a man."

I pursed my lips, shaking my head. "He is not a man," I said. "He is a boy."

"*Mamma*," Orlando said, coming to stand in front of me. "But I, ah—"

"Ah-ah!" I put my finger to his lips, trying not to laugh when he went cross-eyed at me for a second before his eyes looked up and focused on me. I ran my hand through his sweaty black hair. "No excuses. We do *not* hit with buckets."

"He told me, ah, that, ah, I was moving too, ah, slow!"

He had a habit of punctuating his words with *ah* when he became upset.

"It does not matter, son," I said. "We keep our buckets to ourselves. We can respond without using our hands."

"*Bucket*," he said.

"Bucket." I nodded. "Tell him you are not moving too slow, he is moving too fast."

He scrunched up his nose, like he wanted to growl. I told him to go play nice with the other children before he could see me laugh. I kept his bucket, though, because it was the second time he had used it as a weapon.

"*Mamma mia*," I said, watching him run to his sisters like a freight train toward mountains. Ele was helping another smaller child put oranges in her bucket. Alessandra was next to her, watching, trying to direct.

A blood orange dropped in the bucket I'd taken from Orlando. I looked up into the eyes of my husband. The sun broke through the amber, making them turn almost gold. His hair was black, starting to streak with some silver. His skin was warm and tan from working in the groves all day.

"You leave me for one second, and the lions smell fresh meat," he said, sliding his arms around my waist. He pulled me closer, kissing my neck.

"Tell me the truth," I said, thinking back years ago to the day in his office. The day that almost destroyed me. "If Uncle Tito had not sent Rocco to grab the hat he left on purpose... "

"The thought of him sniffing around my family after I was locked behind bars changed my mind. That's why we're here. Why I'm here. Prison wouldn't have killed me. The thoughts would have. The things I would've missed."

We turned together to look at the table full of people on our property. Family and friends gathered around our home to celebrate. Nothing in particular. Just life.

Laughter rose and echoed. Kids ran from one spot to another. A few of the men were drunk and started to sing. The sun was starting to set. Soon hundreds of lights would brighten our property in Catania.

It was the perfect distance to all of our family and friends. We were secluded, tucked away, our own little slice of the world where no one could find us—unless we allowed them to.

I sighed, taking my husband's hands in mine, intertwining our fingers.

Every word I had spoken to him in his grandfather's office was true. I was prepared to spend the rest of my life faithful to him, to our marriage. Not even bars could separate his life from mine. I had a code, too, and I was willing to sacrifice my entire life to see it through.

Though I had known Rocco was one deciding factor in my husband's decision, there was more to it.

*"Didn't I choose you, too?"* Corrado had said to me one night.

I hadn't known what he meant until the next day. We got on a plane to Sicily and never looked back.

The four of us did not exist any longer, not the same way we did before. The plane that was supposed to bring us back to New York crashed over the ocean. We went down with a set of names and came up with a new set of identities.

A new life that came with its own sets of unique wins and struggles.

I rested my head against his chest, looking up at him. "You look tired, *il mio amore.*"

He only nodded.

Even though Alessandro Palermo lived for each new day in his groves, he wrestled different demons every night.

Instead of staying awake, he fought them off in his sleep. Tossing and turning. Saying things I could not understand. Waking up ringing wet with sweat, like he had been to war in his dreams.

His conscience had caught up to him, and the life he left behind never truly left him. It pulled at him like strings to a puppet, demanding that he claim his part again as the puppet master. And his conscience pulled him in a different direction —toward redemption.

"The moon will be full tonight." I smiled up at him. "The grove will be ours."

"I look forward to the madness," he said, leaning down to kiss me. "When the witch comes out in you."

I laughed in his arms and then sighed. "We will stay out until morning," I said. "Until we have to leave. Then we will eat breakfast out on the terrace."

"A new day," he said. "The weather will be cooler."

"Is this the ending you imagined?" I pulled his arms even closer, wishing we could walk around as one instead of two. Maybe Uncle Tito was right. We did walk around as one—his body and my heart. Each day I fell harder and deeper in love with him.

A thousand lifetimes wouldn't be enough.

He took a minute to answer. "No," he said.

"*Papà! Mamma!*"

We turned to look at our three children running toward us. Alessandro smiled, and his Ele returned it.

It took her a little time, but her smile was mostly reserved for her *papà*. She lived up to her name, *light*, when she smiled that way for him.

They circled us, showing us the blood orange they had found, how big it was. Alessandro wrapped his arm around Ele. I pulled Alessandra closer. Orlando stuck himself in between, trying to wrap his arms around all of us. He was grunting, trying to make his arms grow.

I laughed, the sound of it echoing around the groves, as a breeze rustled the trees.

My husband looked at me and grinned. "Now it is."

# EXTENDED EPILOGUE

"You can't get away from me!" Anna said, jumping in front of us with a camera. "On the count of three!"

"One!" Ele shouted.

"Two!" Alessandra held up two fingers.

"*Tre!*" Orlando said, reaching for the bucket, which I refused to let go of.

We all looked at the camera and smiled.

"Wait!" Mari said, coming to stand next to her brother, her entire family surrounding her. "Us, too!"

"*Alla famiglia!*" Anna said, bringing the camera up to her eye once more.

"*Alla famiglia!*" we shouted before she took the picture.

"Now, let's eat!" Donatello "Lima Bean" said, passing us by. "I'm starving."

**THE END**

Yeah, I claimed the name.

Who gives a fuck?

After all, a name is just letters strung together to make a word.

I know who I am.

I'll always be a Don—the boss of this thing we called our life.

## A WORD FROM DONATELLO (ADRIANO):

Shh...let me tell a little secret.

I'm not who I used to be.

The chubby chipmunk described in this book no longer exists.

After Adriano Lima went down and this new man was created from his ashes, I was born again, so to speak.

See, I was addicted to food. I used it as a crutch. I lived to eat, not ate to live.

That life, it came with a lot of things that tore me up inside. Things I never thought I'd have to deal with.

Like my conscience.

I didn't know how to deal with it.

So I ate.

And I ate.

And I ate.

I filled my stomach with food when my conscience felt empty and was growling at me.

It was fucked up—but in that life, it was what it was.

For example. I once ate a bowl of spaghetti while a man was

lying on the floor at my feet, moaning in pain, his intestines hanging out of his stomach after I had caused them to.

You know what I did?

I offered him a bite. Then I described in detail to him how each bite tasted.

But that was then. This is now.

*Now.*

You wouldn't recognize me if you saw me on the street.

I'm nothing but solid muscle—no more chipmunk cheeks to hide my food for later.

What else?

Oh, yeah, I fell for a woman. She's older than me and hates my guts. (Can you guess who she is? I'll give you a hint. Her name was the same as mine, except it ended in an 'a' instead of an 'o'.) Hates the life I used to live. She still accuses me of being a part of it. She acts like I can't be anything else. Like it's in my blood and can't be washed clean.

Adriano would have given up.

The new me? He finds her hate a challenge.

I found something that food could never fill.

Life beyond *the life.*

# AFTERWORD

I hope you enjoyed Mercenary, the last book in the Gangsters of New York series. What a wild ride this has been! Thank you so much for being a part of it!

I wanted to take a moment to point something out about this book. I knew right away that Corrado (the one in this book) and his father, Corrado Palermo, were a lot alike. The sins of the father were visited upon the son. In many ways, Corrado and his father's story ran parallel to each other, but years apart.

Mari recognized the same downfall in her brother, and she knew that talking to him would only get her so far. The scene in the dining room at Emilio's mansion on Staten Island speaks for itself. Actions over words. Corrado chose his wife (essentially his family) over the taste of vengeance—something his father couldn't do.

So after reading Machiavellian, if you've ever wondered about Corrado Palermo and his wife Maria (Mari's *mamma*), this story definitely echoes theirs. Even down to the time spent in Sicily.

The ending to Corrado and Maria Palermo's story was not a happy one. I'm thankful that Corrado and Alcina's ended on a different note.

I hope you enjoyed Mercenary as much as I did writing it. I know I'll always think about the groves, the singing, even the candles and the moon, when I close my eyes and think about them.

Much love,
  Bella

# ACKNOWLEDGMENTS

I truly have no idea where to begin. I have no idea how to truly express my gratitude and thankfulness for what has happened since Machiavellian was released. The amount of love I've received for the Gangsters of New York series has blown me away.

Before I truly get started, let's go back a little, to the moments before I released Mac.

I wrote an acknowledgment in the back of Mac because I had no idea if I would continue on with the series, or stop there. My future in writing was uncertain. I've always been a writer, but I didn't start sharing my stories until 2013 (under a different name). Then I wrote the Fausti Family, and I fell hard and deep for the criminal worlds in my mind. I knew it was something I wanted to keep writing about, and I would have, but maybe not published as often. After I finished writing the Fausti Family, I wanted to jump right back in to that world. I wanted to see if the story strolling around in my head would amount to something equally as great as the love I found between Brando and Scarlett Fausti.

That idea turned out to be Machiavellian—and from that

book forward, what is now known as the Gangsters of New York.

I'm so proud to say that Mac truly resonated with readers, and that it has been described as "not just a mafia romance, but one of the most beautiful love stories."

I could have never foreseen how much love Mac (and the Gangsters) would get. I could have never foreseen how it would change my life as a writer. It gave me a reason to go on. As Alcina would say, "It gave me my fire back."

Writing is not only a passion for me, but a great love. And to receive this amount of love for a book that stole my heart from the very first page...it goes beyond what words can convey.

I have so many people to thank for that, because even though the act of writing is solitary, what comes with it is not.

**First and foremost**, I have a great amount of faith. Without it, I would have given up long before Mac was published. Being a writer isn't easy. It takes long hours of being alone with the people inside of your head, getting to know them from the inside out—what they love and hate; what they would live and die for—and in a blink, it seems like the story is no longer yours alone. It belongs to the world. And that comes with its own set of challenges. I'm so thankful that my faith has brought me this far, kept me strong enough not to give up, and I'm looking forward to whatever the future holds. T.Y.G.F.A.T.Y.H.D.F.M. I. A. Y. E.F.E.V.

**My family.** *La mia famiglia.* The love and strength you find in these books comes directly from my own. I have truly been blessed with the most amazing people to share my life with. I couldn't do this without you all. **I love you all more, and I can't thank ya'll enough for loving me and supporting me as much as ya'll do.**

**To my agent, Stephanie Phillips of SBR Media:** Thank you so much for all that you do for my books and me. Thanks to you, not only will the Gangsters be in audio, but also in

Poland! I can't wait to share these stories with more of the world.

**To my editor, Alisa Carter:** BEFL! You've polished my diamonds in the rough since the beginning. I can't thank you enough for not only being my editor, but a trusted part of my process.

**To my PR team, Buoni Amici Press (Drue and Debra):** Ya'll are every author's dream team. You help me with every aspect of this business, and I can't thank you both enough for the support and friendship.

**To my BETA readers:** Anna, Lashell (who is also my author friend!), Malia, Pam, and Stephanie. You are not only my beta readers, but my friends. You are all immeasurable in worth to me, and I'm so thankful to have gotten to know each and every one of you. Thank you for being a part of this journey with me.

**To Jenika Snow:** Thank you for reading my books, for reaching out to me, and mostly, for all of the support. BAFFAE!

**To the countless bloggers and Instagrammers who have reached out and shown me love and support:** I wish I could list each and every one of you, but you know who you are. Thank you doesn't even seem like enough, but...thank you! You have no idea how much I value your time, your creativity (the edits!), your passion for reading and your support. Keep doing what you're doing. You keep the book world spinning.

**Last but certainly not least:** YOU! Yes, YOU! If you're reading this, you cared enough to take this journey with me. YOU made the Gangsters into what they are—a series of books that I hope everyone will love for years to come. You've given me the opportunity to share these books with the world.

You message me.

You comment on my posts.

You show me so much love that I can't even put into words how much it means to me.

YOU share your love of these books and of reading with the world—and for that, I'll be forever thankful.

*Alla famiglia!*

Thank you so much for being such an amazing part of mine, and thank you for taking this incredible journey with me. I hope you'll be with me for the long-haul, because we're just getting started.

# ABOUT THE AUTHOR

Bella Di Corte has been writing romance for seven years, even longer if you count the stories in her head that were never written down, but she didn't realize how much she enjoyed writing alphas until recently. Tough guys who walk the line between irredeemable and savable, and the strong women who force them to feel, inspire her to keep putting words to the page.

Apart from writing, Bella loves to spend time with her husband, daughter, and family. She also loves to read, listen to music, cook meals that were passed down to her, and take photographs. She mostly takes pictures of her family (when they let her) and her three dogs.

Bella grew up in New Orleans, a place she considers a creative playground.

## ALSO BY BELLA DI CORTE

Made in the USA
Middletown, DE
15 May 2021

39833490R00231